Split Image

Discovering God's True Intention
for Male and Female

Anne Atkins

Hodder & Stoughton

LONDON SYDNEY AUCKLAND

This edition published 1998
First published in Great Britain in 1987
by Hodder and Stoughton
A division of Hodder Headline PLC

1 3 5 7 9 10 8 6 4 2

British Library Cataloguing in Publication Data
A record for this book is available from the British Library

ISBN 0 340 70986 3

Typeset by Avon Dataset Ltd, Bidford-on-Avon, Warks

Printed and bound in Great Britain by
Mackays of Chatham, Chatham, Kent

Hodder and Stoughton
A division of Hodder Headline PLC
338 Euston Road
London NW1 3BH

Split Image

For Shaun
(*Proverbs 11:22*)

Contents

Acknowledgments

I would particularly like to thank Michael Green.

I would also like to thank Elizabeth Crofts, Jill and David Ridgewell, Michael Griffiths, my brother Andrew Briggs and his wife Diana, Jonathan Fletcher, my parents, my grandfather-in-law Austin Fulton, Carolyn Armitage, Elaine Storkey, Colin Wilcockson, Caroline Standing, Chris Ellse, and Chipping Barnet Public Library. For the second edition I am indebted to Chris Peters for his friendship and correction, Francis Gardom for his support, Annabel Robson for her patience, Owen Chadwick for his wisdom, and Martin Hallett for his sensitivity and guidance.

And of course I would like to thank Shaun. After all, a husband 'is a man who stands by you through all the troubles you wouldn't have had if you'd stayed single'.[1]

Foreword

I first met Anne when she was an undergraduate. Beautiful. Artistic. Dynamic. When she joined the Christian
scene in Oxford the *avant-garde* gasped in amazement,
and so did the God-squad. This arresting, happy,
extrovert, and exciting personality threw into high relief
the somewhat lacklustre lives of many of the Christian
Union. Its president realised that something fairly
exceptional was around – and promptly decided to marry
her. It was the best and most far-reaching decision of his
year of office. Shaun went into the Anglican ministry and,
trailing clouds of the Old Vic, Anne went with him.

Given all that, you would expect something exceptional in this book. And you will not be disappointed.
The verve, the humour, the controversial pungency, the
love, the laughter and the sheer ability of Anne the
personality has gone into Anne the writer. The book is
every bit as arresting, as wholesome and as controversial
as its delightful author.

Her thesis is bold and simple. Contrary to general misunderstanding, the Bible teaches the complete equality
of man and woman, their difference but complementarity. She cheerfully takes on the extreme feminist
camp and the extreme Evangelical camp, though she has
strong affinities with both. Scripture does not teach male
supremacy in work, marriage, authority, worship or
preaching: man without woman is incomplete. At the
same time, feminist chauvinism is strongly repudiated.

We need each other. The 'image of God', male and female in interdependence, has been disastrously split. The cry of the book is (hilariously) enshrined in the last brief chapter: it is 'get back to the image'. Singleness and marriage, feminism and male dominance all receive fearless handling.

This proved to be a superb first book when it emerged ten years ago. Since then Anne has written a good deal more and is now also widely known through broadcasting and TV. It is fitting that she should revisit this valuable book and revise it. I am as pleased to see its re-emergence as I was to witness its birth. The issues are just as sharp and even more divisive than a decade ago, and Anne's clarity, sureness of touch, gripping style and biblical understanding make her an excellent guide through the jungle of modern sexual relations.

Since she first wrote, women have been ordained into the Church of England (as she had argued they should), and her 'Thought for the Day' on the BBC about homosexuality created more interest, more correspondence and more controversy than any single contribution during the long history of the programme. It is not surprising, therefore, that she has chosen to re-work her chapter on Authority and offers an entirely new one on Homosexuality. Don't miss them.

This book is forceful, well researched, bold, unconventional and in places breathtaking. Above all, its thesis of male and female interdependence is based solidly on scripture itself. The 'fundamentalists', Protestant and Catholic alike, will have trouble with this sharp exposé of some of their dearest shibboleths. But the general readers, Christian or not, who know full well that for centuries the Church has kept women down, will gain much insight – and delight – from it. Moreover, both single people and marrieds will thank God for its positive radicalism, its candour, its warmth and its sheer good sense.

This book has affected me deeply. Buy it. Give it away.

And then see if you can persuade Anne and Shaun to come and speak at some event. You will find that 'the half has not been told you'.

Michael Green
Advisor in Evangelism to the Archbishops of Canterbury and York

Imago Dei

'So God created man in His own image; in the image
of God He created him, male and female He created
them.'

Genesis 1:27

We are made in God's image. We are also made male and
female. And though the writer of Genesis does not spell
this out any further, there is surely some connection
between these two things.

God is One. So we, the human race, are first described
as one: 'He created *him*.' But God is also 'three'. And
immediately this first statement about us is followed up
with a second: 'male and female He created *them*.' The
suggestion is surely that we as male and female – one
race in two sexes – are in some ways a reflection of Him
as Father, Son and Spirit – one God in three Persons.

Now there are a number of things one can say about
the Persons of the Godhead. They are different,
obviously. They are also absolutely equal. But above all
they are co-operative. They work together. They love, and
serve, and exist for each other. This is what God is like.
And it is also, surely, what we should be like. For as
*inter*dependent vicegerents we can be a glimmer of that
glorious Trinity. As two *in*dependent sexes we are merely
a split image.

ONE

Splitting the Image

*'There is no subject more charged with passion than
the relation between the sexes. In one way or another,
it lies behind most of the poetry and most of the crime,
most of the sublimity and most of the cruelty, most of
the ecstasy and most of the boredom in all our lives.'[1]*

A friend was telling me recently why he preferred an all
male Bible study group as a teenager.

'We wouldn't have discussed our problems in front of
girls,' he said.

'Why not?' I asked him.

'We wouldn't have admitted our failings.'

'But *why*?'

'Why?' He pondered a moment. 'They're beneath us.
They're lesser,' he said simply. 'That's what we really felt.'

So what?

Some people will say that relationships between the sexes
are much better than they were. In many ways this is
true. Much sexual discrimination is illegal, many schools
are co-ed, women and men mix freely with one another
and equal opportunities are supposed to abound. But
these changes sometimes raise their own problems. The
cures can be worse than the original diseases. To our
shame, we Christians have been fairly apathetic about
sexism. Consequently we have had little influence in
finding the solutions. The world has been finding its own

and they have not always been the best.

Instead of encouraging girls and boys to mix freely with each other, our society now encourages them to sleep freely with each other. Instead of elevating motherhood to the position it has in the Bible, society often implies women should not have to 'suffer' it at all, so those who do are still more denigrated. Instead of showing that our differences do not make us unequal, some people try to pretend there are no differences at all. And instead of insisting that men should be less promiscuous, changing moral standards now pressurise women to become more so. It should hardly surprise us if the movement we think of as 'women's liberation' sometimes seems unsavoury; it has had little Christian salt in it to save it from decay.

The fault is largely ours. Many Christians have had little to do with the recent feminist movement. The Church has often shown little interest in the *cris de coeur* many women have been uttering. Until a few years ago the only books you would have found on your church bookstall on the subject would have been saccharine best-selling paperbacks telling you to 'be a woman', by people who have tried.[2] They simply ignore many of the problems experienced by women – and men – today.

But so what? Why should we worry about the way women and men relate? After all, you may say, it is the world's problem; let the world solve it. But we are in the world (John 17:15,18). If our village has the plague we will catch it; if our country goes to war we do too; if our society embraces a philosophy we will come under its influence. It is useless to pretend we are not being radically affected by changing sexual patterns. They are altering our politics, our places of work, and the way we bring up our families. Unless we want to be helpless victims to the new philosophy we must know what it is saying. We must also be salt and light. We must shape the world. We must vote when there is an election and protest when there is injustice. And we need to understand changing trends in our society and know whether to resist or encourage them.[3]

I have heard it said that sexism is not an important issue. And in a sense, of course, this is true. It is not eternal. Sexual relationships and their related problems will pass away. So, indeed, will poverty. So will slavery. So will torture and war, capitalism and socialism. One can legitimately argue that none of these issues is of paramount importance. By far the most important thing in life is the gospel. Whether people are discriminated against, or happy in their marriages, or composing beautiful music is of no importance at all compared with whether their sins are forgiven. But Jesus nevertheless cared about these things. He still fed the hungry and healed the sick and wined and dined with the merry. He was never in any doubt that it was more important to save people than feed them, to teach them than heal them.[4] However, He did feed them and heal them. He did care about these things. We should too. Sexual disharmony can lead to unhappiness, frustration, or injustice. It may have comparatively little effect on our eternal destiny, but it certainly warrants our attention.

Nevertheless perhaps you think that it does not warrant yours. If you are a man you may feel these are women's problems, and you are not involved. Or, if a woman, that they are problems for other, 'feminist', women but not the rest of us. Perhaps you get on perfectly with the opposite sex and never feel misunderstood by them; perhaps you do not mind who wears the trousers or even if nobody wears any at all. But we are told to love and honour one another. We are told to bear one another's burdens (Galatians 6:2). We are instructed to be a body (1 Corinthians 12:12,14). Some Christians are troubled by these issues. Some feel that our cultural, and Christian, heritage is deeply sexist. And we in the Church must nourish and care for each other: a few concerned people cannot overcome the sexism of the rest of us.

This brings us to the crunch. It is often glibly thought that Christian women are 'happy and fulfilled' since Christian men are 'unselfish and understanding'. As a result we tend to think that these 'feminist' concerns are not ours. Alas! all too often they are more ours than anyone else's. The Church seems, in many ways, to be one of the worst perpetrators of sexism. Many women feel that it is amongst fellow Christians, above all, that they are most devalued.

This has been my own experience. I reached the age of eighteen without ever noticing male chauvinism. Then I spent a weekend on a Christian holiday camp. In many ways it was an excellent and godly place; the people were kind, and the teaching, on the whole, was biblical. Yet the women were treated as inferior. We were kept apart from the men and given menial, domestic work. I was deeply shocked. For the first time I experienced that so-called 'envy of men' which we women, according to Freud, are all supposed to feel. I caught myself thinking I would rather be a man. Not because I wanted to change sex, but because I would rather have played tennis in the sun than peeled spuds in the kitchen.

I have often found this kind of sexual inequality amongst Christians since. I know I am not alone. The most pernicious aspect of it all is that unashamed sexual prejudice is sometimes taught as a biblical truth. I have frequently heard frank male chauvinism presented as a creed of our faith.

The answer to heresy is truth. The answer to bogus biblical teaching is true biblical teaching. And the answer to sexism in the Church is a better understanding of what God says about the sexes. We are probably all agreed on this. Why, then, do we still find unbiblical attitudes, even unbiblical teaching, in the Church?

On some things the Bible gives us clear guidance. It is not difficult to see that murder and idolatry are wrong. On others, scripture seems harder to interpret. Are divorce and remarriage permissible? Should slavery be abolished? Sometimes the Bible does not directly apply itself to the issues we face. At other times the answers are staring us in the face, yet we find them remarkably hard to see. None of us comes to the Bible with an unprejudiced mind. Our preconceptions cloud our perceptions. And there are two main reasons for this.

Scripture twisting

The first reason is that we often *want* the Bible to say something. Take the question of divorce and remarriage. I have a friend who was deserted and subsequently, most unwillingly, divorced. He now needs to know whether he is free to marry again. He very much wants to believe he is and this makes his task of interpretation difficult. He will want to cling to the texts which suggest that remarriage is acceptable; he will want to 'reinterpret' the texts which suggest the opposite if he can. Since he is aware of this, if he comes to a favourable conclusion he may wonder if he persuaded himself into it because that was what he wanted to believe all along.

And it is the same with the biblical teaching on the sexes. It is tempting to ignore certain passages of scripture because they are unpalatable. Consider the usual understanding of 1 Corinthians 11:3–15 (pages 90–1). There is an almost unanimous agreement that Paul is commanding women to cover their heads in some way in worship. And yet there is also an almost unanimous conspiracy to ignore this command. It is disregarded as 'culturally conditioned' and therefore irrelevant today. Of course there is common sense in this. However, I suspect the reason most of us interpret the passage like this is not because we have done some hard biblical thinking, but because we find the idea of compulsory headgear repellent.

This 'culturally relative' approach is dangerous. If part of the Bible can be reapplied because it is 'cultural' so can the rest. Much of it is. Paul's words on marriage, women's authority, and women's silence are all susceptible to similar treatment. Often he is written off as the last word in male chauvinism before he has been properly read. More striking still, his revolutionary support of women is totally ignored. All this is because people do not like what he has to say. It is difficult to come to the Bible with an open mind if it is likely to change the way we live. It is hard to be honest about 1 Peter 3:1 if you do not like the idea of submitting to your husband. Of course, much of the Bible may have to be reapplied today, but it is difficult to do this objectively because so much is at stake.

So this is the first reason biblical interpretation can be difficult: we all want the Bible to say certain things. The second reason is this: we all *expect* the Bible to say certain things. There are so many traditional understandings of the scriptures that it is hard to read them without preconceptions. Get a friend who does not know the story well to read through Genesis 3. Then ask her what the couple ate. She will probably say an apple. Get another friend to read Matthew 2. Ask him how many wise men came to see Jesus. He will probably say three kings. Yet the text makes no mention of an apple or any number of kings.

I have seen many examples of this phenomenon. I was studying 1 Peter with some friends and we started the evening by reading the book out loud. Chapter 3 verse 19 (RSV) goes like this: ' . . . in which he went and preached to the spirits in prison . . .' Yet the person reading the passage read: ' . . . in which he went *down* and preached to the spirits in prison'. Though he had never heard of the tradition, he had subconsciously absorbed the patristic teaching that this verse is about Christ's descent into hell. This influenced his, and indeed everybody else's, approach to the passage; almost all of us assumed that was what it was about, though the text itself hardly hints at it.

Another occasion was a talk about Paul's teaching on

sex in 1 Corinthians. Most of the audience would have claimed to know the Bible fairly well and read it regularly. Yet when the talk was prefaced with half a dozen questions, almost everyone gave answers diametrically opposed to the biblical ones. 'Who should govern your body?' it was asked. 'Christ,' they answered, though Paul tells them it is their spouses (1 Corinthians 7:4). 'Is the body temporary or permanent?' To this the unanimous reply was 'temporary', though the Bible clearly teaches that it will be raised immortal and incorruptible (1 Corinthians 6:13,14; 15:42). The preconceived ideas we have about the Bible often hinder our understanding of it. As we studied both the Petrine and Pauline passages, people read all kinds of implications into the texts that were never intended by the writers.

We have the same kind of preconceptions about the teaching on men and women. Read the account of Eve's creation in Genesis 2:18–25 (page 13). Who is presented as the weaker partner? Which of the two would be more helpless, more incomplete without the other? Who is to be the assistant, the follower, the 'number 2' in the partnership? Why, the woman of course. It is clearly taught throughout the passage: she was made for man's benefit; she was a subsequent, junior, version; she was only a tiny bone out of his body; even her name is derived from his. In short, she owes her being to him and exists for his convenience. This may seem an extreme interpretation of the passage, but many of us believe it says something of the sort. We think the writer is saying woman is man's subordinate and created to be his assistant. Why? Is this what the passage actually says?

Try reading it the other way round. Suppose God had made the woman first, and the man out of her. Substitute the woman for the man and the man for the woman, and read the account again. Now who comes over as the helpless, dependent one, the weaker, inferior partner? Why, the woman again of course! She could not cope alone; man had to be made to bail her out. Part of her body was taken away to make him; she can never again be complete on her own. The man was made last, after the plants, after the animals, and certainly after the woman; he is the crown of God's creation. He was made out of human flesh; she is nothing but dust. Even her name ('man' now of course) is a diminutive version of his ('woman'). She is to 'cleave' to him (and, as it happens, this word is 'used almost universally for a weaker cleaving to a stronger';[5] no doubt a great deal would be made of this if the woman were to cleave to the man). Most significant of all, she is to leave her parents and her way of life to join him and adapt to him; she was clearly found to be inadequate on her own.

If we think that the Bible says something we will probably find it there. Church and society have told us for centuries that woman is man's subordinate so we expect to find this in the Bible. And we are not disappointed. As long as we do not look too carefully it is precisely what we do find.

There is another example of this tendency in the very same passage. Again we have been told that woman was made as man's 'helpmate'. You may even, depending on your translation, think it is what you have just read in Genesis 2. The implication is that she is his back-up. He does the work, like an operating surgeon, and she is the nurse handing him the forceps. I know marriages which function on this understanding of the word 'helpmate': vicars' wives, for example, who are expected to have little work other than that of promoting their husbands; whose chief (and often admirable) purpose in life is to facilitate their partners' existences.

And yet this extraordinary word 'helpmate' never appears in the Bible. Eve was created as Adam's 'help'. This word does not imply subordination, inferiority, or in any way a secondary position. On the contrary, it is usually used in the Old Testament to refer to God, as man's help.[6] She is also to be 'meet' for him. The word means 'matching', 'corresponding to', or 'opposite to' the man. So the latter word implies equality, and the former superiority! Yet 'helpmate' is presumably a corruption of these two words. And because of all the connotations of this unbiblical word, when we read Genesis 2 we assume all sorts of things that are not there.

There are numerous such examples. I have heard people ask 'Why did Paul think women more sinful?', though he never suggests such a thing: or 'What did he mean by the word headship?', although he never once uses it.

Conclusion

There is ample reason for addressing ourselves to the question of relationships between male and female, and how we should live together as the image of God. The human race traditionally tends to make a number of mistakes: we often tolerate and even encourage inequality and segregation between the sexes. Our own particular society, although beginning to combat these errors, is now adding more of its own; unless we want to end up worse off than we were before, Christians need to engage in the battle and direct some of the fighting. Lastly, and most to our shame, we in the Church are often the most to blame. Instead of being in the front leading the way, we are often miles behind the back line, dragging our feet unhappily and rather unthinkingly in the direction the majority are going. It is imperative that we study what God says about it all. To do this we must submit ourselves to His word.

But we need to be careful. We must be wary of what we want to find. Perhaps we want to believe that the sexes have different roles, or that husbands have a certain authority, or that marriage should be symmetrical, or women ordained. We may have to surrender cherished views. The Bible is not always a comfortable book to read.

And we also have to be wary of what we expect to find. We tend to think, quite sensibly, that the correct interpretation of the Bible is the most obvious one. This is usually true. However, the 'obvious' can be determined and shaped by all sorts of factors. Sometimes we have heard something so often that it becomes 'obvious'. If we look a little closer it may not be there at all. It seemed obvious to our 1 Corinthians 7 study group that the body is unimportant: almost every other philosophy teaches it, so it was assumed that the Bible did too. It is only the careful reader who sees that this is not the case. We need to come to the Bible with a fresh mind. We must be ready to challenge things we have always assumed to be true.

With this in mind, we will turn to what God says about male and female.

TWO

Difference

'The old war-cry of the sexists – *vive la différence* –
actually implied exactly the opposite; the rigid division
of an infinite variety of people into just two categories,
male and female. '
                              Jill Tweedie, **In the Name of Love**[1]

' "All the women in history have been men." Discuss.'
                              1066 And All That.[2]

We are different. This is mentioned in God's first reference to the human race. We are not just people; we are male and female, and this means we are different. This would seem so obvious it is hardly worth saying, yet it is something people argue about all the time. We assert it. We refute it. Some say the differences between us exist in every sphere of life, others that they hardly exist at all. Whole books have been written insisting there are differences between men and women, as if that had ever been in doubt.[3] Other books are devoted to showing that the differences are culturally induced, as if that suddenly makes them irrelevant.[4]

And people get hot under the collar on this topic. 'Of course, women are more emotional,' someone says with confident omniscience. The particular woman opposite him, sensing some dangerous slight she does not even stop to examine, hotly denies it and passionately insists that women are not emotional at all. Somehow we feel that a great deal is at stake. But what? Why does it matter anyway?

It matters because we link 'difference' and 'discrimination'. If two groups of people can be proved to be different from each other in some way that we think is important, we believe we can treat them differently. Some people like it when women and men are treated differently. Some do not. This is what motivates us to argue the case one way or the other. For years it was assumed that women were more stupid than men. It seemed logical for men to hold offices of government and power and authority. After all, you do not want your country run by congenital idiots. But if it can be proved that there is no significant difference between our IQs we might question a system which favours half the race at random.

Similarly the innate, rather than cultural, differences between the sexes are given importance. If it can be shown that girls are born more domestic and fond of babies than boys, and boys born more aggressive and competitive than girls (rather than both being trained to be so) we might assume that God has made women to stay at home with children and men to pursue competitive careers. The way we are created could be seen to reinforce the status quo. Again some people like the status quo; others do not. This is why they are keen to prove the issue one way or the other.

But there are really two questions. The first is *how are we different?* And the second is *so what?* Do sexual differences indeed mean that we should treat the sexes differently? It is the second question which is the important and interesting one. But we cannot answer it without considering the first. So what exactly are the sexual differences? The relevant text is Genesis 2.

(18) Then the LORD God said, 'It is not good that the man should be alone; I will make a helper fit for him.' (19) So out of the ground the LORD God formed every beast of the field and every bird of the air, and brought them to the man to see what he would call them; and

whatever the man called every living creature, that was its name. (20) The man gave names to all cattle, and to the birds of the air, and to every beast of the field; but for the man there was not found a helper fit for him. (21) So the LORD God caused a deep sleep to fall upon the man, and while he slept took one of his ribs and closed up its place with flesh; (22) and the rib which the LORD God had taken from the man he made into a woman and brought her to the man. (23) Then the man said,

> 'This at last is bone of my bones
> and flesh of my flesh;
> she shall be called Woman,
> because she was taken out of Man.'

(24) Therefore a man leaves his father and mother and cleaves to his wife, and they become one flesh.

(Genesis 2)

This passage tells us that the sexes are different. It is about the making of woman, which means, in effect, the making of sexual differentiation. God, suprisingly, did not make another man. Some theologians think He should have done.[5] But there it is. He did not.

So far so good. We are told that we are different. But that is all. The Bible gives us no clue at all as to what the difference is. A friend of mine spent an entire evening with her church study group, which included an outstanding biblical scholar, trying to discover what, according to the Bible, are the differences between the sexes. They all drew blank. (And also, incidentally, got very cross with each other.)

Between every woman and every man

If the Bible does not tell us we shall have to work it out for ourselves. We must start with what we know for sure; before moving onto the controversial, we should state the undeniable. We are genitally different. Men beget children, or are designed to, and women bear them. There may be other sexual differences, but this is the only one on which everyone is agreed. It is the only one we can be sure of between *every* woman and *every* man.

And its relevance

Where does this get us? We now come to the second, more important, question: what is the relevance of this difference? The answer would seem to be, none. It does not in itself suggest that we should treat the sexes differently. There is no reason why those who conceive children should behave or be treated in any significantly different way from those who beget them.

We could say that the reproductive difference is created by God, so it is good. Attempts to tamper with it are suspect. Two men wanting to adopt a family together, or multi-parent families, as advocated by Greer[6] (not extended families, but households where children do not know which, of the many parents, are theirs), are not God's design. The same goes for the latest plan to do away with sex and reproduce by cloning, so men could be phased out altogether (however attractive some may consider the prospect).

We can also see that a few occupations may be more fitting for one sex than the other: I personally think it is appropriate that midwives, obstetricians and gynaecologists should by and large be women; not because they will do the job any better, but because the work involves such intimacy. A woman doctor is obviously more suitable for conducting internal examinations; apart from anything else, she is free to show sensitivity and tenderness without misunderstanding. Similarly I believe a man should be offered a male nurse for bed baths and other intimate services. However, even this much is mere personal preference: Shaun tells me many men would be far more embarrassed being nursed by a man.

So our reproductive difference could possibly make a few specialised jobs more suitable for one sex or the other. Women should care for rape victims, since they will be more able to sympathise. Men should counsel young boys with sexual problems, since they will be more likely to know what they are going through. Common sense tells us all this, and the fact that we are genitally different does not take us any further.

Between 'masculine' and 'feminine'

There is a second kind of difference. I suggest it tentatively: the Bible merely hints at it so we must use the idea with care.

Male and female are simply genetic, biological differences. 'Masculine' and 'feminine' are more than this. They are poetic symbols; they represent other things. C. S. Lewis describes this well in *Voyage to Venus*. He explains how masculine or feminine ('gender') encompasses far more than mere male or female ('sex'):

> Sex is, in fact, merely the adaptation to organic life of a fundamental polarity which divides all created beings. Female sex is simply one of the things that have female gender; there are many others ... the male and female of organic creatures are rather faint and blurred reflections of masculine and feminine. Their reproductive functions, their differences in strength and size, partly exhibit, but partly also confuse and misrepresent, the true polarity...[7]

The world is full of opposites. There are day and night, strength and weakness, logic and intuition. There are nature and artifice, spirit and matter; and there are male and female. Because this is the best example it is often used as a symbol for the others: earth may be seen as feminine and sky as masculine; or matter as feminine and spirit masculine; or the moon as a woman and the

sun as a man. We can perhaps understand this better by
borrowing from the notion of 'yin' and 'yang'. In Chinese
thinking these opposites are not categorised sexually.
Night and earth, internal things, coolness and co-opera-
tion, are seen as yin. Day, heaven, external matters,
warmth and competition, all belong to the yang.
Feminine is also classed as yin; masculine as yang.[8] The
significance of the idea is its illustration of harmony.
Neither yin nor yang is good or bad in itself. What
matters is the balance of these opposites, without which
nothing can function properly.

This idea is also touched on in the Bible. As we shall
see, there is a suggestion that God has made differences,
which we call feminine and masculine as the Chinese
call them yin and yang, but which are far larger than
mere differences between a woman and a man. It is as if
God has made principles of femininity and masculinity
to express different things about Himself.

Look at it this way. God is both just and merciful.
Suppose He were to make two kinds of creature, both in
His image, each reflecting different aspects of Himself.
Men might express His justice, for example, and women
His mercy – or vice versa. In this way parents often
complement each other, and give their children different
images of God. But it does not follow that every man is
more just than every woman, or any particular woman
more merciful than a particular man. It is not so much
that men are just as that justice, and men, may both be
'masculine'; not so much that women are merciful as that
mercy, and women, might both be 'feminine'. It is not
really to do with individual men and women, but with
certain principles which can be represented by gender
itself.

If we pursue this idea further, we will find that 'masculine' and 'feminine' principles have different functions.
For example a man represented the race in a way that a
woman did not. It is in Adam we all die, not in Adam
and Eve (1 Corinthians 15:22). It is in Christ we are all

made alive, and Christ came to earth as a man (Romans 5:12–19). Some say He had to because of social restrictions on women at the time. Nonsense. When did Jesus care about social restrictions when important issues were at stake? This argument is as unconvincing as the claim that Jehovah revealed Himself as a male God because nobody was thinking in terms of female divinities: on the contrary, there were plenty of goddesses around at the time.[9]

There is more to this than mere coincidence. The fact that 'man' can mean human beings in general, as well as a male human being, is no fluke. Nor is it an isolated flaw of the English tongue. French has the same characteristic. So does New Testament Greek. It could be argued that this, too, is simply another sexist quirk of 'man'-made language. But at the beginning of Genesis we find the same idea, and this time consciously and deliberately expressed. 'Adam' means the human race. The first mention of humanity goes like this: 'So God made adam in his own image, after his likeness he created him; male and female he created them' (Genesis 1:27).

The word meaning the human race is thus deliberately chosen as the name of the first man, as we all know. The woman was called Life, because she is its origin: mortal life in the form of the human race, and eventually eternal life in the form of Jesus, are born through her. The man was called 'Humankind', because he *is* the human race. (As Alex Motyer, an Old Testament exegete, is reputed to have said, 'In Hebrew thought man embraces woman ... Whoopee!') So total is this identification of the male with the whole race that it is hard to know when adam has stopped meaning 'humanity' and started meaning Adam himself. The most striking juxtaposition of the two uses of the word is in Genesis 5:2–3: 'When God created man, he made him in the likeness of God. (2) He created them male and female; at the time they were created, he blessed them and called them adam. (3) When adam had lived 130 years, he had a son in his own likeness, in his own image; and he named him Seth.' It is no mere linguistic mistake. The man, not the couple, represented the whole human race.[10]

I am fully aware that 'man'-centred vocabulary can be used to degrade and ignore women.[11] But this is not the fault of language so much as of male-centred thinking in every sphere. It is true that when we hear the word 'chairman' we think of a man, not of a person of either sex. But until recently the same could be said of 'MP', 'doctor' or 'prime minister'. It is true that most of us, when we hear of the descent of 'Man', think of the descent of a beefy, hairy hunter;[12] that when we mention Neolithic 'man' we envisage a Neolithic male. However, I suspect we would do this whatever we called the species. Calling humanity 'Man' is thoroughly biblical. It has only become sexist because, in the impoverishment of our language and the masculine bias of our culture, 'man' has ceased to mean 'male and female'.

So the first human being, a man, represented the race. I can imagine steam rising out of the ears of some of my readers. Let me hasten to put the other side of the picture – for though the Bible shows ways in which the sexes are different, it also always shows, beneath the difference, a far more profound similarity. Humankind was represented by a man. But it is also, in a different way, represented by something 'feminine'. In its relationship to God the human race is frequently portrayed as a woman. All too often, alas, we are the faithless wife,[13] but we are also, often, called the beloved bride.[14] The way we respond to God is usually represented by a feminine image.

I know this idea might make some people even angrier. I suggested it once to a friend and she got very annoyed with me. After all, this 'feminine response to God' business can be seen as more veiled sexism. By itself, one could argue, the fine, upstanding human race is masculine; in comparison with God it pales into the feminine.[15] This interpretation simply reinforces the idea that male means good, and strong, and self-sufficient, and female means sinful and weak and helpless. Some people seem determined to find any difference threatening, and there is no need for such a tortured interpretation. The human race is neither fine nor upstanding on its own. It is singularly despicable on its own. It is only in its response to God, if you like when it is at its most feminine, that the human race can ever hope to be good, or fine, or upstanding.

(And perhaps at this point it should also be said that arguing God's gender is a singularly fruitless pastime. One can debate the question endlessly: God is always 'He', and we are taught to call Him Father; on the other hand there are many instances of Him behaving to us as a mother,[16] and He cannot be more of one sex than another since male and female are equally in His image. And so on. But God is not any sex at all. Our gender is defined by our genitalia. How can we say that God is a particular sex? He is spirit: He transcends sexuality.)

Its relevance

Thus, as well as the obvious reproductive difference between every man and every woman, there is another, more pervasive but less identifiable difference between the principles of feminine and masculine.

And so to the more important question. What are the implications? Does this difference mean we should treat the sexes differently? It may be frightfully fascinating but will it change the way we live? The answer is no. The information is important, but not of direct practical use. There are two reasons for this.

First, as we have stressed, it is in the realm of abstract ideas, which are simply being expressed in sexual terms. It describes the principles behind gender, rather than people we know. It is concerned with the difference between masculinity and femininity, not the difference between Mr and Mrs Jones. It may tell us that a Man had to represent the human race in salvation because a man represented us in sin; it certainly does not tell us that men in general are more representative of us than women. It may tell us that our response to God can be described as feminine because Israel is described as a wife; it does not tell us that Sarah Smith is more responsive to God than Joe Bloggs. So it does not tell us how to behave towards the Joneses, or Smith and Bloggs.

Second, it is tentative. It is speculative. It is an idea which must be used with enormous care. Though the Bible hints at it, it never states it categorically, and it certainly never applies it. God never says, 'Because a man stood for the race so a man must stand for the country; you must have kings not queens.' Nor does He say, 'Because the Church is my bride women make better Christians than men; you should have women doing Christian work not men.' We will quickly get into trouble if we try to use these ideas, as C. S. Lewis does, to say women cannot be priests because they cannot represent God to man.[17] We could just as easily say men cannot be priests because they cannot represent the human response to God.

This difference cannot dictate our behaviour, but it is still important. Though it cannot command us, it can enlighten us. For example, if God tells us *elsewhere* that women must not be priests this difference could help us understand why not. It is not telling us what to do, but explaining why we might do it. When God comes to earth as a man not a woman this difference can help us see why, and why, as a man, He can represent all humankind. But it does not demand different behaviour or treatment for women and men.

Between the average woman and the average man

But neither of these is what is meant by the difference between the sexes. When people cry 'vive la différence' they do not seriously fear a universal genitalectomy. They do not even consider the more philosophical differences. They mean all the rest. You know. Women are emotional; men are strong; girls are soppy; boys are made of puppy-dogs' tails, and so on. This is what people want to assert or deny – the popular generalisations.

A lot of them are obvious. Most men are taller and stronger and hairier than most women. Some are less obvious. Many little girls like dolls, whereas boys often find them repulsive. Again, some of these differences are clearly and deliberately taught, not innate: in our society girls are brought up to take care of their appearance; boys are expected to be interested in sport. Some differences, on the other hand, have been with the human race so long it would take millennia to undo them: women may once have been as swift or as large as men, but they have surely been physically weaker now for several thousand years at least.

We could devote the entire book to arguing these differences – others do – and for our purposes it would be a complete waste of time. Even if it were conclusive (which is unlikely) the information would be useless because it would not answer the more important question. *So what?* Of what consequence would it all be? The answer is, absolutely none.

Its utter irrelevance

The trouble with these so-called differences is that they are sweeping generalisations. As such they are useless. We cannot discriminate on the grounds of generalisations. We must not treat all men and women differently on the basis of most women and most men.

For one thing it is unnecessary. If girls and boys are really different the differences will surface anyway. We do not need to give girls dolls and boys footballs: if we leave an assortment of toys in the nursery, the children (if they do have preferences because of their sex) will tend to choose appropriate playthings anyway. As J. S. Mill pointed out,[18] we are more likely to be fostering sexual differences because we fear they are *not* there than because we are confident they are.

For another thing, it is unjust. It may be generally true that girls are good at languages and boys at science. Is it therefore right and fair for boys to have better science teachers or more attention in the class? Of course not. A *few* of the girls may be brilliant: why should they suffer because of average statistics? Similarly, it might be possible to prove that more women than men enjoy home-making, either because of the expectations made of them or the hormonal balance. Is it proper or logical for society to educate them for such a role or put pressure on them to adopt it? No. There are always going to be some women who do not like it at all. They are as much 'women' as the others; why should they be made to feel unfeminine because they do not fall within the mean?

Someone who loves being domestic should, of course, be encouraged to run a home. This is not because she is a woman and other women have been good at the job before her, but because she, or he, has chosen it and is good at the job her- or himself. This is an important distinction. It is illogical to say (as I have heard some people do) that women should not be head teachers or barristers or vicars because their voices are not loud enough. Some women's are. On the other hand it may be perfectly reasonable to say that people with soft voices (many of whom might prove to be women) are not suitable for these jobs.

Many people think the Bible says women should not be ordained because they are not authoritative or objective enough. But some women are. If they should not be ordained it is for far better reasons. Some people think Paul says women should not teach or have authority because they are gullible (1 Timothy 2:12–14). This is ridiculous. Paul was a highly disciplined, logical thinker. If he had meant 'gullible people should not teach or have authority' he would have said so.

To sum up then, there are three kinds of difference between women and men: undeniable reproductive differences between every woman and every man; a possible, almost indefinable difference between the 'feminine' and the 'masculine'; and probable, general differences between many women and many men. Again we ask the important question. What is the relevance of this? Can it be used, as is normally assumed, as a reason for different treatment?

The first can. It is a right and proper ground for discrimination. The biological difference between us rules some of us out for certain jobs. Men cannot be wet-nurses. Nor should they be employed to conduct intimate frisking of women. Nor can they earn money as surrogate mothers. Apart from these highly specialised forms of employment, though, there are few situations where the biological difference is relevant. I have been turned down for a role in a film because I was eight months pregnant and did not look the part. Fair enough. People who are eight months pregnant do not make very good athletes, ballet dancers, or in my case, anorexic teenagers. But when it comes to employing traffic wardens, prime ministers, nurses, miners, or indeed almost anyone else, the biological difference is completely irrelevant. It is a good reason for discrimination when it is appropriate. It is scarcely ever appropriate.

The next difference, as we have seen, is no reason at all. The difference between 'feminine' and 'masculine' does not dictate different behaviour or needs for individual men and women. Besides, the Bible never applies it. God suggests it exists. He never asks that it govern our behaviour.

And the third difference is more irrelevant still. Discrimination because of general and controversial observations – the usual grounds for any kind of discrimination – is nothing but unjust prejudice. Each individual must be treated on his or her own merits.

So the differences between the sexes do not mean we should treat the sexes differently. The only legitimate form of discrimination is one that common sense teaches us anyway: any fool can see that men cannot be wet-nurses. This aside, there is no reason why women should not be educated, employed, brought up and treated in exactly the same way as men.

Does this mean we have been wasting our time? If the difference between us is irrelevant, why have we spent a whole chapter on it? Actually, it is not irrelevant at all. It is important. As has been said, God did not make a second man. He made a woman. There was a very good reason for it, but it was not the reason we have been pursuing.

The trouble is, we have been asking the wrong question. We have been asking how the differences might make us discriminate. We had to ask this question because everyone else is asking it, but it does not take us anywhere. Sexual distinctions, like racial ones, do not mean we should discriminate. They do not indicate that we should behave or be treated differently in any way. The question we now have to ask is: 'if the difference does not mean we should discriminate, what does it mean instead?'

The answer is simple. It means we need one another. A singer and an accompanist need each other far more than two pianists do; a socket and a plug are far more use than two plugs or two sockets. We will probably never know all the differences. We do not need to. Their relevance is this: God made us different to complement each other.

We will come back to this in chapter 6. It is, after all, the central theme of this book. First, though, we will examine the other side of what we have been saying. We are obviously different. But we are also equal.

THREE

Equality

'Both sexes are equal, but one is more equal than the other.'[1]

Equal in theory

We are equal. This is the second thing God says about us. Although we are different, He has given us the same value. And biblically this is more important than our difference. Turn again to Genesis 2:18–25, the account of Eve's creation and the making of sexual distinctions. The difference is merely implied. The equality is stressed three times, and in three different ways.

It is first stated in God's purpose. He wants to make someone suitable for Adam, someone fit for him. As we have seen, the word means appropriate (page 8). She had to be right for him in every single way. In other words God wanted someone to balance Adam, to complement him, to be his partner. Someone above him or below him would not be perfectly 'meet'. He needed an equal.

This notion is then illustrated by contrasting the future woman with the animals. Verses 19 and 20, when God brought the other creatures to the man, is placed here as a vivid contrast. It is a graphic example of the wrong thing. The whole point of the naming of the animals at this juncture in the story is that the animals would not do. They were simply not meet. Adam was over them; he was, if you like, their 'superior', just as God was his. But he was in need of help, not another creature to govern;

the animals were rejected. He needed an equal.

Lastly, this interpretation is confirmed in God's method. Because the animals were not right for what He had in mind, He decided to create the man's partner in a new way. He would make her out of him. They would be naturally equal. They were made of the same stuff, the same flesh and blood. The similarity between them was profound, as the man recognised as soon as he saw her. 'At last!' he said, 'this is flesh of my flesh.' At last he had an equal.

So the correspondence between the sexes is more important than the distinction. It is given more emphasis by the writer. This is true to our experience: striking though some of the differences between men and women might be, they are superficial when compared with the similarities. The ways in which we are the same run far deeper, and this essential similarity is what makes us equal. We are equally human, and equally valuable in the eyes of God.

How can we be different but equal? People who are different seem unequal. They may not be equally old, or dark-skinned, or good at football. And men and women are not 'equal' in this sense. But two siblings can be very different, yet equal in their family standing. One is tall and blond and stupid, and the other is short, dark and clever. Nevertheless, they share the same parents, so they are equally members of the family. It is in this way that women and men, blacks and whites, the handicapped and the able-bodied, are equal. We have things in common which are more important than our differences. This lesson is taught throughout the Bible.

We are, male and female, equally good. We are equally created after God's likeness. It is wrong to suggest, as some have done,[2] that a man on his own can be in God's image but a woman on her own cannot. His image is to be restored in woman and man alike.

We are equally bad. We both disobey God, so we are equally sinful (Romans 3:23). The woman took the

initiative, but they both ate the fruit (Genesis 3:6). After
the act was done they were both in the same fallen state.
It is also wrong to suggest that woman is more – or less –
sinful than man.[3]

We are equally judged. We are equally mortal as a
result of sin ('for the wages of sin is death' for everyone
alike, Romans 6:23). As a result, we are considered
equally responsible. I have heard a preacher say that
when you marry a woman you must answer for her sins
(to which a friend of mine replied that he had quite
enough of his own without multiplying them by ten).
This is not biblical. As God gives us the same punishment, He considers us equally answerable.

We are equally saved. Paul makes this point in his
letter to the Galatians. He is primarily talking about the
difference between Jews and Gentiles, which seems to
have troubled the Galatians, but he shows how salvation
ignores other barriers as well: 'There is neither Jew nor
Greek, there is neither slave nor free, there is no male
and female, for you are all one in Christ Jesus' (Galatians
3:28).

It is indeed true that men and women, blacks and
whites, children and the very old are equal in the sight of
God.

Equal in practice?

I doubt if many people would disagree with this. A
theoretical and spiritual equality is something we now
find quite easy to accept. But a belief is useless unless we
act upon it. When God informs our minds it is because
He wants to transform our lives. Doctrine is never of
mere academic interest. If we believe we are equal we
must live according to this belief. This is where we fail. I
know of nobody who denies the sexes equality when the
subject is being discussed. Yet I know plenty of people
who deny it in the way they think and act and feel. We
must change our behaviour to match our beliefs. We

know we are equal; we must treat one another as such.

The Church is not good at this. The following are all comments I have heard, from different women of different churches and different backgrounds, about attitudes encountered among their fellow Christians. None of them was a woman of 'feminist' leanings.

'Being a woman on the PCC is worse than being a worm.'

'His (the vicar's) attitude to women is – well, awful really. Women are expected to make the tea and cook the harvest supper, but they're not expected to think.'

'He (another vicar) wouldn't dream of asking a woman's opinion; they wouldn't have a contribution.'

'He sort of writes off women. He thinks in terms of men. Everything's very male.'

'I was never expected to have an opinion. I was never expected to think.'

Clearly these people feel they are treated as inferior to men. The Christian doctrine of the equality of the sexes is, in practice, being denied. How can we overcome this?

Indiscriminate treatment?

Should we treat everybody the same? This must be the most obvious way of equalising everyone, but is it necessarily right? Parents who have several children know that loving them all equally may mean treating them differently. Because they are not the same they do not have the same needs: one will be reduced to tears by a cross word; another will grin through a thrashing. The older one might want an expensive motor bike for his birthday; the younger one would rather have a box of pencils. In loving them equally, a wise parent will treat them differently.

People sometimes look back in anger on the history of our country and say women were treated as inferior. This accusation needs careful thought. True, until this century they did not have the vote. Until the last they lost control of all their property at marriage, and so on. But this is similar to the way in which we treat children. They do not have the vote. They have no power to dispose of any property they may own. They are not allowed sexual relations. They may not go to pornographic films.[4] Does this mean we consider them inferior, less worthy of happiness, or inessential to the welfare of the country? Surely not. We regard them as important. We believe (for some reason) that they are equally human and have equal human rights. We genuinely think their best interests are served by these restrictions. We may be mistaken, but we are sincere. Although we do not recognise them as full citizens with all the civic rights, we are certainly not trying to oppress them; we are aiming to respect them and treat them as equally valuable by giving them different treatment.

Similarly, cultures which treat women differently do not necessarily hold them in less esteem. It would be rash to assume that Victorian England (for example) did not value its women; in some ways they were looked up to as men's superiors. Nevertheless, there are a number of things which need to be said about treating people differently if we want to maintain their equality.

The first is that they must be treated *on an equal basis.* The parents who treat their children differently are nonetheless treating them on the same basis. They have not said one will be punished through life and the other rewarded; they are acting on the belief that everyone is equally in need of punishment for misdemeanour. They are disciplined differently because they respond differently. Basically, they are being treated in the same way.

This takes us on to the second point. You can only do this with *individuals.* Parents can do it because they know their own children. You cannot do the same with Jews, for example, or with women. It is mistaken to expect women to have different needs from men, and to treat them differently as a class, just as it would be wrong to say that all oldest children must be beaten, and all youngest children merely given a mild ticking off.

But the last and most important point is this: different treatment *must be reasonable*. Children are not given the vote for a reason: we believe they are not yet equipped to use it. They are not allowed sexual experiences for many reasons: quite apart from any moral considerations, they are seldom capable of saying 'no' to an adult, however much they might want to.

It is true that women – and working-class men – did not have the vote two hundred years ago for a reason: only property-holding men were thought to have a stake in the nation. The question is whether this was a good enough reason; for we saw in the last chapter that there is hardly ever a good reason to treat women differently from men. Occasionally our reproductive functions preclude one or other of us from something. That is all. Otherwise there is no reason to treat the sexes differently. So there is no adequate reason not to give women suffrage. There is no biblical reason why a wife should not control her estates. There is no satisfactory reason why women should be discriminated against in any of these ways.

We must indeed treat the sexes the same. This is the first way we should give men and women equality. We must be like God. He treats everyone on the same basis (Acts 10:34). So must we. He shows no partiality (Romans 2:11; Ephesians 6:9). Neither must we. His justice is the same for everyone. Ours must be too. We cannot expect God to use us fairly if we use others unfairly.

I have been told by a clergyman that I do not suffer as much from unemployment as a man does. (He is quite safe in saying this: it would be almost impossible to prove him wrong. Or, indeed, right.) The implication is that it does not matter as much if women are unemployed, so we need not do so much about it. This is not treating everyone on the same basis. It is not just. I have heard another clergyman say we could solve much unemployment by preventing married woman from working. (By contrast this is so obviously true it would not need proving. We could also 'solve' much unemployment by having the same policy towards Pakistanis, or people with red hair, or anyone under five foot four.) Such discrimination against people as a class is injustice, and should never be practised by Christians. We are not to be subject to prejudice (James 2:1–10). We are to be like God. We are to treat everybody the same.

If we look at the examples of sexism quoted earlier (on page 30), we can see the same tendencies emerge. Women are treated differently. For example they are not listened to in public. Many a woman has had a suggestion ignored, only to see it taken up later as a man's idea and adopted with enthusiastic praise. It has certainly happened to me. Or they are not taken seriously. Their problems are belittled or ridiculed. A friend of mine found it difficult being married to someone more success-ful than she. A man in her situation would have received sympathy and counselling. She was just 'being silly'. Again, expectations of women are lower. I was at a dinner party recently and asked my host a question about his work. Because the answer was vaguely technical he addressed it to Shaun (who, having missed the question, was mystified). One incident like this is amusing; an accumulation over the years is first disconcerting and then undermining. It makes one feel puzzled, ill at ease, and eventually simply inferior. These things are all symptomatic of an unchristian attitude. Women are frequently treated as unequal to men by women and men alike. Sometimes they are simply ignored. A friend of mine was giving a talk for a Pathfinder service. The hero of the story was 'Peter Pathfinder'. I asked him why he invented a character called Peter rather than Polly, and he said it would be impossible to base the talk on a girl: the boys would never relate to her. It never occurred to him that the girls might have difficulty relating to Peter – or even, it seems, that it mattered whether they did or not.

All this can cut both ways. Just as women are sometimes expected to be all-round idiots when it comes to anything academic, so a man is often assumed to be inept at the most simple matters relating to his own family. Soon after our first daughter was born a woman in our church was playing with her when Shaun told her what his baby tended to like and dislike. She was indignant. 'How would you know?' she said. 'You're a man!'

All these are examples of people being treated in a particular way because of their sex. Jesus did not do this. In a sense He treated everybody differently. He would sometimes say one thing to one person and the opposite to somebody else (compare Luke 8:38–9 with Luke 9:59). He behaved towards people as if they were all unique. But He never treated a woman 'as a woman', as some people do. As Dorothy Sayers said, 'Nobody could possibly guess from the words and deeds of Jesus that there was anything "funny" about women's nature.'[5] He did not behave differently towards someone because of her sex. Nor must we. A friend of mine had lost her job and was receiving pastoral advice from her bishop. 'Never mind,' he said glibly. 'God is calling you to be a woman, a wife, and a mother. You don't need to be anything else.' He would never have dreamt of offering a man a similar platitude. (How do you 'be a woman' anyway? It tends to happen whether you will it or not.) He was ignoring her individual need and treating her in a certain way because she was a woman. Jesus would not have done this. He treated everyone as an individual. We must do the same.

The simplest way to do so is to ask yourself, in your dealings with a woman, 'Would I treat a man like that?' (or vice versa, of course). I have a friend I am very fond of, whom I tended to call on when I was working near his house. We had many interesting afternoons and conversations and meals together. He was treating me like a normal person – or as he would treat a man. A few months later my situation changed. My job ended. I also became pregnant. His attitude towards me changed completely. I was no longer an ordinary person doing a job of work ('like a man'). I was a Future Mother. Suddenly he started treating me like a woman. We seemed to have nothing in common any more: he would only talk to me about Shaun, and Shaun's work, and any other domestic concerns he could think of. It was months before I could persuade him to have an interesting conversation with me again.

We can apply this rule to any group of people we tend to treat as a class. Children are often at the receiving end of the most extraordinary bad manners: they are ignored in conversation, lied to, laughed at in public, or rushed over their food. We need only ask ourselves 'Would I treat an adult like that?' to see how badly we are behaving.

We must treat everybody on the same basis. When dealing with large groups of men and women we must give them all the same treatment. When dealing with individual men and women we must give them individual treatment. This is the first way we must treat one another as equal. When Christians have learned to do this, we will have done away with almost all the sexism in the Church.

Protection

However, some discrimination is unconscious. If the buttons in a lift are five foot off the ground, children (and dwarfs) cannot use it. Many groups of people are vulnerable in some way – because they are physically weaker, or in a minority, or poorer, or less articulate – so their needs are often neglected. Society tends to arrange itself around its stronger members, around the middle-class, able-bodied, white, adult, educated male. If the rest of us are to be treated as equals our interests must be protected. If handicapped people are to be treated as equal to the un-handicapped, we must have wheelchair ramps at regular intervals along the kerb. This takes some thought.

We usually need to listen to disadvantaged people to discover their particular needs.

Women are vulnerable in some ways. There are obvious and terrible abuses, like rape, which women are subject to; clearly, if women are to be treated as men's equals, rape laws are very important. But there are numerous, less dramatic ways in which women may need protection, or simply consideration. A church I was in had a number of breast-fed babies. Because of the scruples of various members it was awkward for the mothers to feed them in church. This meant the women were disadvantaged. They might not be able to attend a church service for weeks if their babies needed feeding in the middle of a Sunday morning. Nobody was deliberately discriminating against them, or indeed treating women on a different basis, but the church should have catered for their needs (perhaps by providing a screened-off area) if it was to treat them as equals, equally in need of Christian teaching and fellowship.

Men also face disadvantages. It is often harder for them to attend church – perhaps because of an outdated image of Christianity; perhaps, under pressure to be 'macho', it is harder for a man to admit that he is a sinner; or perhaps it is simply because parish timetables are arranged around those who work at home. Whatever the reason, men need more encouragement to come to church. Yet our congregation does the opposite. Each week there are three or four meetings exclusively for women. There are none for men.

So in order to treat people as equals it is not enough simply to treat them as the same, important though this is. We must protect those who are vulnerable in any way, and look to each other's interests.

Positive discrimination

I have a friend who insists he does not want to treat women as inferior. He follows this up by saying 'though

I won't have discrimination in their favour'. Nevertheless, there is a place for positive discrimination. It must be used with great caution, and almost always as a temporary measure, but there is a place for it.

In the past, for example, engineering was considered an unfeminine subject. Women suffered a disadvantage: they would have to cope with others' implicit disapproval and their own reluctance to be 'unfeminine' if they were to succeed in the field. Obviously this is wrong in itself. It is unjust. (The fact that it is not deliberate does not make it any less so.) But there is another aspect of the situation which makes it highly undesirable. The real loser is not the individual woman. If she wants to be an engineer she probably will anyway. The loser is society. We are short of engineers, and have needlessly halved our supply. This is often the case: discrimination or prejudice may be as harmful to the society as to the individuals concerned; if we make it difficult for Africans or Indians to become doctors, we are going to deprive ourselves of good doctors.

The engineering industry has had the sense to spot this problem. In order to redress the balance some engineering firms give women particular encouragement: promising sixth-formers are invited on conferences to promote their interest in the work. Boys are not allowed. This is positive discrimination. And girls are beginning to apply for engineering in larger numbers. Firms and universities now have more good engineers.

There is a place for this in the Church. We suffer from a dire shortage of good biblical teachers. Our need is far more important than that of the engineering industry, yet we have halved the resources available to us. Women have been discouraged from studying theology or teaching the Bible. Almost all the promising young Christian men I know have been encouraged at some stage to consider full- or part-time Bible study and teaching work; I know plenty of equally competent young Christian women who have never had the suggestion put to them at all. If the Church exercised a little positive discrimination we might persuade some of them to take the idea seriously, and the benefits could be enormous. Whether or not we would allow men to take advantage of their skills and be taught by them is another issue (and one which we will come to later), but young Christian *women* could certainly be reaping the benefits. The engineering world has seen that talent is being wasted. It has made the effort to redress the balance. We in the Church have not.

To summarise, there are three ways we should treat people as equals. First, we must treat everybody on the same basis. Women and men should be treated the same. Individuals should be treated as individuals. This is by far the most important point. *Different* treatment accounts for almost all *unequal* treatment.

Next we need to protect disadvantaged members. Women must not be allowed to suffer because they are more vulnerable than men, or indeed men because in some ways they are more vulnerable than women. This is less important, but more likely to be ignored, so it is worth our attention.

Lastly, we sometimes need to use positive discrimination. Because of imbalances that have arisen, an individual may need particular help or encouragement. This is least important of all, and we should always be wary of it lest the pendulum swings too far the other way.

Equal in value

All these are ways of treating the sexes, or indeed anyone, as equal. They are important measures to take. In a sense, though, they do not quite get to the heart of the matter. To do this we need to approach the issue from a different angle. The essence of equality or inequality is not so much the *treatment* we give people as the *value* we put on them. The former is only, after all, an expression of the latter. The worst sexism of all is a failure to value the opposite sex.

I have a friend who is training for ministry in the Church. Her fellow students sometimes tell her it is a shame she is not a man; and they are apt to say this when she has made an intelligent or pertinent contribution. This kind of attitude is far worse than treating a woman badly. The implication is that a man is more use than a woman. Her intelligence would be better employed in him: it is rather wasted on her!

This is worse because it is a criticism, not of women, but of God Himself. Man needed help, God said, so He made woman. To imply that men are more useful, or valuable, or make a more important contribution, is to imply that God made a mistake. He should have made another man. We could have designed the human race rather better than He did.

The most heartbreaking example of this I have heard was from a close friend of mine. He had recently been to a depressing, rather decadent party, and was burning with compassion for the people he had met.

'The only thing in life worth doing,' he said with genuine feeling, 'is preaching the gospel of Christ.' Then he looked at his little daughter. 'Next time we must have a son,' he said to his wife, 'so that he can do just that.' In two sentences he had rendered the female sex useless.

So the heart of sexual equality, oddly enough, is the same as of sexual difference. We come to understand it when we realise our mutual need. It is enough for racial equality to follow the three rules set out earlier, and chiefly to treat blacks and whites, French and English, the same. Sexual equality goes much deeper. The races can survive without each other: the sexes cannot. And it is only when we realise this need that we will realise each other's value, and realise our equality.

Shaun and I are parents. The appearance of the thing suggests I am much more of a parent than he: I have borne them, given birth to them, and fed them for several months. Shaun merely had a few minutes of fun. My part seems more important. Yet this is a false conclusion. Shaun's contribution was different, but vital. We are both *equally* parents, because the part each played was essential. Yet society no longer treats the father as an equal parent (in reaction, it must be said, to the opposite imbalance of a hundred years ago): he is powerless to save his child from abortion (as a court case proved recently). If divorced it is far harder for him to win custody of his own children. And, sadly, I know a number of Christian women who treat their husbands as incompetent morons when it comes to the care of their children. 'I can't leave them with him,' they say. 'He won't change their nappies', or 'feed them properly', or something. But they are his children too. He has as much right to decide what they should eat or when they should be changed as she. It is quite out of place for the mother to assume this superior role, and she has only herself to blame if the father then abdicates from his job.

So this is what equality is really about. It is about recognising the other's value, the other's contribution, indeed realising our helplessness without the other. This is what it means to be the body of Christ: the eye cannot work without the brain, nor the foot without the heart. It is especially true of the sexes. It was not good for man to be alone, so God made a woman for him. She will do things differently, which is why we are indispensable to one another. Because we are both indispensable, we are equal. We must constantly bear in mind our utter dependence on the opposite sex. If we do this, it will be impossible to treat its members as inferior.

And it is this dependence we will now go on to consider.

FOUR

Interdependence

'(11) . . . there is no woman without man or man without woman in the Lord, (12) for as the woman is of the man, so the man is through the woman – but all things are of God.'

1 Corinthians 11

'I was a better man to you as a woman than I ever was to a woman as a man. If you see what I mean. Now I've got to learn to do it without a skirt on.'

Dustin Hoffman in *Tootsie*

The sexes are interdependent. This is the third, and most important, thing God says about us as male and female. We are designed to work together. This is the essence of the biblical teaching about the sexes.

Let us look once more at the account of Eve's creation, at the second half of Genesis chapter 2. That we are different, and that we are equal, are implied or suggested by the writer. That man needs woman is explicitly stated. This is the heart of the account. It is the reason given for making a second sex. 'It is not good for man to be alone.' Man himself was insufficient.

The way this is put is striking. Over and over again, God said He was pleased with creation. He contemplated each new stage and saw that it was good (Genesis 1). When He had finished everything, including the male and female human race, He saw 'it was *very* good' (verse 31). So it comes as quite a shock to hear God say, 'it is not good'. Something was bad. It was the only thing, before the Fall, which was. God had created the garden, the plants, and the animals; He had made man; He had given him work to do and a commandment to obey. It was what some people would think of as a haven of perfection, but it was still not good. Man needed help. God made her.

The teaching in Genesis is reinforced by Paul. Man is not independent of woman (1 Corinthians 11:11). He is born through her (verse 12); every man alive owes his existence to a woman; even the Son of Man Himself entered life on earth through a woman. In a sense, man owes woman everything. The message is quite clear: he cannot live without her; nor should he try. Man without woman is not what God intended.

His need of her is clearly announced in Genesis 2. Her need of him is not. Nonetheless, it is assumed by the text. He is to work alongside her; that is why she was made. Adam is the reason for her creation; he is her partner. And she was formed out of his flesh; indirectly she owed him her existence, as he now owes his to her.

Again Paul stresses this to the Corinthians. She is made 'because of the man' (1 Corinthians 11:9). She is 'of the man' (verses 8 and 12), as the man is 'through the woman' (verse 12). She is not independent of him any more than he is of her (verse 11). And again the message is clear. Woman is made for man. She is not created to live in isolation from him. We are made in need of each other.

It must immediately be said that our mutual need does not mean that we must all marry. This can hardly be stressed enough. Our need for each other is a biblically taught principle, but so is our freedom not to marry. Paul goes to great lengths to establish this before he talks about our interdependence (1 Corinthians 7). The fact that men and women need each other must mean something else. This is obvious as soon as we consider Jesus. He lived in perfect accordance with God's will; He is the very image of God (Colossians 1:15). Yet He never married.

Jesus's example

Indeed it is from His example, even more than from direct teaching on the subject, that we see God's design for us as male and female. There is something remarkable in the way Jesus related to members of the opposite sex. The impact tends to be lost on us because of our ignorance of Jewish society, but in first-century Palestine His behaviour was extraordinary.

By the time He was born, there was a rigid segregation of the sexes. Jewish society aggressively divided men from women. Twentieth-century 'problems of communication' are laughable by comparison: first-century Jews were told not to talk to their wives at all. 'Talk not with womankind,' said the Mishnah.[1] 'They said this of a man's own wife: how much more of his fellow's wife! Hence the sages have said: He that talks much with a woman brings evil upon himself . . . and at last will inherit Gehenna.' A woman could be divorced for talking to another man.[2] Rabbis would normally avoid speaking to women at all (presumably again including their own wives). Some Rabbis today still continue this practice to some extent.[3] There was even a particularly diligent group of misogynists called the 'Bleeding Pharisees': to avoid seeing women at all they walked around with their eyes fixed on the pavement; the more street corners they walked into and the more black eyes they acquired, the more pious they were deemed. Clearly the society in which Jesus lived did not believe in the sexes mixing freely. The segregation was extreme.

It is important to point out that none of this was scriptural. Any sexual apartheid which existed by the time Jesus was born was the result of man's law, not God's. So how did He react to it? Did He approve? Did He consent by silence? Did He go along with it because it was not an important enough issue to offend people over, because He had better things to do with His time than worry about sexual harmony? On the contrary, although He gave no direct teaching on the subject, the way Jesus behaved towards women was revolutionary, and sometimes shocking. Even today, His freedom and intimacy with them might raise an eyebrow. Then it must have been bizarre in the extreme.

It is sometimes said Jesus could not, in that kind of society, have chosen women as His apostles: it would have been quite improper, it is claimed, for women to have travelled and worked, and certainly lived, alongside Him. The evidence is that this did not trouble Him at all. The appearance of impropriety did not deter Him in the slightest. On at least one occasion He took a number of women with Him as He travelled (Luke 8:1–3). Mary Magdalen, Susannah, and Joanna who had presumably left her husband at home, were among the many women who went with him from town to town. I can think of Christians today who would frown at such an arrangement; then it must have seemed unprecedented licence.

Later on in His travels, Jesus stopped at Martha's home (Luke 10:38). No doubt there were others in the house, including perhaps her brother, but it seems to have been Martha who was Jesus's particular friend since it is she who is mentioned and she who welcomed him in. It was also at this house, to her astonishment, that Jesus encouraged her sister to sit at His feet and learn like a man (verses 39–42). Again no woman would normally have been granted such intimacy or, indeed, such a privilege.

This was not the first time Jesus had surprised a host with His freedom with a woman. Simon the Pharisee was shocked by the freedom Jesus allowed to the prostitute who had managed to gatecrash his dinner party (Luke 7:36–50). Despite her profession, Jesus let her kiss His feet over and over again and stroke them with her hair. Again this kind of liberty would have been unheard of between a Rabbi and even a virtuous woman. (Apart from anything else, loose hair was seen as extremely indecent.[4]) It is not surprising that Simon had second thoughts about Jesus. Many Christians today would too.

On another occasion He was touched by an unclean woman (Luke 8:43–8). This would have rendered Him unclean Himself. When she was caught out she fell terrified at His feet, presumably expecting Him to be angry as any other man would have been. Instead He praised her for her faith (verse 48). He did not seem at all bothered to have been touched by an untouchable woman.

Perhaps the most telling comment of all is the reaction of the disciples when Jesus, again most unconventionally, had a long conversation with a woman (John 4:6–30). She herself was surprised, particularly as she was a Samaritan as well as a woman (verse 8). And when the disciples came across them both, 'they marvelled', not because He was talking to a Samaritan, but 'that he was talking with a *woman*' (verse 27).

In all His dealings with the opposite sex Jesus was extraordinarily uninhibited. At a time when most men were ignoring women altogether except for the purposes of reproduction, Jesus frequently included them in His life and work. He was prepared to depend on them for financial support and hospitality. Although He was single, and although the society around Him was extremely strict, He was easy and open with women, and allowed them to touch and even to kiss Him. He talked with them, walked with them, worked with them and stayed with them. He even taught them. He revealed His identity to a woman early on in His ministry (John 4:26). And it was to women, not men, that He first made the most important revelation in history (Matthew 28:8–10, and parallels). Indeed, He ensured that they were included in the Church from the beginning by making their testimony indispensable to the apostles.

It is clear from Jesus's attitude towards women that they are not made to exist in isolation from men. Everything in His behaviour towards them militates against sexual segregation. Everything in His attitude suggests we should be in close partnership with one another. The first Christians clearly were. They worked together as brothers and sisters (Acts 1:14; 16:40, and 1 Timothy 5:1,2, just to name a few of many such examples). We should do the same.

So this is our ideal. Clearly it is not always wrong for men to be alone together, or women to meet without men. There are inevitably occasions, as there were in Jesus's ministry, when the sexes work separately. And clearly too there is a place for common decency. Just because we want schools to be mixed does not mean we want dormitories, changing rooms or showers to be so too. Just because we want men and women to share facilities at work or university does not mean that we want them to share bathrooms or loos. I hope this is common sense.

Sometimes in the name of evangelism we appeal to one sex or the other. Some churches hold meetings for men only as it is the only way they can persuade them to come and hear the gospel. Obviously if this works it is an excellent idea. It is a form of positive discrimination: holding meetings exclusively for men is a way of helping them overcome their image of church as for 'women and children'. (I know of one church, though, which holds a men's prayer meeting for the same reason: apparently they are less likely to come if women are present. Now an evangelistic meeting like this is defensible. A prayer meeting is not. Once people are Christians they should behave in a mature Christian way.) So naturally there can be a place for men's and women's gatherings; the important thing to remember is that the segregation at such events is not good in itself. It can sometimes be a means to a good end.

Similarly, there is evidence that girls are held back, particularly in science and maths, if they are taught in the same class as boys.[5] So it may be advisable to teach them on their own. Again it needs to be said, though, that the segregation itself is not good: ideally it should be solved by treating all the pupils in the same way.

Another reason the sexes are sometimes separated is in an attempt to avoid promiscuity. This was the reason

that Jewish society was so strict: the rabbis believed lust
could only be controlled by hiding women from sight.
But Jesus assumed that it can and must be controlled by
an effort of the will (Matthew 5:27–8). Of course He is
right. This kind of segregation never works. Any man
who has been to a boys' boarding school or in a men's
prison, where homosexuality thrives, knows that sexual
segregation merely results in another kind of promiscuity.
Any woman who has travelled alone in a Moslem, or
even strongly Roman Catholic, country knows that it is
often more hazardous than being in a more lax
environment.

We need to weigh each situation carefully. This teaching, that we are interdependent, could easily be pushed
to silly extremes. There is nothing wrong with women
going out for a meal together or men playing rugby
together, or girls sharing a house. All these things are
good. We occasionally need the company of our own sex,
undiluted. Such activities become questionable when
people start to *prefer* a single sex society, as a general rule,
to one which is mixed.

This teaching could also make individuals feel
unnecessarily guilty: I know of women so disillusioned
by our masculine-biased society that they choose to work
in female co-operatives. I know of men who have had
ten years of single sex education and inevitably prefer
the exclusive company of men. This is a great shame, but
hardly the fault of the individuals concerned. So there
are a number of things our interdependence does not
mean. We are not to conclude that men and women
should never be apart. Nor should we make people feel
unnecessarily guilty. Aiming to work in sexual harmony
does not mean these things. What then does it mean?

Interdependence

First we must *acknowledge our need* of the opposite sex. It
is possible to behave as if the opposite sex is unnecessary

for almost all aspects of life. Until recently, most Oxford and Cambridge colleges were monuments to that arrogance. Many businesses still are. Schools, universities and firms have been run as if women did not exist. And it is a tragedy of the feminist movement that, despairing of correcting men's follies, it falls to aping them: 'These days,' said Gloria Steinham, 'a woman without her man is like a fish without a bicycle.'[6] If she means by this that the female half of the race can exist in isolation, she is being as idiotic as ever the men have been.

Second, we must be prepared to *mix* with the opposite sex. Occasionally there are particularly strong reasons for not doing so, as we have seen, but these are not the norm. We should take it for granted that boys and girls are educated together, that men and women work together, and that we mix for recreation and business alike.

Third we need to *listen* to the opposite sex. It is possible to work with women, and yet continue to work in an exclusively 'masculine' way. Paul Tournier believes our society has put far too much emphasis on what he considers the masculine attributes.[7] About four hundred years ago, he argues, our society chose to go in a particular direction. We decided to value the qualities men tend to have and ignore those more often found in women. Some time after the Renaissance, according to Tournier, women were pushed out of public life and men began to run society; consequently they ran it for men and in a man's way. Our culture, he continues, has become increasingly concerned with logic and reason, with things and machines, with the broad scope of life without attention to the little details. We worship science. We breathe bureaucracy. We ignore people, despise intuition, and chase after materialism at the expense of the quality of our everyday lives. This, Tournier asserts, is because we value men's contributions and have no time for women's.

He may overstate his case, but his theory makes good

sense. If women and men are different – and we must agree they are – our difference has a purpose. We must have different contributions to make. We express God's image in complementary ways and these two ways are equally important to His purpose.

Fritjof Capra argues a similar thesis.[8] He uses yin and yang for illustration. We can do the same; it is not uncommon to find biblical truth echoed in alien philosophies, and listening to foreign ideas sometimes helps us understand the familiar. The particular concept of yin and yang is helpful for two reasons. There is no suggestion, in the Chinese philosophy, that men ('real men') have certain attributes, and women ('ladylike' women) have others. 'All people, whether men or women,' says Capra, 'go through yin and yang phases.' So there is no implication that a woman who has yang qualities is 'butch' or a man with yin qualities 'effeminate' – as there might be if we said they had masculine or feminine characteristics.

More important, however, is the teaching that 'what is good is not yin or yang but the dynamic balance between the two; what is bad or harmful is the imbalance'. Capra's diagnosis of our society echoes Tournier's. He too thinks we have become unbalanced. He too sees excessive emphasis placed on the masculine qualities (and incidentally on the scientific and technological approach to life). Once again the problem with this is not that masculinity is not as 'good' as femininity, but that, as God says in Genesis 2, 'it is not good' on its own.

And of course if feminine and masculine are created by God to complement each other, it is essential that they work in harmony. Let us take an obvious example. Intuition is one of Capra's yin qualities and rationality is one of his yang ones. Since women are supposed to have more yin strengths, we may find their intuition tends to be sounder than many men's. Men may sometimes be brought up to think more logically. The observation is often crudely made: 'men are logical, women intuitive.' Its importance is overlooked. Reason and intuition are of very little use without each other. When Western society decided, two centuries ago, to value its own human reason above every other form of enlightenment it led, not only to a further devaluation of women, but also to the conclusion that there is no God. Of course. How can God be proved by human logic?

The limitation of masculine logic was well illustrated at Simon the Pharisee's dinner (Luke 7:36–9; 44–50). Simon's logic was not at fault. He knew the woman was a sinner, he knew she must be condemned by God; he also knew a prophet should have discernment and should judge as God would judge. And yet Jesus did not condemn the woman. There was only one possible logical conclusion: Jesus could not be a prophet.

But the woman's intuition summed the situation up better. She sensed her hopeless condition. She sensed she had good cause to mourn. And somehow she instinctively sensed that Jesus would accept and forgive her; she realised how much she would owe Him, and she poured out her gratitude in love and tears and ointment. Nobody explained anything to her. As far as we know no words were exchanged with her at all until Jesus forgave her sins and dismissed her. Yet she had saving faith while Simon doubted. On this occasion a woman's intuition got the better of a man's logic.

Jesus possessed these two qualities in perfect balance. He read people's hearts with unerring intuition (Matthew 22:18), and sprung their traps with faultless logic (verses 20,21). We should be combining these gifts in the same way. God has made excellent provision for us to do so. If one of these talents is largely found in one sex and a complementary one in the other it is clearly important that men and women work in harmony. When they do their matching gifts will harmonise.

Shaun and I have seen this graphically illustrated. If 'masculine' characteristics do indeed exist, we should expect a profession dominated by men to be influenced by masculine values. It will perhaps tend to be efficient in a rather analytical, bureaucratic way. (This, according to Capra, would be a yang approach.) A field dominated by women, however, is likely to be shaped by 'feminine' qualities, and may have, for example, a more personal, caring touch. (This gentler attitude would be described by Capra as yin.)

Almost everything in our society is run by men. But there is one profession which has retained a strong feminine influence. It is midwifery; throughout history most midwives have been women. If there is such a thing as a feminine approach, we are likely to find it here. Doctoring has traditionally been done by men, so masculine methods, if they exist, are likely to have thrived amongst doctors. An increase in women doctors is unlikely to change this overnight. (Like women prime ministers and executives, they have to behave like men in order to succeed in a masculine field.)

We noticed a significant difference of approach when we had our first child. We wanted her born at home. The doctors all disapproved. This is quite sensible if you view people en masse: the policy of encouraging everyone to have her baby in hospital has no doubt saved many lives; it can be safe, efficient and easy to organise. The midwives, on the other hand, were enthusiastic. Again this makes sense if you regard each person as an individual: in my case a home birth was perfectly safe and likely to be far more enjoyable. One approach deals with people in their thousands, the other with one person at a time.

This difference was noticeable throughout the births of all our children. Because they were all at home they were supervised entirely by the same midwife. And because of this they were conducted according to her intelligence, intuition and experience rather than a set of hospital rules. Medical guidelines lay down how long it is safe to be in labour; this is obviously important and useful information, but it is bound to be based on the average woman and the average labour. Our midwife, however, knew exactly how long would be safe for me.

Her 'personal touch' seemed infallible. She would say we needed some music. She suggested a pot of tea. She told Shaun to go downstairs and have a drink with his mother. These details would be beneath a doctor's notice; he is concerned with the technical safety of his 'patients'. But the details are important: a relaxed and confident mother is far more likely to give birth without complications. This approach was much more pleasant for us than the official, clinical way in which some labours are apparently organised.

There are two things which need to be said about our experience. The first is fairly obvious: this 'feminine' aspect of midwifery is a good thing. When competent midwives are not interfered with, they can treat people as people and give them individual and intuitive care. Labour can be easier, less frightening and safer. If a large number of men become midwives, or midwifery becomes more institutionalised, it may lose this 'feminine' characteristic. We may all be made to feel we are giving birth to our babies as machines do to sausages. This would be a great loss. We must struggle to preserve the feminine approach.

The second thing which needs to be said, though, is every bit as important. Midwifery owes a great deal to the 'masculine' contribution to medicine. Men may have institutionalised labour, but they have also made it a far less terrifying, and painful, and dangerous business. Some time ago midwives may have held sway in the matter of childbirth. A great many women and babies suffered terribly under their care. A great many died.

Both contributions are vital. We were lucky: we had the full benefit of the masculine mastery of science and the feminine care of me as an individual. Both are of limited use on their own. Together, they are the perfect combination, the partnership envisaged at creation.

Again we see in Jesus's life and example the essential value of both. Because He was perfect Man (by which I mean of course perfect humanity) He had all human characteristics in perfect balance. There is a tendency in rather hearty brands of muscular Christianity to react against the 'gentle Jesus, meek and mild' of our Sunday School days. But He *was* gentle, meek and mild. Though He could be a ravaging scourge (Matthew 23:23–36), He was also the epitome of patience and humility (Luke 2:51). He was tough, living among wild beasts without food or shelter (Mark 1:13): but He was protective, longing to care for Jerusalem like a mother bird (Matthew 23:37). He endured a succession of tortures which would kill many hardened warriors, and was still able to think and speak clearly (John 19:26,27): but He delighted in little children, going quite against 'manly' Jewish behaviour (Mark 10:14,16). He courted violent death (John 8:58,59): He cooked breakfast (John 21:12). He fought (John 2:15): He wept (John 11:35).

Throughout His behaviour we find this balance. And of course Jesus ought to contain such harmony, since God made both sexes in His image. Both feminine and masculine characteristics have their origin in Him, so we would expect Jesus to exemplify both.

We might go on to think we cannot hope to imitate this since we only have the gifts we think appropriate to our sex. But the fruit of the Spirit includes a list of qualities normally thought of as feminine (Galatians 5:22,23): patience, peace, gentleness, faithfulness and self-control. Christian men are to have these so-called 'feminine' qualities. Perhaps we should each try to copy Jesus's blend of masculine and feminine strengths.

Where it matters most

The importance of masculine and feminine is that both are vital. Women and men should be partnering one another in everything they do.

Yet look around you. Is this what you see? We have girls' schools, gentlemen's clubs, ladies' coffee mornings, men's training colleges, Women's Institutes and Boys'

Brigades. And we show great reluctance to change this. For nearly twenty years my father ran a boys' preparatory school. For more than half that time he battled to turn it co-ed. His experience in education had taught him that to separate girls from boys was as illogical as dividing redheads from blondes (and rather more harmful). He was resisted on all sides: governors, onlookers, and most of all the pupils themselves were passionately against it for no better reason than it had been this way for five hundred years. Ten-year-old boys lay down in the school drive in protest. What is amusing in prep school boys is ridiculous in adults, but sadly it is often as rife: many people cling to sexual division because 'it has always been this way'.

And this is nothing. Every afternoon outside my window I see armies of women, their pram wheels glinting in the sunlight, mobilising at the school gates opposite. These women never get the chance to share a day's work with men. When Shaun went to theological college there was not a single female student. Those men were hardly ever able to work alongside women. From stockbrokers to infant teachers, nurses to car mechanics, people can be found in work which is the preserve of their sex. There are still many jobs in which the sexes work alone, though it is in work most of all that we are created to be together.

Work is the context of Eve's creation. It was in tending the garden that Adam needed help. '(15)The LORD God took the man and put him in the Garden of Eden to work it and take care of it.' And then, two verses later, '(18) The LORD God said, "It is not good for man to be alone. I will make a helper suitable for him." ' It was in his labours that he was not to be alone. The Lord did not observe that Adam was sexually frustrated or lonely or unable to reproduce; He gave him work, and said he needed help. So Eve was not primarily created to be the man's friend or lover. First and foremost she was his colleague; his 'helper', not his sweetheart. So segregation at work is the most serious form of segregation. Yet this is what we have. Although the law now allows both sexes to do most forms of work, custom still dictates much of our choice. Miners are men. Housewives are women. Politicians and professors are usually men. Cleaners and health visitors are women. Where is the 'help' God envisaged for Adam? She is usually elsewhere, in the kitchen or typing pool.

As a result we miss out on the feminine angle. Many people, from Lysistrata to the Greenham Commoners, believe having more women in government would mean waging fewer wars; women are wary, it is argued, of sending husbands and sons to their deaths. Indeed, their influence might improve many other areas of life. Look at modern architecture. Who knows most about houses? And yet who designs most of the houses we live in? It is usually men, who spend far less time at home, who decide what our homes will be like. And we all know what the result is; my mother knows an architect who built a house with four floors and only two staircases. The examples could go on *ad infinitum*. It is impossible to know how much we have already lost by neglecting the feminine touch for so long.

How has this happened? And are we doomed to a masculine bias? If men are stronger and more forceful than women, are we bound to have everything run in a masculine way unless they are deliberately kept out of certain fields, as they were for some time from midwifery?

Tournier shows how we have become increasingly masculine in our outlook because women have been excluded from political and business life. Since our society has become industrialised and work has moved away from the home, men's and women's work has become more and more rigidly determined according to sex. Marxist feminists argue the same point. They criticise this divorce between public and private, where 'public' work is recognised and paid for and 'private' work is not even seen as work, and its essential contribution to the economy goes unacknowledged. In the public sphere so-called 'masculine' virtues are rewarded and 'feminine' ones penalised; it is no good hoping for promotion in some professions by being co-operative and sympathetic and gentle, however appropriate these qualities might be. Private work, on the other hand, requires what are thought of as feminine qualities: aggression and fierce ambition are not much use to a housewife. It is this division of labour into 'men's' and 'women's' work which has resulted in a widespread segregation of the sexes, and an accompanying division of masculine and feminine qualities.

Many people strongly believe in these divisions. Some say they are biblical. After all, there are two ways in which we can be interdependent. We can do the same work in different ways, by having male and female doctors; or we can do different work together, by having male doctors and female nurses (or vice versa). We can see our mutual need in terms of different contributions or different roles. Many Christians think the latter is more biblical. A man, they believe, contributes to the home by supporting it financially and imposing discipline; he needs to spend time with the family, but not nearly as much time as the mother. She contributes by feeding, loving, washing, and being a bosom and refuge from the world; she rears the children and runs the home. She needs him and he needs her; the children need them both. This is obviously a form of sexual interdependence. Is it the correct one? This is the next question we will consider.

FIVE

Work

'Home is the girl's prison and the woman's work-house. '
George Bernard Shaw, **Women in the Home**.

'I don't want to play the pimp and educate her just for marriage. If I do that and she remains single then she'll just become one of those embittered spinsters. On the other hand I don't want to train her for some masculine vocation that'll take years of study and be completely wasted if she does get married.'
Strindberg, **The Father**.

Shaun and I were on a weekend houseparty with some friends. Our host and hostess were talking about marriage, and giving us all some advice. Shaun asked how their ideas would work out in a family in which the woman was the breadwinner and the man the 'home-maker'. (Apparently 'housewife' is now derogatory. Not that this is new of course: 'hussy' is derived from it.) They were shocked at the idea. The biblical pattern, they said, is this: the man provides and the woman runs the home. They considered any deviation from this norm a per-version of nature; they thought it morally wrong and likened it to homosexuality.

Most of us in Western society expect men and women to adopt these roles. We assume a man's first commit-ment is to his job, and a woman's to her home and children. As a result she may be asked, when she has a

Split Image

baby, 'Will you go back to work?' No one will ask this of her husband. She may face the agony, and the luxury, of choosing between work and home. He does not have the option. She may meet the child's needs first and only return to work if she can find adequate childcare. He will stay at work regardless. We are largely intolerant of the sexes 'swapping roles': a man who stays at home with young children is freakish; a woman who does not is still frowned on in many circles.

Because we live in society we Christians have absorbed its assumptions. Indeed, they are often presented as biblical teaching. Some Christian books state categorically that a woman's first duty is to the home.[1]

Is this true? Does the Bible teach that there are different roles for women and men?

Before we address the question we must admit that these so-called 'traditional' roles are no longer entirely successful. This is not to say that they cannot be, nor is it to deny that some couples are blissfully happy with them. But they do present us with serious difficulties in the modern world.

If earning a living is to be a man's career it is easy to prepare him for it. You train him for a job and he does it till he is sixty-five. He will probably marry and support a family but it does not matter if he chooses not to do so. His life has been a success. Of course, if he fails to find employment he is not a 'real' man, and after sixty-five he is no longer seen as useful. But apart from this, the system can still work quite well for men.

If running a home and rearing children is a woman's natural sphere she should be prepared for it too. She should be taught to cook and be domestic and love babies. She will also, in this egalitarian age, be given an education – just in case she wants to become a career-girl, or find a part-time job when her children are grown up, or by some misfortune fails to marry. Nevertheless, her schooling is not seen as so important or vocational as a boy's, and her parents quietly hope she will 'settle down'. So she reaches her teens and marriage becomes her ambition. She shows interest in the boys. One of them is to be her ticket to success: without him, she cannot do *real* woman's work.

Now suppose she meets the man of her dreams, gets married, and starts a family. She is happy. She has 'arrived'. Naturally, she invests more of herself in her marriage than her husband does. His work is to earn money, win promotion, and be a success outside the home; his marriage is a pleasant bonus. Her employment, though, depends on him; her marriage is vital to her work. Without her, he would lack a little something; without him she would lack purpose and meaning and usefulness.

This puts pressure on them both, since the partnership means more to her than to him. He has to make an effort to remember wedding anniversaries, to come home when he would have liked to stay working, to make a fuss of her. She must try not to be 'clingy', or jealous of his time. But they ride these minor irritations, and when the children are born the situation becomes more balanced; she spends her time and energy on them, and has her own work – as he has his. The serious problems start when their youngest leaves home. Suddenly she faces virtual unemployment for the rest of her life. She may be under forty, and her working life is over.

She is the lucky one. Another girl may not have 'made it' at all. Like her sister, she wanted to marry. Unlike her brother, she was unable to do anything about her ambition. She had to wait for her work to materialise. It never did. She is not only a failure, but also out of place; she is a woman, but she is not doing women's work. She is doing third-rate men's work.

For if homemaking and childrearing are a woman's work, marriage, of necessity, becomes her aim. Not only can this put a strain on those women who do get married, but it can also have a devastating effect on those who do not, or on those who cannot have children, or whose children leave home. A man can prepare for, and do, man's work all his life. A woman's usefulness is seen to depend on catching her man. We have enslaved women in a situation from which Paul says explicitly he wanted them freed.[2]

It is also difficult for a woman to train for her working life. If she prepares for domesticity she may be disappointed all her life. If she prepares for 'man's work', and succeeds and does well, she faces an impossible choice; she must either forgo what most human beings long for – a lifelong partner and children – or the work she is doing so well. If she decides on some kind of compromise she may be mediocre in both roles.

In addition, our society offers those of us who work outside the home an increasing variety of choices. We no longer have to do the jobs our parents did; we can do other things if we enjoy them more. There is a lot of status in many of these jobs: by and large, the harder the jobs are to do or get, the more money they bring with them and the higher the status they carry. However, a housewife is always a housewife is always a housewife. She receives no pay. It is an easy job to qualify for (though not to do). Any woman is considered capable of it. The status is almost nil. Small wonder, then, if women are heard to say 'I'm just a housewife'.

And 'woman's work' can be lonely work. As Genesis 2 makes clear, for most of us work needs to be a social thing. It is not good to do it alone. One of the satisfying things about work is the fellowship it gives us with others. Housewives work with no one but their children and Hoovers. The children are often at school and not their mothers' workmates anyway. It is not much use to say they could chat over the garden fence and pop in on each other for coffee:[3] housewives can mix together, but they do not work together. Two businessmen, or MPs, or miners, are working on the same project, but two housewives are not cleaning the same house. They share this problem with a number of others: research students, clergymen and gardeners, writers and road sweepers, can all find themselves working alone; some of them, like some housewives, can be the loneliest people in the world.

This analysis may seem simplistic and hopelessly old-fashioned. Many girls are ambitious, successful and accomplished. Many men do some of the household work. But the underlying expectations are still there. There is more of a stigma attached to spinsters than bachelors, and to unemployed men than women. I have often witnessed tensions resulting from the above assumptions.

A veterinary student asked me recently if she should throw in her training, which she enjoys and is good at, in case she might one day get married. My best friend at university believed women should not receive higher education: they are likely to waste it when they have children. A teenager told me she does not know how to plan her future: should she take up a career at the risk of losing it at marriage?

It is hardly surprising many people are re-evaluating. Some women have expressed discontent. Many are frustrated. They feel torn between work and home. They may find a single life difficult: society persuades them they have 'failed'. They can find married life worse: they may be given low status, and either stuck in domestic work which might not suit them, or doomed to mediocrity in the office because of their extra duties at home. On paper, we may have sexual equality. In reality, it is difficult for women to work alongside men.

Of course it can work well for some people. And it can work in certain cultures. In a society where no one has a choice about employment, 'women's work' need not be unprestigious; where families live in extended households several women can run a house together, and those who are single or past child-bearing can look after other people's children; where polygamy is acceptable, or men have a duty to marry (as in Islam or ancient Judaism) every woman can get married. In some societies it can work beautifully. But in ours it does not.

These problems do not mean that we can necessarily abandon the roles. If, as is often taught, they are the biblical pattern, we must embrace them; but we must also make them work. It is not enough simply to tell women to get back into the kitchen. We must solve the problems which have driven them out.

However, there is one more objection which cannot be so easily dismissed. Under the present system many areas of work are dominated by one sex. This does mean the sexes are depending on one another, which is biblical: if an office is managed by men and dusted by women, both men and women are needed for the business to function smoothly. But it also means we are often segregated, which is not biblical: the men run the business between nine and five; the women clean it after six. This division is not God's plan for us. Jesus did not encourage it. Yet it is exactly what we have created. Men work largely with other men; housewives work on their own. The work is bound to be impoverished. Governments are run along masculine lines. Homes are dominated by femininity. Business standards conform to men's ideas. Children are moulded and shaped by women. This is a more serious charge. It is difficult to see how this shortcoming can be solved at all if men and women are to be in completely different spheres of work.

But we must leave the problems on one side for a moment and return to the question. Are these supposedly 'traditional' gender roles designed by God?

NATURAL?

Your reaction to this question may well be a 'gut' reaction. You may 'feel' it is right; you 'sense' it is proper. If pressed further, you may say it is 'natural'. Our feelings, our instincts, are not necessarily to be despised. They often tell us when something is right or wrong. On the other hand, they can also easily lead us astray. If you are angry with someone it may feel right to give him a black eye: this is also 'natural', but it is seldom right. The fact that we are moral beings means we are capable of moral decisions: if we are to decide whether something is right or wrong we must examine and question the 'natural'.

Poor Nature is often given rather vague responsibility for a great many things. What exactly do we mean when we say it is 'natural' for women to be domestic, to rear children and to run the home?

The animal kingdom

We may mean 'natural' is what the animals do. I have heard this argument used to persuade women to care for their children. 'Females of other species do it' the argument goes, 'so human females should do so too.' The fact that females of many other species totally ignore their young is overlooked. So too is the fact that females of some species eat their lovers after the sexual act [4] – I have yet to hear this practice recommended as 'natural'. Other animals do all sorts of things. In many species, it is true, the females look after the young. In others it is the males who have this responsibility.[5]

However the argument is not wholly ridiculous. Amongst non-human primates (by which, of course, I mean 'monkeys', not 'archbishops'), the group of species considered nearest to our own, the care of individual infants is almost exclusively the work of the mother. She carries, suckles, feeds, loves. The males merely tolerate.

Can this lead us to the conclusion that we must do the same? Does it mean it is 'natural' for us too? One could conceivably argue this, but where do you draw the line? Male gorillas and chimpanzees do not provide for the females or the young. They do not recognise their own offspring or show them particular affection. A male orang-utan or gibbon may mate with one female one day and another the next; if he is 'top ape' he will probably enjoy them all. Are we saying that this is 'natural' and therefore recommended for us too? And why, of all the animals, should we choose to copy the apes? Other species may be far worthier to set us an example. Whereas apes are promiscuous, swans show a lifelong faithfulness to their mates. Surely we would do better to take our standards from them – yet swans share the care of the young equally between cob and pen.

The trouble is, of course, we are turning God's creation upside down if we start judging our behaviour by the animals'. Yet this is what people are doing when they say, as I have heard them do, that certain gender patterns are 'natural' (and therefore right) because they are found in the animal kingdom. Human dignity has sunk low indeed if the creatures who were put under us have become our teachers. If we decide what is right or wrong on the basis of animal behaviour, like a parent asking a baby for moral guidance, the whole of creation will be in a mess.

Human behaviour

What is 'natural' could also be understood to be what human societies do. If women look after children in every culture perhaps we can conclude that it is natural because it is universally practised, and therefore essentially human. I have been told that every society enforces the sixth commandment in some form: there is a worldwide taboo against murder, though murder may be variously defined. If all peoples also have the same gender roles there may be a good reason for it.

But all peoples do not have the same gender roles. Alaskan Eskimos share the care of the children equally between mother and father; for them it is no more the woman's work than it is the man's. Male Cheju Islanders care for their children while their womenfolk go out to work.[6] The same is true of the Alor Indians.[7]

And which particular 'universal' or 'natural' trends are right? No doubt aggression and greed are found in almost every culture. No doubt they are often rewarded (as indeed they are in ours). Are they therefore good? We find the same problems in imitating other societies as we have in imitating the animals: which particular society do we choose as our model, and which of its qualities are we to value?

Again, of course, we are turning God's plan upside down. Just as it is degrading if we humans take our standards from the animal kingdom, so it is foolish if we Christians take our standards from non-Christian cultures. We are 'not of this world' (John 17:16). This does not mean that we are not to be involved with this world, but we do not have to take our standards from it. We are not to be moulded by human mores (Romans 12:2). We are to be salt (Matthew 5:13). We should set the standards. The reason we do not kill is not because others think it wrong, but because God has spoken. The fact that others think it wrong too is an interesting incidental – no more. We decide what is right and wrong by what God has said, not by what others do. So this argument is as invalid as the first.

Biology

The third possible meaning of 'natural' is what our bodies, our biology, can teach us. If God has created us a certain way it is because He expects us to function a certain way. This would not be taking our standards from others but from God Himself. So what does biology tell us? That one man and one woman are necessary for conception. And that a woman will bear, give birth to, suckle, and incidentally quite often die from the birth of a baby.

That is all. It does not tell us who will clean the house. Or who will care for a three-year-old child. Or who will change the nappies. Nor indeed who will bring home the bacon. We assume that the parent that bears the child must do all the other things for it because that is how our society is structured. We also assume, for the same reason, that the other parent will earn money. Neither of these norms is biologically dictated, or 'natural' at all.

Our biology also tells us a man can father twenty children, by different women, at once. And that a woman can bear children from different men. And that a father can ignore his children, yet they can survive. It tells us he can kill a woman with his bare hands. Or impregnate her against her will. And so on. Do we really want to be dictated to by our biology? We are very foolish if we think that because something can be called 'natural' it must be right. Of course, the truly natural must have been right, but the whole of nature is now fallen, and we are not to be enslaved to it. God has given us a moral law so that we can be freed from our fallen 'natures'.

So whatever Nature says – and what she says is by no means clear – we are free from her dictates. We are free to make up our own minds on the basis of what the Bible says. It is only there that we will find the answer. Whether something seems 'natural' to us is quite beside the point. The truly natural is the way God intended us to be, not the way we are now; and we will only know what He intended by listening to what He says.

BIBLICAL?

So what does the Bible say? Are certain types of work more suitable for one sex than the other?

Let us define, for convenience, three kinds of work. 'Breadwinning' is providing money or its equivalent means to live; since industrialisation, Western middle classes have largely considered this to be man's work. 'Homemaking' is turning this money into food and a pleasant home; again, in recent history we have considered this to be woman's work. And 'childrearing' is caring for children; this can easily be combined in our society with homemaking but not with breadwinning. So it is also thought to be woman's work.

It is important to realise that these assumptions are recent ones; they became necessary when work moved away from the home. Until industrialisation, work was not rigidly divided in this way. Men and women alike earned a living and ran the home.[8] And it was not until after the Second World War that a woman was likely to have the sole care of her children.[9] Many people think these roles are 'traditional' or 'universal', so there is a subconscious tendency to expect to find them in the Bible. But they are not. They have been with us for about two hundred years. If they appear to be in the Bible we must examine our interpretation carefully, in case we are making the kind of assumptions we noted in chapter 2.

Genesis 3

The only biblical passage which might suggest that 'breadwinning' is the man's job and 'homemaking' and 'childrearing' the woman's is the second half of Genesis 3. The woman and the man have disobeyed God's word and He pronounces judgment:

(14)   The LORD God said to the serpent,
         'Because you have done this,
            cursed are you above all cattle,
            and above all wild animals;
         upon your belly you shall go,
            and dust you shall eat
            all the days of your life . . .'
(16)   To the woman he said,
         'I will greatly multiply your pain* in
                                     childbearing;
            in pain you shall bring forth children,
         yet your desire shall be for your husband,
            and he shall rule over you.'

(17)   And to Adam he said,
        'Because you have listened to the voice
                                        of your wife,
            and have eaten of the tree
        of which I commanded you,
            "You shall not eat of it,"
        cursed is the ground because of you;
            in toil* you shall eat of it all the days
                                        of your life;
(18)   thorns and thistles it shall bring forth to you;
            and you shall eat the plants of the field.
(19)   In the sweat of your face
            you shall eat bread
        till you return to the ground,
            for out of it you were taken;
        you are dust,
            and to dust you shall return.'
Genesis 3, Revised Standard Version.
(*'pain' and 'toil' – which can also be translated as
'labour' – are the same word in Hebrew.)

At first sight there seems to be an assumption here. The
woman is cursed in her sphere, the man in his. Her
'labour' is having children. His 'labour' is tilling the
ground and getting food from it. I have heard people
interpret the passage in this way. God expected woman
to be doing one thing and man another. This is what it
might seem to suggest. But it suggests this to us largely
because it is how our society is organised. If we read the
passage more carefully we can see that the expectation is
not there at all.

The two curses are not on the woman and the man in
their spheres of work, their 'labour'. The curses are on
the snake and the ground. The snake's curse is addressed
to the snake (verses 14 and 15), and the ground's curse to
the man (verses 17–19). The curse on the snake need not
concern us here.

The curse on the ground is a curse on us all: the whole

of creation is under it and we all suffer from it. We all die (verse 19). The man does not endure this any more than the woman. It is not a punishment on him in his sphere of work; it is a punishment on us all. It is simply *addressed* to the man. There is, as we shall see, a significant assumption here; but it is nothing to do with work.

The woman, on the other hand, receives individual treatment. She is given a specific punishment. Childbirth will be painful. This is relevant to her alone; nothing else in creation seems to be affected. She will suffer as much as the man from the curse on the ground; in addition, she will suffer her own punishment, presumably because she disobeyed first.

There are two assumptions here, though not about work. The first is that women have babies. Now I know of no one who seriously disputes this. We must confess they are better designed for it than men. But there is no assumption about housework, cooking, home management, or even child care. God, like our biology, says nothing about the nappies. However, when God assumes women have babies we jump to the conclusion that they run homes and families too. This is ludicrous. Everybody knows women have babies. It is all the other jobs we are trying to find out about, and there is no mention of them here.

The other assumption, though, is often missed. God addresses to the man the curse which affects us all. Not to the whole of creation, or even to the man and woman together. Only to the man. The assumption is that he is responsible. It is because he fell that the whole world is fallen (verse 17). He represents the world. This follows the point made in chapter 2, that the man was deliberately named with the name of the human race. He stands for us all. It is not clear whether this was God's original plan or the result of the Fall; now, though, the man is addressed in place of all of us.

Whatever the implications of this may be, they are nothing to do with work. They do not tell us about the man's particular occupation. We all eat in toil. We all find life a struggle. We all go back into the ground, and we all return to dust. The animals also suffer and die. We all find work spoilt by this curse: it is frustrating, unpleasant, and often meaningless for us all. There is no assumption that the man does any more work, just as there is no assumption that he is going to do any more dying. So there is no suggestion in these verses that 'work' is a man's responsibility, and 'domesticity' a woman's.

So what does the rest of scripture say? It is often thought that the overall biblical picture is that women do indeed run homes and care for children, and men provide for them. These roles are often vaguely connected with the idea of the man being the 'head of the household'. If pressed, no one seems quite sure what the connection is. As we shall see in a later chapter the idea of a husband's 'headship' is often associated with a number of concepts which are not biblical at all. One of these is that 'headship' is something to do with making money. This idea is not found anywhere in the Bible. An unemployed or incapacitated man can be fulfilling his duties as a husband and a father just as faithfully as a man on £50,000 a year. The biblical teaching that a husband is the head of his wife has nothing to do with breadwinning.

So let us see what the Bible says about each form of work – breadwinning, homemaking, and childrearing – in turn.

Breadwinning

Is this a man's domain?

We must immediately acknowledge that a woman who earns money or works for a living is not condemned in the Bible. Lydia was a businesswoman. She is described as 'a dealer in purple-dyed [clothes], and a worshipper of God' (Acts 16:14). There is no indication that this is strange, or dubious, or unwomanly. Nor that being a businesswoman and worshipping God are incompatible. Nor that when she was converted to Christianity she changed her lifestyle and became more domestic. (Nor, incidentally, that she was a widow or unmarried. Her household was baptised with her, as the jailer's was with him (verse 33). It is sometimes assumed with spectacular male arrogance that because her husband is not mentioned he did not exist – no one makes the same assumption about the jailer's wife.)

Priscilla was a tentmaker (Acts 18:3). She and her husband Aquila were in the trade together; the account specifically says '*they* were tentmakers by trade'. This is how Paul became friendly with them: he was a tentmaker too, so the three of them worked together. Again, there is no suggestion this is inappropriate for a wife and a Christian, or that she would have been better employed running a house or caring for children.

Lydia, presumably, provided for her household. Priscilla and Aquila earned money together. These women are in no way criticised for the work they do. However, neither are they held up as examples for us to follow. There is a difference between tolerating the occasional businesswoman and expecting or even commanding women to provide for their families. After all this is surely what men are told to do. Paul says 'anyone who does not provide for their own people, and especially their family, has denied the faith and is worse than an unbeliever' (1 Timothy 5:8. I am afraid I have sacrificed English grammar for the sake of a more accurate translation of gender). This is usually taken to mean that a man must provide for his wife and children. In the context this meaning is forced, to say the least.

For one thing the Greek has no suggestion of the sex of the person described. To translate it as 'he' throughout (as is normally done) is to assume that then as now men were thought of as the providers. A few verses later Paul shows that this is not his assumption.

For another, Paul is not thinking in terms of exclusive 'nuclear' families. He is saying Christians must support widowed mothers and grandmothers (verse 4). He is not talking about a man working for his wife and children.

Lastly, Paul makes clear that he expects women to provide for their families. Indeed he commands them to do so. 'If any believing woman has widows [related to her] let her relieve them, and not let the church be burdened' (verse 16). Those of us who are able-bodied are to support those in our family who cannot support themselves. We are not to sponge off the Church (or perhaps in our case the state). Women are in no way exempt. They are to provide for their families.[10]

But the best example of biblical expectations of a married woman is found at the end of Proverbs (31:10–31). She is called the 'good wife'. She is the ideal. She has all the best qualities a wife could ever have. (It is amusing, because of this, that people sometimes quote this chapter and say, 'You see! the ideal woman is domestic.' This hardly follows: she is the good *wife*, not the good woman. The ideal husband would also be seen in terms of his domestic contribution since this is what would make him a good husband.) So if a man were to dream up the best wife money could buy, this, according, to the Bible, is the woman he would come up with.

I am reminded of a recent talk about men's and women's roles. By and large the audience believed a good wife stays at home while her husband goes out to work. We turned to this passage. Members of the audience were asked to read it through carefully and say what struck them about her. Which of her qualities is most often mentioned? What seems to be the talent for which she is valued most?

There was a stunned silence. One could see most of them coming to the same conclusion.

'She works.'

'She earns money.'

'She trades.'

It is impressive. The ideal wife is a working wife. Her husband trusts in her 'and he will have no lack of gain' (verse 11), presumably because her business deals are successful. She buys a field and plants it 'with the fruit of her hands', money she has previously earned. She is strong (verses 17 and 25). She is diligent (verse 27). She gets up early in the morning (verse 15), and works well into the night (verse 18). She negotiates with merchants (verse 24), sells them her own produce (verse 24), and makes sure she is making a good profit (verse 18). She is generous (verse 20); she can afford to be. She is a worker.

The first thing that is said about her is that she is valuable (verse 10): her husband will never be poor (verse 11). The last thing said about her is more note-worthy still. 'Give to her the fruit of her hands,' says the writer, 'and let her works praise her in the gates.' Let what she earns be her own reward, and the work she does her own eulogy. The ideal wife is a working wife.

We must not be anachronistic. Of course this does not mean careerists are praised and housewives condemned. Housewives are some of the hardest workers in the world. Nor does it mean women, or men, must rush out to work in droves and leave their children inadequately cared for. The 'good wife' did some of her work at home; and besides she had a house full of servants (verse 15). But it does mean that 'breadwinning' is a feminine role. It means that women are expected to earn a living. It means that they, like their husbands, are to support their families.

So much for breadwinning.

Homemaking

What about 'homemaking'? Which sex, in the Bible, is expected to run the home? Is it the man or the woman who is to manage the household affairs?

There is no doubt that a woman is to care for her home. She is responsible for the welfare of her children, her guests, and her employees. Again the 'good wife' of Proverbs 31 is exemplary. She provides food (verses 14 and 15), clothing (verses 21, 22), and work (verse 15) for her family and her servants.

Paul, in his letters to Timothy and Titus, is unequivocal about the duties of married women. A widow is not to be supported unless she has performed certain duties, which include showing hospitality and bringing up children (1 Timothy 5:10). He goes on to say a married woman should rule, master, or be the head of her household (verse 14).[11] To Titus he says young women should be taught to love their husbands and children and to be 'home-workers' (Titus 2:5).[12] Since we do not know what the household work would have been, or how many servants the women in Titus's church would have had, we must assume they were to ensure that their houses were smoothly run. Like today, for some women this probably meant doing every chore themselves, for others (like the woman in the Proverbs) it meant ensuring that the work was done by employees or servants. It is not clear precisely what work each woman would have done. But it is clear that a married woman is considered by the biblical writers to have a duty to her home. She is to make sure it is properly organised, well managed, and hospitable. She is to be a 'homemaker'.

So is a man. One of a married man's duties is to see that his household is managed. Like a woman, he is also to run the home and bring his children up properly (1 Timothy 3:4). Paul specifically says that he is not fit to be an elder (or bishop) unless he copes with his household duties (verse 4). He then says the same thing all over again with reference to deacons (verse 12). If we took these commandments more seriously, quite a few of our clergy might be defrocked.

This is remarkably similar to what he has said of a woman. It is clearly a married man's responsibility, as it is a married woman's, to organise his household. This does not necessarily mean each husband and wife must

perform identical functions. To a large extent this
depends on the culture and personality. I, for example,
cannot pack. Neither can my father. Nor could my grand-
mother. We depend on our spouses to do this for us. Some
Arab couples I used to teach assumed that men should
do the shopping; they would not have dreamt of
exposing their women to the public eye. Until recently,
many English couples would have assumed the opposite.
We do not know how Paul's readers would have divided
the household jobs. It does not matter. The point is that
both sexes are responsible for the home. They are both to
manage it, rule it, and make sure it is well and hospitably
run. Married men and married women alike are to be
'homemakers'.

Childrearing

Finally what about the most important job, the care of
the children? Who is responsible for them? Are they
largely the work of the mother, as our society has for
some time assumed? We have already touched on their
care in discussing the running of the household. Women
are to 'bring up children' (1 Timothy 5:10). Men are to
manage, or care for, or rule their children (1 Timothy
3:12),[13] and have them in subjection (verse 4). Again, we
are not told what this will entail. Different things will be
appropriate for different cultures. The important thing is
that both are responsible.

But it is in the Old Testament that we find the bulk of
the teaching about mothers and fathers. When it comes
to the duties of respective parents the differences are
imperceptible. Hastings' *Dictionary of the Bible* says 'the
constant co-ordination of father and mother in such
passages' (references to parents in the Bible) 'practically'
(i.e. in practice) 'places the mother on the same level as
the father with regard to the children'.[14] Throughout the
Old Testament mother and father are mentioned together,
or in the same way (for example 'honour your father and

mother, that your days may be long in the land . . .'
Exodus 20:12). Both are to be given honour and respect
(Leviticus 19:3; Deuteronomy 5:16). Both are to be obeyed
(Proverbs 6:20; 30:17). Both parents teach and instruct
their children (Proverbs 1:8; 6:20; 4:1; and 31:1). As
Hastings says, 'the utmost respect and obedience to both
father and mother are insisted on'.[15]

If anything is equally shared between the sexes
it is the duty of being a parent. Again, this does not
necessarily mean both parents do the same for their
children or even spend the same amount of time with
them. However, their care, discipline, and teaching is the
job and responsibility of both.

There is not the slightest suggestion, when we are told
to multiply and subdue the earth (Genesis 1:27) that one
job (multiplication) is the responsibility of one sex, and
the other (subduing) the responsibility of the other. The
idea is not a biblical one. There is no biblical reason why
the woman not the man should wash the clothes or do
the shopping, or why the man not the woman should
earn the higher or only income. In fact one could go so
far as to say that these ideas are often anti-biblical. They
are responsible for many men's abdication from their
God-given work of running their homes and caring for
their children. They are responsible for many women's
feelings of guilt at their natural desire to work and
provide for their families.

Before we conclude there are one or two important
things which must be said about our labour. We are all
created to work. So we all have a duty to work. But we
do not have a duty, or indeed a right, to a *career*. This is a
totally unbiblical concept. We are expected to do an
honest day's labour and support ourselves and others.
We are not expected to scramble for a place in the rat-
race, put in overtime instead of coming home to our
husbands or wives or children, and agonise over whether
we are in the most fulfilling job possible. Plenty of men
have sacrificed their families to their careers. If women

start doing the same they will merely be adding one disaster to another. We are to *work*, not be promoted or successful or careerist.

As we have seen, there are different kinds of work. It can be paid (breadwinning) or unpaid (homemaking, childrearing, and of course voluntary work). For some time now our society has equated 'work' with bread-winning. Those who are not paid to work are assumed not to work. As a result people are sometimes asked the absurd question 'Do you work, or are you a housewife?' A previous vicar of ours honestly believed that seventy-five women on the electoral roll 'sat at home all day doing nothing'. The distinction made is not between work and idleness, but between a pay packet and lack of it.

This attitude is disastrous. Those who fail to secure the wages are made to feel unproductive. Christians must fight this wholeheartedly. The 'unemployed' must be supported in any work they do; whether it is housework or helping neighbours, mowing the lawn or writing poetry, it must be taken seriously as work. Increasingly, housewives also need this kind of support. This is where feminism has sometimes failed. Women who stay at home to raise a family are given little encouragement: they are doing unpaid, sometimes lonely, and usually exhausting work. Consequently they often suffer depression brought on by low self-esteem, fatigue and 'loneliness, frustration and boredom'.[16]

Christians must never allow housewives or the un-employed or the retired to feel inadequate, insignificant or guilty because they are not being paid. The involuntarily unemployed support their families with money from the state to which they are entitled as members of it; nobody should ever be made to feel a 'failure' for providing in this way. Housewives support their families not only directly by the work they do, but also indirectly by freeing their partners to work full-time. Nobody should ever be allowed to feel inferior for giving this kind of provision: housewives do some of the hardest, most important, and often most unrecognised work in the country.

Conclusions

What does all this mean in practice? The most significant implication is the wide range of choices it gives us. Society can be a tyrant, and on this issue it has done its best. My brother tells me that where he lives (amongst Oxford intelligentsia) it is not really acceptable for a young mother to stay at home. Where we used to live (North London suburbia) it was barely acceptable to do anything else. I realised this when I visited him carrying a baby on my back; I was introduced to an academic who asked me 'What do you do?' Such a question would be inconceivable where we lived in Persil Country. Wherever one lives one is liable to be bullied by expectations. These are not necessarily biblical, and when we realise this we can cease to be dictated to by them.

Some friends of ours recently wanted some advice. They had postponed the idea of children because he had been hoping to study for three years. His plans had fallen through; he would not be able to do the course for several years, if at all. Should they wait so long to start a family? Should they contemplate it now? They were put off by the uncertainty of his position: he had taken a job but might lose it at a moment's notice.

But her job is completely secure. She is a doctor. So in fact there is little problem. If he is still working when the baby is born she can either leave medicine and become a housewife, or stay at work and employ a nanny. If he loses his job they will not be able to afford help, but then he will be free to stay at home himself and look after the baby while she returns to work.

This latter choice had not occurred to them, although it is a perfectly legitimate one. It is just as much his job as hers to bring up the family. It is as much her job as his to provide for them. Because she has secure and well-paid work he will be set free to stay at home if he wishes. Of course this choice, like others, is not without its hardships. Society does not encourage the option: if he takes his child into a public lavatory to change a nappy he will find no facilities to help him. Christians may not be supportive either: some will tell him categorically that he is abdicating from his 'headship'. And he may well find his task frustrating and even humiliating (as many women have before him) so he will need support and encouragement from his partner, just as many women do.

Another couple we know, on the other hand, have made a different choice. They are both highly qualified scientists, and they have two tiny daughters. They too each have a duty to bring them up, to manage the home, and to provide. It would be difficult for both to do all three. They have made the conventional choice: she is a housewife and his work continues as before. Temperamentally they are well suited to this, and they had no reason to opt for anything else. Yet this too is not without its difficulties. She will never again be as high-powered as he. He may not be as close to the children as she. They have halved their income; she has a low status; he is no doubt tempted to work long hours and neglect his other duties; she will need appreciation and company from him since she may not get enough from anyone else. And so on. These difficulties can also be overcome, but he will need to give her much of the support which society has taken away.

It is often the parent who stays at home who has the harder time. This is particularly true of certain professions. Some housewives undoubtedly have more rewarding jobs than their husbands. Others experience considerable frustration, even if to work at home was a voluntary choice. So the 'breadwinning' partner has a responsibility to the other. He (for it is still usually he) must provide much of the company, stimulation and support other people tend to receive from their colleagues.

It is not always necessary for either parent to be the sole housewife. A lecturer at a theological college near us shares her job with her husband. They both teach, and they both look after the children. In many ways this is ideal: both are enjoying the wide variety of work for which they were created; the children (and indeed the college) are getting the benefit of both, including the different contribution each sex brings to a job; and they will be able to understand each other's setbacks and joys at work. They are true 'helps' to one another.

There are many possible combinations, and we often give ourselves unnecessary problems by conforming to certain patterns. A couple told us of their dilemma about starting a family. She is a solicitor and he a clergyman.

She is reluctant to become pregnant because she is fond of her work. It would be almost impossible to find part-time work and difficult to return to law after some years' break. Someone asked if it had occurred to them to get an au pair or home help.

He objected. 'You can't push your children out on others.'

'You wouldn't be pushing them out,' it was pointed out to them. 'You work at home most days. You have afternoons free because you work in the evenings. You could look after the children much of the time. The au pair would free you to work, but you'd often be around if you were needed. If you still disapprove, you could work part-time. It would be easier for you than for a solicitor!'

He laughed. 'My mother would be horrified!' he said. Again, it had not occurred to them that they had so many options.

We have not addressed ourselves to the question of nannies and childminders. It is not the place of this book to do so. The Bible does not tell us much about them, other than suggesting that Rebekah was closer to her nurse than to her mother (Genesis 24:59). Despite this, many people think parents who employ professional help are abdicating from their responsibility. This may sometimes be the case but is not necessarily so. There are three things which need to be pointed out.

First it is preferable and biblical for parents to be the main influence on their children. Their upbringing is chiefly the responsibility of the mother and father. This is a God-given responsibility, and for those of us who have children it is perhaps more important than any other work we do. There is no excuse, for men or women, for neglecting our children because we have taken on other work which is too demanding.

Second, though, parents are never going to be the only influence on their children unless they live on a desert island: grandparents, godparents, teachers, and society itself are also responsible. Schools have a large part to play. The good parent is not necessarily the one who minimises other influences – for example by teaching the children at home – but the one who chooses it with great care. The same applies to nannies, au pairs and childminders.

Third, being a good parent cannot necessarily mean being a full-time one. It is impossible for every parent to be full-time: someone has to earn a living. A man can be a superb parent even if he only spends evenings and weekends with his children; the same must also be true of a woman. So it is perfectly possible for parents to employ professional help in caring for their children and still to be the best of parents.

Christians sometimes talk about 'different roles' for the sexes. It is thought that the Bible says we have particular parts to play. No one seems to know exactly what those different roles are. People are either vague about them or else claim, as biblical, certain rather dated cultural trends.

But 'roles' is a misleading word which means different things to different people. Some people mean we have different contributions to make. This is absolutely true.

God made us different to complement one another. But other people mean we have different jobs to do. This is false. The Bible does not suggest different work for the sexes. Except for those which are biologically defined in reproduction, the tasks are not different for women and men; the ways of doing them may be different. We play our respective parts by doing the same work in different ways, we do not need to know what the respective roles are. They will come quite naturally to us because they depend on the way we are created.

Are there any exceptions to this? It is sometimes thought that in two areas, the Church and the family, God has given the sexes particular and different duties to do. Let us look at these in turn, beginning with the Church.

SIX

Authority

'Woman taught once and ruined all.'
St John Chrysostom [1]

MAGISTRATE: I'd rather die a thousand deaths than
obey someone who wears a veil.
LYSISTRATA: If that's all that's bothering you,
here, take my veil, wrap it round your head and shut
up.[2]

On certain topics in this book the Bible is clear. On some
(sexual difference) it says little. On others (interdependence) it leaves us to apply the principles. On a few
(marriage and singleness) we are given practical, unambiguous commands. On this topic alone, the teaching
seems opaque if not downright contradictory.

It has traditionally been understood to say that women
cannot have authority over men. But society now says
that they can. Women are trained, educated and expected
to do jobs the Bible has been thought to forbid. And they
have proved themselves competent. Some women, like
some men, are clearly gifted in positions of leadership.
They can teach and govern and direct. If the traditional
interpretation of the Bible is right then these particular
skills should not be used. It is difficult to know what to
make of this: to us it seems like a waste.

We have also learned to accept certain inconsistencies.
We tolerate women in schools, business, and Parliament,

but when it comes to preaching or parochial administration we go into paroxyms of verse-quoting indignation. We accept a woman as Supreme Governor of the Anglican Church, with authority over every man in it. Yet we baulk at a woman running a parish. Again this is confusing. Why should talented women be allowed to run the government or publish works of theology, but not preach the gospel? Why should the world, not the Church, be allowed the full benefit of their skills?

I find myself, I suspect like many others, caught between the devil and the deep blue sea. The Church seems to be ignoring abilities, embracing double standards, and presenting a sexist image. I am bound to appreciate a society which allows my sex to lead government. I naturally feel deeply uneasy when I hear people say women should not lead the Church. I cannot help noticing a few women who would make far better vicars than many of the vicars I know. And yet there are Christian leaders I greatly admire who say the traditional view is right.[3] The last thing I want is to be in disagreement with them, but I have yet to be totally convinced by their arguments. The last time I heard a sermon on the subject the speaker made three points: first, women have an important ministry in the Church; second, they must be encouraged to exercise it more than they have been in the past; and, third, we have no idea what it is since they cannot do anything involving authority. I have heard from several eminent Christians that women have a vital contribution, different from a man's. I have never yet heard what that contribution is. It seems to me we have more thinking to do. I do not know if my interpretation is right either, but perhaps, at least, it will contribute to the debate.

There are three possibilities. The first is that women should never, under any circumstances, have authority over men. That is, at a glance, what the Bible seems to say (1 Timothy 2:12). Yet I know of no Christian since John Knox[4] who has had the courage to say so:

after all, it would mean we should object to police-women, women doctors, a former prime minister or indeed the Queen.

The second possibility is that there is more than one kind of authority. There is 'secular' authority which women may have over men: they can be monarchs and generals and surgeons. And there is 'spiritual' authority, which they may not: they should not preach, run a church, lead a Bible study, or even pray or prophesy if to do so involves authority over men. This is the position many Christians have adopted.

The third is that God makes no sexual distinction when it comes to authority. He can give it to people regardless of sex (or race or skin). If this is true, then those who object to women's ordination on the grounds of authority are mistaken.

So we must ask whether God allows women authority over men. If He does, we must then ask what kind of authority it is.

The nature of authority

We cannot consider the question until we have a biblical understanding of authority. There are three things we must get clear.

First, authority comes from God (Romans 13:1). Most people assume it comes from man. Authority gets confused with an 'authoritative' personality. Some people are born authoritative, as others are born red-haired. This is a good quality in a leader but it is not the same as authority. Authority comes from above. A soldier, no matter how 'authoritative', has no authority over his commanding officer. Both men are under a higher power, and if one has command over the other it is because he has been given it from above, not because he has a force-ful personality. So authority is like grace. It is not something we have by nature or right. God can give it to anyone, and sometimes He gives it to people who seem wholly unsuitable (Exodus 3:11 and 4:10,13; Judges 6:15). He can even give it to people who do not have qualities of leadership at all.[5]

Second, it is given for a purpose. Moses was given authority to lead the people out of Egypt; the apostles were given it to preach the gospel; at one point seventy disciples were given it to cast out demons. It is always given to do a job of work. So two people can have authority over each other. When you leave your place of work, your boss loses authority over you. If he plays in the cricket team you captain, you sometimes have authority over him. There is nothing contradictory in this. And two people can have authority over each other simultaneously. A man may be ordained in his parents' parish: he and they will both, in their respective roles, have authority over each other. The Queen may submit to Prince Philip as her husband, while he submits to her as his monarch. The authority goes with the job and 'you salute the uniform, not the wearer.'[6]

And third, that job is servile. True authority always involves service. If you have authority over someone it is for his or her benefit not yours. You must put his interests first; you must become like a slave. Jesus was given all authority in heaven and on earth, and He knelt down and washed our feet. Those of us in authority must be prepared for the most unpleasant and humiliating of jobs; one of the first tasks a parent learns, after all, is to change a baby's nappy.

When we have a biblical understanding of authority, we can see a number of things.

Authority can be given to anyone: it does not depend on personal qualities. That some men may or may not be more 'authoritative' than women is neither here nor there. That some people may find it harder to obey a woman is the most irrelevant of objections; you would hardly be prepared to face a court-martial because you think your sergeant-major lacks a bossy enough personality. You 'salute the uniform'.

All authority is 'spiritual'. It all comes from God. A traffic warden or a prime minister ultimately receives power from Him (Romans 13:1–7). Anyone disobeying an individual within the confines of that authority is disobeying God. It is a spiritual matter.

Authority is not something we are born with. It is not part of our natures, an abstract quality endowed on some of us for no reason. No man simply 'has authority' except Christ Himself, its origin. So it is unbiblical to suggest that authority resides in one sex or the other. God gives it to us for a purpose and to do a job. Men will not have some vague or permanent authority over women. Whether husbands have authority over their wives is another question, and one which we will turn to in the next chapter. If so, it will be for the particular job of loving their wives and will not affect the issue any more than a mother's authority over her sons or a queen's over her subjects: neither of these relationships suggest that women in general have authority over men.

And authority is not enviable. This is the last and most important implication. If God never asks women to exercise authority this should pose no threat to us at all. Because it is given as a responsibility not won as a prize, having authority does not mean we are better people than those who are 'under' us. Because it goes with a job and does not rest in a person it does not mean we are any more important in ourselves. Because it means slavery to those in our care it is not something we need ever covet. It is perfectly possible to believe God never gives authority to women without abandoning the biblical doctrine of the equality of the sexes.

Now we can address the question. What kind of authority, if any, does God allow women over men?

WOMEN'S AUTHORITY – CAN WE FORBID IT?

Scattered throughout the Bible are a few verses which suggest limitations on women's authority. It is usually these, rather than the broad sweep of scripture, which cause people reservations. They are not numerous, so we can look at them each in turn.

Genesis 3:16

The first is Genesis 3:16. It is after the Fall. God is telling the woman the consequences of her actions. Childbirth will be very painful, but she will desire her husband and 'he shall rule over you'. The comment is sometimes taken as an indication that women are not to be in charge: God specifically gives men authority over women for the rest of time.

In fact the verse implies no such thing. For one thing, God tells Eve her husband will rule over her: there is no suggestion that every one else's husband will too. Your mother rules over you: does that mean every other mother in the world should too? This verse is set in the context of marriage; it does not necessarily refer to the relationship between the sexes in general.

For another thing, there is no indication whether this arrangement will be good or bad. We do not know whether the man's rule is a merciful provision or a disastrous result of the woman's sin: whether God has just arranged it or is merely warning her it will happen. (If you shoot yourself you will die: you can hardly say I am killing you simply because I have warned you what may happen.) The suffering in childbirth is God's work (as He says) yet we use all our scientific knowledge to overcome it. We do not know whether the husband's rule is God's work or not, but it is assumed we cannot improve upon it. We give women drugs for the pain of childbirth, but nod approval when their husbands rule over them. This is illogical.

So Genesis 3:16 tells us that a husband will rule over his wife. It does not tell us whether he should or not, and it does not say that men in general will rule over women.

Isaiah 3:12

The next text in question is Isaiah 3:12, sometimes translated as follows: 'Youths oppress my people; women rule over them.' The context of this verse is a list of disasters. Women in authority are seen as another misfortune of the people and a sign that they have turned against God. The situation is clearly seen as undesirable.

But to argue from this verse that women should never have authority over men is to stretch the text to breaking point. Isaiah is referring to Ahaz, the contemporary king. Ahaz was probably twenty when he came to the throne (2 Kings 16:2) and strongly influenced by his mother and the other women of the court. Isaiah frequently criticises him; he saw the king as weak and compromising, and the whole nation as idolatrous (see, particularly, Isaiah chapters 1–8). It is as if a prophet in the 1940s had said, 'Germans oppress my people'. He would not necessarily mean a German should never have authority over a Jew.

God is not saying that young men, and women, should never be in authority. No criticism is implied of Josiah because of his age ('Josiah was eight years old when he began to reign . . . and he did what was right in the eyes of the LORD' 2 Kings 22:1,2). Timothy was another young man; and in Paul's first letter to him, in which the apostle clearly expects him to command and teach in the church, he tells Timothy to let no one look down on him because he is young (1 Timothy 4:11,12). And yet if we understand this verse in Isaiah to be saying women should not have authority we must also understand it to mean young men should not have authority. We cannot use it to question a woman's authority without also questioning Timothy's authority.

In any case, the verse is sometimes translated completely differently: 'Money-lenders strip my people bare, and usurers lord it over them'. One text (the Hebrew) talks about youths and women. Another (the Greek translation, the Septuagint) mentions money-lenders. Scholars and translations disagree as to which version should be preferred.[7] So we could not rest any case on the basis of this passage anyway: we cannot have Christian doctrine founded on an uncertain translation of one text.

I Corinthians 11:3–15

The next relevant text is in 1 Corinthians 11:

(3) . . . but I wish you to know that every man's head is Christ and a woman's head is the man, (or 'husband') and Christ's head is God. (4) Every man praying or prophesying with anything over his head shames his head, (5) but any woman praying or prophesying with an uncovered head shames her head, because it is one and the same thing as a woman who has been shaved. (6) Because if a woman is not covered, let her be cropped as well, but if it is a disgrace for her to be cropped or shaved, let her be covered. (7) For indeed a man ought not to cover his head, being the image and glory of God, but the woman is the glory of a man (or 'husband') (8) because man is not of woman, but woman of man; (9) for indeed man was not created because of the woman, but woman because of the man. (10) Because of this the woman ought to have authority (or 'power') over the head because of the angels. (11) Nevertheless there is no man without woman or woman without man in the Lord, (12) for as the woman is of the man, so the man is through the woman as well, but all things are of God. (13) Judge among yourselves: is it appropriate for a woman to pray to God uncovered? (14) Does not nature herself teach you that, indeed, if a man wears

his hair long it dishonours him, but if a woman wears her hair long it is a glory to her, because the long hair has been given to her as a covering?

Paul's message here was no doubt crystal clear to the Corinthians. To us it is like mud. Hardly a commentator approaches the passage without some excuse or apology; it is common to claim that this is the most obscure passage Paul ever wrote.[8] The interpretations are numerous. Some say all women should be 'covered' by a man's authority.[9] Many have believed women should wear hats in church. One has recently asserted that women should have longer hair than men.[10] All this should make us wary: as with the verses in Isaiah, though for a different reason (here it is not the text's reading which is in doubt but the interpretation), we should be slow to claim anything dogmatically from a passage over whose meaning there is so much disagreement. However there are a couple of things we can say with reasonable certainty.

Women do have authority to pray and prophesy (verses 5,13).[11] Praying in public means to some extent representing the Church to God. Prophecy is harder to define: it is not always easy to know what is meant by New Testament prophecy, but it surely involves bringing God's word to His people. It is for upbuilding and encouragement (1 Corinthians 14:3). It edifies the whole Church (verse 4). It convicts. It judges (verse 24). It necessarily implies some authority over its hearers: when God speaks, we must listen. So women can have a certain kind of authority over men.

And they are to have authority over their heads (verse 10). In 'popular' interpretations of the passage this verse has often been grossly misunderstood. Paul says a woman 'ought to have authority . . .' Whenever this Greek idiom is used, in the New Testament or anywhere else, it always means holding authority. It cannot mean being under authority. Even the most conservative scholars[12] insist that the Greek cannot be twisted into such a meaning. Such a 'grammatical distortion of *exousia*' (authority) 'to mean not power . . . but powerlessness' is condemned by commentators.[13] M. D. Hooker criticises interpretations in which *exousia* 'is . . . given a very strange meaning, since the head covering is not being understood as a symbol of authority but, quite the reverse, as a symbol of subjection'.[14] W. M. Ramsey called such an abuse 'a preposterous idea which a Greek scholar would laugh at anywhere except in the New Testament, where (as they seem to think) Greek words may mean anything that the commentators choose'.[15] No reputable scholar takes this sentence to mean a woman must be under someone else's authority. The only authority mentioned in the passage is that which is hers. Whatever we make of the rest of Paul's argument, we can be sure there are occasions when a woman 'ought to have authority' (verse 10).

For the purposes of our present enquiry it is not necessary to examine this passage any further. When seen as restricting women's authority it is usually because of a misunderstanding of the Greek idiom in verse 10. Nevertheless, it is interesting to pursue Paul's idea. He says a woman should 'have authority over her head'. What did he mean by this and why is it so important?

We must read the passage in the light of the first premise. '*I want you to know*' he insists (verse 3), that man's head is Christ, woman's head is man, and Christ's head is God. If we forget this series of metaphors we are likely to miss his entire meaning. Throughout the passage we must be conscious of the meaning of the 'head' which Paul has taken such care to establish. When the man's head is referred to, we must remember his head is Christ. When the woman's head is mentioned, we must remember her head is the man.

In verse 10 Paul tells us 'the woman should have authority *over her head*'. He has told us unequivocally (verse 3) that her head is the man. Surely he is telling us therefore that the woman ought to have authority over the man?

And, indeed, when one pursues Paul's argument carefully it is not difficult to see why. What does he tell us about the man? First, his head is Christ (verse 3) and, second, that he is the image and glory of God (verse 7). As we saw in chapter 2, man and woman represent the race in different ways. In Genesis 2 (to which Paul is referring in verses 9 and 12) man stands for the whole human race; his very name means 'Humankind'. It is in this sense that he is God's glory. He is His representative on earth, and the crown of His creation.

So, Paul tells us, man should not cover his head (verse 7). This is logical. He is God's glory. To cover his head would presumably be to hide that glory. When a man prays or prophesies (verse 4) he should not cover himself and thus hide the glory of God. And man's head is Christ. Unlike the woman, he obviously should *not* have authority over his head. He should not cover himself, because this would shame his head (verse 4).

So much for the man. He should pray to God uncovered. What about the woman? Again Paul establishes two things. First, her head is the man (verse 3); second, she is man's glory (verse 7). She presents a different aspect of the human race. She is the crown of man himself, the glory of the glory, as it were. As (dare one say it?) the more glorious member of mankind, she shows forth its glory. After all, says Paul, she was made for man, just as mankind was made for God: she was made as his glory, as we were all made as God's. As one commentator has said, 'Of all the lovely things in this world of beauty, the loveliest of all is a woman. In a world of beautiful things which proclaims God's love of beauty, she is the crown.'[16]

So, Paul says, she should be covered in worship (verses 5 and 6). Again this is logical. She is man's glory (verse 7). If she is praying or prophesying (verse 5) she should not be glorifying the human race. She should cover herself, lest she give glory to man, not God. In addition, her head is the man. Whereas it would be quite inappropriate for him to have authority over his head, the woman, according to Paul, *should* have authority over hers.

It is not difficult to see why a woman should have authority over her head. Anyone praying or prophesying must do so with the appropriate authority or not at all. If a woman has distractingly lovely hair[17] the men in the congregation, in particular, are likely to be concentrating not on God, but on her; not on the divine, but human; not on the message, but on the messenger. Clearly this is wrong. She must have command of her congregation if she is to proclaim God's will. Let her hide her own glory, and have authority over her head, the man.

It is hard to see how this passage restricts women's authority. Any careful reading points us in the opposite direction. The only authority mentioned is the authority of the woman. And that authority would seem to be over the man, her head: there are times when women must have authority over men. So the authority in this passage cannot legitimately be taken to be authority *over* the women. Verse 10 does not speak of her subordination at all.

1 Corinthians 14:34–5

But this does give us problems three chapters later. If nothing else, Paul has surely been endorsing women's vocal contributions. They can hardly pray or prophesy without speaking. And yet we read:

> (34) As in all the churches of the saints let the women in the churches be silent, for it is not allowed for them to speak, but let them be subject, as even (or 'also') the law says. (35) But if they wish to learn anything, let them question their own husbands at home, for it is a shame for a woman to speak in church.

* * *

Again we must be careful. This passage is almost as ambiguous as the last. It offers at least six interpretive problems in about as many lines.

First there is a textual question mark over these verses. A few manuscripts reproduce them later in Paul's argument (after verse 40), which might make the emphasis slightly different.

Second, he quotes the law, but he does not say which one. Bibles with cross-references usually mention Genesis 3:16. There is no good reason for this. Presumably it is done because no other text fits better. Nowhere does the Old Testament say that women should not speak; it is certainly not to be found in Genesis 3:16. Nor, as we have seen, does this verse say women *should* be subordinate (simply that they will be), but if it did, it is not clear how this would support the case. Subordination does not easily suggest silence: you are subject to your parents, but I hope you talk to them. There is no law in the Old Testament relevant to Paul's argument.

Then he does not say to whom the subordination is to be. It is automatically assumed that he means subordinate to men, or perhaps to husbands. Again there is no good reason for this. If he had said 'men should be subordinate' we would never have dreamt that this would mean subordinate to women. Paul may be talking of subordination to God. Perhaps he means subordination to the Church?

Fourth, we do not know which women are included. All of them? We know some were not married (1 Corinthians 7:8); how can they ask their husbands? Or does he mean only married women? We know some were married to non-Christians (1 Corinthians 7:13); how can they ask them questions about the faith? Or only women with Christian husbands? Why should they be silent and not the others?

And what kind of speaking is forbidden? 'Laleo', the word Paul uses, can mean idle, empty chatter; perhaps the women were simply gossiping. But Paul also uses 'laleo' throughout the letter when referring to the spiritual gift of languages; this usage, some say, would make him unlikely to use it for something so trivial.[18]

And lastly, of course, these verses seem to contradict the assumption three chapters earlier. How can women pray or prophesy if they are not allowed to speak? To resolve this, as some do,[19] by saying that they can speak as long as they do not exercise authority makes little sense. In chapter 11 he says they *should* have authority. Here he says they should be absolutely silent, not simply quiet or respectful.[20] This is the most puzzling problem of all.

The trouble, of course, is that we rip these sentences out of context and apply them to an issue they did not address. That is why we have such difficulties with the sense. Here, Paul is not concerned with the rights and wrongs of women in authority, as he was to some extent in chapter 11. Throughout chapter 14 he is talking about church order.

The Corinthian services were a riot. They were babbling in unintelligible languages (verses 6–12). They struck outsiders as crazy (verse 23). They all came with different contributions (verse 26). Several people would speak at once (implied, verse 27). They even brought their dinners to the communion table and some of them were getting drunk (chapter 11:20–22). We would never call it a dead church, but it was a hopelessly chaotic one. Paul was making a perfectly reasonable attempt to check the spontaneous racket and confusion which would erupt in place of a sober Sunday service.

So grow up, he says (verse 20). Don't talk languages which no one understands. Build the church up. Do things for edification. Don't have more than two or three people speaking languages, and don't let them all talk at once. Let someone interpret. If no one can, let the language speaker 'be silent in church' (almost exactly the phrase he uses to the women). Don't have more than two or three prophecies, and then think about them and weigh them up. And if someone else gets up to say something 'let the first (speaker) be silent'. It is all common sense and decency. And don't let the women chatter interminably, as they could when they sat apart from the men and were not taking part in the services. Don't let them interrupt with endless questions they could just as easily ask at home. Paul implores them, 'Let all things be done decently and in order' (verse 40). This is the context of verses 34 and 35. As Calvin said, 'The discerning reader should come to the decision, that the things which Paul is dealing with here, are different, neither good nor bad; and that they are forbidden only because they work against seemliness and edification.'[21] In the light of this can we resolve our earlier questions?

First, the textual uncertainty need not really concern us. We certainly would not wish to dismiss these words in verses 34 and 35 as un-Pauline since they appear in every manuscript. If they were indeed written after verse 40 this makes little difference (except to render even more far-fetched the already unconvincing explanation that the women can speak as long as they do not judge the prophets).[22]

Second, why did he quote the scriptures if they do not support his case? In Pauline usage, 'the law' does not necessarily mean the Torah, the first five books of the Old Testament, or even the Old Testament as a whole. Sometimes it can mean a secular law, or even an accepted custom.[23] Here, in fact, he is quoting a non-biblical rabbinic law. He repeats almost verbatim a tradition of the Pharisees: 'It is a shame for a woman to let her voice be heard among men.'[24] The suggestion he is making is that 'even' or 'also' – in addition to common sense or decency – 'even (non-scriptural) law says you should be quiet'. He is not quoting the Old Testament at all.

So, third, he is not referring to subjection to men. Nor does he suggest it. The most natural reading is that women should be subject to the Church, and to church order. After all this is the only subordination which would suit Paul's purposes and induce the women to be quiet. In the same way, those who speak in languages must submit themselves to the Church, and to the interpreters. Those who prophesy must also submit themselves to the Church, and to those who judge.

Similarly, women should submit to the Church. It is reasonable for Paul to tell them to be silent, just as he tells prophets and speakers of languages to be silent when they, too, are being disruptive. It is part of the mutual submission of all of us to one another (Ephesians 5:21).

But it is not reasonable of us to take this as a contradiction of his earlier assumption that women will pray and prophesy. Women are not *always* to be silent, any more than the first speaker in verse 30, who is told to be silent in church, is expected never to speak again. We cannot push Paul's words to such extremes or we will find ourselves with absurd questions like 'can unmarried women speak since they have no one to ask at home?'

Some understand Paul to be saying here, on the basis of Genesis 3:16, that women as a rule should be in subjection to men. This is not the case. He does not refer to Genesis 3; he does not mention subjection to men; he is insisting on orderly services for 'God is not a God of tumult but of Peace' (verse 33).

So far we cannot say that God restricts women's authority.

1 Timothy 2:11–15

But the passage which persuades many people that women should not be in authority is still unexamined.

It is the last and most frequently quoted text on the subject:

(11) Let a woman learn in quietness and all subjection,
(12) but I do not allow women to teach or use authority

(or domineer) over a man, but to be quiet, (13) for
Adam was formed first, then Eve, (14) and Adam was
not deceived, but the woman, being deceived, came
into sin; (15) but she will be saved through childbirth,
if they remain in faith and love and sober holiness. (1
Timothy 2:11–15)

At last something directly on the subject! It looks as if
Paul has specifically addressed himself to the question
of women's authority. And the prohibition seems clear
enough. The text certainly appears to say that women, at
least in church (since corporate worship is the context)
should not have authority over men.

The popular understanding of the passage goes something like this. Women should quietly give way to men
and never be in charge. This is argued from creation and
the Fall, so it is not culturally conditioned and it is still
binding on us today. There is even, for good measure, a
suggestion thrown in that women's proper occupation is
not trying to take over the men's role but being loving
and good and having babies.

On closer examination, however, this interpretation is
not without its problems. It leaves a number of questions
unanswered.

What does verse 15 mean? Some take it that good
Christian women will not die in childbirth. History can
quickly prove this wrong. The Greek wording suggests
that women will be saved by having children. Common
sense and the rest of the gospel tells us that this must be
nonsense. The traditional interpretation does not
adequately account for this verse.

Then, we can see that Paul argues something from
creation. But what? The fact that Adam was formed first
does not seem to support his case. It is possible that his
seniority implies authority. But this is not immediately
apparent here, or even hinted at in Genesis 2: the animals'
seniority over Eve certainly suggests no such thing.

Lastly, her deception seems even more of a red herring.

Is she more culpable than Adam because she sinned in ignorance, while he knew what he was doing? Surely not. As we have seen, it was Adam not Eve who was blamed for the fall of the world (1 Corinthians 15:21,22). Even less likely is the idea that Paul thinks all women are gullible. It is patently not true. And if this were his argument we should have to allow any exceptions – any discriminating women – to have authority after all.

So it is a little too facile to claim that Paul must be talking about permanent gender patterns because he mentions creation and the Fall. We must discover *why* he mentions them. What is he saying about Genesis? What point is he illustrating, and how?

It is also all too easy, in this 'straightforward' interpretation, to ignore one or two details of the Greek text which might be significant.

Paul says he does not allow a woman 'authority' over a man. But what kind of authority does he mean? He has not used the noun (the *exousia* of 1 Corinthians 11:10) which is normally translated as 'authority'. Here he uses the verb *authentein*. This word appears nowhere else in the New Testament. Elsewhere it can refer to a prostitute's authority in the latest techniques of sexual naughtiness.[25] If this is what Paul means it is hardly surprising he is unenthusiastic about it. Many believe a better translation would be 'domineer'. The noun from this verb originally meant suicide or murder, and the verb still had the suggestion of 'self-willed arbitrary behaviour'.[26] So a woman should not be bossy. But neither should a man. No Christian is to lord it over another (Mark 10:42–5). Church leaders in particular are not to domineer over their flock (1 Peter 5:3). It should not surprise us then that women are also told not to domineer. And it does not necessarily mean they should never have authority over men if they are mature and responsible about it. In other words, it can be argued, 'the manner in which the wife should not instruct her husband is the subject dealt with. It is not the question of instructing or teaching him, but the manner of doing it.'[27]

This quotation brings us to another point. The words given as 'woman' and 'man' can equally legitimately be translated as wife and husband. The words 'wife' and 'woman' are the same in Greek, as are 'man' and husband'. (There is another word for man which can also mean mankind; it is not used here.) The sense of these words is determined by the context. Unfortunately in this case the context does not make it clear. The mention of Adam and Eve may suggest Paul is thinking of a 'wife' and 'husband' though the fact that he has been talking about men and women in general (verses 8–10) might imply that he means 'woman' and 'man'.

Most translations tamper with the text slightly in order to enforce the latter meaning. The Greek is: 'I do not permit a woman/wife to . . . have authority over a man/ husband.' The RSV translates this: 'I permit no woman to . . . have authority over men.' This suggests a different situation: no longer two individuals (who may have a particular relationship) but a blanket prohibition on any woman having charge of a group of men. (Small wonder if it sounds, from this translation, as if women should not be church leaders.) The Good News version similarly changes both words to the plural, thus moving from the individual to the universal. However, not allowing a wife to domineer over her husband is very different from never allowing a woman authority over men. The former may be all Paul means.

There is another characteristic of Paul's wording, however, which is not lost in translation. It so clearly throws doubt on the traditional application of the passage that I am astonished it is not usually mentioned. Paul says he 'does not permit' (or 'is not permitting') a woman to do so-and-so. He is not saying that it should never be permitted. Whether he is talking about women or wives, sexual licentiousness or authority in the pulpit, wholesome Christian leadership or selfish domineering bossiness, in his words to Timothy Paul does not forbid it. He does not tell us to forbid it. He does not say it is wrong. He simply tells us what he does. It is descriptive, not prescriptive. An observation, not a command.

Come now, you may protest: that is splitting hairs. No it is not: not at all. If we have any kind of belief in the inspiration of scripture, we must surely believe its wording is inspired. Paul was perfectly capable of saying 'they must not have authority' or 'do not let them have authority'. He does not. He says, 'I do not permit it'. What we have here is an account of Paul's practice. He tells us what he did in the circumstances of the time. It is not necessarily what he would do today, or what he would have done in his own day had the situation been different. He does not tell Timothy he is necessarily to follow Paul's example.

Now of course we are to imitate Paul. Of course we must follow his example. Of course, as an apostle, he is a model for us. But we are to imitate him *intelligently*. We are not all to be single (1 Corinthians 7:7b). We do not all speak in languages (1 Corinthians 12:27–30). We know this because he says so. But different circumstances can make us depart from his practice too. Paul sent an escaped slave back to his master (Philemon 10–16). If we lived in the eighteenth-century Deep South we would not necessarily do the same. He told Timothy to drink wine as well as water (1 Timothy 5:23). Living, as we do, in an age when alcoholism can be crippling, we might not necessarily insist that all Christians do so too.

We must of course be very careful of this kind of hermeneutics. We want to be obedient to scripture. If we start saying God's people avoided certain practices only because of current cultural taboos we may soon (albeit illogically) be allowing adultery, occultism, homosexuality, and even stealing from the DHSS or the tax man. But we must be careful in the other direction too. If we believe unthinkingly that because the apostles did something then we must too, we would have to conclude that no Christian should eat black pudding because the first

Christians were not to eat blood (Acts 15:29).

There is clearly a wide difference between God saying, through Moses, 'you must not commit adultery', and saying, through Paul, 'Take a little wine for the sake of your stomach'. We need to work out which kind of statement this one to Timothy is. It will help to know why Paul behaved as he did, and what he was conveying to Timothy; whether he intended a permanent restriction on the Church, and if not, why he said these words at all.

Let us attempt to look at the passage afresh. When you read it before, what struck you? What, to your twentieth-century Western eye, was the statement which seemed most memorable and important? I imagine it was that a woman should be quiet and submissive and not 'teach or have authority over a man'. This is what we think of when we mention this passage; it is this pronouncement for which it is well-thumbed. In a society which is beginning to take for granted women as professors, judges and prime ministers this is bound to jump at us out of the page as the heart of Paul's meaning.

But this is anachronistic. It ignores Paul's main concern. What was likely to have been going on in Timothy's church? Consider this:

'It was debated whether or not a man should give his daughter a knowledge of the Law . . .'

'Not only was a woman not to be instructed in the Law, but the rabbis made it explicit that her obligations to it were limited.'[28]

Women could depend upon men for guidance: 'The husband seems competent to transmit the knowledge of the law to his wife' (Hypothetica 7:14).[29]

These attitudes were not unusual. It never really occurred to anyone that women should be taught: 'Women were not subject to education in the ancient pagan world. Although the Greeks had the highest standard of culture, they did not educate their women.'[30] The Jewish rabbis went further, expressly forbidding women any direct access to God's law. They are not

commanded to study it, says the Talmud, which then
continues 'the wise men have commanded that no man
should teach his daughter the law for this reason, that
the majority of them have not got a mind fitted for study,
but pervert the words of the law on account of the
poverty of their minds. The wise men have said "Everyone that teacheth his daughter the law is considered as if
he taught her transgression".'[31]

Rabbi Eleazer added, 'Let the words of the law be
burned rather than given to a woman.'[32]

This is the context in which Paul wrote. These are the
assumptions of his day. It is hardly likely, in view of this,
that Timothy's church would seriously have been considering a teaching or authoritative ministry for women.
Indeed 'rabbinic prohibitions even ruled out a mother's
teaching the Torah to her own children'.[33] It would surely
not occur to them that women would take any important
part in the life of the Church at all.

Now read Paul's words again:

Let a woman learn quietly in all submission. But I do
not allow women to teach or have authority over a
man, but to be quiet. For Adam was formed first, then
Eve, and Adam was not deceived, but the woman was
deceived and entered into sin; but she will be saved
through childbearing, if they remain in faith and love
and holiness with sobriety.

What is the heart of his message, the surprising – even
extraordinary – idea, indeed the only *commandment* in his
words to Timothy here? Why, *let a woman learn!* This is
what is important. At last the barriers are down
(Galatians 3:28); even women can be full, baptised
members of God's covenant. And the equality must go
all the way. They must indeed have access to God's law
and learn along with the men (as, indeed, they did in the
past before men started adding to God's commandments
– for example in Deuteronomy 31:12).

When we realise what would have struck Paul's contemporaries on reading these verses, rather than what strikes us in a completely different social context, the whole passage suddenly makes sense. Everything falls into place.

'Let a woman learn', Paul is saying. What immediately follows now sounds like a caveat. She must do so 'quietly and submissively'. Indeed anyone should learn quietly and submissively; rowdy pupils are a thorough nuisance. And 'I do not allow a woman to teach or domineer over a man, but to be quiet'. Of course. Most women at the time were ignorant, illiterate and strangers to any form of education. It would be thoroughly inappropriate for them to teach or have authority. Paul is being reassuring. He is firmly, but very gently, insisting that women learn; nevertheless, he is not going berserk. He says he does not use them as teachers or leaders (although in fact he sometimes did, as in the case of Priscilla and Phoebe). Not yet: it would be crazy, as anyone who thinks about it will realise.

Now he returns to his real theme. Let a woman learn. Why? 'Because Adam was formed first, then Eve . . .' The traditional interpretation is that Adam, not Eve, came first, so he not she must be in charge. The Genesis writer does not suggest this. Nor in fact does Paul. He does not say 'Adam . . . not Eve', but 'Adam . . . *then* Eve'. Look at the sequence of events in Genesis 2. God made Adam (verse 7). He commanded him not to eat out of the tree (verse 17). *Then* He made Eve (verses 18–22). As far as we know, she did not hear directly from God the warning about the tree. Presumably she only heard through Adam. She may not even have received the information accurately (Genesis 3:3). Similarly, many women in Paul's day would only pick up what teaching they could glean from their husbands. But the result of this was disastrous: ' . . . and Adam was not deceived but the woman was deceived and entered into sin'. So, from now on, let a woman learn! Teach women as well as men.

Alternatively, Paul may simply be drawing attention to the fact that Eve was created at all. As we have seen, contemporary men behaved largely as if women did not exist. But after Adam came Eve, says Paul: 'Adam was formed . . . then Eve'. Mankind did not stop at man. Jewish education was conducted as if it did. The importance of learning had long been recognised, and rightly so: to some extent it is what our spiritual lives depend on; we cannot obey God unless we know what He has commanded. But it had only been recognised for men. Paul's insistence on Eve's creation reminds us that women exist too; they need teaching just as much.

Either of these interpretations is reinforced by the next verse. Eve was deceived. This is an inevitable result of ignorance. So she sinned. This is the result of deception. The solution is obvious. Let women *learn* and they will not be so easily deceived. They will be better equipped to recognise sin. Paul's logic is clear. Teach the women. And teach them directly, not just through their husbands. Let them have open access to God's word.

He sums up with what is almost an aside to his argument. His mind is still on Genesis, but now on chapter 3. Sin came into the world through woman. 'But she will be saved through childbearing.' He is surely thinking on to the promise of Genesis 3:15. Salvation will also come into the world through a woman, through the birth of the Christ to a young girl or virgin (Isaiah 7:14). And that salvation is available to all, to men as well as women, 'if they' (there is no gender here) 'remain soberly, in faith and love and holiness'. So in case we should be tempted to blame women because their ignorance helped cause the Fall, we should be quick to thank women because it was a woman's childbearing which brought our salvation.

Paul may even see this as an additional reason for their learning: creation, the Fall and redemption all argue for women's spiritual education. She was made, as man was, so she should learn. She was deceived, as man was not, so she must learn. She gave birth to the Son of God Himself, as man could never do, so she is even entitled to learn; what excuse could we possibly have for keeping the mother of God in ignorance?

This, I believe, is the correct interpretation of the passage. Paul is one of the few men of the ancient world to insist on women's education. He argues it logically and consistently from Genesis, and does not impute back to the Old Testament a meaning which did not appear to be there.

Seen in this light, verse 12 is almost in parenthesis. It is still there and we must not lightly ignore it, but we may apply it differently now we can see Paul's real concern. There is often tension between God's ideal at creation and what the restrictions of society may make desirable; so Moses allowed divorce, and Paul, prepared to oppose Peter in order to abolish circumcision, still had Timothy circumcised. We can see this tension illustrated by the fact that, some years earlier (1 Corinthians 14:35), Paul had suggested that women asked their husbands for answers to their questions. The ideal is that they should be properly taught like the men. Until they are, and to avoid the assemblies getting out of hand, let them also be helped at home by their husbands.

Paul insisted on a slave's obedience. Yet it is generally agreed that it was the underlying principles in the New Testament which eventually overthrew slavery and made his words unnecessary. Can we not hope for the same for women? He was cautious about their leadership, but dare we not believe that the principles he laid down about their equality and the importance of their education might, some day soon, render such caution superfluous?

Summary of the texts

None of these passages definitely prohibits a woman's authority. The one which most strongly suggests restrictions is the last one. Yet even with this text there are other

possible and equally legitimate interpretations. He may
be talking of a husband and wife. He may mean bossiness, not true authority. He never categorically forbids it
anyway. And the force of his argument is elsewhere. So
to say on the basis of these verses that women should
not teach or lead in the Church (or in the world) is to
hang a great deal on a very thin thread.

To be fair, the texts often used to claim that women
should be given authority are ambiguous too. Some say 1
Timothy 3:11 is talking about women deacons. This is
probably the most natural reading of the text: the context
is deacons' qualifications; the phrase is, 'Similarly the
women . . .' But, as we have seen, we often cannot
distinguish between 'wives' and 'women'. So 'deacons'
wives', not 'women deacons', may be the intended meaning (although we certainly have no right to translate the
word 'wives', as many versions do).

We do know that Phoebe was a deacon (Romans 16:1),
but this does not necessarily tell us she was in authority.
There is no job description for the office: the word simply
means one who serves. (Though again there is no justification for translating it as 'servant' when it refers to
Phoebe, but 'deacon' or 'minister' when it is Paul or
Tychicus!)

Junia was 'notable among the apostles' (Romans 16:7).
Some take this to mean she was an apostle herself. This
is not necessarily the case. We are simply told she was
notable among the apostles. In Greek, as in English, this
may mean that as an apostle she was notable; or it may
simply mean she had a good reputation in the apostolic
circle. We cannot argue anything from this. (Besides, as
the critics never tire of telling us, she may have been a
man . . . like all the other women in history.)

It all seems fairly inconclusive. We have not proved
women can have authority in the same way as men. All
we have shown is that we cannot be dogmatic in saying
they cannot. Yet this is important. Those who disapprove
of women's authority on biblical grounds can sometimes

be very dogmatic. They can also be self-righteous: there is a tendency to think that those who hold firmly to a traditional interpretation of scripture are holding more firmly to scripture itself; that those who exclude women's authoritative ministry are being more obedient or biblical. This is not necessarily true. There are sincere and intelligent people on both sides of the debate. Both are equally trying to understand and obey scripture. So there is no room for arrogance or even assurance on either side: from the texts examined so far, we simply cannot say whether women should or should not be in charge of men.

WOMEN'S AUTHORITY – CAN WE PERMIT IT?

So we can have no certainty that women should not be in authority. There is no text which absolutely forbids it. But have we any reason to believe that they should? If we can find any examples, however rare, of women in the Bible being allowed or commissioned by God to hold positions of authority over men then we will know that it cannot be wrong.

And as well as knowing *whether* women can have authority we will also want to know *what kind* of authority it may be. As we have seen, authority is always given for a particular function. If women can have authority over men, the next question is naturally going to be 'to do what?' The reservations people most frequently have – no doubt because of 1 Timothy 2:12 – are whether women can have authority to teach and lead in the Church. Let us now look at these questions in turn.

Authority to teach

We certainly find women teaching men in the Bible. Chapter 31 of Proverbs presents a woman's teaching (see verse 1). Timothy received the faith from women

(2 Timothy 1:5). And Priscilla taught Apollos. Apollos was a fine speaker, accurate teacher, and zealous Jewish convert to Christianity who was 'well versed in the scriptures'. But he did not know the whole gospel (Acts 18:24,25). So, along with her husband Aquila, Priscilla took him and 'expounded the way of God to him more accurately' (Acts 18:26). It is not unseemly then for a woman to correct and instruct a man. But Priscilla's authority in this instance was limited. Though Apollos owed her respect, he was under no obligation to obey her. And authority to correct him in private as a friend is not the same as authority to do so officially in public before the Church: the prime minister's wife correcting her husband over the breakfast table is not the same as her doing so in a press conference. Thus Priscilla had informal authority to teach and instruct but, as far as we know, no formal authority demanding an immediate response, or public authority as a church representative.

But women also had authority to teach their sons, and not only to instruct them but also to expect obedience to that instruction. A man is not at liberty to reject his mother's teaching (Proverbs 1:8 and 6:20). Nor, indeed, is he at liberty to disobey her. Throughout the Bible we are told to honour our parents. It is one of the Ten Commandments (addressed incidentally to adults not to children: Exodus 19:25; 20:12). And Paul lists disobedience to mothers with crimes like murder and hating God (again referring to adults, since he has just mentioned their homosexual activities: Romans 1:26–30). So a mother had fairly extensive authority over her grown sons. Her teaching is to be listened to and she is to be obeyed.

A mother's authority to teach is formally instituted, and much more far-reaching than Priscilla's. But to us, in a society which has greatly 'privatised' the home (compared with a tribal society where family life *was* public life), authority in a domestic sphere will still seem limited. Could women have authority over men on a scale we could call 'public'?

Authority to lead

We can see from the case of Deborah that they could. She was judge over Israel (Judges 4:4). As such she would have had authority not only to judge, but to lead in war, govern in peace, and keep Israel faithful to God. Judges were chosen by Him and representative of Him. Like the king, they were deliverers as well as rulers. Indeed, 'we may see in them a type of Christ, who came to be our Saviour, is with us as our leader, and will come to be our judge'.[33]

Deborah was one. Throughout Judges 4 we hear of her using her extensive authority to save Israel. She summoned Barak, commander of the Israelite army (verse 6). She commanded him (verses 6 and 7). She told him when to attack (verse 14). And the result of her leadership was superb victory (verse 23).

1 have occasionally heard the insinuation that there was something 'second best' about Deborah as a leader of the people; that she was only chosen because there was a shortage of suitable men; or even that having a woman leader at all was a sign of Israel's hopeless degeneracy. There is no suggestion of this anywhere in the text. All the judges were raised up and chosen by God Himself (2:16). They were God's answer to Israel's need (3:15). And Deborah is no exception: 'The people of Israel cried to the Lord for help' (4:3), and He replied by giving them Deborah. There is not the slightest hint that His choice of Deborah was in any way different from His choice of any other judge. (Besides, He chose some very odd people as judges. Samson and Gideon are hardly what we could call 'suitable'. There does not seem to have been such a thing as a 'suitable man' as far as God was concerned, so there can hardly have been a lack of one.)

Nor is there much evidence for the theory that Barak is criticised for bowing to Deborah's authority. In verse 8 he says he will not fight without her. She replies by promising to go with him, and adds that he will not win glory himself, since someone else, a woman, will kill the enemy commander. This is sometimes seen as a rebuke to Barak for not claiming his 'manly' authority, and for wrongly wanting a woman by his side as his boss. Even if this somewhat forced interpretation were correct it simply reinforces Deborah's authority. What was Barak's fault but that of failing to obey her promptly? As we see in the gospels (Matthew 8:5–13), if someone has sufficient authority his presence should not be necessary for his word to be obeyed. If Barak was in the wrong it can only have been because Deborah's commands could just as well have been carried out in her absence.

So Deborah was given authority by God over the whole country, including an army of ten thousand men. A woman can therefore have full public and official authority to lead men on a large scale.

And there is one other element in Deborah's leadership which is very important. Israel's victory as a nation was directly dependent upon the Israelites' obedience as a worshipping people. Because of this, a judge's authority was not simply civil and military, but also religious. They were not only to save Israel from invasion but also from idolatry. Failure to listen to them resulted in a departure from the way of their ancestors, a breaking of the commandments, and widespread unfaithfulness (2:17). So, as a judge, Deborah was expected to be a spiritual leader as well as a temporal one. Indeed she was exceptional among the judges in being also described as a prophet (verse 4). Her commandments came directly from God Himself. Her first words to Barak were 'The LORD, the God of Israel, commands you . . .' (verse 6). She told him what God was going to do, had done and was doing (verses 6, 9 and 14).

From her example, we can see that a woman can be a

political, military and religious leader of God's people. She can judge in law, command in battle, and proclaim God's will and message. As His spokesman she can insist on obedience from men. And she can do all this nationally, in a public, official capacity.

Authority to preach

Deborah's authority resembles what we would expect of a preacher. To expound God's will and word to His people, and tell them what to do in the light of it, is surely what faithful preaching is all about. And in Huldah we have an even better example. She too was a prophet (2 Kings 22:15–20, or 2 Chronicles 34:22–8). She too was appealed to by men for her authority (2 Kings 22:15–20). In her case the chief man involved was a king; he sent a number of ambassadors to her, including his secretary and the high priest, to discover God's will for himself, his people and the whole of Judah (verse 13). She was expected to instruct the entire nation in its worship and moral behaviour. Nor is there any doubt that this authority was from God. The men were sent to 'Go, inquire of the LORD' (verse 13); they immediately went and inquired of Huldah (verse 14). In her reply to the king, she said, 'Thus says the Lord' four times in the same number of sentences.

In a sense, Huldah was preaching to the whole country. As with Deborah, there was no suggestion that she was chosen only because there were no suitable men available. Indeed Jeremiah had already been prophesying for four years and was living only a short distance away in Anathoth; he could easily have been consulted instead. So we cannot say women were only given this kind of authority because there were no men around to exercise it. Huldah and Deborah were appealed to and obeyed regardless of their sex. It is also interesting that both of them were married. Their husbands must have come under their authority like anyone else in the country. So their marriages, like their femininity, were no barrier to their leadership or authority.

As prophets, then, women can preach God's will to His people on a public and official scale. And there are women prophets throughout the Old and the New Testaments. Miriam was not only a leader of the Israelites, along with her brothers Aaron and Moses (Numbers 12:2), but also a prophet. Anna was another (Luke 2:36). The Corinthian church presumably had several (1 Corinthians 11:5), and Philip had four daughters who prophesied (Acts 21:9).

Authority to lead in Church

As we saw in 1 Corinthians 11, women were also expected to lead the Church in meetings. Paul assumes they will be praying and prophesying, and says that they must have the proper authority to do so.

Therefore, according to the Bible, women are free to perform many of the functions often thought barred to them. They can teach, and expect their teaching to be obeyed; they can govern, judge and command as God's representatives; they can publicly preach and prophesy to His people; and they can lead the Church in worship. God clearly chose women to have all these different kinds of authority over men and does not see this as in any way a contradiction of Genesis 2.

Nevertheless, there are one or two things we do *not* find them doing in the Bible. However much authority a judge or prophet may have had, she (or he) could not offer sacrifices. This was firmly restricted to the priests; Saul, who had considerable authority as a king, was condemned for usurping the authority of a priest in this matter (1 Samuel 13:8–14). And a woman could never be a priest. Nor, indeed, do we find that any of the twelve apostles were women. Jesus chose these people very carefully to pass on His teaching and history, and deliberately chose only men. Does this mean there are things that women should not have authority to do today?

We must first look at the functions of priests and apostles. Priests had various duties, including the teaching and instruction of the Law, but their one exclusive role was the offering of sacrifices on behalf of the people. And this is why the priesthood has now been abolished. The great Sacrifice has been paid; we no longer need priests to offer sacrifices for us. We have a perfect High Priest; we no longer need any others (Hebrews 7:11–28). And we do not have an exclusive priesthood any more; we are now a 'priesthood of all believers' (1 Peter 2:5).

Similarly, apostles, in the way that Paul and the eleven were apostles, were appointed for a specific purpose. They were the foundation of the Church (Ephesians 2:20). They were to preach the faith to the world (Romans 1:5). And for this they were attested by 'signs, wonders and mighty works' (2 Corinthians 12:12) and had to be eyewitnesses to Jesus and His resurrection (Acts 1:21,22; and 1 Corinthians 9:1, where Paul, in order to give weight to his apostleship, says he had seen the risen Lord). Obviously then, just as we no longer have priests in the Old Testament sense of the word, we no longer have apostles in the sense that the eleven and Paul were apostles. They have founded the Church, given us their first-hand accounts and teaching, and left us.

We no longer need priests or apostles, but if we did, they would not simply have to be men. Priests were all Levites, members of only one tribe. No woman could offer sacrifices, but no male member of the tribe of Benjamin or Judah could either. Similarly, the apostles were all Jews. The old covenant was exclusive: it was made through circumcision, so only with male Jews. The New Testament repeatedly tells us this is over; the covenant is now made through baptism, so it is for anyone who believes. And yet Jesus chose for His apostles only members of the old covenant. He deliberately built the new Israel on the foundation of the old. So both priesthood and apostleship were considerably restricted.

There are denominations today which call their leaders 'priests' or 'apostles'. Obviously these are not priests or apostles in the way we have just defined them. But it would be easy in such a church to think women cannot be church leaders because they were never priests or apostles in the Bible. By this argument, however, the only priests we can have are Levites, and the only apostles, Jews. I doubt if these churches would find this acceptable. These restrictions are no longer relevant today; but if they were, they would not only rule out women, but most men as well.

There is one more position in the Bible which, it is said, women never held. This is the position of elder (or bishop, which was much the same thing, as is clear from Titus 1:5–7). Actually, we do not know that there were no women elders. When 'elders' are mentioned the word is always in the masculine plural. But this is also true of 'saints' and 'brothers' (and the latter should usually be translated in the New Testament as 'brothers and sisters').[34] Yet we know these terms included women. This is a feature of the Greek language, like modern French; a crowd of men and women, even if there are fifty women and only one man, is still referred to in the masculine plural. We cannot deduce anything from the fact that elders are referred to as masculine.

In Acts, when the Church was very young, the elders were all men. When Peter and James address them (15:7,14) they actually say, 'Men brothers . . .' *(andres adelphoi)*. But later on, in the epistles, we simply do not know if there were any women elders. It is possible that the 'older women' of 1 Timothy 5:2 were elders since Paul used the feminine form of the word 'elder' *(presbuteras)* rather than the word which can mean 'older women' *(presbutidas)*. The context, however, does make this extremely unlikely, since Paul seems to be talking about older and younger men and women in general.

The important thing is not whether there actually were any women elders at the time, but whether the practice is prohibited. Is there anything to suggest that they will always be unsuitable for eldership? We are told that elders and bishops are to be 'the husband of one wife' (1 Timothy 3:2; Titus 1:6). This could mean that they should be male and married: I am told that in the Eastern Orthodox Church parish priests must be married men (though their bishops, strangely enough, have to be single). It is more often taken to mean that *if* an elder is married he should only have one wife; he should not be polygynous, or divorced and remarried. In this case, Paul simply expected most elders to be married men, but was not insisting that they must be. Either interpretation is legitimate. Perhaps we should assume that elders will usually be married and male, but make exceptions in the case of outstanding women or bachelors, as Paul would probably have done himself.

We know there were no women priests or apostles. They could not be the former, and were not chosen as the latter. We do not know that there were no women elders. Even if we think it unlikely in the social conditions of the time, there is no restriction to suggest that they could not be elders when circumstances might make it appropriate.

Implications

Most of the teaching, preaching, leading, ruling, governing and prophesying in the Bible is done by men. But not all. Women are found doing all these things, and are approved by God in them. The implication is not that there should necessarily be *as many* women in authority as men, but that *it cannot be wrong.* Yet there are church denominations and individual Christians who forbid it. This is surely mistaken: if God does not disapprove of something, how can we?

So the most obvious implication is in the realm of church leadership. There is no part of a church leader's work which, on theological grounds, a woman cannot do. We find God commissioning women to rule, judge, command, proclaim His will, correct, reprove, teach, and train. It is hard to see what is left out. There is no prohibition or lack of example to prevent us ordaining women to teach and lead in the Church. Yet in many churches this is still not done.

Why is this? Why are some people still unhappy about it? Sometimes it is because of 1 Timothy 12. This is the most convincing reason for not ordaining women: Paul did not allow them to domineer, and this is seen as an indication that they should never have spiritual authority. However, though I respect this conclusion, in the light of the rest of the scripture I do not think it is right. Men are not to domineer either. And women in the Bible are seen to do plenty of things which involve spiritual authority over men.

Often, though, people are not even sure what their objection is. Sometimes it is only half-articulated, which makes it difficult to examine, but one frequently hears something like this.

'A woman can *help* run the Church or preach an occasional sermon, but she should not have ultimate authority.' This may be argued from various notions about the family. It might be said that women have a limited authority over their children, not ultimate authority: this is in the hands of the father, so in the Church it ought to be in the hands of a man. Or it may be argued from a man's 'headship': a man is the head of the household, so he ought to be the head of the Church; a woman cannot represent Christ in this way because she is not head of the home. Or perhaps it is claimed a woman always needs a man to submit to, a 'head' in this sense, so she should never be at the top of any organisation; there should always be a man over her.

A number of different ideas often get mixed up in these kinds of arguments. Concepts about 'headship', authority itself, the family and the Church can all become somewhat confused, so we need to examine each in turn. First we should dismiss once and for all the idea of every woman needing a 'head' in the sense of someone to submit to. Paul's use of the word head has been grossly abused. It is given all sorts of meanings the apostle never gave it himself. A fashionable one at the moment is to suggest a woman needs a man, a 'head' over her and responsible for her, in order to flourish and use her gifts and feel secure in the Lord. Not only is this an insulting and emotionally dangerous teaching for single women, but it is thoroughly unbiblical. In 1 Corinthians 11 Paul uses the concept to insist on a woman's authority, not her submission to or emotional dependence on men. And in Ephesians 5 he teaches quite clearly that a head should lay down his life for his body. No one suggests every bachelor should have a body, a woman to adore and give his life for, though people seem to say that every spinster needs a head. In 1 Corinthians 7 Paul is at pains to free single women from the pressure to marry. Do we want to enslave them instead to an equally tyrannical pressure: to find a head, though not a husband, and possibly even to share with him his rightful body, his wife? Whatever Paul may mean by 'head' he never suggests a woman must have a man over her in this way. If Lydia was indeed single, who was over her in the church at Philippi?

The next question to answer is whether women should have ultimate authority. And of course the answer is no. No one should. God is the ultimate authority. Any authority we may have is derived from Him for a specific purpose to which it is limited. Someone who has the authority to preach has no authority to book you for a parking offence, and vice versa. All human authority is limited. None is absolute or ultimate, nor should it be. This applies to men in leadership as much as to women.

Next, we should understand the family properly if we are going to apply it to the Church. We must know whether we are talking about a man as a *father* or as a *husband*. As a father his authority is the same as his partner's. There is little distinction – for example in the

Ten Commandments, or Proverbs, or Paul's teaching about the family – between the authority of the two parents; both are owed equal honour and obedience, and a mother has as much authority as a father in this respect.

The Church is indeed the family of God. But we are not His aunts or uncles or grandmothers or cousins. We are His children. And we are all His children. We have all been adopted as His heirs (Galatians 3:26–4:7). It is almost blasphemous to suggest that a man, a mere minister or servant of the Church, is in some way the father of God's family. I hope most ministers would blush to hear it suggested. We are specifically told to call no man 'father' (Matthew 23:9). God is now our Father, and this gives us a glorious equality (1 Peter 3:7). Paul, who was in many ways in the position of father to the churches he founded, and indeed to subsequent Christians since we owe so much of our faith to his writings, nonetheless calls us his siblings far more often than he addresses us as his children. We are the family of God, but we demonstrate this by living as brothers and sisters; it is in our love for one another, not our power structures, that the world will see we are His family (John 13:35).

On the other hand, when we talk of a man as husband, or *head*, we are referring to his relationship with his wife. As we shall see in the next chapter, Paul does not talk of a man as head of his household or children, or dog and car and four-bedroomed semi. In the context of the family, head is synonymous with husband. He is head *of his wife*. We must have this clear in our minds when we apply 'headship' to church structures. 'Headship' is about the relationship between a man and a woman.

And the Church, like a woman, is also described as a bride and a body (Ephesians 5:22–32 and 1 Corinthians 12:12–30). As a wife, the Church does indeed have a husband. As a body, she does indeed have a head. But her head, her bridegroom, is Christ and Christ alone. Again it is verging on the blasphemous to say that a man can be the head (and therefore the husband) of the Church. A man's relationship with his wife is a picture of Christ's love for the Church, but this does not mean that a minister is to behave towards the body of believers as if it were his wife. If we start drawing unbiblical principles from a biblical image like this we are asking for a Church in which there is one man at the top and lots of women in the pews. (And alas, all too often, we get what we ask for.)

These metaphors – the Church as the family, or the wife, or the body of the Lord – are never used in the Bible to maintain that a man should be in charge. They are used to teach almost the opposite: that God alone is head of the Church, and that we are equal and united in His service.

We must, of course, be sensitive to any uneasiness felt over women becoming bishops or elders in the Church. There are numerous other objections given by people who feel unhappy about it. I have heard many of them.

'I don't think it would be proper.'

'I would feel very uncomfortable.'

'It just smells wrong.'

'I don't think they'd be any good.'

Most of these come down to the same thing in the end. We simply would not *like* it. This is surely what C. S. Lewis is unwittingly referring to when he talks about 'an inarticulate distaste, a sense of discomfort which [we] find it hard to analyse'.[35] Many people would have felt the same two hundred years ago (and might even today) about a black clergyman, or a woman doctor. It is a gut reaction. And if we are truthful, it is often simply prejudice. This is why many of us object to clergywomen, but not to the Queen as Supreme Governor or to women working as missionaries in places men will not go. We are accustomed to those things; they seldom threaten us, so we seldom question them.

To be honest, many of the reasons on the other side spring from the same thing, too. We must be careful of going along with the spirit of the age. Our society is increasingly treating men and women the same; inevitably we are going to want to follow suit. Perhaps this is why I feel defensive when people say that women should not be in charge. Perhaps it is because it feels to me like misogyny, and quite simply, I do not like it.

So the Church is right to exercise caution. We may be free to employ women as leaders and teachers in the Church, but we still have cause to pause. We may be free to. But we are also surely free *not* to. The issue is highly controversial. The relevant texts are difficult. I do not think they are usually interpreted correctly. I am uneasy to be in disagreement with Christians I respect, although I must admit I am more uneasy with their interpretations. However, I think there is more room for humility on either side of the debate; there are sincere, biblical, dedicated Christians in both camps. For this reason none of us should be dogmatic.

The Church has often survived without women's leadership. Though the New Testament allows and indeed I believe encourages it, it does not insist upon it. We must conclude that, though permitted, it is not essential.

A majority vote to ordain women?

Just as others remember where they were when Kennedy was shot, so I remember what I was doing when the vote was cast and counted in the General Synod of the Church of England on 11 November 1992, after the debate on the ordination of women. I was in the kitchen, listening to the radio over tea, hoping it would be on the news but not sure if it would be.

It must have been shortly after four o'clock when it was announced. The required two-thirds majority had been reached; Parliament permitting, there would now be no bar to women being ordained to the Anglican priesthood. At some point we were also told that it would only have taken two or three people to have changed their minds and the vote would not have gone through.

When I heard the result I was astonished by my own excitement. Extraordinary though it may seem, I felt as if, for the first time in my life, the Church of England had become a Church which belonged to me, where I was welcome and accepted and a full member. I had not the slightest intention of getting ordained. But I hadn't realised how excluded I had felt, and how much I had cared, until that moment. When I went out later I wanted to hug everyone in the street and tell them to celebrate with me.

And yet my other, simultaneous, reaction was just as much of a surprise. Even in my joy and delight, the first thing I said to myself was, 'Thank God I wasn't on Synod.' Because I could not have voted for the motion. Being realistic, I doubted that I would have the courage of my convictions to vote against it; I would have had to abstain, and was very glad God had not given me that responsibility – especially as the vote was so close.

I am aware that, at first, this may seem a contradiction of much that has been argued in this chapter. I am in favour, indeed passionately in favour, of the ordination of women. But not at the expense of other principles which the Bible holds more dear. And in Synod on that historic day a very important biblical principle was completely steamrollered.

If you have followed, and agreed with, my reasoning in this chapter so far, you will be able to say with me that we have seen good, biblical reasons for ordaining women in the Church.

But what does Paul say in his first letter to the Corinthians over a comparable issue? 'Not everyone has this knowledge' (1 Corinthians 8:7). 'Be careful, in case your freedom (literally *authority*) somehow becomes a stumbling block to the weak' (verse 9). 'For the weaker brother, for whom Christ died, is destroyed by your knowledge' (verse 11). 'Everything is lawful, but not everything is a good idea. Everything is lawful, but not everything is edifying. No one should seek things for himself, but for others' (10:23–4).

The situation in the Church in first-century Corinth was remarkably similar to that in the Church of England in the late twentieth century. The point of contention in Corinth was the eating of food previously sacrificed to idols. Some members of the Corinthian church believed it wrong to eat it because of the idolatrous overtones. Others did not. Similarly, some members of our Church believe it is wrong to ordain women, because they think it contradicts the Bible and the received teaching of the Church. Others do not.

As it happens, Paul says, there is nothing wrong with eating food offered to idols. It is just food, and won't do your faith any harm. But if your Christian brother believes it to be wrong, then your love for him means you should never make him eat it, or even eat it in front of him, because to do so would be to make him go against his conscience. The point is this: the brother or sister who does not think it wrong is the one who can afford to be generous. The other cannot, because to do so would be to do something he believes to be wrong.

Let me give another example. One of my elderly relatives lost a brother who died of drink. Consequently she believed alcohol to be wicked, and strongly felt that Christians should not drink it. We, the rest of her family, did not think so, believing that, if used properly, it can be harmless and give great pleasure. She was not free to drink it. We were. But we were also free *not* to. We could please her on this matter. She could not please us, since to do so would involve doing something she considered wrong. We had the choice. She did not. Consequently, if we went to a party in her house we did not drink – or not in front of her anyway. If she came to a party at ours, or that of any of her relations, no drink was served where she could see it. This is straightforward love and common sense. We can survive without alcohol, by the use of a little judicious unselfishness. But she could not be comfortable with it, or even stay in a room in which it was being served; not by exercising unselfishness, or generosity, or anything other than an uneasy conscience. No Christian has a right to ask this of another over something which is not essential.

It is exactly the same with the ordination of women. I believe we are free to ordain women and that women can teach, lead, run churches and dioceses without disobeying God. I could be wrong, but this is what I think. But I *know*, without any shadow of a doubt, that we are free not to. It may be very galling to live in a Church which does not have women ministers in this day and age, but it is certainly not *wrong*. I can be a member of a Church which does not ordain women: not happily, not comfortably, it is true, but with an easy conscience. I may feel intensely exasperated, but I will not feel guilty. But those who believe the ordination of women is contra-indicated by scripture and the teachings of the Church *cannot* exist in a Church which ordains women, except by compromising what they understand to be the truth, and therefore their own consciences.

And yet, when Synod voted to ordain women to the priesthood in the Church of England, almost a *third* of General Synod voted against it: a quarter of the bishops, slightly more clergy, and all but a third of the laity. Can you imagine Paul saying: 'Food offered to idols is not wrong. So get a two-thirds majority confirming this and you can make the other third eat the stuff. Tell them not to be so silly.'

You see why I could not have voted for the motion. For a unanimous verdict, yes; even a 95 or 98 per cent majority, yes. But *two-thirds*? What about the other third? Is it not their Church of England too? It is a Christian principle that we need to care for those who are more vulnerable. Paul says that some Christians may have 'weaker consciences' (verses 7–10). My conscience on this is strong. I need to care for my weaker brethren.

It will be said that provision was supposedly made for them. But what provision can you make for someone who believes his Church has just voted in a change which God has forbidden? And over and over again I have heard accounts of the ways in which those who cannot accept the ordination of women are now discriminated against within the Church of England. Would-be ordinands, ordinands, and ordained men seeking posts have been asked their views on the subject in interviews, and when they have given the 'wrong' answer have been told there is no place for them. A friend of ours who was at theological college when the vote was taken was told, by her bishop no less, that there was no longer a job for her in the Church of England as she was not prepared to be ordained as a priest. These people are not bigoted misogynists, but sincere, godly Christian men and women who cannot reconcile women's ordination to their received faith.

Sadly, I am not surprised at this outcome. One of the foremost speakers in favour of the motion telephoned a close friend of mine a few days before the debate because she had seen his name on a petition opposed to it. During the course of their conversation she said, 'Do you really think there will be a place for you in the Church of England if you oppose this?' She is an old friend, but her words and the implied threat behind them made his flesh creep.

Michael Green, who kindly wrote the foreword to this book, has recently come back from Canada where he was the Professor of New Testament and Evangelism at the University of British Columbia. Michael, like me, is far from opposed to the ordination of women, but he says that in many North American churches now, which are a few years ahead of us on this issue, almost the only credal doctrine left is an essential belief in the ordination of women.

It was said at the time that once women were ordained people would come round to it. Give the Church a trial period and everyone will see how well women do. But of course women do well. We always knew they would. No serious opponent of women's ordination is so because he thinks women incompetent. And the measure has had the opposite effect on me. I have seen what it does to a Church when we make a change for unchristian motives in an unchristian way.

For we did it for all the wrong reasons. People campaigned for women's ordination using the language of 'rights', 'justice' and 'careers'; because they felt 'hurt', 'marginalised' and 'misunderstood'. But Christians are called to be marginalised and misunderstood. Do we really want ordinands who are concerned about their own *rights*? These sound like the words of spoilt children. Do we honestly consider ordination the only way to serve God? Or was serving God always a secondary consideration?

Living as I do with someone who has given his life to the ordained ministry, I did not recognise any of this language. He never sought a 'right' to be on call twenty-four hours a day, to take a fraction of the pay otherwise available for similar qualifications, to share home and family, sometimes with people who help themselves to what they find, or who are dangerous or threatening or totally exhausting, to have his health impaired, possibly permanently, because of the demands of God's work. This is what I understand by a willingness to serve God in the ordained ministry, having lived with it for fifteen years. It is noble and good to be prepared for it. But, having experienced this, I simply did not recognise whatever 'career' it was which a number of women were arguing for on the grounds of 'self-fulfilment' and 'recognition'.

Of course not everyone campaigning for change was doing so for these reasons, or with this strident tone. Most of the women seeking ordination were no doubt driven by a desire to serve the gospel. But those who are genuine in this determination will never be thwarted simply by

being ineligible for ordination in the Church of England!
Certainly those ministers I most respect would hardly
bat an eyelid if the Anglican Church turned them down:
they would take this as guidance and serve God some
other way.

Significantly, some are now saying that because they
supported women's ordination for reasons which were
less than biblical, they now feel a duty to do the same for
practising homosexuals. It is only 'fair'. But true
Christian service has nothing to do with a desire to have
'fairness' for oneself. The best, and only legitimate,
reasons to ordain women are the biblical ones. Unfortunately, these were not always the ones used at the time.

There is also now talk of 'promotion'. I agree it is
illogical to have women priests and not women bishops.
It is arguably more insulting to women than not ordaining them at all; we are saying, in effect, there is no
essential theological reason why women are ineligible for
the priesthood, but we don't want them getting too
important and using smart letter paper in the House of
Lords. The situation is absurd. Nevertheless, because of
Paul's words to the Corinthians, because of the
sensitivities of others who love the Lord Jesus, at present
I would vehemently oppose legislation to allow women
to become bishops until others in the Church are ready
for it.

I believe the passing of the motion, at that time in that
way, was less than Christian. Christian unity is far more
important than ordaining people of one sex or the other.
The gospel is infinitely more precious than women's
rights. On that day in Synod, by putting our freedom in
Christ before the consciences of our brothers and sisters
in Christ, I believe we put so-called women's 'rights'
before the glory of God.

Nonetheless, because I don't consider the motion
wrong in itself, I don't think the situation is hopeless.
My heart goes out to those who now find their consciences uneasy in the Church of England, and I am very

glad and profoundly grateful that so many of them have stayed in. We *must* do everything we can to keep them in: the integrity of our Church depends on how well we look after them, and we will be infinitely the poorer without them. I hope, and pray, that they will come round to accepting the ordination of women.

But I also believe God could have changed hearts more quickly and less painfully, and given us a genuine unity on the matter, if we had only had more patience, more faith, and more love for our brothers and sisters who interpret the scriptures differently.

For many years I hoped for my Church to see women as 'joint heirs of the grace of life' (1 Peter 3:7) on earth as well as in heaven, valued as equally capable of preaching God's word and leading God's people; used by God as our biblical predecessors, Deborah and Huldah, clearly were. So I ought to be proud to be a member of a Church which now ordains women to the priesthood. And I am. But I am not at all proud of the way we are treating the dissenters.

SEVEN

Marriage

'Marriage is popular because it combines the maximum of temptation with the maximum of opportunity.'

George Bernard Shaw, *Marriage*.

There is nothing more relevant to our theme than the biblical picture of marriage. Nor can there be any human relationship more exciting. And yet the subject has been overlaid with more prejudices, unbiblical assumptions, and just plain unnecessary conventions than almost anything else.

The other night we were talking to some friends about the pressures on marriage. We all agreed that the hardest thing to adjust to was other people's expectations. 'Others have no right to tell you what your marriage should be like,' says Patricia Gundry in *Heirs Together*.[1] And yet others are telling us all the time. Or, worse still, they do not tell us but then disapprove when we do not live up to their expectations.

In addition, many are saying that the biblical teaching on the subject is no longer relevant. If the Bible says wives are to be submissive we should dismiss it as hopelessly old-fashioned, goes the theory; they are no more to obey their husbands now than slaves their masters. Now occasionally, it is true, reinterpretation of scripture can be right. Elsewhere some understand Paul to be giving teaching for a particular situation (' . . . because of the present distress . . .' 1 Corinthians 7:26); as we have seen he is also capable of making pragmatic concessions which are in contradiction to a more important argument (1 Timothy 2:12, or Acts 16:3). But there is no suggestion of either in his teaching on marriage. The real answer to this argument, however, must come as we examine the teaching itself, and see whether it is argued from contemporary circumstances or from something more fundamental.

LOVE AND EROTICISM – The Song of Songs

What marriage is

Perhaps the most beautiful and poetic book in the Bible is the Song of Songs. It also strikes people as one of the most problematic. The first remarkable thing about it is its apparent immorality. It describes a couple making love without any of the impedimenta we think necessary to make love-making proper. They are not recognised as a couple by society, they do not live in the same home, they seem to have no plans for children, and they are not bickering; by our standards they are not married. We know God does not approve of extra-marital sex; how can He approve of this?

Is it conceivable that our definition of marriage is wrong? The most explicit biblical description of the relationship is in Genesis 2:24. 'A man leaves his father and his mother and cleaves to his wife, and they become one flesh' (verse 24). Our society has of course reversed this, and expects the woman to leave and cleave. She is supposed to adapt to him emotionally, psychologically, and domestically; I know someone who recommends that a woman should not marry until she has seen her fiancé 'on the job' and knows what she is letting herself in for. This is not biblical: the writer of Genesis expects him to leave his family and his way of life and give himself to her.[2]

However, the climax of the wedding – 'they become one flesh' – is mutually active. This is the essence of marriage. He has left those whose flesh he once was: he has joined her whose flesh he will become. The cycle is to be completed; the body which God divided will become one again. She was once part of him, his side: he will be part of her, her head. She once came out of him: he re-enters her. And the moment of marriage is the moment this happens, the moment they become one flesh, the moment they first make love.

Now of course there is true lovemaking, and there are many distorted imitations. Lovemaking as God designed it in Genesis 2 is heterosexual, exclusive, and lifelong. When it steps outside this definition in the Bible it is roundly and unequivocally condemned. But in its true form it is synonymous with marriage. Marriage is agreeing to make love to someone for the rest of your life.

Seen in this light, the Song of Songs is a glorious celebration not only of the erotic but of marriage itself – which is, of course, the same thing. The relationship is heterosexual. The couple's love is exclusive (the references to Solomon being surely poetic allusions, not serious suggestions that the woman is a member of his harem).[3] And they intend a lifelong commitment: for 'love is as strong as death, jealousy as cruel as the grave' (8:6).

In God's terms the couple is married. The wedding ceremony is even referred to at the end of chapter 3, when the shepherd is described as a king coming through the desert with the crown with which his mother crowned him: 'on the day of his wedding, on the day of the gladness of his heart . . .' And after this celebration he frequently refers to his lover as his bride.

There is nothing immoral about the poem at all. But because our marriages are plagued with convention, we do not see the Shulamite and her beloved as husband and wife; they do not appear to eat breakfast together or share a bank account. We burden ourselves with as many expectations and requirements when we get married. I know plenty of people who become overweight after marriage because they suddenly feel they must eat 'properly'.

My sister once invited me out for the day with her and another girlfriend. Then she hesitated: 'But you'll have to make Shaun's lunch,' she said. Her friend had just as long-standing and stable a domestic relationship as mine; wouldn't she have to cook lunch as well, I asked?

'I wouldn't expect her to,' my sister laughed. 'They're not married; they're living together!'

Now of course cooking someone's lunch, or buying red roses, or giving up a lifetime's work to nurse someone through illness, is often part of making love as surely as having children is. But these things do not *make* a marriage. They are not an essential part of everyone's relationship. What makes a marriage is the commitment to be one flesh. This is given formal expression in our society through a church or registry office, and worked out year by year as a couple learn to give themselves to each other. The point is we do not necessarily have to invest in houses or washing machines together, or adopt certain domestic roles in order to be properly married, as many people seem to think.

What marriage illustrates

Even more important than what marriage is, however, is what marriage illustrates. For the other extraordinary thing about the Song of Songs is its apparent lack of reference to God. There is no mention of Him at all. Yet we are told all the scriptures speak of Christ (Luke 24:27). Dare we conclude that erotic love between a woman and a man can somehow, of itself, imitate Him? That it is, even unconsciously, a picture of the divine? C. S. Lewis suggests something of the sort when he talks of ' "the Pagan Sacrament" in sex'.[4] We would perhaps not presume to pursue this idea were it not confirmed in

Ephesians 5. Paul quotes Genesis 2:24, ' "For this reason a man shall leave his father and mother and cleave to his wife, and the two shall become one flesh" ' (verse 31); then he says 'This is a great mystery, and I take it to mean Christ and the church' (verse 32).

It is perhaps the most exciting imagery in the Bible. It promises that the love between mere mortals can resemble an immortal relationship with God. So our concern must be how we can live up to this honour. If God has chosen erotic love as an image of divine Love we should not take our part in it lightly. We should be concerned that our eroticism is thoroughly Christian. For the world inevitably spoils and twists and distorts this 'Pagan Sacrament' as much as it can. There are obvious ways in which this is done, like rape and promiscuity, adultery, divorce and homosexuality, but there are also more subtle ways which Christians are more likely to fall for.

One of the most common fallacies to be found throughout Christendom is the view that sex is either not good or not important. The Corinthian church was suffering from this delusion, so married couples felt free to abstain for no good reason (1 Corinthians 7:1-5), and extra-marital sex was not seen as particularly serious (1 Corinthians 5:1). These are two sides of one coin: if true lovemaking is not seen as important its abuse will not be seen to be either. We have the same attitude in our own society. We think we are 'liberal' in turning a blind eye to sexual immorality; in fact we simply do not see sex as an essential part of marriage. I often hear people say that an affair would not hurt their relationship; they would still be best friends, which is the most important thing. But if marriage is making love, an affair attacks its very heart. Sex is important, says Paul. Married couples should not abstain. (Unless they both agree to, for a short time, for prayer. But even this, he continues, I only say as a concession to you; you must come back together again, or you are asking for trouble, 1 Corinthians 7:5,6.) Otherwise married couples are actually robbing one another: they owe each other the 'debt' of their own bodies.

We must also realise that making love means giving oneself away. Again, our society tends to think in terms of self-gratification. Of course this is a pleasant bonus to making love, but it is not the driving force. 'I am my beloved's and my beloved is mine' says the Shulamite (Song of Songs, 6:3). They have given themselves to each other. The entire poem is full of possessive pronouns: 'my sister, my love, my dove, my perfect one'; (5:2), 'my beloved', 'my fair one', 'my bride'. This is the desire behind their desire; a longing to give themselves away. It is not difficult to see why Paul says a married couple have authority over one another (1 Corinthians 7:4). If we bestow ourselves on each other as this couple do we keep nothing back for ourselves at all. It is inconceivable that these two would refuse one another anything.

And their giving is mutual. We still tend to see sex as male-centred. He is taking; he is satisfied; he is the one who 'has sex' while the woman acquiesces. Christians easily fall for this attitude too. In her book *The Mark of a Man* Elisabeth Elliot includes two chapters entitled 'Masculinity means initiation' and 'Femininity means response'; the man, according to many Christian books, is supposed to take the active role and the woman the passive one. Similarly, versions of the Bible which ascribe speeches in the Song of Songs to one partner or the other tend to call the man the lover and the woman the beloved; it is assumed that he does the loving and she the receiving. But this is not the picture of the goat swain and her shepherd at all. She starts the song. She frequently refers to him as her beloved, and as 'him whom my soul loves'. She searches for him repeatedly. She holds him and refuses to release him. She takes him to her mother's bedchamber. She woos him and makes love to him. He is not slow to respond, but the initiative is hers; she is the lover.[5] Our society puts great pressure on men to 'perform' in bed, to be the expert and the one who does all the wooing; but (having done an extensive field study of one) I know that men sometimes long to be made love to, and to be allowed the passive, receptive role.[6]

Perhaps the most striking aspect of the song is the sheer delight of it all. Throughout the poetry there is an intoxicating extravagance of beauty and enjoyment. This is the overwhelming example they set us. They drown in the pleasure of one another's company: 'Eat, O friends, and drink: drink deeply, O lovers!'

This is not merely a narrow kind of eroticism resulting in a momentary physical climax. It is also a deep and lasting friendship (5:16). And it is a fruitful partnership; there are several reminders of conception, the natural result of this kind of love (3:4 and 8:5).

For this is the love which imitates Love Himself. Doubtless it does this in many ways. God is all-knowing: in lovemaking we 'know' each other. God is faithfulness: love stays faithful to the grave. He gave Himself up for us: we find sexual fulfilment in complete self-surrender. And God is three in one, three Persons in one Godhead: we become two in one when we make love, two persons in one flesh.

But perhaps supremely there is also something God-like about a couple when they have children. When God made the world, Father, Son and Spirit were all working together (Genesis 1:1–2; John 1:1–3). When parents have children, male and female work together. They have to. It is the only form of human creativity in which two people are absolutely and involuntarily dependent on one another. So, like God, when parents bring their own image into the world they do so as an interdependent team.

C. S. Lewis has said, when describing what he called 'the Pagan Sacrament' of making love, that 'within the rite or drama they become a god and goddess'.[7] There is indeed truth in this. It is partly in what lovers receive from one another – a surrender no human being has a right to expect. It is partly in what they can create with one another – new human beings in their own image. But above all the similarity lies in what they give to one another; it is in its overwhelming self-sacrifice that marriage most nearly comes to resemble the divine.

LOVE ENACTED: CHRIST AND THE CHURCH – Ephesians 5

And for this the husband and wife are given different parts to play. For there is a sense in which, as well as the relationship imitating Christ, each partner in the relationship enacts a different role. 'Husband and wife,' said a friend of ours when preaching from Ephesians 5 at a wedding, 'should be visual aids to each other of Christ and Christian discipleship.' A husband should remind his wife of Jesus: she should remind him of the Church. As we saw in chapter 2, the idea that God and His people are like husband and wife is fairly common in the Old Testament. Paul is using an established biblical picture and taking it further: not only is Jesus like a bridegroom, but a bridegroom is to be like Him; not only are we like a bride, but a bride is to be like us, the Church.

Preparation

Our marriages will never illustrate God's love if we ourselves do not. So before telling us how to live as Christian wives or husbands Paul tells us how every Christian must live.

First we are to imitate God (Ephesians 5:1). Whether we are husbands or wives, or slaves, or children, we are all to be like Him. We must immediately ask ourselves, *how* are we to imitate God? Are we to be an avenging, angry judge, as God undoubtedly sometimes is? Of course not. We are not to imitate God in every way. Paul tells us exactly how to be like Him. 'Walk in love, as

Christ loved us, and gave himself up for us as an offering and sacrifice . . .' (verse 2). We imitate God by imitating Christ, and we imitate Christ in self-sacrifice. Not by ruling over one another with any kind of authority, but by giving up our lives for one another in obedient humility.

So the first commandment to all of us is to be Christlike. This is a common New Testament command. It does not mean that we are to be in authority over one another, as Christ is in authority over us. As Paul clearly says, it means we are to lay down our lives for one another. It is important that husbands get this clear: Christlike love is singled out as a husband's particular duty. And he must know that by 'love' Paul does not primarily mean 'responsibility', or even sweet nothings or sexual desire. He means self-sacrifice.

The second command to us all is to submit. We are to be 'subject to one another in the fear of Christ' (verse 21). Respect for Christ means submission to Christians. This is also essential to our Godliness: it is part of Christian wisdom and worship (verses 15–20).

So Christian marriage is set in the context of Christian love and Christian submission. The first is commanded at the beginning of the chapter; the second at the beginning of the passage itself. The two are different sides of one coin. Christ's own life was a life of submission; He was obedient to the Father in everything. It was also a life of self-sacrifice; He gave everything up for us. This is how we *all* have to be.

So, although we have our own individual roles to play, there is a sense in which we are also both to play both parts. All Christians are to be Christlike; all are to lay down their lives as He did. So – although a husband is specifically told to do this for his wife – simply by virtue of being a Christian a wife is also to lay down her life for her husband. And all Christians are to be submissive: all are to put other people's wishes first. So – although a wife is specifically told to submit to her husband – simply by virtue of being a Christian he is also to submit to her.

And God has provided us with an excellent preparation for this. 'Children, obey your parents in the Lord,' says Paul, 'for this is right. "Honour thy father and mother," which is the first commandment with a promise, "so things will go well with you, and you will live long on the earth" ' (Ephesians 6:1–3). Every time we do something for our parents we are preparing ourselves for marriage. As we put our wishes aside for theirs we become more self-sacrificing. As we obey them we become submissive. As we learn to please them we are learning to please our partners. Good children are likely to become good lovers.

Sociologists tell us that we will repeat our parents' mistakes. If your father hit his wife you are likely to beat yours. If your mother was unfaithful you will be tempted to be too. But God's commandment carries a promise. If you 'honour your mother and father . . . things will go well with you'. Be Christlike and submissive, however reasonable or unreasonable your parents are, and when you marry a partner who makes impossible demands (as every partner does) you will have been well-trained in your role.

So this is how we prepare. Husband and wife are given different roles to enact in 'the Pagan Sacrament', but first we are both to learn both parts. We must all be like Christ *and* like the Church. Before we can hope to be good husbands or wives we must learn to be good Christians. We must all become self-sacrificing and submissive.

Husbands

(25) Husbands, love your wives, as Christ also loved the church and gave himself up for it, (26) so that he might sanctify it, cleaning it by the washing of the water by the Word, (27) so that he might present the church to himself glorious, not with a spot or wrinkle, or anything like that, but so that it might be holy and

unblemished. (28) This is how husbands ought to love their wives, as their bodies. He who loves his wife loves himself; (29) for no man ever hated his own flesh, but feeds and looks after it, as indeed Christ does for the church, (30) because we are parts of his body. (31) This is why a man shall leave his father and his mother, and cleave to his wife, and the two shall be one flesh. (32) This is a great mystery, but I say it is about Christ and the church; (33) nonetheless you should each love his wife as he loves himself... (Ephesians 5)

... In the same way, husbands, each of you live considerately with your wife as a weaker vessel, giving her honour as a co-heir of the grace of life, so that your prayers are not hindered. (1 Peter 3:7)

I suspect that most husbands, when they read the Bible and see that their wives are told to submit to them, are tempted to feel a slight glow: it is rather pleasant to think of oneself as the ordained recipient of such behaviour, and it is rather a relief that God does not demand such an attitude from you. The trouble is that we are all more interested in our spouse's obedience to the marriage teaching than our own; it is much easier to see how your partner would benefit from Paul's words than to see how you would. So it is worth bearing something in mind.

Paul seems far more concerned with a husband's behaviour than a wife's. He spends much more time on it. This could be because he thinks it more important. It could be because it is harder. I suspect it is partly because, then as now, the subject was superbly and successfully neglected. The question usually prompted by Ephesians 5 is whether a wife can still be expected to submit. But if we expounded the passage as we should we would be asking instead, mouths agape, whether a man could *ever* have been expected to love in such a way. Paul's emphasis is on him. We have cleverly drawn attention away from the husband's behaviour by making his wife's controversial. I noticed a similar thing happening recently during a Bible reading on Ephesians 5. Because Paul concentrates on a husband's behaviour rather than a wife's this talk tried to do the same. But when a friend was talking to me afterwards he let fall a couple of comments which indicated that he had simply received the same old message. All he had heard was 'wives submit'.

Husbands should beware. The weight of the Pauline teaching is directed towards them. Before a man worries about whether his wife ought to be submitting to him in this day and age he should ask himself whether he is behaving towards her as the Bible tells him to.

His duties are threefold. He is to love like Christ, care like a head, and honour as an equal. Before we turn to the practical implications of this we must get something absolutely clear. We must understand exactly what Paul means when he says a husband is *like* something. A wife is to be like the Church; obviously, though, I am not supposed to cultivate spots and wrinkles (apart from anything else, I don't need to: the resemblance comes naturally). Yet there are many popular understandings of a husband's role and duty which are just as inappropriate. Take an absurd example. A husband is a head; Paul says he is to cherish his wife as his own flesh, to care for her as a head does for its body. Elsewhere he tells us that he, Paul, treats his own body severely and subdues it like a slave (1 Corinthians 9:27). One would have a plausible case for saying this is how a husband should treat his wife.

Common sense shows us this is daft. Neverthless we constantly do the same kind of thing. Paul is quite specific in applying his images. A man should treat his wife as his body by nourishing her and cherishing her (Ephesians 5:29). If we ignore his specific application and invent our own then we can infer that a man should govern his wife and be in control of her, as he should govern and control his own body. Yet this is not Paul's use of the image at all. Similarly a husband, according to Paul, is to be like Christ (Ephesians 5:25). And again he is quite specific in what way he is to be like Christ. But it is easier to lord it over your wife than to lay down your life for her, so we ignore Paul's use of the simile and substitute our own: he has authority over her, and should rule her. Once again, this is not how Paul applies his image.

Of course when we start introducing our own applications rather than using Paul's the whole thing becomes controversial. We would all like to infer different things. Some say there are clear instances of the word 'head' being used in the sense of 'boss'; this is part of Paul's meaning in Ephesians earlier on when he refers to Christ as 'head over all things' (1:22) as the context makes clear. So, argue some, the man is to be boss over the woman.

Their opponents point out that in the same letter, and much closer to the teaching about marriage, Paul employs the meaning 'source' not boss, since he talks of 'the head . . . Christ, from whom the whole body . . . makes bodily growth and upbuilds itself' (4:15,16); in this sense the source of a river is spoken of as its head. So it is argued instead that a man is merely the origin of his wife as Adam was the origin of Eve. This argument is attractive, but even more absurd than the last; how is a husband supposed to behave like the head of a river to his wife?[8]

The most puzzling thing about the debate is why neither party refers to what the text itself says. When Paul uses this image he tells us exactly what he means by it. We have no excuse for adding our own suppositions. We are not to conclude, for example, that because a husband is to be like Christ he can wash away his wife's sins; such a suggestion would be blasphemous, and make Christ's sacrifice unnecessary (for married women). Nor that he can have many wives, just as Christ can have many members in His Church. Nor that he is necessarily to be in authority over his wife as Christ is in authority over the Church, unless Paul actually says so. We are not to think the husband is to be like Christ in any way we fancy. As C. S. Lewis said, just because we are told to be like doves does not mean we are to lay eggs.[9] A likeness is only of any use if we understand *in what way* it is like the original. Just because a man is his wife's head does not mean he necessarily has her brains.

Paul's teaching has been charged with all sorts of unbiblical ideas and connotations. 'Headship' has become the catchphrase. No Christian discussion on marriage is complete without it. Everyone wants to know whether it involves authority, what it means in everyday life, and how a couple (or, more often, a husband) should put it into practice. In fact this very emphasis is not biblical. Even the word is not. Like many of the ideas which go with it, it is never used by Paul. He describes a husband as a 'head'; he never talks, as so many do, about some abstract quality known as 'headship'. So we must stick to the meaning he gives the word, or we will be in danger of imposing totally unbiblical applications onto the biblical image. We must be quite clear what 'head' does – and particularly does *not* – mean.

A man is never told to be the 'head of the household'. People with street questionnaires are fond of this phrase; they ask for the 'occupation of head of the house', by which one is socially graded. From time to time I have quizzed them as to what they mean by this. They are usually not quite sure. The senior man? Well not necessarily... The husband? Yes. At least, if he is in full-time employment... Oh, the chief wage-earner? Probably. Unless that's a woman. And then possibly... It is all fairly vague. The general idea is of someone who, as we say, 'wears the trousers'; the person who holds the purse strings; probably the man unless he is unfortunate enough to be unemployed or have a well-paid, bossy wife.

And sadly Christians are often just as vague. There is

an impression that the Bible says a man should be the 'head of the home'. He should in some way be in charge: earn the basic salary, make important decisions, and be the ultimate threat when the children are naughty. We are often remarkably ignorant about what the Bible does say. Shaun and I went to a party where the guests had to dress as pub signs. He, of course, wittily went as himself (The Nag's Head). When, after three hours, no one had guessed who he was we gave the clue that he was the something's head. People tried everything. The family, the household, the house (which, if one could build such a monstrosity, might win an architectural award), and even, most oddly, the church. No one suggested he might be head of his wife.

The Old Testament does sometimes describe men as the heads of their families. This means that they were tribal chiefs. Their sons and grandsons, though they might be married with children, would not be 'heads' in this sense (indeed they would come under their mothers' as well as their fathers' jurisdiction). We should never confuse this with Paul's concept of a husband as 'head'. The only time he uses the word which could be translated as 'head of the household' he applies it to young women; he advises them to marry, have children, and 'rule' or 'be head of their households' (1 Timothy 5:14).[10] In fact the concept of head (meaning ruler) of the home or family is scarcely found in the New Testament, since tribal society was no longer prevalent. Paul talks of a husband as the head of his *wife*, not his family or his home. He sees every husband as the head of his wife, whether he is the senior male running the household or not. And he does not describe this kind of head in terms of being in charge. The popular notion that a man should be 'head of the home', a kind of chief of his nuclear semi-detached two-car tribe, has no basis in biblical fact. Paul is not advocating a patriarchal hierarchy which goes husband, wife, children, dog. He is talking about one person's care of another.

We also ought to be clear that a husband is not told to do anything about his 'headship'. For one thing he is never commanded to be his wife's head. He *is* her head whether he likes it or not. It is permanently true. Those who tell husbands to 'assert their headship' are talking nonsense. A man's headship cannot be asserted or denied: it is fact. It is not the result of certain behaviour but its basis. And the behaviour it affects is not the husband's. When Paul mentions his headship he is not talking to him but to his wife, as the preceding and following verses show (verses 22 and 24). It determines her attitude not his. It is relevant only to wives. A husband's proper concern is not his own 'headship' but his wife's 'bodyship'. His worry should be that she is nourished and cherished. All he needs to assert is his own altruism. A husband's 'headship' is, in fact, none of his business.

And, as I hope has been made clear, his 'headship' is never linked with authority. The only time authority is mentioned in the context of a man being head it is authority given to the *woman*, as we have seen (1 Corinthians 11:10). Being someone's head is about looking after her, not being in control of her. A husband is to imitate Christ in His death, not His government; His selflessness, not His supremacy.

Love like Christ

What, then, is a husband's duty? It is simply and supremely to *love* (Ephesians 5:25). This is how he is to be like Christ. For he loves, not as a man who desires someone or admires her or wants to feel she belongs to him, but ' . . . as Christ loved the church . . .' And not as He loves her by governing her, but as He 'gave himself up for her'.

As the Church on earth lives to serve Christ, so He lived on earth to save her. This is how a husband is to enact the role of Christ. Not by being placed in a manger.

Not by teaching and healing and performing miracles. Not in leadership and authority, but in self-sacrifice. It is not enough for him to know that he is to be like Christ. He must also know what the point of similarity is to be. It is not by being in charge or leading or taking decisions; these he is never told to do. It is by laying down his life for another. This is the greatest love a man can have (John 15:13), and it is this he is to show to his wife.

And how did Christ do this for us? He gave up everything. He too, like a husband, left His parental home, 'who, though He was in the form of God, did not count equality with God a thing to be grasped'. He too surrendered everything to cleave to another, and 'emptied Himself, taking the form of a slave'. And He too became one flesh with the one He came to serve, 'being born in the likeness of humanity. And . . . humbled Himself and became obedient unto death' (Philippians 2:6–8).

Everything He did on earth was for us. Every mile He travelled, every breath He drew, every word He spoke was to serve the Church. He put us first in everything. He even put our relationship with God before His own, and was cursed while we were saved. This is the kind of sacrifice a husband is called to make. It is staggering. In taking on the role of Christ he has been asked to give up everything he has. His work, his family, his career, his friends, his very self is to be sacrificed for her. His concern is no longer how to please the Lord; he lives now in order to please his wife (1 Corinthians 7:33).

Most men, if asked why they love their wives, would no doubt answer 'because . . .' Because she is clever; because she loves me; because she is beautiful, or has borne my children, or is always fun to be with. But the supreme answer is not because of anything. Christ did not love us 'because'. He loved us *in order* to clean us, and make us 'holy and without blemish'. So a man's love for his wife should not depend on anything in her. Happily for us Christ did not love us for any qualities on

our part. In the words of C. S. Lewis, 'This headship . . .
is most fully embodied not in the husband we should all
wish to be, but in him whose marriage is most like a
crucifixion; whose wife receives most and gives least, is
most unworthy of him, is – in her own mere nature –
least lovable.'[11]

He does not love her, then, because she is beautiful,
but in order to make her so. He reverses the natural
process. The day a bride marries she is probably young
and gorgeous; the day she dies she will look blemished
and wrinkled. But lovely as she looked, she was full of
sin; and, decrepit as she will one day be, under the
influence of her husband's love she can become holier
and more splendid year by year. The more a man loves
his wife the lovelier she can become.

His model is not simply a man who pleased His bride,
but one who sanctified and cleansed and beautified her
(Ephesians 5:26–8). This is the Love he is to imitate.
Whereas a wife lives to please her husband (1
Corinthians 7:34) he lives to benefit as well as please her.
He must constantly put her interests before his own. He
must always be asking himself 'how can she best be
served?' This must be the reason behind his work, his
worship, and everything he does. Every decision he
makes should be for her. If he is offered a new job the
question he should ask is not whether it will lead to
promotion, or be more interesting, or help the firm or be
more use to the church, but whether it will better serve
his wife. If he is asked to join a church committee or play
football or stay late at work, his first question must be
whether it is in her interests.

Paul's teaching is often turned inside out. We knew a
couple who were fairly new Christians. He had been
made redundant and was at home looking after their
small baby. His wife had a job which was demanding
and enjoyable, as his had been. Naturally enough he
sometimes found his position trying. He often felt
frustrated and depressed, as many housewives do, and

was glad of opportunities to be away from the house and the baby. Sometimes when his wife came home he would escape to the pub for a blissful hour of adult company. His wife, although distressed at his difficulties, was otherwise happy and fulfilled.

The elders in his church saw what he was going through and told him to assert himself. He must exercise his 'headship'. His wife must give up her job, and they must move somewhere where he would have a better chance of employment. It was chilling to hear the passage which calls a man to lay down his life being twisted to make him 'assert' himself. He understood what it meant to be the head of his wife. He even had the courage to put it into practice. And his elders had no idea. He gave up his job, his happiness, and even his abilities so that hers could be used instead.

I was telling this story to a friend, when he objected, 'A man should work for his wife's holiness, not her happiness,' he said; 'her sanctification, not her career.'

Of course. A husband's supreme concern is his wife's spiritual welfare. This is far more important than whether she is in suitable employment. But I wonder whether the men who say this really have their wives' interests at heart. A wife will be sanctified through making sacrifices, this husband could have said to himself. It could be a most convenient doctrine. But so far we have only been talking about the first part of a husband's duty: loving as Christ loved the Church. He is to lay down his life for her holiness. Then, in case he is tempted to elevate this to a 'spiritual' plane (by which we often really mean purely theoretical or even irrelevant) Paul goes on to use a far more earthy image. He is to love her as his body (Ephesians 5:28).

Cherish as a head

She is his flesh (verse 28). As the head lives to serve the body so he must live to serve his wife; as the head cares for the body so he must care for her (verses 29,30). And the teaching is drawn from the essence of marriage, from the fact that they are 'one flesh', from love-making itself, so we can be confident it is relevant today. Once before, at creation, man and woman were one flesh: on their wedding night they became one flesh again. A husband has no separate identity of his own any more: his body is his wife. He should be able say, with Charles Williams, 'love you? I am you'.[12] For 'he who loves his wife loves himself' (verse 28).

It is a superb complement to the earlier image. Christ's love for us was often painful and exhausting. A man's love for himself is natural and instinctive. You seldom have to think about it. You sleep when you are tired, feed when you are hungry, and wrap up well when you are cold. If you are sensible you also make sure your body gets regular exercise and is working as well as it can. If you are treating it as you should you never stop listening to it and caring for its needs.

A husband's love for his wife is the same. He should tend to her needs all the time just as he tends to himself. Like his body, she need not be pampered, but her well-being should never be neglected. If she needs friends her husband should look for them; if she is unhappy he should ask himself why; if she is ill he should care for her; if she has gifts he should ensure she uses them. All these are things one would do for oneself. This is why it was right for the husband I mentioned to put his wife's work before his own; he was doing what any man would instinctively do for himself.

And this is why the church elders were so wrong in their advice. The husband was depressed and miserable. They thought he should swap places with his wife and make her depressed and miserable instead. I know Christian husbands who make a sincere attempt to love in the conventional way, yet whose wives are doing work the men would not dream of stooping to. Their husbands, I believe, think this is all right because it is 'women's work'. But they are supposed to love their wives *as themselves*. They should never expect their wives to do something they would not be prepared to do themselves.

God calls a husband to be ready to give up everything for his wife. He should put her wishes first in choosing their holiday. He should put her job first when they decide where to live. He should put her family first when they issue Christmas invitations. He should put her judgment first when it comes to the children's education.

You protest. Your wife is as thick as two short planks. you might put her welfare first, but you cannot be expected to put her *judgment* first. After all, Jesus did not put our judgment first when He put our interests first. He loved us as He knew to be best, not necessarily as we would have liked the best. And a wise head, though it will always listen to its body and usually follow its inclination, will occasionally overrule it.

Honour as joint-heir

But this is where we turn to a husband's third duty. He is to honour his wife as an equal; to live with her in the knowledge that she is weaker, giving her honour because she is a joint-heir (1 Peter 3:7). And almost all women are weaker than their husbands, on a purely physical level. In the last analysis a man can usually enforce his wishes on his wife. Even if he never lays a finger on her, he will almost always be capable of bullying her to get what he wants. Ultimately, in a disagreement, he can lay down the law. Whether this is because his muscles are stronger, or his income is likely to be bigger, or society still expects him to have the last word, hardly matters. We should simply face up to the fact, on the basis of Genesis 3:16 and empirical evidence, that a husband almost always has been, and almost always will be, in a position to command and exploit his wife. He can usually get his own way.

But he is to honour her, says Peter, as a joint-heir of the

grace of life. She is weaker physically. But she is equal eternally. She is more vulnerable than he is on earth, but she is not his inferior in heaven. She is co-heir of the kingdom of God, so she deserves his full honour and respect (1 Peter 2:7). He must treat her as his equal. And this is where the analogy with Christ breaks down. The average husband is not infallible. He is no more likely to have better judgment, or be right on any issue, than his wife. On some things she may be far more knowledgeable. It is a Christian principle to 'consider others better than yourself' (Philippians 2:3), so he should always be ready to put her opinions before his own.

Besides, if he has such a low view of her judgment, what was he doing marrying her in the first place? Paul is quite clear in saying that a man will live to please his wife (1 Corinthians 7:33). The Bible is quite explicit in saying he must lay down his life for her (Ephesians 5:25). Obviously he should have married a woman he respects enough to honour and nourish and put before himself.

So because of a husband's superior strength or position his wife is likely to be at his mercy. Her welfare and happiness will probably to some extent depend on him. He can of course take advantage of this and decide to be 'boss in his own home'. But this is not the Christian way. Christ's example teaches him to neglect his own desires and lay aside his power; it tells him to use all he has for *her* benefit; it shows him that any advantage he may have over her is to enable him to serve better. The Fall gives a man a certain power over a woman which he can easily use at her expense. His 'strength' can be his wife's enslavement. Christ's life should inspire a husband to make it her liberation.

Suppose they are both doctors. In the normal course of events it will be a wife's work that takes second place. She will be out shopping while he is keeping up with extra study; society will expect this. A Christlike husband will lay aside this 'right' and free her to become the best doctor she could possibly be. Or perhaps she is a housewife. Expectations will tell him to put his feet up when he comes in while she continues with her day's work for the next hour or two. Jesus's example tells him to take over from her so she is the one to have some free time. She may be a mother. Normally she will be doing boring chores like stacking the dish-washer while he has the fun of reading to the children or playing with them. But a Christian husband should be asking himself how he can free her to enjoy the children and be the good mother she was made to be.

A truly Christian wife may come in for scorn. A truly Christian husband almost certainly will. Christ neglected His power to suffer humiliation for our sake. A man must be prepared to endure the same for his wife. We have a friend who is one of the finest Christian husbands I know. He comes home from one demanding job and immediately starts another. As soon as he gets in he is carrying the baby, putting another child to bed, emptying potties, cleaning up vomit and doing other pleasant jobs so dear to a father. His domestic duties sometimes keep him from church activities. His spiritual 'superiors' think he is not 'keen'. His peers say knowingly 'I married a wife' when he declines from some church meeting or other. Everybody thinks he is henpecked. He is the least henpecked man I know. He is making sacrifices for his wife and children. He is freely obeying God's commands. He is living to liberate his wife: he is a truly liberated man.

It is not surprising Paul refers to a husband as a saviour. If men were to give themselves for their wives, the question of their wives' submission would almost never arise. No one in their right mind can grudge Christ the total submission He demands; He has done so much for us we must be overwhelmed with gratitude. Husbands who behave as Paul tells them to would surely find the same. A man who lays down his life for his wife and frees her to be herself would find himself married to a woman overwhelmed with gratitude too. She would surely *want* to entrust herself to him wholeheartedly and unreservedly. There would be little question in her mind about submitting to him. She would know it was in her interests to please a man who cared more about her than about himself.

Wives

...(21) Submitting yourselves to one another in the fear of Christ; (22) the wives to their husbands as to the Lord, (23) because the husband is the head of the wife as Christ is also the head of the church, and is himself the saviour of the body. (24) But as the church is subject to Christ, so also should wives be to their husbands in everything ... (33) ... let the wife make sure that she fears her husband. (Ephesians 5)

(1) In the same way, wives, submit yourselves to your husbands, so that even if any disobey the word they will be won through the behaviour of their wives, (2) seeing your pure behaviour in fear... (5) For indeed in this way then the holy women who hoped in God adorned themselves, submitting themselves to their husbands, (6) as Sarah obeyed Abraham, calling him Lord; you became her children, doing good and fearing no terror: (1 Peter 3)

There is no doubt about it. A wife is to submit to her husband. Having seen how he should behave towards her, however, we should hardly be taken aback. He is her head (verse 23), caring for her needs all the time; of course she should trust herself to him just as a body trusts its head. He is even her saviour (verse 23), putting her interest first in everything he does; of course she should submit to such sacrificial love even as the Church submits itself to Christ.

This is not culturally relative, as many people try to argue nowadays. As we have seen, he is not her head because of any legal or social set-up. He is her head because they are one flesh. His love for her as his body springs from the essence of marriage itself, from love-making; her submission to him as her head is argued from the same principle.

Nor is it dependent on his sinlessness, as others some-times try to tell us. It is true that there is a sense in which a wife's behaviour is prompted by her husband's. She submits to him because he is Christlike; she obeys because he loves. So, one sometimes hears it said, if he is not a Christlike husband she need not be a submissive wife. (In which case, of course, we would all be off the hook.) But in Peter's letter a wife's submission comes in the context of suffering, turning the other cheek, and obeying even oppressive governments and masters and husbands. Both before and after his words to wives, Peter stresses that submission does not depend on kind treat-ment. 'Servants,' he says (1 Peter 2:8), 'submit yourselves to your masters in all fear, not only to the good and forbearing, but also to the perverse.' He tells the wives to do so even though some husbands do not obey the word (3:1). In fact this is one of the reasons he gives for submissive behaviour. Even if it involves suffering you are to do it, for 'if indeed you do suffer because of righteousness, you are blessed' (3:14).

Peter even suggests a further reason for submission; a wife may win her husband over to the Lord (1 Peter 3:1). When he sees her submission to him he sees how he should submit to Christ. When he sees her reverent and chaste behaviour he sees how his behaviour should be reverent and chaste. She is a living reminder of what he should be. If this can be true of a non-Christian husband (as Peter says) how much more must it be so of a Christian one? He will recognise the allusion; he will know what she illustrates; his conscience will tell him he should be as she is.

But what does Paul have in mind when he tells wives to 'be subject'? What does it mean for a woman to submit to her husband? There are a number of things it does not mean. Unfortunately much of the behaviour advocated for wives in the name of submission is nothing of the kind. We tend to think of the submissive wife as quiet, domestic, passive, and – dare we say it? – rather dull. Yet no qualities could be more irrelevant to true submission. Who was more obedient to God than Elijah or John the Baptist? Who more submissive to Christ than Paul? Indeed, who has ever submitted more humbly than Jesus Himself? These people should be our models for submission; yet they were tough, outspoken, unconventional, and courageous in the extreme. There is nothing soppy about submission.

Nor does submission mean silence. In 1 Corinthians 14:34, Paul does not mean you stop talking to your husband (indeed, he advises to the contrary). If you hate spending Christmas with your sister-in-law, say so. If you don't appreciate a mobile telephone glued to his chin over dinner, tell him. If his job keeps him away from home too long and you believe he should give it up; if the family needs to move house so you can get better employment; if he does not look after the children properly or the meals he cooks are disgusting, then explain what you expect of him. This is not inconsistent with submission; David spends much of his psalms moaning about God's treatment of him, yet he was 'a man after God's own heart' (Acts 13:22). Obviously there is a difference between communicating and nagging; the latter in a wife is like rain on a wet day (Proverbs 19:13, and 27:15). But again we have a matchless model for submission: Jesus asked if the cup might pass from Him, but He was well prepared for the answer no. This is how a wife should be.

And submission is not financial or emotional dependence. The submissive wife is not necessarily the one with the helpless little girl image. Obedience to God should never mean abandoning all thought of earning a living or making decisions or growing up. Similarly, submission to your husband should not mean these things either. It is not necessarily unsubmissive to earn a bigger income, get a better degree, have more intelligent opinions or correct a man when he is wrong.

Nor does submission mean domesticity. It is not a 'job' in this sense. Submission does not mean you keep a beautiful home, or give up your job, or become a housewife when you have children, or cook the meals, iron the shirts, do the dishes, or plan the shopping. A wife is a picture of Christian discipleship; since when has this entailed full-time domestic service? She submits to her husband as to Christ; since when has this meant darning. His socks? Her supreme model is Jesus Himself; since when do we look to Him for examples of housewifery? The truly submissive wife is not necessarily the domestic one.

And submission is not manipulation. This is a disgraceful abuse of Paul's command which is popular at the moment. People do this with God as well as their husbands. 'How to pray to get what you want' is the thrust of much of our teaching on prayer.[13] This is not prayer at all; how to pray to get what God wants should be our concern on our knees. Similarly, how to submit to get what you want is the substance of a number of books for wives. Say yes to everything he ever utters, scribble sexy messages in his lunchbox, greet him at the door in high heels and not much else and you will have him wrapped around your little finger. Such advice is degrading to husband and wife alike. Submission means doing his will, not tricking him into yours.

For just as a man has power over his wife which he can use for his own self-importance, so a woman can have enormous influence over her husband which she can employ for her own ends. She can dictate many of his opinions; she may make or break his career; she is likely to shape what kind of a father he will be. And I have frequently heard women suggesting one should exploit this. It is the power behind the power; the 'hand that rocks the cradle'. A woman is thought to have a

'right' to get her own way through subtlety; to persuade
her husband to a certain course of action and make him
think it was his idea. Again, this is not the Christian way.
The Christian way of submission is to give up all thought
of self altogether, to put aside any devices one might use
for one's own profit, and to put one's entire life at
someone else's disposal.

But there is a more subtle form of 'submissive' manipulation which is just as erroneous. It is often thought
that a wife's submission implies a husband's leadership.
This is not so: Christians submit to one another, but this
does not make every Christian into a leader. There are
husbands who do not particularly want to govern their
wives; a man might have good reason for wanting his
wife to take decisions or discipline the children or run
family prayers. A submissive wife will see what he wants
and fit in with it. There is nothing wrong with this. Those
who think 'headship' means 'authority' will say he is
abdicating from his role. Men must take a lead, they say,
or women cannot submit properly. So women have to
manipulate men into leadership; they are told that on no
account should they undertake anything which might
be a man's responsibility, and eventually their husbands
will be forced into their 'role'. I have heard the same idea
applied to the Church in general; if only women would
stop taking part in Christian work men might come
forward and fulfil their duties. I very much doubt if this
theory works anyway, but even if it does it is no more
submissive than wearing skimpy négligés to manipulate
your man into taking you to the Bahamas.

Occasionally there may be exceptional situations in
which a wife should not submit. Women can be raped,
robbed and beaten by their husbands. They can be asked
to steal or lie. They can see their children abused. Where
must they draw the line? Our first allegiance is always to
God. Any obedience in the Bible, whether to masters or
parents or governments, is subject to this. If a woman's
husband wants her to do something contrary to the word

of God she must stand up to him. Sapphira failed to do this when her husband attempted to deceive the other disciples, and 'immediately she fell down . . . and died' (Acts 5:10). Her sin, presumably, was the same as Adam's (Genesis 3:17): she listened to the voice of her spouse. She did not oppose her husband when he was doing wrong. She submitted to his plan and, like Adam, received fairly speedy judgment.

If a man is doing something which is *without any question* wrong, then his wife should not submit to him. This is also the one situation in which a husband should oppose his wife; Eve's suggestion to Adam was clearly contrary to God's command. But this does not include instances of mere disagreement or difference of opinion between husband and wife. A woman may think her husband mistaken, but this is not the same as seeing him obviously going against the written word of God.

I know of a woman whose husband beats their children fairly regularly and without any signs of repentance. This is clearly wrong (Ephesians 6:4). I believe she should take them away from him, and I deplore the pressure being put on her, by Christians, to stay by his side. I know another whose husband has run her into debts of thousands of pounds. Again this is obviously wrong, and she should not allow him to continue to do so. Wives of men who are violent or unfaithful, criminal or mentally ill, may all have cause to oppose and sometimes to leave them. Christians must be entirely supportive. Such women are already in a distressing position: their consciences as well as their husbands may torment them for what they cannot choose but do; the last thing they need, and sadly often the first thing they receive, is condemnation from Christians.

Happily most husbands do not come into this category. To the ordinary, run-of-the-mill, imperfect, selfish, sinning husband a woman should submit as she would to Christ Himself.

But what is submission? One might as well ask what

is Christian discipleship. It is everything. This is why marriage is, in some ways, the most supreme example of sexual interdependence. How should a wife submit to her husband? 'As the church submits to Christ', Paul says. And in case we should miss the point, he continues ' . . . let wives be subject to their husbands in everything' (verse 24). In fact it is the same kind of behaviour that he says slaves should give their masters (Ephesians 6:5).

The Church's *raison d'être* is Christ's service. Her ambition is His pleasure. Everything she does must be to gratify Him; every decision she takes should be according to His will; every work she undertakes ought to be to His greater glory. Every course the Church ever follows should be the one which will most please Christ. If a wife is to submit to her husband as to Christ she must submit her whole life to him. There is nothing she will do without conscious or unconscious reference to her husband. The work she does, the friends she has, the clothes she wears, and the hobbies she pursues will all be in keeping with what he would want for her. Being a wife is like being a Christian: not so much a matter of performing particular duties as of embracing a completely new attitude. There is no self any more. There is only living to please another. This is what it means to be one flesh: total and absolute surrender.

Such is a wife's submission. Everything she does will be in order to please her husband. Consistently we find she should treat him as if he were Christ. Her model is Sarah, who called Abraham 'lord' (not merely 'sir' as is sometimes claimed, but the word used throughout the New Testament of Christ Himself); who submitted to him and obeyed him. Her proper attitude is to 'fear' him (not 'respect' as gutless translations would nowadays have us believe), and then she need fear nothing else (1 Peter 3:6). And her concern is to please him (1 Corinthians 7:34); her preoccupation is his pleasure when once it was only Christ's. Her submission to her husband is to be like her submission to God Himself. It is astonishing. If it were not there in front of us in the Bible we should think it blasphemous.

Great mileage is often made out of the fact that the Bible never tells wives to 'obey'. Strictly speaking this is true – although Peter suggests wives should take Sarah as their model, and she 'obeyed Abraham' (1 Peter 3:6). The word used for wives is 'submit', which is also used for the mutual giving way to one another which all Christians do (Ephesians 5:21). But this does not mean a wife is living to please her husband any less than if she were told to 'obey'. On the contrary, submission is far more all-embracing than mere obedience. Obedience simply means doing as you are told (and by careful manipulation you can often be told the right things) but submission to Christ, the image Paul uses, is total. It involves not only our actions but also our attitude. It is willing and joyful and cheerful, like our trust in the Lord.

Now of course this is not always easy. We do not take kindly to submission. It means putting someone else's will before your own. It sometimes means making someone else's mistakes instead of your own. It may occasionally mean doing things you think are stupid. And in fact many people will not respect a woman for submitting to her husband. For there is a movement abroad at the moment which says people have a primary duty to themselves. If your husband is not allowing you to be fulfilled or reach your potential or 'be yourself' it is unreasonable to submit to him. A husband is an ordinary sinner; it is possible that submission to him may occasionally involve frustration, annoyance, or even a waste of his wife's abilities. It would be deceitful to claim, as some books do, that the reward for submission is a fully guaranteed bed of roses, and a husband so gratefully doting that he strews his wife's days and nights with Black Magic. Peter took it for granted that righteousness can involve suffering (1 Peter 3:14). No doubt some women submit to their husbands and are taken for granted, or even treated badly, in return.

However, the balance of scripture, and experience, tells us the opposite. Usually when we make sacrifices for each other we find a glorious fulfilment; we tend to be happier people ourselves, and our marriages are much more rewarding. Peter clearly takes this to be the norm. A wife's submission may disarm her unbelieving husband without a word (1 Peter 3:1), and she will have nothing to fear (verse 6). Submission can be extra-ordinarily liberating. Instead of being enslaved by our own desires, we are free to live our lives for another. Instead of worrying about our own requirements, we are able to spend our lives pleasing someone else. A married woman is indeed in a privileged position. She never needs to think of her own happiness, because someone else has been commissioned to think of it for her. She never needs to be concerned about her own fulfilment, because he has been charged with taking care of it. All she needs to do is to make his task of loving her possible by giving herself to him without reservation.

It is indeed like being a Christian. Submission to Christ often involves a struggle. He calls for a surrender on our part which seldom comes easily. If He asks us to give up a particular course of action, or take up another, we often go through agonies at the time – which is partly what makes the reward afterwards such a blessing. A wife who submits to her husband is sometimes going to find it difficult to put his wishes before her own. But unless she does so how can his love find full expression? Unless she puts herself in his hands how can he care for her? Unless she trusts herself to him completely how can he dedicate himself to providing her with the fullest possible liberation?

LOVE AND AUTHORITY – 1 Corinthians 7:4

There seems to be something missing. We have discussed a husband's and wife's respective roles, but we have surely left something out. What about authority? Where is the husband told to have authority over his wife? Where is he told to be in command? Where indeed? It is nowhere in the Bible. He is never told to rule over his wife or command her.

Surely, some say, it is *assumed* in all the biblical teaching. It was so taken for granted at the time that the Bible did not need to mention it. This kind of teaching is very dangerous indeed. If we start drawing things out of the Bible because we think they were assumed at the time we can draw out anything we like. If it could be taken for granted that husbands had authority over their wives it could also safely be taken for granted that wives had to submit to them. Nonetheless, Peter and Paul both saw fit to tell them to.

As it happens there is talk of authority in marriage (1 Corinthians 7:4), but the only mention of it is mutual. Paul recognises that a married couple have authority over each other. A married person has no power over his own body, he says; it is governed by his spouse.

So husbands are not *told* to have authority over their wives. Paul does not command it; he simply recognises it. ' . . . the wife must pay the debt [of sexual intercourse] to the husband, for the wife has not got authority (or power) over her own body, but the husband has . . .' (1 Corinthians 7:4).

At first glance it looks as if Paul is just talking about sex. What he is saying seems to amount to no more than this: whenever a husband wants sex his wife should make sure he gets it. It seems fairly sound marriage counselling.

But he is saying far more than this. The *reason* she is to give her body to her husband whenever he wants it is *because* she has no rights over it herself. Paul has just established that we do not own our bodies. 'Do you not know,' he says (6:19), ' . . . that your bodies are from God, and that you are not your own? You were bought with a price . . .' The price was Jesus's body, which was exchanged for ours. Our bodies belong to him. But when a woman gets married, her body, which by rights is Christ's, is handed over to the husband for his care and enjoyment. She does not own it. She owes it to her husband.

Surely, though – one could argue – the husband has authority only over her body? He does not have authority over her mind or her soul. He has no say over what she thinks or says or does, other than in bed. This kind of thinking is unbiblical. A man or woman cannot be broken up into body and mind and soul. What a man thinks will affect his behaviour. The God he worships will change his mind. What he says is an indication of what he believes and who he is and how he feels. The idea of dividing someone up into compartments is a Greek one and is foreign to the biblical view of humankind – indeed, the thrust of much of Paul's message in chapters 6 and 7 is that our bodies matter because our bodies *are* ourselves. The commandment to love God with all your mind and soul, body and strength, does not imply that it is possible to do one without the others. It simply means that you are to love God in every possible way. You cannot worship God 'only in your soul'.

So if a man has power or authority over his wife's body, he has power or authority over his wife. This is common sense. If he commands her body he commands what she says, how she behaves, where she goes to church, and even what she feels. He has power over every area of her life. This is fairly comprehensive authority. A husband, then, *does* have authority over his wife.

Those who know the Corinthian letter will see where we are heading. So far this teaching about the husband's authority may not be surprising. 'Reactionary', perhaps to some people; 'chauvinist' or extreme, maybe. But since Paul is supposed to be such a frightful misogynist, not particularly astonishing. But we have not yet finished the sentence. It is very revolutionary indeed; powerful stuff, even today: 'the husband should pay his debt to his wife', he says, because ' . . . in the same way also the husband does not have authority over his own body, but the wife does'. In other words exactly as the husband has power or authority over his wife, so the wife has power or authority over her husband. Everything we have just seen about the wife's body is true also of the husband's. He too was bought with a price. He too is not his own. When he got married, he too was handed over to his wife for her pleasure and use as long as they both live. She has authority over him just as he has authority over her.

When it comes to authority the marriage relationship is absolutely symmetrical. Those who say that the husband has some kind of authority over his wife are right; but they should never say this without also adding that she has the same authority over him: '(3) The husband must pay the debt to the wife, and also the wife, in the same way, to the husband. (4) The wife does not have authority (or power) over her own body, but the husband has, and the husband does not have authority (or power) over his own body, but the wife has' (1 Corinthians 7).

Making love to someone means giving your body to her or him; and giving your body to her means giving yourself to her without restriction. As we saw, the Shulamite and her beloved give themselves to one another without reserve: of course they have comprehensive power over each other's lives. A married person retains no right over himself at all. His wife has authority over him. He has authority over her. And it is absolute authority. If a man's wife asks him to take regular exercise he should do so. If he asks her to go to church with him she should do so. If she asks him to give up his job; if he asks her to stop smoking; if either partner asks anything of the other he or she has no right to withhold it. Our bodies, our very selves, are not our own. We must live every day with that knowledge. The unmarried person does not *own* his or her body, but is in charge of it. The married person has given that charge over to his spouse. It was bought by the death of Christ and made over to his partner. She or he governs it. He or she is in charge of it. Each has authority over the other.

This is why the erotic relationship is the ultimate in mutual dependence. Indeed it is more than mere dependence: it is complete loss of self. A friend of mine criticised this idea as an 'idolatry of marriage'. And that is almost what it is: not for nothing does a groom say amongst his vows, 'with my body I thee worship'. God has allowed marriage this astonishing status. This is how we become 'like a god and goddess'.

People will of course object to this. We all have very convincing reasons for not giving ourselves to our partners.

A woman may say, for example, that she tries to submit to her husband. For his part, though, he does not seem to recognise his duties. He would never give up his job, or even his bi-monthly duties on the PCC for her, and would not dream of doing anything she says. This is probably true of most Christian marriages to some extent since one half of this teaching has been stressed much more than the other for the last two thousand years. (Everyone talks about 'headship', and a wife's submission; no one mentions bodyship, and a husband's sacrifice.) But this is no reason not to submit, as Peter's letter makes clear. A husband's obedience to scripture is his responsibility, not his wife's. She need only answer for her failings on the day of judgment, not his. She should do her part and submit. If he fails to lay down his life for her it is ultimately between him and God.

A man may say his life's work is more important than giving himself to his wife. He is, perhaps, ordained to serve the gospel – if he behaved as she would like him to he would be less effective for Christ. He should have thought of this before he married. Marriage is demanding as well as fulfilling, and the cost should be carefully weighed up beforehand. After all he had no excuse not to do so. This particular result of marriage is quite clearly spelt out by Paul: 'The unmarried man cares for the things of the Lord, how he may please the Lord; but he who is married cares for the things of the world, how he may please his wife, and he has been divided' (1 Corinthians 7:32).

Others will say that this teaching will result in anarchy. You cannot *both* have authority over each other. Someone must be in charge or there will be chaos. If this is all the faith we have in God's specific commandments our faith is worthless. You could say the same of throwing your life away, or seeking only the Kingdom of God, or any of Jesus's sayings which involve a little risk. You might expect them all to end in disaster. Followed half-heartedly they are almost bound to. All I can say is, I dare you to try. Taste and see that the Lord is as good as His word. There are many strange and thrilling visions in the Bible, and this revolutionary idea of marriage, in which two people have total command of each other, is surely one of the most inspiring.

Applications

People sometimes ask how this kind of teaching works out in practice. What does it mean in terms of disciplining the children, spending money, housework, washing up, careers, and all the other heartaches the married flesh is heir to? As I hope was clear from chapter 5, there are no sexually prescribed roles in these areas. It simply does not matter who takes on what jobs. They are the responsibility of both partners; how we share them out is up to us. Sadly, as Patricia Gundry points out, most people 'never even consider that *they* can determine what kind of marriage they want and then create it themselves'.[14] Yet God has left us free to decide these things. The couple in the Song are by no means conventional or even socially acceptable, yet they are the biblical model of erotic love.

The scriptural guidelines for marriage do not concern themselves with divisions of labour. They are far more radical. They will affect our behaviour more than any external structures, but not in such predictable ways.

I knew a couple who were married for several years without children. She was not ready for them. Her work was important to her, and it would have been jeopardised by pregnancies and small children. But he had wanted children for some time. One or two Christian leaders I know would have told him to 'assert his headship'. As it happens this is exactly what he did; Christlike, he put her welfare first and never mentioned the subject.

Eventually she realised he wanted to start a family. She was apprehensive at the idea, but realised that 'a wife has no authority over her own body but the husband has'. She believed she should submit to him in every-thing. She told him so. She left the matter up to him, and put herself in his hands.

He took her at her word and they stopped using con-traception. She then discovered she was so apprehensive about pregnancy that she found sex physically painful. So she asked God to help her submit in feelings as well as actions. It was not until then that she was able to make love to him willingly, despite the risk of pregnancy. As a consequence she found the experience more liberating and exciting than ever before.

As it happens she did become pregnant. The struggles started again. She was depressed at the thought and sometimes found herself antagonistic towards the baby. Again she prayed. Again she eventually won through. Now she has three children, and loves being a mother. It is sobering to realise that if she had had her own way they might never have been born.

A story like this is in danger of sounding saccharine but it is a practical example of the surrender God asks of married people. It is bound to be painful at the time. My friend put her entire future in her husband's hands. Total trust in someone involves risking everything: losing our lives for Christ can be just as frightening. Yet this is also how we find that freedom from ourselves which she found so intoxicating.

Her children now give her undreamt-of happiness. Her husband, because he made the decision to have them, takes responsibility and care for them in a way which frees her to enjoy them to the full. And when it came to a decision about his future he put himself in her hands in the same way. He was due to change jobs, and in his turn realised that 'a husband has no authority over his own body but his wife has'. He too risked his future, his work and his happiness. He too was prepared to hand her complete control of his life, and gave her *carte blanche* for the next decade of his life.

This is where the biblical teaching applies itself. Not who does the shopping, but who owns your life. A friend of ours married someone who was not as secure a Christian as he. After a few years of marriage she was not going to church regularly any more. Children, or Sunday lunch, or cleaning always seemed to get in the way. So he stayed behind to help her instead of going himself. Many would see this as a recipe for disaster; he ought not to let his wife disrupt his spiritual life in this way. But he was imitating Christ who gave up everything for the sake of our relationship with God; she realised he was making a sacrifice and eventually organised herself to go to church with him again.

This kind of love, however, should never be forced from one partner by the other. A man, for example, is never called upon to insist on his wife's submission, or even to ask for it or expect it. Parents are to rule or govern their children (1 Timothy 3:4), so if their children are unruly they should discipline them; their unsubmissive behaviour should not be tolerated. But husbands are never told to rule or govern their wives. They are not responsible for their wives' submission in the way that they are for their children's, so they are not to ask for it. A wife's submission is much more of a glad and willing thing – a voluntary placing of herself under her husband's love and care – than is always possible for employees or slaves, or even sometimes for children. For a man to try to force such behaviour from his wife would be as inappropriate and ineffective as a woman trying to insist that her husband lay down his life for her.

We know a couple who disagree about abortion. She, if she gets pregnant, will want amniocentesis tests to see if the child is normal: she does not want to carry a handicapped baby. He believes abortion to be wrong and would be unhappy with any such tests. Perhaps one day she will say to him, 'My body belongs to you; you make the decisions.' Until she does, it is not his place to ask her for such a sacrifice. If he is wise he will allow the tests (and pray they will not be positive).

This is how marriage works out in practice. She will do anything for him. He gives up everything for her. Both give the other complete power in every area of their lives. It is total interdependence.

I have often heard an explanation of the husband's 'headship' which goes something like this: by and large a couple should decide things together but if they simply cannot agree the husband has the casting vote. This always strikes me as a very sad and impoverished picture. It also makes little sense. Paul specifically draws the doctrine from Genesis 2, *before* the Fall (Ephesians 5:31 and 1 Corinthians 11:8,9). However, presumably, before the Fall Adam and Eve were in perfect agreement. They never would have needed 'deciding votes' or 'emergency measures'. *In practice*, Adam would not have been Eve's head at all; if 'headship' means having the final word in a disagreement, a couple who always see eye to eye are not head and body at all since he never needs the last say. A husband who is always putting his foot down, on the other hand (to continue the anatomical metaphors) is very much the head of his wife according to this interpretation, as he is constantly needing to insist on his casting vote. Surely this is wrong. Headship, like bodyship, is a continuous not an occasional thing. It means a husband is constantly loving his wife before himself.

People often ask whether husband and wife perform the same roles. Are their functions identical? And in a sense the answer is of course not. A head and body are not the same. (The head does all the talking, and the body does all the work!) The Church and Christ are not the same. She submits: He loves. So a wife does everything in her power to please her husband. He gives up everything, not only to please her but to make her beautiful, holy, happy, fulfilled, and reaching her maximum potential. They are like an actress and her agent: if she has a good agent she will put herself completely in his hands; if he is a good agent he will spend his time developing her talents and furthering her work. He exists to serve her. She recognises this and submits to him. Small wonder a woman is her husband's 'glory'; we will know he is a good husband by the beauty of his wife (1 Corinthians 11:7).

There has been an attempt lately to say that the marriage relationship is symmetrical. In the interests of women's equality some claim we must reinterpret the scriptures to present a wife's and husband's duties as identical. We would be well advised to leave the scriptures as they are. Though she was made for him, he is now to live for her. Though Adam was formed first, he lays down his life for Eve. If we are worried about women's equality we would do better, not to change what God has said, but to expound it truthfully.

Yet there is something remarkable about this asymmetry. It is like lovemaking itself. Of course it is not symmetrical: a woman and a man have different sexual functions. Yet in true lovemaking there is little difference between the way they make love to each other: both woo, both win, both surrender authority to the other. And perhaps the most important thing about the head and body imagery is not their difference but their mutual dependence; a separation at the neck means instant death for both.

Indeed the more fully we accept our separate roles, the more we realise they are much the same. The distinction between the Church's behaviour and Christ's should be lessening every day: the difference between a wife's attitude and her husband's also fades as they both become more like Christ. After all, there is not much to choose between total submission and total self-sacrifice. Body and soul, mind and strength, are given over to someone else. And this is what both lovers do.

EIGHT

Singleness

'Sing, O barren woman,
    you who never bore a child;
burst into song, shout for joy,
    you who were never in labour;
for more are the children of the desolate woman
    than of her who has a husband,'

says the LORD.
(Isaiah 54:1)

'Virginity is . . . a blessed thing . . . if conferred to those
frequent incumbrances of marriage.'

Robert Burton

There is no doubt whatsoever in the Bible that being
unmarried is good. Single people can have fewer worldly
preoccupations, be more single-minded Christians, and
even be happier than the married (1 Corinthians 7:32–4;
40). Small wonder Paul advises them to stay as they are
(verse 27).

Yet we find the teaching shocking, or simply incompre-
hensible. We seem to think everyone wants to be married.
The idea that anyone could be happier single is something we refuse to believe. And although in our society it
is allowable, if eccentric, to choose singleness, our
attitude to the single life is negative. Though we never
ask ourselves, 'Why on earth would Josephine want to
get married?' we often say to each other 'I wonder why
poor Jane never found a husband . . . after all, she's very

attractive.' It never seems to occur to us that perhaps 'poor' Jane believes the Bible, enjoys being single, and prefers to stay that way.

This pessimistic view of the single life is unbiblical, unchristian and faithless. Paul, by contrast, is very positive about staying unmarried. He stresses the values and joys of the life, and he practised what he preached: he chose to stay single himself, although this was quite contrary to Jewish practice at the time.[1]

He addresses himself to the issue in 1 Corinthians 7:

(1) Now, concerning the things you wrote about: it is good for a man not to touch a woman, (2) but because of sexual immorality each man should have his own wife, and each woman her own husband . . . (He then talks to married people about sex) . . . (7) I would like everybody to be like myself, but everyone has their own gift from God: one this, another that. (8) Now, I say to unmarried and to widows, it is good for them to stay [as they are], as I do, but if they are not controlling themselves they should marry, because it is better to marry than burn . . . (Paul goes on to talk about being married to non-Christians) . . . (17) Only everyone should live the life the Lord has given him or her, as God called him. I command this in all the churches. (He discusses being called in different situations, circumcised or uncircumcised, slave or free.) (23) You were bought with a price; do not become slaves of people. (24) Brothers and sisters, let everyone stay with God in the state in which he was called. (25) About virgins I do not have a command of the Lord, but I give my opinion as someone who, by the Lord's mercy, is faithful: (26) so I suppose, because of the inherent need, it is good for someone to stay as he or she is. (27) Have you been bound to a wife? Do not try and be free. Have you been freed from a wife? Do not try and find one. (28) If you marry, though, you are not sinning, and if a girl marries she is not sinning; but you

will have worldly troubles and I would spare you that. (29) The time has been shortened though, brothers and sisters . . . (and we are to live in the light of this) . . . (32) I want you to be without anxieties. The unmarried man cares for the things of the Lord, and how he can please the Lord, (33) but the married man cares about the things of the world, and how he can please his wife, (34) and he has been divided. Also, the unmarried woman, the virgin, cares for the things of the Lord, so that she can be holy both in body and in spirit, but the married one cares about the things of the world, and how she can please her husband. (35) So I say this for your advantage, not to put a restraint upon you, but for good order and undistracted attention to the Lord. (36) However, if anyone is not behaving properly towards his virgin, if their passions are strong (or possibly 'if he/she is past the bloom of youth') and so it ought to be, let him do what he wants; he would not be sinning; they ought to get married. (37) He who does not have this need, though, and stands firm in his heart, and has his will under control and has decided in his own heart to keep her as she is, will do well. (38) So both the one who marries his virgin does well, and the one who does not marry does better. (39) A wife is bound as long as her husband lives, but if he sleeps she is free to be married, only in the Lord, to whom she wishes; (40) but she is happier if she remains as she is in my opinion, and I think I have the Spirit of God as well (1 Corinthians 7).

Oddly enough some people think Paul is being a kill-joy, laying down the law with impossibly difficult teaching. Nothing could be further from the truth. He wants us to be without anxieties (verse 32). He bends over backwards not to burden or restrict us. Although he suggests we stay single he insists we are free to marry. And he specifically says his advice is 'for your advantage', and 'not to put restraint upon you' (verse 35). He is offering us Christian liberation. He wants us to be free to enjoy our situations to the full, and to live the particular lives the Lord has given us (verse 17).

LIBERATING COMMANDS

Freedom from marriage

This chapter in its entirety is not addressed only to the single. It is relevant to us all. And central to Paul's message is a command he gives everywhere. 'Let everyone live the life the Lord has given him' (verse 17). This does not just apply to the question of being married or single but, in context, this is one of its major applications. God has given you a way of life. Live it to the full.

What is my way of life? Perhaps I have a strong desire to be married. I feel sure this is my 'gift'. If God would hurry up and give it to me I would enjoy it to the full. Or perhaps I am not sure quite what my 'gift' should be. Some days I like being single; some days it drives me mad. If God would tell me what my particular life is to be, what my special 'gift' is, I would do my best to enjoy it.

This kind of thinking is unbiblical. We have already been given a gift, a particular situation. It is not the same as a 'calling'. Our calling is to God. We are called to serve the gospel. The only Christian vocation is the vocation to be a Christian. And our calling never changes; it is the same for all of us. This should never be confused with our individual way of life or our particular occupation; our 'gift'.

Quite simply, our 'gift' is the one God has given us. Our way of life is the one we have. If you are single your gift is singleness. If you are married it is marriage. And our gift, unlike our calling, is not particularly important. It does not actually matter whether we are slaves or free, Jews or Gentiles, married or single. It matters very much indeed that we are godly. And of course our gift may change. Just because God gives you one gift now does not mean He cannot give you a different one later. I have been given marriage. Tomorrow I may be widowed. I would then be given a single life. Perhaps you have been given singleness. In five years' time you might be married. But now, whether you are fourteen or forty, you have been given a single life. Live it.

On reflection this may seem an absurd command. 'Live the life you are living.' Surely we have no choice. Why are we told to do something we cannot help but do? The point is there is a way of life appropriate to each gift. The single life, like the married life, is easily spoilt.

The first way to spoil it is not to see it as a gift. All too often people are persuaded to think of the single life as a curse. Paul tells us repeatedly it is good. Yet people refuse to believe it. The culprits are often not unmarried people themselves; the real culprits are those who assume everyone wants to be married. I am constantly hearing people say, 'If only poor so-and-so could get married . . .' This kind of comment is offensive in the extreme. It assumes on the part of so-and-so a disobedience to God. He has given single people a gift and told them to enjoy it, but it is difficult to do this if everyone keeps telling you to change it.

A friend of mine has recently become engaged. A member of her congregation congratulated her, saying 'I'm so glad you're getting married at last: you've got so much to give!' This unbiblical well-wisher would do well to study Paul. The idea that one is more useful, or even better off, with a partner is contrary to his teaching.

So the first freedom Paul gives us is freedom from marriage itself. In most societies – including, I imagine, Corinth at the time – it is assumed everyone will be married. In many Moslem countries, for example, there is little choice: it is the men's duty to marry, while the women are considered useless if they are not bearing children. Jews were under the same kind of obligation. But in Christ there is a new freedom. There is no such pressure on us. We can do as we like.

We need not be 'slaves to people' (verse 23) in this way. Paul clearly sees the single life as a kind of freedom (verse 27). And this it can certainly be. Those of us who are married know that it 'ties you down'. It is a glorious captivity, but it is one all the same. You can no longer be undivided about the cares of the Lord. Once you are married you also live for someone else. But Christians are free to choose another way of life.

Many people are so determined to idealise marriage they refuse to accept Paul's attitude. His words were only for the Corinthians, they say, and are no longer relevant. (Why we keep them in our canon of scripture is anybody's guess.) 'The inherent need' (verse 26) is translated as 'present distress',[2] and interpreted as first-century persecution; in which case they would have had good reason to be thankful for singleness.

Admittedly a country under persecution is the worst place to be married. Your partner and your children may be tortured for your beliefs. But as it happens, there was no persecution that we know of in Corinth. Paul may mean, by 'present distress', the restrictions placed on all of us. We are bound to find tensions in life. We will have trouble and distress before we get to heaven. None of us lives in ideal circumstances: it is necessary, common sense, and normal Christian practice to rejoice in whatever we have. And even if you take Paul's words here (verses 25–31) to be only for those under persecution, he has already laid down the principle that we are to lead the life God has given us. Corinthian or not, we accept what we are given.

We are to enjoy and appreciate our gift. Paul goes further. We should not even try and change it. Whatever your gift was when you were called as a non-Christian, stay in it now you are a Christian. If you were circumcised when called, stay circumcised; if you were uncircumcised, stay uncircumcised; if a slave, stay a slave; if free, stay free (verse 18–22). 'Brothers and sisters, let everyone stay with God in the state in which he was called' (verse 24).

'Are you bound to a wife?' (or, we can assume, a husband). 'Do not try to be free. Are you free from a wife?' (or husband). 'Do not try to find one' (verse 27). If you are free, stay free. Do not look for a partner.

This makes sense. There is nothing which detracts from enjoyment of a single life more than trying to get rid of it. The most successfully single people I know are those who have no thought of marriage. Someone we know, when he was a young man in his first curacy, used to waste considerable emotional energy assessing the nubile fauna of his parish. 'Is *she* the one?' he was constantly tempted to ask himself, before deciding her nose was too long or her legs too short. It was not until he put this thinking behind him that he was able to enjoy his job and his situation. Now he loves being single. He has more friends, more time, and far more freedom than a married man could have.

It is only when we forget marriage that we can make true friends of the opposite sex. A friend of mine in her twenties was plagued with thoughts of finding a partner. Every possible man was assessed as soon as she met him. This made true friendship with any man next to impossible. Those who were ineligible were dismissed as no good. Those who scored higher were only seen in terms of future partners, not cultivated as present friends. Again it was not until she freed herself from this attitude that she could enjoy the opposite sex. We are all tempted to do this, and it tends to cripple our chances of deep fellowship with either sex. I could have had far better boy and girl friends as a teenager if I had not been trying to pair myself off.

So Paul sets us free from the need to find a partner. This is the first way to enjoy your particular life. See it as a gift. Do not look for marriage. Live the life God has given you.

Freedom from sex

The second way to enjoy singleness is to embrace celibacy. For Paul also sets us free from the tyranny of sex: 'It is good,' he dares to say, 'for a man not to touch a woman' (verse 1). Again we find this teaching so repellent many try to explain it away. The most common excuse given for it is that he was repeating some crackpot idea of the Corinthians. Now it is quite possible he was quoting something they had said in an earlier letter, but if so he endorses their statement; he qualifies it by ruling out abstention for married people, but he does not contradict the initial idea. It is good to go without sexual experiences! It is actually good to be celibate. It is not necessarily superior to marriage, but it is certainly not second-best. This is liberating stuff. It means the world is wrong. There *is* life without sex. We are free to live without it.

This is most unconventional teaching. Our society tells us we need sex, and cannot be fulfilled without regular sexual expression. I saw a headline in a paper the other day which ran: 'Too much sex can be as dangerous as too little.' That too little is dangerous is taken as accepted fact. It is considered essential: without it we cannot be normal, socially acceptable, or psychologically healthy. It is inconceivable to the world that anyone who has a choice in the matter could use it to abstain. And, from what we know about first-century Corinth, I doubt if it was very different.

Paul's comment is not only liberating for single people; it is also a doctrine of great freedom for homosexuals, for the impotent or frigid, and those who are unattractive to the opposite sex. Society tells them they have failed. A single person may one day marry, but Christian homosexuals are 'doomed' to life-long sexual frustration if they want to be obedient to God. This is not failure, says Paul. It is good to live without sex. There is no need to think of this as disaster.

No one is pretending it will be easy. We are designed to make love, so those of us who are celibate are bound to feel tempted and frustrated. There is no convenient answer to this. Some find it a life-long struggle; others are hardly bothered at all. But contemporary 'liberal' attitudes to sex tend to render the struggle far harder.

Paul tells us in no uncertain terms to 'flee immorality' (6:18). He wants us all to be like him (7:7): we are all to be sexually pure. Some of us have one gift and some another: some are married and some single (7:7). But we are all to be like Paul: we are all to flee immorality. Married people do this by giving themselves to each other; single people do so through stringent self-control (which the married, of course, will sometimes need as well). We are all to be alike in our chastity, and we are to achieve that chastity through our different gifts.

This has been made difficult for single people in our society. Paul tells us to flee immorality, but he does not tell us how far to flee. He tells us to use self-control, but he does not tell us how much of ourselves to control. Nowadays it is possible to dip one's toes into sexual intimacy without taking the plunge. Teenagers can kiss. Couples can canoodle. Young people can disappear into cars or quiet corners at parties for a little physical self-expression. And none of this is seen as 'having sex'.

Nevertheless these things are all erotic, and the biblical picture of the erotic is one of unconditional surrender. There is no reserve in lovemaking. Everything is given to one person and one alone. If you want erotic intimacy with a woman you give yourself to her, body and soul, for the rest of your life. We have somehow divided the erotic into various degrees of seriousness. If you are under a certain age or president of your Christian Union you will not go far; if you are engaged, or not such an exemplary disciple, you will experiment a little more, and so on. This would appear to be our current 'Christian' ethic. If you are married you go the whole way but only with one person; if you are single you can go part of the way with anyone you like. The problem then, of course, is knowing when to stop.

Non-Christians are at least consistent. Secular society now more or less allows anything with anyone. We Christians practise double standards: two men would raise eyebrows if they were kissing and cuddling in the dark, as would two people married to others; but unmarried teenagers are told to indulge in any amount of slap and tickle as long as they are not 'having sex'.[3] Yet these things are all sexual; and sex belongs to marriage.

This supposed liberality does not help the unmarried. Paul's advice is compassionate. Celibacy is hard. Abstention is never made easier by tasting tiny morsels of a dish we want to devour. Lovemaking is designed to be enjoyed without restraint. Sampling it is likely to be more frustrating than avoiding it altogether.

Obviously, in the present climate we all want to know how far we can go with immorality before we have gone too far. But Paul tells us to flee it. In normal usage that means to run away from it, to have nothing to do with it all. The erotic is for marriage. If you are married enjoy it; if you are single flee it.

It would be easy to make Paul's words sound hard, but he is not being legalistic or unfeeling. He knew from personal experience what tensions single people can be under. As he says, he is telling us something for our benefit; he does not want to put restrictions on us. If we find it impossible, and other options are open to us, he suggests alternative advice. His 'strict' teaching is indeed liberating. I know several people who wish they had heard it when they were younger: it never occurred to them they were free to save themselves for marriage; they never realised they could go through their teenage years without even kissing a girl. As Paul has already said, 'All things are lawful', but not all things are *helpful*; all things are lawful, but we do not want to be enslaved to them (6:12).

Nor is Paul trying to burden us with guilt. He is telling

us how we should live, not telling us off for how we have lived. Sexual folly, like any folly, can be repented of and forgiven. We are rare if we have no regrets about previous misconduct. The answer is simple: 'Go, and sin no more' (John 8:11).

'Flee immorality.' But this never means flee the opposite sex. Unfortunately those churches which encourage young people to be truly celibate often encourage them also to shun half their peers. This is a pity. A teenage boy, for example, should have among his friends several girls to whom he can talk quite openly. A single woman in her late thirties ought to know a number of men of her own age, married or single, well enough to call them good friends. Much of the frustration single people experience is because they are often not allowed to make real friendships among the opposite sex.

This is surely another reason why Paul tells us to flee immorality. I knew a teenager who worked through a long succession of boyfriends. No one had told her she was free to do anything else; it had never occurred to her that she could choose 'not to touch' a man. All these relationships were frustrating. None lasted. They were pale shadows of marriage rather than honest friendships in their own right. The only relationships which survived from her teenage years were of the kind we tend to call 'platonic': with her girlfriends, and the only boy who was not a 'boyfriend'. This is common to many people's experience. As soon as we begin expressing physical attraction towards a member of the opposite sex we start a course which ends in either marriage or estrangement. It will seldom end in friendship. Yet deep friendships with members of the opposite sex are just what we need. By and large we are only free to make them when we have ruled out erotic possibilities.

Single people, particularly teenagers, sometimes ask about 'girlfriends' and 'boyfriends'. Can I go out with a non-Christian girl? Is it right to have a boyfriend? The questioners usually assume that any close relationship with the opposite sex must be pseudo-erotic. But a pseudo-erotic relationship is not a real friendship at all. Anything truly erotic belongs to marriage; any imitation is merely a mockery. We should all have male and female friends and Christian and non-Christian friends. Some of these should be intimate. But if any is an erotic friendship it is time to question whether we should still be single.

Freedom to marry

For this is the third freedom Paul gives us; freedom from singleness itself. People always seem to go overboard stressing one half of his teaching or the other. Either single people are made to feel that they have not 'made it', or married people are made to feel they have fallen for 'second best'. Because Paul emphatically says the single life can be better, people somehow assume the married life must be worse. Yet he repeatedly says this is not the case. Those who say it is 'second best' are contradicting him. Marriage is not a sin. Paul stresses this several times (verses 28–36). A man who marries a woman is doing a good thing (verse 38). Just as some people do better to stay single (verse 38), some do better to get married (verse 9). This is why Paul, twice, tells them to do so.

But if you have been told to enjoy and stay in the single life how will you ever know to leave it? It is sometimes thought that if we were really faithful to Paul we would never marry. If we were keen, hard-boiled, strong-willed Christians we would steel ourselves and remain celibate for life. The human race would quickly and obediently expire. Because we are not all perfect, it is suggested, Paul allows a counsel of compassion for the fallen: if you simply cannot live without sex you might as well give up and look for a wife. In other words, although you are unmarried, have no available partner in mind, and all appearances point to your being at present well and truly single, you may come to the conclusion despite the evidence that your 'gift' is marriage after all.

This interpretation does not make sense for a number of reasons. First, it is in utter contradiction to Paul's main argument. We have established that those who are single have the gift of singleness. If we start thinking it is not our gift simply because it is sometimes difficult, we make nonsense of Paul's teaching. I imagine some of the Corinthians with the gift of slavery did not always feel like being slaves.

In addition Paul tells us to enjoy the life we have. Suppose you decide you have too much libido to do so. You start to look for a spouse. Unfortunately it takes you a decade to find one. You have then wasted ten years – or two, or five, or even half a lifetime – hankering after marriage when you could have been enjoying the single life.

And, finally, sexual frustration is not the only or even the chief reason many people long for marriage. Some want companionship, or children. Why are those with uncontrollable lusts to give in while those with other equally difficult desires stay frustrated? Besides, if we followed this interpretation we would probably find that more men than women would be getting married. The situation would be laughable: it would be the beginning of Christian polyandry. This cannot be how we should understand Paul's advice to some of us to marry in verses 8 and 36.[4]

For one thing about Paul's advice is absolutely clear. He is addressing those with a particular partner in mind. The situation is this: a couple are free to marry; they very much wish to; their passions are strong, they are even behaving badly, and they feel as if they are on fire. They are longing to give themselves to one another in the fullest possible way. In short, one could safely say they are a couple in love. In which case, Paul says, as any sane man would, 'it ought to be, let him do what he wants . . . they should get married'.

But he only says this to those *who have a prospective spouse already.* The couple have a well-established relationship. They are already committed to one another. There is even a suggestion that they are going too far sexually (verse 36). This is very different from someone rather disliking living alone. Deciding to marry because you are in love is sound. Deciding to marry because you do not like being single is no reason at all. This is how to destroy your peace of mind and throw away your gift. Once in the Bible, it is true, a man went looking for a wife (Genesis 24). But the situation was hardly normative. He was not seeking a wife for himself. The idea was the groom's father's; the search, choice and proposal were his servant's; and the girl accepted the offer without meeting the man himself. He was the only person who had no say in the affair at all. His courtship is hardly a model for us. So we are not to go looking for a partner (verse 27). If you are in love, consider marriage. If you are not, do not. You will never enjoy being single if you are trying to find a mate. If you want to marry a particular person Paul suggests you do so; if you simply want 'marriage' he does not.

So it is good to stay single, and if you can 'stand firm in your heart' you will find the rewards very great. But it is also good to get married, and if you are burning with passion for someone you are probably well advised to get on with it. If you are both in love, go ahead. Get married if you want to.

But there is a problem here. It seems probable that the Corinthians were all betrothed by their families from an early age anyway; Paul's advice is appropriate for those who only have to decide between marriage and singleness, not between one future spouse and another.[5] People thinking of marriage often tie themselves in agonising knots over this question. 'Is he God's man for me?' 'Is she the partner the Lord wants me to marry?' For of course it is possible to fall in love with someone quite unsuitable. Paul seems to give little help in such a situation. This is because it would not have concerned the Corinthians; they may have had no say in the selection anyway.

However, there was one group of people amongst his listeners who seem to have been able to choose their future partners: when talking to widows Paul assumes they can select for themselves. If we want advice about choosing the right person we must turn to what Paul says to widows. This is where we find the biblical guidance on the matter. And he gives remarkably little information: a woman who wants to remarry should choose, 'in the Lord, whom she wishes' (verse 40). That is all. If you have found someone in the Lord whom you wish to marry, go ahead. Naturally it is common biblical sense that he or she should also be of the opposite sex and free and willing, but otherwise there are no rules or even particular guidelines on the matter.

Now obviously some choices are wise and some foolish. A woman is wise to choose a man she can submit to, since this is what she will have to do for the rest of their lives; if she has no respect for his values and no time for his opinions she is going to find marriage an uphill struggle. And a man is wise to choose a woman he can love and lay down his life for; if he thinks her judgment poor or her ambitions idiotic he is going to find life very frustrating. So there are certainly silly choices to be made when it comes to marriage. However such 'mistakes' are hardly morally wrong. We are free to marry, in the Lord, whom we wish. There is no 'right' or 'wrong' person in an absolute sense. There are people who are likely to make us happy and people who are not. But there is none who can make us ungodly. We can always be obedient husbands and wives even if we are not blissfully happy ones. So we can take plenty of helpful non-biblical advice as to whom we should marry. The only biblical word of advice, however, is to choose, in the Lord, whom we wish.

It is sometimes thought that marrying for love is a

totally modern concept. But Jacob worked for fourteen years to marry the girl he loved (Genesis 29:16–30). Samson married for love – not once but twice. (Judges 14:1–3 and 16:4. Both occasions were disastrous . . .) And what is the Song of Songs if it is not a love story? Of course other kinds of marriage are valid too: in tribal Pakistan or in Nepal, where marriages are arranged and love matches have never been heard of, the practical implications of Paul's teaching would be different. For us, in our society, this particular application is the appropriate one.

And falling in love is not something you can ever plan. So plan to stay single. Aim to stand firm. One day you may be swept off your feet and your plans will have to change.

PROMISED BLESSINGS

Paul tells us repeatedly the unmarried life is good. Yet for some this may not ring true. You may love being single and not want to change for anything in the world. On the other hand you may often feel frustrated or resentful, and wish you could be married.

Of course. This is natural. In fact it is probably far more common than feeling satisfied and grateful for singleness. We are created to make love, so most single people will feel sexually frustrated. We are created to have children, so many single (and some married) people will feel their parental instincts are being frustrated. And we are created to be in partnership with the opposite sex, so single people – particularly in our 'nuclear family' society – may often feel unsettled or lonely without the lifelong commitment of marriage.

What we often tend to forget is that everyone is frustrated. We are also made to work, so the unemployed are frustrated. We are made to subdue the Earth, so the powerless are frustrated. We are made to serve God, so those of us who are married will sometimes, according to Paul (1 Corinthians 7:32–5), feel frustrated too. I have a friend who works a great deal amongst women, and she finds considerably more frustration in the lives of her married colleagues than her single ones. It is foolish to pretend we are not frustrated, but it is equally foolish to forget that everyone else is frustrated too. Some constraints on our freedom, like unemployment and slavery, are not good in themselves. Singleness is. Paul says so. When we find it trying it is important to bear in mind the advantages it has over marriage.

A single person can be 'carefree'

Paul describes a single person as 'free' (verse 27). You can be happier (verse 40). You need not have worldly cares (verse 32). The other day a friend and I were discussing Paul's commands in Ephesians 5 on marriage. As we talked of the teaching which is so often neglected, the total self-sacrifice God demands of a husband, his face began to fall.

'She'd better be good,' he said. Then he thought a little more. 'I think I'll stay single after all.'

We saw in the last chapter what marriage means. A husband has given his life away; someone else has authority over him (verse 4); his concern is his wife's pleasure (verse 33). Small wonder Paul describes him as 'divided'. He is rightly torn between giving his life to a woman and giving it to God.

Shaun and I experience these tensions every day. He works in the evening; he often has meetings to attend. If he were single he would stay talking afterwards, help wash up, walk home with a friend and perhaps ask him in for coffee; then he might do some work at his desk. All this is part of his job. Afterwards he would probably eat, have a bath, go to bed at twelve and read for an hour. He could give himself to his job and live as he liked. Because he is married he comes home sooner than he wants, goes to bed earlier than he wants, and turns the light out before he has read what he wants. If I were single I would go to bed at ten, get up at the crack of dawn, and work for several hours before breakfast; because I am married, I am awake late at night and get up tired in the morning.

This is a small example of the numerous constraints on married people. When I was single I loved my work and gave myself to it wholeheartedly; as soon as I got married it started to suffer. When Shaun was single he was dedicated to his work and found few tensions in pursuing it; since marriage he has often felt called away from it by his family. To be more accurate, our work has changed. Now we have other responsibilities as well as our individual careers, which must often stand aside. So I have lost many jobs because I no longer wish to travel anywhere or work any hours. And Shaun has lost many hours of work in his study because of having children to bath or to play with.

These things are not begrudged; one would not marry if one were not prepared to give oneself to another. But those of us who are not married will appreciate our way of life far more when we realise the advantages it offers. Single people are much freer in their work, their worship, and their lifestyle. They will still, of course, have obligations and commitments to others: some have lodgers for whom they feel responsible; others are looking after parents; all should be caring for friends and other members of their church. Nevertheless a single person has not given himself away in the same way. You have not granted another authority over you, a right to your body, and a claim on your life. As a result you can give the Lord your 'undistracted attention' (verse 35). Instead of laying down his life for his wife as Christ did for us, a single man can lay it down for God. Instead of submitting to her husband 'as to the Lord', a single woman can submit to the Lord Himself.

Of course it is good to give one's life to someone else; of course it is deeply satisfying to have a lifelong partnership with another human being. But it is far better to give one's life to God; it is far more satisfying to enjoy eternal friendship with Him. In this the unmarried person can be free and undivided.

A single person can have 'children'

Unmarried friends have sometimes told me they would like to be married not so much for marriage itself but for children. This is important. Paul says it is good to live without sex; he does not say it is good to live without children. Some people are going to find this difficult. Again, however, in exchange for this deprivation the single person has a corresponding blessing greater than the loss.

The commandment given to us at the beginning of the Old Testament is to go forth and multiply (Genesis 1:28). Consequently, throughout the Old Testament children are seen as a wonderful blessing (Psalm 126:4,5; 128:3,6). Great joy is the result of obeying God's commands.

In the New Testament we are given a new commandment. '(19) Go therefore,' Jesus said, 'and make disciples of all nations, baptising them in the name of the Father, and the Son, and the Holy Spirit, (20) teaching them to observe everything I have commanded you . . .' (Matthew 28). We are no longer simply commanded to bear natural fruit; now we are told to bear spiritual fruit too. Abraham was promised as many descendants as the stars (Genesis 15:5). We, too, are told we can increase a hundredfold (Matthew 13:23).Whereas the Old Testament emphasises the joy of having children, the New Testament recognises a new joy of having disciples born again. Paul constantly gives thanks to God for those he had brought to Christ (1 Thessalonians 1:2; 2 Thessalonians 1:3,4). He recognised Timothy as his 'true child in the faith' (1 Timothy 1:2) and he longed to see him, day and night, because of the joy that Timothy brought him. But he could not have given himself to others in this way if a woman had had a prior claim on his life.

We have a friend who has many spiritual children, as Paul had. She prays for them regularly and teaches them the Christian faith. She goes on holiday with them, spends days playing tennis with them, and takes them out to the theatre. She even advises them in their choice of university, or career, or marriage partner. In many ways she cares for them as a parent does for a child. And they in turn look to her for Christian love and guidance. The relationships are deeply rewarding on both sides. Yet she could not do this if she were married: she would have a husband to spend time with and her own children to pray for.

Some may remain unenthusiastic about this. Perhaps new believers do not bring you much joy. You have known one or two people become Christians, but you would hardly look on them as your children or a source of extraordinary happiness. But children are a great commitment. They involve prayer, love, self-sacrifice, expense, and considerable hard work. They also involve a lot of fun. If you want the fun, though, you must be prepared for the rest. Paul went to enormous trouble, suffering and deprivation not only to bring people to Christ but to keep them with Him, as anyone who reads Acts or his letters can see. Consequently, he found his Christian children very rewarding. E. J. H. Nash, the man who brought the writer and preacher John Stott to Christ, started on a five-year weekly correspondence with him when he had met him only once as a non-Christian schoolboy. He also prayed for him every day, apparently for the rest of his life.[6] I imagine he was eventually very proud to have such a spiritual son. Having children is a costly and painful blessing. If you want the joy you must first face the hard work. But those of us who are single (or otherwise childless) need not be deprived: Jesus's disciples, His spiritual children (and even probably Paul's) are surely now as numerous as ever Abraham's were.

Marriage is good and offers great rewards, but there

are better opportunities and greater rewards available to single people. Partnership with God is better than partnership with any other; new Christians born in the spirit are better than new babies born to the flesh; and eternal life through salvation is better than a lasting name through one's children:

> To the eunuchs who keep my Sabbaths,
>   who choose what pleases me
>   and hold fast to my covenant –
> to them will I give within my walls
>   a memorial and a name
> better than sons and daughters;
>
> (Isaiah 56:4,5)

DIVINE EXAMPLE

The greatest encouragement of all to single people must be the life of Jesus Himself. Whenever we are tempted to think there is something second best, or unfulfilled, or inferior about singleness we have only to think of Him. His life was perfect, yet He never shared it with a woman. He is our example for living, and He stayed single all His life. So we have a great deal to learn from His example as a bachelor.

We can learn from His chastity. Jesus was above reproach in His behaviour with the opposite sex. He was accused of being a drunkard, a glutton and a blasphemer, but He was never accused by His contemporaries of being sexually immoral. This is all the more remarkable when we consider His intimacy with women, and the freedom He allowed them to express their affections towards Him. Yet it was inconceivable even to His enemies that He ever had an erotic entanglement with anybody. His physical contact with men and women was absolutely pure.

We also need to learn from Jesus's partnership with

women. He never shunned them, as some bachelors do
who are trying to live good Christian lives. He travelled
with them, stayed with them, and above all worked with
them. We are to enjoy a similar partnership with the
opposite sex. It is good for a man not to touch a woman,
but it was not good for the man to be on his own. Single
people are to be celibate, not unsociable; Christian
bachelors should be chaste, not misogynous. They can
and should be intimate with women friends and
colleagues as well as with men.

And of course we must learn from Jesus's relationship
with the Father. His was truly a life of single-mindedness
and dedication. We can never hope for the same intimacy
with God, but if we aspire to the same obedience we will
enjoy some of the same divine companionship.

So single people have an excellent model for their
lifestyle in Jesus. If we live as Jesus did we are bound to
find fulfilment and liberation in singleness. Our aim is
to be as free with the opposite sex, and as pure. After all,
in Christ we are all one family; we should treat each other
as brothers and sisters (1 Timothy 5:2–3).

As well as having Jesus as our example, though, it
helps to know others who lead exemplary single lives. I
have a friend I would happily take as my model if I were
single. His secret seems to be his readiness to share
himself. Because he has no wife he is free to give himself
to others. He is constantly available. He is extremely
hospitable. He spends his holidays with other single
friends. He is often to be found caring for those younger
than himself. He shares his life, his time, his money and
his house with other people. He is also self-disciplined
in his sexual behaviour. He never blights friendship with
women by pointless entanglements with them. In every
way, he lives his single life to the full. As a result he
seldom seems lonely or frustrated.

He also fills his house with lodgers. One of the greatest
difficulties for single people in modern life is the way we
have structured our families. In cultures where

grandparents, nannies, uncles and slaves also made up part of the household, single people could care for children, help run a house, and be part of a domestic unit. Our society does not encourage this. Families are split up. Teenagers or young adults leave home. Households tend to consist solely of parents and schoolchildren.

One way round this is for single people to live together with some commitment to one another. A friend of mine discovered recently that one of her lodgers is a liar and an alcoholic. Instead of asking her to leave my friend considered it her duty to care for her. Her household is like a loose-knit family, with responsibility for its members.

It is also good when couples and families share their homes. When we were first married we lived in a house with half a dozen single friends. It was not a deliberate choice, but we all enjoyed it and learned from it. We too were like a large family. We ate together, prayed together, and shared our money with one another, as the first disciples sometimes did.

Since we have had a home of our own we have also, for most of the last fourteen years, had people living with us. At first we did not look forward to our loss of privacy, and even thought it might be detrimental to our family life. It has proved exactly the reverse. It is enriching for the children to have other adults to relate to. It is refreshing for us to have the company and insights of other people. And those who have lived with us have also sometimes told us they have found it a valuable experience.

None of these suggestions is an imperative for single people. But the single people I most admire tend to have these things in common: they share their lives, their homes, their possessions, and even their most private moments with other people; they are sexually disciplined in the extreme; and they show a lasting and prayerful responsibility for others. Of course all these attributes will make them excellent spouses if they ever marry. And all these things were characteristic of the most exemplary single life of all.

Some people think Jesus failed in His mission because He did not marry. Sun Myung Moon has based his religion on this premise. A perfect man, he claims, should have married and left perfect descendants to carry on his name.

Yet as soon as we ask ourselves why Jesus lived like this the reason is obvious. Clearly there were many pragmatic advantages. Like Paul, if Jesus had had a wife He could not have travelled as He did, or given Himself to His followers as He did, or even have been free to die as He did, since He would have given His life to His wife. But there is a far more significant reason for Jesus's celibacy. If He had married a woman how could He have been our bridegroom? If He had had natural descendants what would our status have been in comparison? We are His bride, and His true descendants. We are the wife He loves and cherishes, and the offspring He teaches and disciplines. Jesus has indeed married and left descendants to carry on His name.

Obviously this aspect of Jesus's life is no example for us. We are not married to the Church. But it tells us something about the single life. Jesus, as a single person, was free to be one flesh with us; we visualise the relationship every time we take communion. We can be free for the same kind of communion with God Himself. The single life (like marriage) is seldom easy, but it can be a very great privilege.

The Old and New Testaments clearly teach that marriage is a wonderful thing; it is made by God, and good, and the source of a great deal of happiness. You may be given it for part of your life, and it is a gift and a blessing. But the New Testament also teaches that singleness is wonderful too; it is a life of dedication and happiness, with the blessings of spiritual children. We are all given it for part of our lives, and it is also a gift and a blessing.

The single person who lives singlemindedly for Christ need never fear that he or she will miss out. When Jesus told His disciples that marriage was for keeps, they said, presumably in astonishment, that it would be better not to marry (Matthew 19:10). He did not contradict them. Instead, He confirmed that this is true for those who can remain single; there are those, He says, who have done so for the sake of the kingdom of heaven (verse 12). A little later on, Peter points out how much he and the others have given up (verse 27). Jesus reassures them (verse 29). Everyone who has left homes or families, possessions or children for His sake, 'will receive a hundredfold, and inherit eternal life'.

NINE

Homosexuality

> '*Homosexuality. There is probably no other word in the English language which is so symbolic of controversy and which so quickly triggers emotional reactions.*'
>
> Gary Collins, ***Christian Counselling***.[1]

> '*Should some young and lusty bystander overhear us as we propose it [a ban on sexual licence, including homosexuality] he might probably denounce our enactments as impracticable folly and make the air ring with his clamour . . . Things have come to such a pass today that no such result is thought possible . . .*
>
> '*Would you like me to show that the proposal is feasible? . . . Athletes made no hardship of denying themselves this "heaven of bliss" [sex with women or boys] for the sake of a victory in the ring, or the racecourse, or the like. And are our pupils to fail in endurance for the same of a far nobler victory?*'
>
> Plato.[2]

I did not want to write this chapter.

Because of a brief religious broadcast I made a year ago,[3] it has sometimes been claimed that I must be someone who dislikes homosexuals and wishes to campaign against them. Certain newspapers (not always disingenuously) have labelled me 'homophobic'.

Nothing could be further from the truth. Instinctively, I have a strong sympathy with gay people. Like many women, by and large I find gay men easy to get on with, and often more sensitive and less threatening, sometimes more humorous and almost always less aggressive and competitive than many heterosexual men. I am aware of gay relationships which are, as far as I can tell, beautiful and good; I know some who say that 'coming out' was the most important and healing thing they have ever done, who seem much happier and more whole once they have accepted their homosexuality and had it accepted by others. I have met lesbians who have tried heterosexual marriage, who find it is only when they are loved by women that they feel truly understood, accepted and genuinely feminine. And every so often I hear a 'gay' argument, perhaps a homosexual interpretation of some verse of scripture, and believe – indeed wildly hope – that the traditional understanding of homosexuality might be mistaken.

So I have tried to minimise public comments I make about homosexuality, partly because I haven't wished my name to become linked to this particular issue, but also because it is frighteningly easy to do more harm than good, to make homosexual people feel more hated than loved by what God says.

Nevertheless, some things have to be said. If God requires certain moral standards of Christians, we Christians need to know what they are. Over the last decade a considerable amount of confusion has arisen on this particular topic, which has never, as far as I know, existed in the mind of the Church before. So old truths need to be reiterated, and young Christians re-taught them. Not to do so would be unkind and unfair, as well as irresponsible.

And it is supremely in the context of male and female relationships – and especially within the teaching about sexual interdependence which this book is about – that the Christian teaching about homosexuality needs to be given. Simply to state God's negative prohibitions on homosexual practice might seem, in the current cultural context, harsh and unloving. It sounds so unfair. But when seen in the light of all that God says about the complementarity of the sexes, the Judaeo-Christian teaching about homosexuality makes good sense.

First let me explain how I came to the subject myself. As a child I was privileged to meet the writer E. M. Forster, living as he did in King's College, Cambridge, to which my father was attached. I barely remember him, but I grew up to be an enthusiastic fan of his writings, so when his novel *Maurice* was posthumously published I fell upon it greedily. I must have been a young teenager at the time. The book tells the story of a Cambridge undergraduate, in the days when homosexual acts were still illegal, gradually realising his homosexual orientation, and of his love affair with another man. It is commonly presumed to be in part autobiographical and Forster left instructions that it could be published after his death. Like all Forster's books it is beautifully written, and I recommend it strongly; it certainly helped me to begin to understand the homosexual dilemma. But at the age I was when I first tried to read it I couldn't cope with it. I felt a distaste, an instinctive revulsion and, disappointed, I put it on one side.

Let me immediately add that I, and all my class at school, experienced a similar reaction to the idea of heterosexual sex when it was described to us in a biology lesson when we were twelve. My mother had already explained sex to me when I was younger, but when our teacher gave us the full details we were unanimously disgusted, and scandalised that people as respectable as our parents should have sunk so low. I say this to make the point that we mustn't conclude something is wrong just because many of us initially *feel* it is wrong. (And also, perhaps, to illustrate the fact that at the age when I was genuinely homophobic I was also strongly heterophobic.)

I tried *Maurice* again a few years later, when I was

about seventeen. I attempted to come with a more open mind, and I was amply rewarded. This time I loved it and found it a profoundly moving book.

A year or so after that, before going up to university, I went to live in Paris for a few months. Some friends took me to a gay nightclub where we were entertained by slick and very professional drag queens and where, for the first time, I met a large number of openly gay people. We went back for drinks to the house of one particular male couple. They seemed middle-aged to me, but I suppose they might have been in their thirties or a little older. I thought them quite delightful. They had been together for some time, and had an apparently stable and mono-gamous relationship; one fulfilled a domestic role, cooking and running the house, while the other went out to work to support them both. Such a set-up may seem impossibly old-fashioned and cosy nowadays. To me, as a young Christian teenager in the seventies, it seemed fine.

So by the time I went to university I had discovered that I liked homosexual people, and I believed homo-sexuality to be healthy, acceptable and normal. I had not done any Christian *thinking* on the subject. But my *feelings*, my instincts, were all in favour.

Chris was the first, and (apart from Shaun) the best friend I made at Oxford. He spotted me straight away as a vaguely enthusiastic but hopelessly ill-educated Christian, took me under his wing, and set about reading the Bible with me weekly to try to help me think my faith through. Sometime in that first year the subject of homosexuality came up. He happened to say that it was not an option for a Christian. I was appalled. I argued with him vigorously and told him in no uncertain terms that he must be wrong. I probably accused him of rejecting people who had been born that way. I'm sure I must have told him he was bigoted. I refused to countenance his views. Patiently, graciously, he made me open my Bible and read what God has said.

Not once, not twice, but many times over several weeks.

Like most people, I don't like admitting I am wrong, and do not do it readily. But I had no choice. Rebellious I might have been; blind I was not. I had to concede that Chris was right and I was wrong. Active homosexual practice is not an option for a Christian.

I have spent a lot of time since then trying to understand why not.

CLARITY AND COMPASSION

One of the best books I have read on the subject of modern homosexuality from the Christian perspective is Thomas Schmidt's *Straight and Narrow*.[4] It is biblical, extremely well researched, and above all lives up to its claim for 'compassion and clarity in the homosexual debate'.

For, when it comes to moral debate, compassion and clarity are what the Christian and the Church need in equal measure. Society tends to err on the side of one or the other. Sometimes we have strong moral values, but are unkind to those who fail to live up to them. A hundred years ago no one was in much doubt that sex outside marriage was not appropriate Christian behaviour. But the price paid for this was that those – particularly women – who were caught out as having failed were treated harshly, sometimes cruelly, and given little chance of repentance and a fresh start. Their children suffered considerably as a result. Nowadays, those who don't live up to the ideal are treated far more compassionately, but consequently we seem to have forgotten that extramarital sex is wrong, so that 47 per cent of children in Britain are now born out of wedlock, with all the disadvantages and insecurity which that entails.[5] Again, it is innocent children who suffer.

There is no place for either of these errors in the Church. Sadly, because Christians are not perfect we are always likely to incline one way or the other, or both. Plenty of Victorian churchmen and women were as unkind and judgmental as the worst prudes of their day. Plenty of modern clergymen, bishops and theologians are as woolly, muddle-headed and unchristian in their thinking as the most mealy-mouthed politician trying to get elected on a 'liberal' ticket.[6]

Jesus, as always, gives us the supreme example of the two – compassion and clarity – held in perfect balance. John 8:2–11 relates the occasion when a group of upright, religious Jews brought to Jesus a woman who had been caught in the act of adultery. (Presumably this means her partner had been too. It is telling that only the woman was exposed.) Jesus accepts the despised outcast. He knows that, in some ways, she is not as bad as those who are judging her. And yet He makes no attempt to condone her behaviour. Adultery is wrong. She must stop.

This is the balance we must strike. We must teach the Bible accurately in every detail, but also in all its rounded fullness. On the one hand, if something is sinful we must say so; but on the other, we are all sinners so there is no room for complacency or self-righteousness in any of us.

THE BIBLICAL TEACHING

Let us start, then, with the clear biblical teaching on the subject. And, contrary to some popular opinion, there is no real ambiguity on the subject of the Bible and homosexuality. In this respect the debate about ordaining openly practising homosexuals is very different from the debate about the ordination of women. Over the ordination of women, as we have seen, it is possible conscientiously, legitimately and obediently to interpret the texts either way. When considering ordaining practising homosexuals it is not.

And very few people, on either side of the debate, seriously think it is. Let me give a couple of examples.

Some months ago Francis Gardom, who founded Cost of
Conscience, kindly asked me to take the platform with
him in a South London deanery synod open evening; the
two of us expounded the orthodox Christian morality on
homosexuality while a feminist and a gay priest appealed
for the Church to abandon her traditional teaching. We
were each given five or ten minutes to put forward our
case. The gay priest opened by telling us that he would
not be arguing from the Bible but from his own life
history and experience.[7]

Similarly Richard Kirker, founder of the Lesbian and
Gay Christian Movement, said on the radio recently that,
'Christians simply cannot be allowed to get away with
believing that the Bible is going to provide them with the
answer to this issue . . . You have to look elsewhere.'[8]

These are both typical. I have never yet heard anyone
convincingly argue the 'gay' cause from a coherent
biblical viewpoint.[9] For, although homosexuality is
mentioned less than a dozen times in the whole of the
Bible, every single reference to it is vehemently negative.

It is often argued that the Bible is only condemning
homosexual promiscuity, or homosexual rape, or the
breaking of ancient hospitality laws. If this is so (and,
sadly, it is very hard to be convinced) it would have been
helpful, to say the least, if God could have given us one
or two examples of a faithful, loving, sexually active gay
relationship which He found acceptable. He does not.

Whenever homosexuality is referred to in the Bible, it
is because it is being condemned. Hard though this seems
when we first look at it, it does make sense in the context
of the biblical teaching about the sexes.

Genesis 2

The essence of the biblical teaching on homosexuality is,
naturally enough, found in the passage about the creating
of two sexes in Genesis 2 (page 13). As we have seen, this
tells us much about men and women. It also tells us a

considerable amount about men, or women, on their own. It *was not good* for man to be on his own. He needed somebody different, not somebody the same. The whole thesis of this book is that male and female are complementary. We need each other.[10]

This is true in society, at work, in the family, and in marriage and sexual intercourse, which in many ways is the epitome of all social intercourse. God has created us to relate, supremely, to someone who is other, dissimilar, distinct from ourselves. He has created lovers, partners, parents to be different from each other, not the same; complementary, not symmetrical; *'appropriate'* (Genesis 2:18), not identical. When two human beings engage in the act of sex together they reflect God in the act of creation; the different persons becoming one in a loving, productive union. If this is a symbol of God Himself we distort it at our peril.

Now, as explained in the chapter on 'Singleness', there is liberty in the New Testament to forgo that most intimate of human relationships, the erotic, in favour of a whole-hearted relationship with God. But if we choose to become one flesh with another human being, that human being is to be different from ourselves.

We can see various reasons for this, both in generalisations and in specific instances of people we know. For example, there is a saying that 'men's love is stronger, women's lasts longer'. Clearly, as with all generalisations, there are plenty of exceptions. But let us concede, for the sake of argument, the observation that men love more passionately, and women love more permanently. One can see the evolutionary purpose to this when one considers that the male of the species needs to spread his seed as widely as possible for his genes to continue; an urgent sexual desire is an evolutionary advantage to the male. Women, on the other hand, need to provide their young with stability and security to aid their survival; a preference for a long-lasting 'meaningful' relationship makes evolutionary sense in a female. It is probably true, broadly speaking across different cultures in different ages, that men are more likely to be tempted to have extra-marital affairs, enjoying sex for its own sake; whereas women seem more naturally to set a high premium on fidelity, seeing sex as part of friendship and commitment.

If God has made one sex more inclined towards emotional stability and fidelity, and the other more interested in giving the relationship sexual expression, then same-sex relationships may become unbalanced. Homosexual men are likely to become more interested in the sexual act, with more and more different partners. Homosexual women are going to have stabler and more emotionally satisfying relationships, but find it harder to sustain interest in giving them sexual expression. Which, again broadly speaking, is exactly what happens.[11] It is observably true that the male homosexual lifestyle is one of considerably more promiscuity than the average heterosexual one. Is this not precisely what we would expect? (Obviously, as with all generalisations, there are exceptions to the rule: I know lesbians who have several partners a night, and gay men with committed, faithful and stable relationships.)

To go from the general to the particular, I imagine every reader is acquainted with successful marriages which are based to a large extent on the complementarity of the two people involved. This is particularly important in the bringing up of children. Shaun and I conform to one particular sexual stereotype in that I am fairly 'touchy-feely' and emotionally extravagant, whereas he is much more reserved and careful. Both qualities have something to recommend them, and both are necessary in the bringing up of children. I can teach our offspring that they can be emotionally open, and, in the appropriate social context, say anything they like. Shaun can teach them qualities of discipline and self-control.

One of our sons is very like his father with regard to his feelings; his natural inclination is to pay little attention to his emotions and just get on with life. Left unchecked, this can be quite dangerous. Once or twice he has found himself suddenly overwhelmed by powerful negative feelings which he had no idea were creeping up on him. We have told him that he sometimes needs to be aware of his feelings and give expression to them, and it has been delightful, and very exciting, to see the maturing process as he goes against his natural grain and becomes far more expressive and self-aware. In one parent he sees someone like himself, so he knows he is normal and lovable and acceptable; in the other he sees someone unlike himself, so he can see how to change. I believe it is not an exaggeration to say that such a boy – by no means untypical – brought up by two men, two people like himself, would almost certainly grow up emotionally crippled. Reared by two women, both different from himself, he would probably feel that his natural reserve made him odd or even inferior.

Of course, two people of the same sex can have very different, complementary personalities. But there are other implications. A boy brought up by two lesbians grows up without an immediate domestic role-model. This is true even if his mother and her partner have close male friends or 'uncles' for him to relate to. The unit he experiences teaches him that a family, and, by extension, society itself, can function perfectly well without someone like him. He is not essential. He is freed from responsibility; he is also denied any vital role. He may grow up thinking his whole purpose is pleasure, since no one needs him for anything. He may have low self-esteem, because no one depends on him. The potential is there for him to feel both inadequate and irresponsible, as a result of not having an essential role-model of his own sex in his childhood household.

No doubt we can all think of people brought up by widowed mothers, or single fathers, or indeed by homosexuals, who have grown up to be happy, rounded, emotionally healthy people. God can work in all circumstances, and mercifully make provision for our inadequacies. But the normal way He does this is by providing children with two complementary parents, of different sexes; when this is not possible we can trust God to help us, but we should not expect Him necessarily to bail us out if we deliberately flout His laws.

Genesis 2 is the core of the biblical teaching on the norm of sexual complementarity. But God can make exceptions to the norm. He does this in 1 Corinthians 7 when Paul says quite clearly that not everyone needs to get married. So if God had given us any positive examples of same-sex sexual activity we could say that Genesis 1 is merely a generalisation, and exceptions are morally legitimate.

Let us look at the Bible's instances of such activity.

Genesis 19 and Judges 19

These are the first references to specifically homosexual activity. The two episodes are remarkably similar. And pretty shocking stuff they are too, to the modern reader.

In the Genesis passage, Lot is visited, at his home in Sodom (from which the term sodomy has its origin) by two male guests. In the Judges story a traveller arrives at Gibeah with his concubine and servant and asks for hospitality from a resident. On both occasions men of the city surround the house and demand sex with the male guest or guests. Lot copes with this by offering his virgin daughters for the men to rape instead. The host in Gibeah proffers his own virgin daughter and his visitor's concubine. The men of Sodom refuse the substitutes, while the men of Gibeah reluctantly accept the concubine, and then rape her to death.

The unavoidable conclusion from both accounts is that the hosts, in both Old Testament episodes, were in no doubt whatsoever that almost anything – including the rape of virgin girls and even manslaughter – was preferable to homosexual sex.

Of course, one could not argue from these stories alone that all forms of homosexual sex are wrong. First and foremost they are talking about sexual force and abuse, and no reputable campaigner for gay rights would dream of demanding that this kind of homosexuality should be considered acceptable. The majority of gay rights activists are asking for the right to have adult consensual sex without being disapproved of. (It is true that many also consider promiscuous sex acceptable; and some promote the idea of 'intergenerational sex'[12] – what the rest of us would call pederasty or paedophilia – but the latter are not the majority.)

It has also been argued, with some conviction, that the reason Sodom and Gibeah were both treated so harshly by God after these episodes was not so much because the intended abuse was homosexual, as because it was an infringement of the rules of hospitality of the time. There is, however, some special pleading here. It is true that the requirements of hospitality were extremely important in a time and place where the withholding of aid to the traveller could result in his death. But the intended offence was undoubtedly homosexual. If there is nothing offensive about homosexuality *per se*, then demanding it of a guest would not have been seen as so scandalous.

But these arguments need not concern us too much. It is dangerous to argue any doctrine from a historical account. We are not told whether God approved of Lot's suggested substitute, or of the sacrifice of the unwilling concubine. I sincerely hope – speaking as a woman – that He did not. But I simply do not know, from this account, because it does not say.

These episodes may be of interest in the light of other teaching from the Bible on the subject, but in themselves they do not tell us much about the rights and wrongs of different forms of sex.

Leviticus 18:22; 20:13; 1 Kings 14:24; 15:12; 22:46;
Deuteronomy 23:17–18

These Old Testament passages condemn homosexuality
and male prostitution.

The verses in Kings and Deuteronomy tell us that God
considers homosexual temple prostitution detestable.
The Law in Leviticus lays down the death penalty for
any 'man who lies with a male as with a woman ... [it
is] an abomination; they shall be put to death' (20:13; also
18:22).

I have heard this explained away in the most creative
of ways. In one church discussion at which I was present
it was dismissed in a sentence by a member of the clergy
(himself gay), as 'just an Old Testament law'. When he
was pressed on this he said, 'No one takes any notice of
any of those any more.' He apparently considered God's
Law completely irrelevant. Yet Jesus said heaven and
earth would pass away before one jot or tittle of the Law
(Matthew 5:17–20).

If Old Testament Law is really irrelevant we ought to
cut it out of our Bibles. But it is not. A vital purpose of
God's Law is to tell us about His character. His character
does not change. If He considered sexual immorality an
abomination several thousand years ago the chances are
He still does not like it today.

We still need the Law to guide us and tell us what
God is like. But for the purposes of this chapter we need
not dwell on a detailed application of Leviticus. A fuller
treatment of these references can be found in books
devoted to the subject of homosexuality.[13] If this were all
the Bible had to say about it the Church might have
serious doubts about whether homosexuality is always
wrong.

But the Christian understanding of homosexuality is
not primarily derived from the Old Testament texts. It is
strange how many, even Christians, think it is. In a
conversation I was having with my prayer partner some

months ago (rather along the lines of Chris's conversation with me all those years ago) my friend said, 'If homosexuality is so wrong, why is it never mentioned in the New Testament?' She was amazed when I told her it is. A vicar's wife had also told her that female homosexuality is never referred to in the Bible, which of course it is.

1 Corinthians 6:9–10; 1 Timothy 1:9–10; Romans 1:26–7

It is sometimes claimed that, since Jesus never condemned homosexuality, we should not either. The fact that Paul did so simply proves what a misguided – and unchristian – old codger he was. We need to be more like Christ and accept the gay lifestyle.

But (apart from the fact that if we dismiss what Jesus's friends and apostles tell us we shall have no Christianity left) it is unthinkable that Our Lord Himself would have accepted something which the Old Testament condemns. On questions of morality, He obeyed the Old Testament in every particular. He never accepted as permissible sexual behaviour which the Old Testament forbids.

It stands to reason that we have no record of His addressing the question of homosexuality. Quite simply, we have no record of His coming into contact with any practising homosexuals. His ministry was among the chosen, the children of Israel, the Jews, who all *knew* homosexuality was wrong, 'an abomination', because they had been brought up in the light of Leviticus 20:13. You do not need to tell people who can see, that the sky is blue. He never addressed the question of intergenerational sex either, or rape or torture or patricide or suicide, or the nuclear destruction of a vulnerable nation. These things did not cross His path. Nor did homosexual practice.

Jesus took it for granted that those who were not married would not be sexually active (Matthew 19:1–12). Interestingly, Martin Hallett, once an active homosexual, said, 'When I became a committed Christian, it was looking at the life of Jesus and the moral issues He addressed which convinced me that He would not be happy with my homosexual relationships.'[14]

God had already ruled out homosexual acts, and that was enough for His Jewish hearers. It would never have occurred to any of them that it might be acceptable. It was not until the gospel went to Gentiles, with Gentile moral standards, that the question arose again. This is why it is Paul, the apostle to the Gentiles, who deals with it. And each time he mentions it he roundly condemns it, just as the writer of Leviticus had.

> Don't you know that the unrighteous will not inherit the Kingdom of God? Don't be deceived: neither fornicators nor idolaters, nor adulterers, nor passive homosexuals (*malakoi*, 'effeminates') nor active homosexuals (*arsenokoitai*, 'those who lie with men'), nor thieves, nor the greedy, nor drunkards, nor slanderers, nor extortioners, will inherit the Kingdom of God.
>
> (1 Corinthians 6:9–10)

> . . . the law is laid down for the lawless and unruly, for the impious and for sinners, for the unholy and profane, for parricides and matricides, for murderers, fornicators, homosexuals (*arsenokoitai*), kidnappers, liars, perjurers, and anything else which is contrary to healthy teaching, according to the glorious Gospel of the blessed God with which I was entrusted.
>
> (1 Timothy 1:9–10)

There does not seem much doubt about it. Paul does not see homosexual activity as a Christian way of life.

The most powerful passage is in Romans 1:26–7:

> Therefore [because people refused to acknowledge the existence and sovereignty of God] God gave them up to dishonourable passions. Even their women ex-

changed natural relations for unnatural ones. Similarly the men abandoned the natural use of women and burned in desire for each other, men committing shameful things with other men and receiving back in themselves the due penalty for their error.

It is a description of our time. Widespread atheism and apostasy in Western civilisation have gone hand in hand with an escalating increase in homosexuality, certainly in its tolerance and probably in its practice. This is true even among women. And, sadly and most tragically, this has resulted in terrible consequences for the homosexual community in the form of disease and early death, particularly with the onset of AIDS.

The whole of society is to blame. It is not individual homosexuals, but an entire nation which has turned away from God, which must take responsibility for the breakdown of our morals. When HIV and AIDS were first diagnosed many people asked the question, 'Is AIDS God's punishment on homosexuality?' Not according to Romans, it isn't. AIDS – and indeed many other sexually transmitted diseases, as well as psychological and emotional suffering – are the natural consequences of sexual promiscuity. Paul's explanation is that it is abandonment to homosexuality itself which is God's punishment for rebellion. The individual homosexual is the casualty, not the culprit.

Our hearts should burn with compassion for those who are reaping the harvest of our godless culture. If Paul is right in describing the homosexual lifestyle as more of a punishment than a sin, our responsibility towards homosexuals themselves is considerable and awesome.

I have a dear friend who has struggled with homosexuality all his adult life. As well as emotional problems with regard to his failed marriage and confused children, he has endured continual psychiatric strain and several suicide attempts. The last time I heard from him he had 'given himself up' to his homosexuality. Knowing him as I do, I very much doubt that it will make him happy. Recently he told me that he needed psychiatric help because he had tried to do as friends in his church advised, and cope for a whole year without sex. This had messed him up so badly that he needed hospitalisation. I was profoundly shocked: I know plenty of heterosexual Christians who find abstinence very difficult, but I don't know any who think it would render them in need of psychiatric medication. It seems to me that my friend is in the grip of something more painful and damaging than the lust experienced by my heterosexual friends. It is senseless and uncaring to see this as his fault. But it is equally senseless and uncaring to think that it doesn't matter, or to believe that, if we were only to find homosexuality acceptable, there would be no problem.

Same-sex love in the Bible

But what about other biblical passages describing people of the same sex who loved each other? Twice on the radio in the last few months I have heard those campaigning for a more relaxed moral attitude in the Church referring to 'homosexuals' in the Bible. The examples given were of Ruth and Naomi, and David and Jonathan.

Ruth and Naomi certainly loved each other. 'Where you go I will go,' Ruth said to her mother-in-law, as she clung to her. 'Your people will be my people, and your God my God. Where you die I shall die, and there shall I be buried. May the Lord deal with me, no matter how severely, if anything separates us' (Ruth 1:14–17).

The love between David and Jonathan is even more remarkable. Jonathan was 'one in the spirit' with David, and loved him as himself (1 Samuel 18:1). David said of Jonathan, after his death: 'I grieve for you, Jonathan my brother; you were very dear to me. Your love for me was wonderful, more wonderful than that of women' (2 Samuel 1:26). But to claim that such love was 'homo-

sexual', in the way we understand the word, is such a
distortion as to be almost heartbreaking. The love the two
men felt for each other was strong, even passionate; it
was also precious, good, and as far as we know wholly
approved by God.

And there is no evidence at all that it was 'homosexual', or indeed that it would ever have occurred
to either David or Jonathan that there was anything
sexual or erotic about their love at all. I have been asked
whether I think David and Jonathan were ever homo-
sexually tempted. I have no idea, but I very much doubt
that the idea ever crossed their minds. The fact that we
can no longer contemplate love between two people
without imagining them in bed together shows how
impoverished our society has become.

I was on one of the radio shows when this example
was given,[15] and I protested at the innuendo put on it.
Nowhere does the account suggest that David and
Jonathan were lovers, and given the Jewish context, such
an idea is preposterous. When I said this, my fellow guest
said that there is more to homosexuality than homosexual acts – and he is in a better position than I am to
know this. But it is only homosexual *acts* that are wrong.
Love between two men is not wrong. If this is what is
meant by homosexuality I hope none of us has any objection to it. God certainly does not. But 'homosexuality'
does not normally mean love between two men, just as
incest does not mean love between a brother and sister.
Neither of these is wrong. What is wrong is sexual
intercourse between these people.

When my father was at school he shared a study with
his best friend, Frank. He and Frank loved each other
dearly. Frank gave his life for his country during the war,
and even now, nearly sixty years on, my father cannot
talk about Frank, or look at his much-treasured letters,
without tears. The suggestion that there could have been
anything 'homosexual' about this love between them is
so outrageous as to be grotesque. The fact that I know

very few men of my own age who would be able to admit
to such a love says something profoundly sad about the
present day, and illustrates how one 'freedom' (to have
homosexual sex) can deny us another (to love our friends
deeply).

When I was at university my best friend from school
wrote to me saying, 'I love you, Anne.' A friend saw
her letter on my desk and teased me. I ignored him,
assuming he had no experience of such friendship.
Only half a generation has passed since then, but I do
not believe two women could write to each other so
unselfconsciously today.

There is no doubt about the biblical attitude to same-sex
genital intercourse. It is wrong. The assumption of this
book – and of the Church throughout the ages – is that
the Bible is God's living word, and should be obeyed.
The inevitable conclusion of this is that it is not a
Christian option to be a practising gay or lesbian.

Nevertheless, we must immediately follow this up by
saying two things. First, homosexual *activity* is a sin. But
there is nothing in the Bible to suggest that homosexual
temptation is sinful. If you believe you have a homosexual
orientation there is no reason to feel guilty or shameful
or that there is any need to hide the fact. You may choose
to keep quiet about it, and certainly your sexual orientation is not something you are obliged to share if you
prefer to keep it to yourself; no one has the right to 'out'
you, or publicise the way you feel. Indeed, if you
maintain a Christian lifestyle no one will ever be able to.
I have a clergyman friend who thinks he is homosexual,
but he has never put his desires to the test, nor told
anyone other than a few close friends. OutRage! will
never be able to expose or embarrass him because there
is no sexual behaviour in his private life of which he
needs to be ashamed.

We are told that Jesus was tempted in every way, just
as we are (Hebrews 4:15). I imagine this means He knew

and understood homosexual temptation too. And, as the writer to the Hebrews makes quite clear, Jesus was without sin; so temptation in itself cannot be sinful.

So we must make a distinction between those who choose a homosexual lifestyle and those who find themselves – usually involuntarily – with homosexual desires or orientation. We have looked in an earlier chapter at discriminating against people on the basis of who they are, and why it is wrong. This is very different from discriminating against what people choose to do.

It is acceptable, in certain circumstances, to 'discriminate' against some forms of behaviour. I can say, when choosing a nanny, that I don't want one who smokes, uses her fork like a spoon, or has sex with her boyfriend. This is reasonable and fair. I might think her example would have a negative effect on my children; and she does not have to smoke, scoop up her peas, or have sex if the job is important enough to her. This is not the same as saying I won't employ her because she is black, or Scottish, or anything else which it is not within her power to change.

Similarly, there is a world of difference between homosexual *practice*, and homosexual *orientation*. The Church of England has always recognised that it is not appropriate to employ, as a minister within the Church, anyone who persistently and unrepentantly engages in extramarital sex, whether heterosexual or homosexual. In other words, we cannot and should not ordain practising homosexuals. But if someone finds himself with a homosexual orientation this should never in itself be considered a bar to ordination. Indeed, it would be a great shame for the rest of us if we had none amongst the ordained clergy who had experienced and understood homosexual temptation.

Second, as we have seen, homosexual activity is a sin. But so is lying, being greedy, disobeying our parents, or malicious gossip. These are all mentioned, by Paul, in almost the same breath as homosexuality (Romans 1:29–

31). Which one of us can cast the first stone? I have been appalled by the self-righteousness of some in the Church who seem to think they are being biblical in expressing their hatred of homosexuality – and, dare I say it, sometimes of homosexuals themselves. One otherwise delightful, charming, godly friend of mine shocked and sickened me recently when we were discussing the proposed lowering of the age of consent for homosexual sex. I could hardly believe my ears. 'I think they should put them all on an island,' she said sweetly, 'and drop a bomb on them.'

This is not Christian. We are commanded to love one another (John 13:34–5), not to be self-righteous (Luke 18:14), and to care for the oppressed. Jesus often condemned hypocrisy and self-righteousness more than prostitution and fraud. By extension, He might have been far more scathing today in exposing homophobia than homosexuality.

Nevertheless, that does not make homosexuality right. Somehow we must hold in tension the Christian teaching to care for others, particularly the despised and rejected, with the moral teaching that extramarital sex is wrong.

THE GAY PHILOSOPHY

In talking and writing about the issue of homosexuality I have frequently been dismayed and saddened by a common response.

Let me give an analogy. I love riding. I know it is an absurdly dangerous sport but I love it anyway. Because of this I need to know how dangerous it is. If a journalist were to write an article telling me that every time I get on a horse I have a one in a hundred chance of killing myself (say), I should be grateful. I would probably still keep getting on the creatures, but I might employ greater precautions, abstaining while I have young children in case they are left motherless, and taking extra safety

measures for my children when they decide to follow
my ridiculous example. The information has given me
greater freedom, and greater responsibility.

The article might also go on to tell me that riding is
incompatible with ballet dancing because it uses different
muscles, and I would then be in a position to make a
further choice. Which would I rather do? Again, I would
be indebted to the journalist. I very much doubt that
many equestrian enthusiasts would object to a piece like
this, or feel threatened by it, or bother to put pen to paper
to protest.

But try writing an article suggesting that there are risks
associated with homosexual activity. Dare to imply, moreover, that it is incompatible with any other choice, for
instance Christianity. You will receive a backlash of angry,
hurt letters; you will probably be the subject of
complaints to the Press Complaints Commission; you
will be accused of homophobia; and most distressing of
all, almost all homosexuals reading your article will
assume that you don't like them.

One could suggest a number of reasons why this is so.
Homosexual people feel hurt and unloved already, so are
more sensitive than people who simply ride horses;
society has condemned homosexuality for so long that
homosexuals are understandably likely to assume they
are being criticised. And so on. But I understood this
phenomenon far better after hearing a critique on contemporary 'gay philosophy' by the journalist Rachel
Tingle. The gay movement which was born in the sixties
in America has an ideology. This ideology is threatened
when certain things are said, even if they are facts published in the interests of truth and compassion. So an
article which is intended as objective and informative can
be perceived by the gay community as a statement of
war.

Obviously many, probably most, gay people just want
to get on with their lives quietly without being intimi-
dated and persecuted. Nonetheless there is a political

militancy behind gay rights which has profoundly influenced our thinking in the late twentieth century. It has successfully led us to make assumptions which may be based more on 'political correctness' than on actual fact. These are important to the gay rights movement in its aim to persuade the rest of us to accept homosexuality as a valid alternative.

None of these assumptions makes any difference to the biblical moral position on homosexuality. Whether or not you can change your sexual orientation does not alter the fact that homosexual practice is always wrong. But it makes a very big difference to individual homosexuals, especially if they are trying to lead Christian lives. For this reason, we need to examine some of these assumptions and challenge them if they cannot be substantiated.

1. Homosexuals are born homosexual

This is a double-edged sword from the gay rights point of view. In an age of abortion-on-demand, if such a thing as a 'gay gene' or gay biology could be identified prenatally many parents would exercise their 'right' to the termination of a potentially homosexual baby. (I hope it goes without saying that this would be a monstrous abuse of human rights, and must be vigorously opposed by the Church.) Also, some gays prefer to suggest that homosexuality is a positive life choice. But the advantage of the genetic assumption is that it enables homosexuality to associate with the legacy of the American Civil Rights Movement. If people are born gay it is part of their essential, involuntary identity, like being black, or female; it has all the right political overtones.

But there is no conclusive proof of any biological cause for homosexuality. Significantly, studies done before the gay rights movement had politicised homosexual origins indicated that only 9 per cent of gay people thought they had been born gay. By the 1980s, this figure had risen to

35 per cent.[16] Nevertheless, in 1993 researchers at the New York State Psychiatric Institute found 'no evidence to support the biologic theory'.[17]

A number of factors which are nothing to do with biology or genetics are known to increase the incidence of homosexuality. One study says that being raised in a town increases the chances threefold.[18] A 'same-sex psychological deficit' or lack of the same-sex parent, through absence, death, or emotional withdrawal, is known to cause a longing for intimacy with a same-sex partner, which can take the form of homosexuality. Many researchers think there is a significant – and alarming – link between 'inappropriate sexual interference' of children and young people by adults, and the subsequent prevalence of homosexuality in those who have been abused. (The abuse can be as simple as subjecting a child to pornographic pictures or images.) There is considerable evidence to suggest that homosexuality can be caused, at least partly, by external factors.

And increasingly, as it becomes fashionable, it can simply be chosen as a trendy thing to be. The term LUG – Lesbian Until Graduation – is now used on some American campuses for women who opt for a homosexual period so they can get their studies done without male interference, before settling down into marriage and family life once they have their careers under way.

2. *Everyone must have sex*

This assumption is not, of course, confined to the gay philosophy. But it is crucial to it. Once celibacy is seen as a valid alternative to sexual activity, one of the most important justifications for the gay movement collapses.

But the belief that we must have sex is not a Christian one. Paul specifically says that celibacy is good (1 Corinthians 7:1; see pages 180–81). No harm will ever come to us from voluntary, conscientious sexual abstention. We sometimes look back on previous centuries, and marvel at how stupid they were. I wonder what future generations will think of our unscientific but widely held superstition that sex is necessary to our well-being, as well as unavoidable, and that abstinence is not only downright impossible but also dangerous and harmful.

3. Homosexuals cannot change

It is even seen as an abuse of gay rights to suggest that they can. I have frequently heard Christian counselling centres written off (by gay groups) as 'ex-gay'. Strictly speaking, this simply means some of the counsellors have led a homosexual life and now turned their backs on it. But the reason it is such a venomous criticism is because of the implication that it is possible to change the orientation itself, which some 'ex-gays' have done.

In 1994 the American Psychiatric Association tabled a motion to discourage psychiatrists from helping patients to work towards heterosexuality.[19] This was done for political reasons rather than scientific or medical ones: it is part of the propaganda which is crucial to the gay rights movement. I know homosexuals who have experienced change in their orientation (for instance Lance, mentioned later in this chapter) who are then told by other homosexuals that they cannot have been truly homosexual in the first place.

This denies homosexuals the medical help and expertise to which they have a right. Christians believe God can change us. He always changes us to some degree when we turn to Him and obey Him. Homosexuals do sometimes experience an alteration in their orientation, particularly as a result of conversion to Christ. It is not an inevitable result of obedience to God, and may depend on a number of factors, including age and previous experience (particularly sexual experience). But it can and does happen.

4. Homosexuals have no choice

This follows on from the first three. If homosexuals are born, not made, must have sex, and cannot change their orientation, then it is clearly unjust to discriminate against anyone on the grounds of homosexual practice. And this is increasingly being accepted in European law. Churches, Christian youth groups and Sunday schools may soon not be able to turn down would-be 'Christian' workers who are living flagrantly unchristian lives.

Another implication of this philosophy is that it is impossible to persuade or seduce young people to the gay way of life, because the tendency either is latent in them or it is not. This can be a potent argument for legalising intergenerational sex.

Again, the gay movement has been remarkably successful in getting this message across. I was watching a television programme the other day in which working-class men were being filmed talking in a pub. They were discussing homosexuality and one of them said, in passing, 'I know they can't help it.' It is widely accepted now that homosexual activity is involuntary.

5. Homosexuals are 10 per cent of the population

This figure was first suggested as a result of a survey done by Kinsey in 1948.[20] Again, it is important to the gay rights movement. If, in a class of thirty children three of them are latently, inherently homosexual, some kind of appropriate sex education for homosexual children ought to be provided.

The idea has caught on. I read an interview in the *Daily Telegraph* with a prominent gay who explained homophobia by saying that if 80 per cent of the population is heterosexual and 20 per cent is homosexual, the majority is going to give the minority a hard time. His assumed statistic, which he probably believes himself, went unchallenged by his interviewer.[21]

But Kinsey's findings were discredited years ago.[22] It was a highly flawed study, using an unrepresentative sample of volunteers, which included sex offenders. Over and over again recent, detailed and far more reputable studies have shown homosexual incidence to be between 1 and 3 per cent of the adult male population (on average about 1.5), and rather less than 1 per cent of the female population.[23] And yet the myth persists. In 1996, publicity for the Lesbian and Gay Christian Movement claimed that 10 per cent of the population is gay. If the LGCM is genuinely unaware of the more recent figures and research it is disturbing. If it is deliberately suppressing the truth it is even more so.

6. Homosexuals must 'come out'

This is important to help promote homosexual conscious-ness, increase the numbers of visible homosexuals, raise the profile of gay rights, and make people part of an inclusive, supportive gay community of which they will want to be a member. It also makes it less likely that they will want to leave their homosexuality, and indeed harder for them to do so.

'Coming out' is done in the name of honesty and integrity, and one sometimes gets the impression that 'a failure to come out' is seen by the homosexual community as the only sin which needs repentance. This philosophy has sometimes led to 'outing' others – making their homosexual orientation public against their will. Many gays disapprove of this. It is an infringement of privacy and can cause considerable distress.

7. Gay is just like straight

The only difference, of course, is the sexes of the people involved. This was certainly what I assumed until I knew more about the gay lifestyle; that gay couples are much like others, wanting stability, fidelity, domesticity, and perhaps children if possible. The reality sometimes seems rather different.

Certainly I have never heard of any two gay men who were virgins when they met and have stayed faithful to each other, who have therefore only had each other as sexual partners. However, I can think of dozens of heterosexual couples, in my acquaintance alone, of whom this is true (though admittedly they are almost all Christians).

A study in 1978 found that three-quarters of male homosexuals had had more than a hundred partners, and over a quarter had had more than a thousand.[24] Some studies cite men having sex with up to 25 partners a day.

These are only statistics, and we should always be careful of them; naturally there are gay people who are not interested in casual sex. But even a cursory reading of gay literature frequently reveals the same trend. *The A to Z of Gay Sex* (incidentally promoted by the Lesbian and Gay Christian Movement) says, 'Who said that human beings are supposed to be monogamous, anyway? Why, some boring old fart in the Bible, that's who!' Edmund White, in his autobiographical book, *The Farewell Symphony*, talks of reaching the 'thousand' mark, and describes a homosexual friend who, every month, would invite to his flat the thirty new people he had had sex with that month. White does not even comment on this habit; he seems to consider it commonplace.[25] A friend of ours, who has been in and out of the gay lifestyle, talks of several partners a night, not even exchanging names as they have a few minutes of sex in a public lavatory before moving on. The last time I was at a party full of lesbians, two who had just met had sex in the cubicle next to mine in the Ladies, and talked freely about it over the canapés five minutes later.

A number of my heterosexual friends are promiscuous, but I know none who lives like this.

8. Gay is good

This is the most painful item to write about, and yet perhaps the most important. It will be perceived as the most homophobic, though in fact is the most necessary for reasons of compassion towards homosexuals.

The truth is this: the homosexual life can be an extremely harsh one. Even many homosexuals admit this. A gay friend once told me he did not know a single homosexual who would not become heterosexual overnight if he could. This is probably less true than it was now that homosexuality is more widely accepted, but even so, in a recent survey 34 per cent of gay men *admitted* regret at not being heterosexual.[26]

The gay lifestyle has implications. Promiscuous sex is a health hazard. So is anal sex. When alternated with oral sex, with different partners, it is even more so. The combination of the three, widely common in the gay community, is literally lethal. Others have described in detail the sexual practices common among homosexuals.[27] I have no intention of doing so here, but if the following resultant statistics seem farfetched, the sceptical reader need only set them in context by researching the day-to-day realities of gay sex, and they will seem not only unsurprising but perhaps almost inevitable.

One study has estimated that the life expectancy of an active homosexual is reduced by *25 to 30* years as a result of regular homosexual intercourse. Another, extensive, study done in 1994 and written up in an American medical journal, found that the life expectancy of a gay man *without HIV* is 42 years (with HIV it is 39). Fewer than 2 per cent of active homosexuals survive to old age, defined as 65 or older (compared with 80 per cent of married men and 85 per cent of married women).[28] Alcohol and drug abuse, violent death, depression, sexually transmitted diseases and psychiatric disorders are all far more common amongst the homosexual community.[29] Gays are twenty-four times more likely to commit suicide.[30]

Again, of course, these are 'mere' statistics. Sometimes statistics need interpretation. The 1994 survey, for instance, was based on obituaries (admittedly over 7,000) in the gay press; it is conceivable that gays who are well known enough to be written about are those who lead a more promiscuous life than those who live quietly at home. However, these statistics are all very extensively and reputably researched, and must not be ignored.

Schmidt sums them up by imagining a household of ten average American homosexuals. He bases his findings on studies which are either neutral or sympathetic to the gay cause, and consistently opts for the most 'homosympathetic' statistic. Statistically speaking, the composition of the household would be as follows: four are in relationships, of whom only one is faithful to his partner and he will not be by the end of the year; six have regular sex with strangers, and the whole group averages two partners per month per person; three take part in orgies, one is a sado-masochist, one a paedophile; three are alcoholics, four have a history of acute depression, five use illegal drugs; three have seriously contemplated suicide and two have attempted it; eight have a history of sexually transmitted diseases, eight carry infectious pathogens, at least three are HIV positive and one has AIDS.[31] Presumably none will survive to old age.

These figures will be greeted with howls of incredulity and cries of 'homophobia'. Fair enough. I would not want you to be persuaded simply by my say-so. I was not convinced the first time I read it. It is right to be sceptical. Look at the research for yourself. If you are gay I would particularly urge you to do so. It is well-attested, compelling and very frightening. And you have a right to know.

In the meantime, think of your own gay friends. How many of them have lasted to old age? I think of some of mine. Of the first half dozen that come to mind: one is young and happy; two have lives that almost anyone would describe as 'screwed up'; one is in regular need of psychiatric help; two are dead. I do not like seeing my friends suffer like this. Nor do I like losing them in this way. It makes me increasingly angry that more was not done to help them. White's *The Farewell Symphony* is so called because death has claimed so many of his gay friends that he is, symbolically, the only one left.

But if these statistics are true, why are they not more widely known? Why are gay people, and young people, not made aware of the risks? Why? Because it sounds 'homophobic', that's why. If the government withheld, for political reasons, information about the dangers of smoking, it would (rightly) provoke an outcry. But if it were to make available what is known about the dangers of the homosexual lifestyle it would be hated, picketed, lobbied, despised, targeted as homophobic and voted out at the next election.

None of the above makes any difference to the biblical teaching on homosexuality. But it certainly throws light on Paul's assessment of gay life in Romans 1.

Tragically, the gay life is all too frequently anything but gay.

9. Moral is the opposite of caring

The reason God hates the sin is because He loves the sinner. Sadly, however, the society we live in now believes the terrible lie that if the Church says you are doing something wrong, it must be because the Church hates you.

Jesus was outspoken in His condemnation of sin, but loving and compassionate in His acceptance of sinners. The Church, at her best, echoes this. Christians were among the first to care for those with AIDS, nursing them and running hospices for those who were dying. This is as it must be. Homosexual practice is wrong. But we must love and accept practising homosexuals.

THE PRACTICAL IMPLICATIONS

It is a Christian principle that we should always be more critical of ourselves than others (Matthew 7:1–5). Paul's description of homosexuality in Romans 1 is immediately followed by a thundering exposé of judgmentalism. Since the vast majority of readers will be heterosexual, it stands to reason that we should be far quicker to condemn heterosexual sins than homosexual ones. And because most of us are heterosexual, the overwhelming majority of sexual sins – fornication, infidelity, lust, rape, adultery, and child abuse – are committed by heterosexuals. Some, for instance adultery, do far more obvious damage to innocent people than many homosexual sins. Yet over and over again I have heard those engaged in heterosexual sin condemning homosexuals. I have one friend, who broke up someone else's marriage with his adultery, who applauds the Church for its moral stand on homosexuality; and another, who lives with her boyfriend, who says she agrees with the Church's teaching.

We must make clear God's view of homosexuality. But it is hard to do this in a Church which now all but accepts divorce and remarriage without comment. If we do not stand firm against other sexual failures we will rightly be called hypocritical.

Homosexuality in ourselves

First let me admit straight away that I speak from inexperience. This does not, in itself, mean I should not speak at all. There is a certain amount of posturing at the moment by heterosexuals in the Church trying to be politically correct, saying they cannot talk on the gay issue because they are not gay. This is nonsense. One does not need to have tried adultery to see the effect it has or expound what God says about it. If what I have to say is not particularly profound or helpful it is not because I am heterosexual. I know nothing of the struggles of singleness, having got married long before being single became a trial to me, but single friends have kindly told me they found the chapter on singleness in this book the best and most helpful one.

Now, as we have seen (Hebrews 4:15), to be tempted is not to sin. It is not wrong to long for a homosexual partnership, just as it is not wrong to fall in love with someone else's wife. Nor is it sinful to experience a homosexual orientation or desires which are outside our control. It is what we do with those temptations which will determine our godliness and shape our character.

The gay movement has had a profound effect on homosexual identity. Until modern times there seems to have been no concept of a 'homosexual person', either in the consciousness of society or in the mind of anyone who felt homosexual desire. There were homosexual *acts*. Some people committed them, or were tempted to. Many went through a phase, particularly as teenagers, of experiencing and sometimes acting on those desires. Many grew out of it, or combined it with marriage and children, as Oscar Wilde did.

But now there are homosexual *people*. Politically, of course, this has tremendous force. And on the personal level it can help homosexuals feel less wretched, lonely and isolated. But it can also be a trap. Nowadays, your homosexual desires are thought to define you as a person. It is no longer simply a question of how you feel – much less how you sometimes feel – but of *who you are*. You are not first and foremost a brother or a son, a milkman or a professor, perhaps not even primarily a Christian, but a *homosexual*. The implication is that there is no escaping it, ever. You can no more be free of homo-sexuality than a black woman can become a white man.

But this is not true. Some people have changed their orientation; others have found it possible to live a fulfilled and rounded life without sex. Homosexual people are being denied this freedom.

In addition, if anyone disapproves of homosexual acts it is now claimed that he or she must be 'homophobic'; the word is indiscriminately applied to anyone who expresses any reservations about homosexual activity. This is not only absurd, but pernicious. You may dislike smoking, and even forbid it in your house, but this does not mean you dislike smokers. There are those who disapprove of homosexuality, often for religious reasons, who do not necessarily dislike homosexuals any more than orthodox Jews dislike people who eat bacon. Recent studies have confirmed that the majority of people[32] still consider homosexual acts to be wrong. If this is really because we are all homophobic the inevitable conclusion for the individual homosexual is that most people do not like him. This will make homosexuals feel closer bonds with the gay community, the one place they know they are accepted, but I can hardly believe it helps their self-esteem. The homosexual life is hard enough already without inventing homophobes who are not there.

Worse than either of these is the interpretation put on our relationship with God. If 'homosexual' is who you are, and gay sex is an involuntary part of your identity, then the unavoidable conclusion from God's prohibitions on gay sex is that He has forbidden you to *be*. Presumably this means even God is homophobic. He Himself does not like you. This is too terrible to bear. You have no choice but to rewrite God or be damned.

But none of this is true. God loves each and every individual. He gives us His laws because He loves us. They are wise, compassionate and right. I have several friends of homosexual orientation who have obeyed God and stayed chaste. Each of them, without exception, is convinced his life is much more blessed than it would have been had he given in to his desires.

Lance Pierson, the Christian writer and actor, realised he was homosexual at the age of fourteen. (He himself puts this down to having lost his father at an early age.) He grew up longing for an intimate sexual relationship with another man. Lance now believes he was very fortunate to be young at a time when homosexuality was still not generally acceptable. When he became a Christian at the age of eighteen he had not had any sexually active homosexual relationships. The Christian teaching he then received was clear: the options are heterosexual marriage or abstinence. At no stage did he feel rejected by this teaching because he realised the prohibition condemned homosexual *practice*, not people. He never expected his orientation to change, and after he became a Christian he assumed he would always be celibate.

Lance told very few people about his orientation, not because he was ashamed of it but because he didn't want to go through the teasing he had experienced at school. But he prayed earnestly, for ten years, that God would change him. And at about the age of twenty-eight or twenty-nine he found his feelings were indeed beginning to be different. He married Sue when he was thirty-two and has genuinely never looked back. He now has two teenage children and one of the happiest marriages I know.

He compares this, with chilling realism, with how things might have been if he had been twenty or thirty years younger and growing up today. He believes he would almost certainly have had some homosexual experiences before he encountered Christianity. It would have been almost impossible, humanly speaking, for him to have heard the gospel if he had been in a homosexual relationship, or involved in the gay culture. In addition, it would have been far harder for God to have changed his orientation if he had already led a homosexual life. He is in no doubt that, if he had not exercised the Christian gift of chastity which he found difficult and painful at the time, he would never have experienced the blessings he enjoys today. God's restrictions often seem harsh at the time, but He is loving and good and far wiser than we are.

Lance's is a very happy story. Other homosexual friends of mine have not had their prayers answered in such obvious ways. Another is thirty-six. He prefers to remain anonymous because he says there is far more to him than his homosexual orientation, and in the current climate many would consider his homosexuality the most important thing about him. He is chaste and celibate, and has never had a sexual relationship because he too has held fast to the Christian teaching on the subject. He does not think God will change his orientation now, and has given up expecting Him to.

Nevertheless, he is glad of, and thankful for, God's prohibitions on homosexual practice, though he has not found it easy. He has been in love, and ached to consummate the relationship. But when he considers the experiences of his non-Christian homosexual friends – the stress, the frequently short-term relationships, the grim reality – he thanks God for His commandments.

So, to the homosexual reader we must say, 'Don't give up on God.' The rest of us can only guess what struggles you will go through. But you are not alone. There are a number of organisations, listed at the end of the book,[33] run by and for those with a homosexual orientation who wish to live chaste Christian lives.

One of these counsellors, a very wise, loving man and homosexual himself, believes that the first step towards healing, for a homosexual, is to learn to love and accept yourself – and therefore, of course, to accept yourself as a homosexual. Perhaps this is why homosexuals describe such a feeling of wholeness and freedom when they 'come out', or join groups like the LGCM; because they suddenly feel accepted, first and foremost by themselves. Also why some find they can change their orientation when they turn to Christ, because at last they know they are lovable and loved as they are.

And don't necessarily believe what you are always being told, that your trials are much harder than everyone else's. To some extent, we all face lives of frustration. Very few people would describe themselves as perfectly content on this earth. Those who do, tend to do so not because everything around them is perfect, but because they have learnt to be content in any circumstances. Like Paul, they have learnt to rejoice whether well fed or hungry, in plenty or in want (Philippians 4:12).

I have heard it said that a homosexual faces more despair than other celibate, single Christians, because he or she must accept the prospect of *never* having a satisfying sexual relationship. But this is not necessarily so. It was what Lance thought, but he was changed. And there are others who share the same fate. Some fall in love with people who are already married. I once met a man who was so badly disfigured from a facial burn that he said no woman would ever look at him, let alone want to make love to him. Some are divorced against their will and consider remarriage wrong. Many women after wars have faced certain spinsterhood. These all experience a similar temporal 'hopelessness' with regard to sexual satisfaction.

But Jesus has not promised us fulfilment here and now. He *has* promised us that the wait, for Heaven, will be worth it.

Homosexuality in the Church

Jesus gives us a terrible warning. 'Be careful,' He says (Luke 17:1–3): 'If your brother sins, rebuke him.' If we fail Him in this, it would be better for us if a millstone were tied around our necks and we were cast into the sea.

Paul makes it quite clear that we are not to tolerate immorality within the Church (1 Corinthians 5:1–2). Church leaders especially are to be above reproach (1

Timothy 3:2). It is unacceptable to have elders in the Church, ordained members of the clergy, who are not living a life of Christian morality and example.

A homosexual lifestyle is not a Christian lifestyle. It is therefore wholly inappropriate to consider ordaining to the clergy those who deliberately, repeatedly and avowedly engage in acts of homosexual sex.

The official position of the Anglican Church is biblical. In 1987, General Synod almost unanimously passed a resolution affirming 'the biblical and traditional teaching on chastity and fidelity' and in particular affirmed 'that homosexual genital acts . . . are . . . to be met by a call to repentance'. In 1991 the House of Bishops produced a statement entitled 'Issues in Human Sexuality', which reiterated that scripture views 'sexual activity of any kind outside marriage . . . as sinful, and homosexual practice as especially dishonourable' (p. 18). It also makes it absolutely clear that 'the clergy cannot claim the liberty to enter into sexually active homophile relationships' (p. 45).

This document has been widely misrepresented. It is unambiguous in saying that homosexual practice is wrong, and that ordained members of the clergy are not free to engage in it. However, it also attempts – quite rightly – to be pastorally sensitive towards homosexuals among the laity who do not accept the biblical teaching. Its shortcoming is that it is not as clear as Jesus and Paul are in saying we must correct our brothers and sisters who are sinning. But it is right to make a distinction between Christian leaders and teachers who must be above reproach, and those who come to the Church for sustenance and fellowship who are not yet living Christian lives. The *reductio ad absurdum* of the statement to 'Gay is fine for the laity but not for the clergy' by groups as disparate as gay rights organisations, orthodox pressure groups and secular journalists, is at best ignorant and at worst mischief-making.

Sadly, however, the Church's practice is not living

up to its teaching. The last Anglican Archbishop of Canterbury, Lord Runcie, publicly admitted to knowingly ordaining practising homosexuals. There is a considerable amount of hypocrisy and political expediency with regard to the subject.

Some months ago Shaun and I visited a senior churchman who assured us that he, and indeed the entire unanimous House of Bishops, was orthodox on the subject, and in agreement with the Bishops' statement. We questioned him about one bishop in particular, and he assured us that this man had a biblical, orthodox understanding of homosexuality. Within a few weeks this same bishop had recommended in print that the Church should bless same-sex 'marriages'. Within a few months one of the authors of the statement retracted much of what had been said. At about the same time, the churchman we had visited appointed to his staff a clergyman who has been publicly and unashamedly proclaiming his own active homosexual lifestyle for many years. I remain completely mystified as to why he told us one thing and did another.

Nevertheless, Church practice is bound to be inferior to its doctrine. It always has been. The Church is full of sinners. The vast majority of Christians and churchgoers in Britain know that homosexuality is wrong. They are also, incidentally, dismayed and discouraged by the cowardice and muddle-headedness of their bishops and 'leaders' and pastors in what appears to them to be their failure to stand up for biblical morality.

If we care about our Church, we must pray. God listens to His people, and if we cry to Him to save our Church from heresy He will heed us. So we must make it a cause for urgent and continual entreaty.[34]

Homosexuality in society

Christians living in a secular society, as we are now, frequently have to compromise one Christian principle

for the sake of another. Modern Western democracy is
based on the Christian premise that everyone is valuable,
and that no one individual should hold too much power
because we are all subject to sin and corruption. In
addition, the Bible teaches that internal regeneration,
rather than external compulsion, is the basis for Christian
morality. So Christians rightly believe in government by
consent. This means that, for the sake of democracy,
Christians will sometimes agree to, and even support,
laws which are in conflict with Christian morality.

An obvious example is adultery. Half-way through the
last century adultery was decriminalised. As a Christian
I believe adultery to be always wrong. It causes considerable suffering and instability in our society, and I very
much doubt that decriminalising adultery has increased
the sum total of human happiness. In addition, I would
far rather you stole my car than my husband, so in some
ways I would prefer to live in a society which punished
adultery more than theft. Nevertheless, I would not
campaign to recriminalise adultery in our society because
it would not have the consent of the majority. It might be
a reasonable idea in absolute terms, but for modern
Western society it would be daft.

This logic can be extended to the laws governing
homosexuality. I believe homosexual practice to be
wrong, because God has said so. I consider it unlikely to
be in anyone's interests to encourage something which
God has condemned. I am far from convinced that the
1967 Sexual Offences Act has increased the total well-
being of homosexuals. But I presume the current law,
more or less, to be what most of Britain wants.

I am also expecting our representatives in Parliament
soon to agree to lowering the age of consent for homosexual sex from eighteen to sixteen. Again, I very much
doubt that this will benefit sixteen-year-old homosexuals.
Many teenagers go through a phase of homosexual
attraction, and I believe it is more compassionate to
encourage them to do this through abstinence than with

experimentation. I think of Lance, who believes his life would have been ruined if he had experienced homosexual sex when he wanted to. So I will use my democratic right to argue against this change as forcefully as I can (and have done so[35]). But I will also accept the democratic decision when it comes, and I can understand why some Christians, for instance Lord Alton, have agreed to vote for it.

In addition, the message given by this law may be more important than the law itself. In truth, a law which allows heterosexual sex at sixteen and homosexual sex at eighteen is not unjust. It does not discriminate against persons, but against acts. The law is frequently misrepresented, as 'straight kids can have sex at sixteen, gays at eighteen'.[36] This is not true. It is like saying, 'Smokers are not allowed in this train.' What we mean when we say this is that smokers *are* allowed on this train, but they may not smoke on it. We are not banning the *people*, but the *behaviour*.

Similarly, the different ages of consent do not discriminate against people, but against acts. Any teenager, gay or straight, can have heterosexual sex at sixteen and homosexual sex at eighteen. If Peter is caught having sex aged sixteen, what matters is not whether he can prove that he is straight rather than gay, but whether the sexual act was heterosexual not homosexual.

So the law is not unjust. But gay political pressure has successfully convinced us that it is. It is popularly perceived to be a law which discriminates against an oppressed minority. This being the case, it may be more important for Christians to be seen to be on the side of perceived justice rather than sexual morality. The teaching that we should protect vulnerable minorities and love those who are hated and work for justice and oppose unfairness is reiterated far more often in the Bible than the teaching about homosexuality. It is perhaps a more fundamental Christian principle. We must not tolerate homosexual practice in ourselves, and are not at liberty to tolerate it in the Church; but we can and perhaps should tolerate it in society, if we live in a democracy which sees it as acceptable. (Though the best solution all round might be to campaign for the age of consent for heterosexual sex to be raised to eighteen.)

Regardless of what stand we take on changing this particular law, Christians must fight to protect homosexuals against injustice. 'Gay bashing', taunting, unkindness and inappropriate discrimination in the job market are all an anathema to the genuine Christian. It is right and proper that Christians should have been among the first and some of the most energetic in combatting AIDS and HIV. When we do this, we will usually be received with open arms by many who feel that society, for all its token tolerance, really despises them.

Some months ago I was taking part in a discussion programme on lesbianism. I was asked my opinion of a case which had recently been in the news in which a woman was thought to have been given a particularly harsh sentence for a murder charge because she was a lesbian. The presenter clearly expected me, as the token Christian on the show, to take a 'homophobic' position, presumably defending the judge. But the judge's position was indefensible. Lesbianism is not illegal. It is no more of a crime to kill a man if you are gay than if you are straight. There is no justification for such injustice. When I said so the presenter challenged me: surely the Bible has something to say about lesbianism. Sure. But it has far more to say about injustice.

Our 'moralising' on homosexuality will be seen as just that, if we are not equally committed to other issues with which the Bible is also concerned.

Homosexuality in our friends

Some time ago I was working as a member of a theatre company. There was a fellow actor, Tom, whom I liked immediately before I even realised he was gay. He, knowing I was a Christian, was more wary of me, assuming I would disapprove of him. It is a tribute to him that we nevertheless quickly became good friends, as actors often do, spending many hours in each other's company. We had much in common; as the Christian and the gay we were both on the social fringes, tolerated but different from the others.

One day he asked how our friendship was possible, since he was living a life which I, as a Christian, must have considered wrong. I had never stopped to ask myself this question, as my fondness for him had been instinctive and unhesitating. But it was an interesting one. As I thought about it I began to realise that every member of the company was leading an 'unchristian' life. One man had sex with a number of girls during the course of the season. Another (still a good girlfriend of mine) was living with someone else's husband. A third had an 'open' marriage; a fourth would collect lunch receipts and tell the tax man it was business, and so on. Why on earth should I pick on the gay lifestyle to disapprove of? He at least was in a stable relationship and was not stealing anyone else's partner.

If we have non-Christian friends we must expect them to lead non-Christian lives. If we find it impossible to be friends with anyone who is not living in accordance with the Bible we will have no friends at all.

And far more important than Tom's sex life was the fact that he did not know the Lord Jesus. This is a much more serious sin than anything he could have got up to in bed. Sexual sin is negligible compared with not knowing God. Unbelief cuts us off from God far more effectively than the most unimaginably wicked orgies anyone could invent. Obviously this does not mean that atheists are necessarily more wicked than serial killers or axe-murderers, or indeed Christians. It is simply that not knowing God is a far more dangerous, life-threatening sin to the person committing it than is fornication or adultery or homosexuality or pederasty, or anything else.

Our non-Christian friends will only hear the gospel if we tell it to them. It is imperative that we know and love and accept friends who are not living Christian lives. I loved Tom because he was my friend. It grieved me that he did not know Jesus. But his homosexuality made no difference to me at all.

We must make friends with those in all walks of life. If we are to love them we must take them as they are. It would be not only impertinent, but also very foolish, to disapprove of the comparatively tiny error of homosexuality in our non-Christian friends, and thereby be unable to influence them in the grip of another which will ultimately prove to be fatal – atheism.

Conclusion

Compassion does not mean being economical with the truth. Clear biblical teaching is not unkind. Clarity and compassion are two sides of the same coin.

In every age the Church is called to be prophetic about the difficult issues of the day. Paul tells us that 'anyone who wants to live a godly life in Christ Jesus will be persecuted' (1 Timothy 2:12). If we protest about poverty in the Third World no one will mind, because no one will take any notice; society will nod approvingly and go on spending billions on the Lottery. But if we stand firm on the issue of homosexuality we will discover the truth of Paul's words for ourselves: it hits too near home.

And we must. We owe it to Jesus, to one another, to our children, but most of all to our homosexual brothers and sisters. We must love and accept them with open arms, but with all the brilliant clarity and profound compassion of Jesus Himself. We must befriend and care for them. We must never be judgmental, but we must also never lie.

With our gay friends, perhaps more than with anyone else in our society, we must be patient and kind, not boastful, arrogant or rude, nor irritable or resentful, not rejoicing at wrong, but rejoicing in the right. For them we must bear all things, believe all things, hope all things and endure all things. We must delight in the truth. We must always protect, always trust, always hope, always persevere.

This morning I was a guest at a church meeting to discuss the family in modern society. Afterwards a small, grey-haired lady came up to me, turning her back in such a way that others could not see her expression. She told me her thirty-year-old son is gay and described how he had spent the previous weekend sobbing in her arms.

Fighting back the tears, she said, 'Please tell people the truth. There is nothing gay about it.'

TEN

Feminism

HELMER: . . . *What duty do you mean?*
NORA: *My duty to myself.*
HELMER: *Before everything else, you're a wife and a mother.*
NORA: *I don't believe that any longer. I believe that before everything else I'm a human being.*

Ibsen, **A Doll's House.**

'*All feminists are angry young men.*'

Anon.[1]

I was at a party given by a tutor at a theological college. His wife was talking to me about the feminist movement. 'What we want,' she said, 'is a biblical approach. *Christian* feminism is what we need.'

One of her husband's students overheard her. 'There's no such thing,' he said. He showed no hesitation. In his mind Christianity and feminism had no possible common ground.

Many Christians face a hard choice when it comes to feminism. They have two equally unacceptable options. One is a set of 'traditional' Christian expectations. Like bygone missionaries, their elders sometimes preach a certain culture along with the gospel. Christian women seem expected to behave in a certain way. There is a suggestion their 'femininity' should be rather more demure and domestic than its secular counterpart. I received vivid proof of this in a somewhat backhanded compliment; a Bible college asked me to do the readings for a film they were making.

'All our women are so demure,' they complained. 'We thought you could be a bit more . . . well, you know . . . aggressive.'

Many Christian women find this stereotyping irksome. If they have an ounce of history they will know that the so-called 'traditional' roles are not traditional at all; if they have an iota of common sense they see that some of their elders' and betters' assumptions are so much bunkum. Secular society in some ways offers them more respect, more sympathy, and more freedom to be themselves. They feel the gentle stirrings of rebellion against such rigid archaic roles.

But if they leave this cosy and irritating frying pan they may find themselves in the fire. Their fellow Christians may be wrong, but at least they are vaguely sincere. They believe their assumptions to be godly. The world has no such pretensions. Its god is itself. It has no one else to please. Should Christian women, and men, ignore the expectations of people in the Church and risk being moulded instead by the worldly philosophy of 'women's lib'?

It is difficult to know what our attitude to these changing trends should be. Undoubtedly, modern mainstream feminism has become secular. This means if we embrace its values we are bound to accept some of the world's assumptions. On the other hand there is also no doubt that feminism has achieved much in our society which is good. It is helping to bring legal, political, and educational equality to women. If there had been no twentieth-century feminism half of us would still not have the vote. Obviously we do not want to reject the entire movement; but we will also want to be wary of endorsing it wholesale.

ANTI-FEMINISM

Many Christians are less than supportive towards the women's movement. The anecdote at the beginning of this chapter is just one of many such examples. Elaine Storkey, in her book *What's Right With Feminism*, illustrates the aggressively anti-feminist position adopted by some leading figures in the Church, particularly in America.[2] Many books have been written by Christians trying to reinforce the 'traditional' roles feminism has criticised. For its part feminism is often mistrustful of the Church: Judaeo-Christianity is frequently blamed for sexist structures and assumptions. This ought to give us pause. What is the reason behind this antagonism? Is there something at the heart of feminism diametrically opposed to the Christian faith? Are Christians against it simply because it is wrong?

We must admit there is a considerable lack of knowledge in the Church about the women's movement. Storkey herself says, 'it is my firm conviction that most of these authors *have never read* any of the feminist writers they criticise and have little understanding of what they are saying.'[3] Elisabeth Elliot, for example, who is most unsympathetic towards the feminist movement, is under the impression that a feminist is someone who believes the difference between the sexes is merely physiological.[4] This is simply ignorance. Many feminists passionately believe there are other differences. Indeed female chauvinism, the hallmark of extreme feminism, would be impossible without it. A vicar told me the other day that the latest feminist wheeze is to give boys and girls the same names. I have never heard such a notion from a feminist herself. One quite often hears people pontificating about feminism without having any clear idea of what feminism is. If we knew more of its history and origins we might not be so scornful. If we bore in mind what it has achieved in our society we might not be so ungrateful. And if we bothered to find out what it stands for, we might not be so antagonistic. We in the Church are often ignorant of the Christian, Evangelical convictions which inspired the feminist movement in the nineteenth century.[5] We frequently forget, for example, the contribution it made to the abolition of slavery. We ignore the feminist protests of Florence Nightingale and domesticate her image until it is acceptable to us. We forget that feminists fought tooth and nail to combat alcoholism; that they campaigned consistently for the poor and inarticulate; that they hated immorality, were intolerant of prostitution, and even discouraged contraception.[6] When we condemn feminism, we ought to realise that we condemn a movement originally built on Christian principles.

We also tend to forget what it has achieved. I wonder how many women who profess apathy towards feminism would really like to live in a society without universal suffrage? How many would want to be without the Married Women's Property Act? How many would genuinely be happy to be paid less for doing the same job of work?

And we show a remarkable capacity to ignore what it believes in now. Feminists are not women trying to be men, as many anti-feminists pretend. Feminists are women trying to be women. 'The whole point is that they want to live an oppression-free *woman's* life.'[7] Women are equal to men. They have as valuable a contribution to make. They should be granted the same human rights. This is what feminism stands for. A feminist is not someone who wants to abolish good manners or call her daughter 'John' or emasculate men. A feminist is someone who believes that women are equal to men and that they should be treated as such.

To a large extent anti-feminist attitudes in the Church spring from ignorance. In truth, most of us have sympathy for feminist causes and respect for feminist achievements, but a horror of aligning ourselves with the feminist name. It has an almost leprous image. When we

think of feminism, we seldom call to mind Christabel
Pankhurst or John Stuart Mill. Instead we envisage a few
braless wonders on the edge of the post-sixties movement, squatting at Greenham Common or demonstrating
about abortion. If we are to shun feminism it should be
on the grounds of a rather more informed analysis.

So the first criticism we should make of the anti-
feminist lobby is its distortion of feminism itself. As far
as I know, no one in the Church has attacked feminism
from a position of knowledge. Those who are well
acquainted with the movement are largely sympathetic.
Those who are critical of it seem to be criticising a grossly
inaccurate caricature.

Our second charge against anti-feminism is more
serious still. It has misrepresented feminism. It has also
misrepresented Christianity. Plenty of books have been
written from a supposedly Christian position, reinforcing
certain sexual roles, which make almost no reference to
the Bible at all. The writers invent doctrine out of their
own preferences and present it as Christian teaching.
Worse still, those who wish to lend credibility to their
anti-feminist position are not above a flagrant abuse of
scripture to provide a supportive text.

Elliot, for example, in trying to prove that 'what is right
for men is wrong for women', not only quotes some
highly misleading translations (for example '[women's]
role is to be receptive' in place of Paul's injunction to
silence in 1 Corinthians 14:34) but also – I can only
imagine deliberately – quotes half of 1 Corinthians 7:4 in
order to misrepresent Paul. He is being astonishingly
egalitarian: 'The wife has no authority over her own
body, but the husband does; in the same way, the
husband has no authority over his own body, but the wife
does.' Elliot stops the quotation half-way through. This
is bad enough. Then she has the gall to say: 'There you
have it, the contrast between what is expected of men
and what is expected of women. The lists are *different!*'[8]

Tim LaHaye does something similar. 'All men possess

leadership tendencies,' he says. 'This characteristic is one of the many areas where a man differs from most women.' To illustrate the case he quotes Genesis 1:26, saying that man – *he* according to LaHaye – was given dominion over fish, fowl, cattle and all the earth.[9] Yet it is quite clear from the next verse that 'man' means men and women. 'So God made man . . . male and female.' Has LaHaye not read the next verse? Or is he deliberately suppressing the truth? I am not sure which is worse.

The reactionary position of the anti-feminist is not the one we should adopt. It tends to ignorance and dishonesty. But is it wrong on all counts? Should we have no reservations at all about the secular feminist movement?

SECULAR FEMINISM

Feminism is difficult to define. The doctrines of Christianity or Marxism or Islam can be described. They are what the founder (or his immediate disciples) taught. But what is feminism, and who says so? A few extremists can daub the whole movement with their war paint. No doubt one or two feminists hate men or believe in total anarchy (though I suspect they are more myth than fact: I have never met any of them) but this is hardly the essence of feminist belief. What are its fundamental creeds?

The only doctrine to which all feminists subscribe is this: a belief in *the essential value of women.* This is the basis of feminism. Women have an intrinsic worth. Because of this they should not be treated as men's inferiors. And this is the only point of absolute feminist agreement. Some feminists believe we will never have sexual equality without abolishing capitalism. Others believe in sexual separatism because men always dominate a mixed group. Others again are simply asking for scrupulously fair treatment. But anyone who calls her (or him)self a feminist believes that women should be thought of and treated as human beings of value.

This is not only the common ground on which all feminists stand, but the reason behind most forms of feminist activity. For example, denying women the vote can imply that women are less intelligent or important; the suffragettes were fighting this form of inferior treatment. Or allowing contraceptives can result in women being used for men's convenience; nineteenth-century feminists fought this kind of inferior treatment. And not allowing contraceptives denies women the sexual 'freedom' men can have; twentieth-century 'libbers' have fought this sort of inferior treatment. All these different battles spring from the same conviction. Women should be treated as men's equals.

And of course this is also a Christian conviction. As John Stott says in discussing the feminist movement, 'every complaint of injustice and every cry for justice should make the Christian sit up and take notice'.[10] With this, the most basic of feminist ideals, the Christian has the deepest sympathy. Women and men are equal, and should be treated as such. This 'cry for justice' is the mainspring of the women's movement. Christians must heartily support it.

So Christians should be behind the feminist cause. Its first goal is also a Christian one. Whenever we hear an appeal for sexual equality we must indeed sit up and take notice. We should go further. We ought to give active help and encouragement. We should feel genuinely abashed at our Christian apathy. Shame it was the world, not the Church, which brought about many improvements for women. Shame it was only women, not men too, who usually caused the necessary outcry. It is time we redressed the balance.

We should also acknowledge our debt to feminism. Sexual equality is a biblical doctrine. Unfortunately in latter decades Christians have done little to make it a reality. As Stott says, the contemporary liberation of women is largely due to Jesus, but 'the shame is that it did not come earlier and that the initiative was not taken more explicitly in His name.' [11] Feminism has done much of the work Christianity should have taken on.

So far so good. We agree with the basis of feminism. We too want sexual equality. Obviously we will not agree with every application of the principle. Some women say sexual equality means that women should sleep around as freely as men have done. Christians will say the opposite: men's moral standards should be as high as women's have had to be. Some say sexual equality means abortion on demand. Christians will say the reverse: a father, too, should take the responsibility for an unborn unwanted child.

It is on these points that Christians and feminists disagree. But feminists themselves do too. By no means all believe in legalised abortion or unrestricted sex. The pioneers of the feminist movement would have been horrified at such a notion.

The fact that these outworkings may be unchristian does not mean we should dissociate ourselves from the movement. It means the opposite. We must involve ourselves. We are in agreement over the aim; we must encourage a godly pursuit of it. Christians have a vital contribution to make to feminism. The fundamental principle is biblical. It is only Christians who will make the outworkings of it biblical too. As was pointed out in chapter 1 it is because our voice has gone unheard that 'Women's Lib' does not have a particularly Christian tone.

Thus far, then, we can endorse feminism. We are fully in agreement with its basis; both Christians and feminists want justice. We will want to work alongside the movement in pursuit of sexual equality. We want equal pay for equal work, the same opportunities for the sexes, paternity leave for fathers, and so on. We are in disagreement with some conclusions of some feminists: we do not believe in separatism or Marxism or lesbianism. We do not see sexual equality in terms of a mother's right to kill. However, such considerations do not rule out the possibility of Christian feminism. These are not essential feminist tenets; one can be a feminist without being a Marxist or a lesbian.

But are these the only points of disagreement? Are there, perhaps, more profound aspects of 'women's liberation' we may have overlooked? After all feminism has become a secular movement. It was not always so; once there were women with Christian beliefs at the forefront of the campaign. Now its main writers and thinkers are not Christian, and this means they are not likely to argue from within a Christian framework. Christians and feminists are agreed in wanting the job market to be fair, but we are not agreed on the purpose of life itself. Yet this is surely more important. Underlying worldly assumptions about the purpose of our existence are more dangerous to the unwary Christian than, for example, outspoken attitudes towards sexual morality.

Any secular movement is ultimately going to be in disagreement with Jesus's teaching. There is indeed an essential difference between Christianity and feminism, but it is a difference we have not just with the women's movement but with almost any philosophy in our society. We do not live for the here and now: we believe in a hereafter. We cannot live to please ourselves: we have a Lord in heaven. We may not simply work for a just society: we have a gospel to proclaim which is even more urgent. This means that we are profoundly at variance with almost every worthy cause around.

I personally have every sympathy with, for example, the Campaign for the Protection of Rural England, the Society for the Protection of the Unborn Child, Road-peace, and the fight against world poverty. I believe Christians should be involved in all these causes. But they must see them from a Christian perspective. They will seldom, for example, have justification to break the law; however concerned we are about vivisection, for example, we must think carefully before jeopardising Christ's witness by stealing property or using violence. I remember hearing on the radio that the leader of Christian CND had just left his wife; he regretfully explained that his work for peace had destroyed his marriage. Again, I myself support his cause. But I believe he has it quite out of proportion: in fighting these lesser battles, for justice or peace or the environments or the arts, we are never called to abandon a greater war.

Yet this can easily happen. I know Christians who care more about women's rights than the Lordship of Christ; who are more concerned to show the Bible to be egalitarian than to expound it truthfully; who would rather hear a talk on 'humankind' than a sermon on God. I heard a lecture at a Christian festival some time ago on the subject of sexual oppression. The speakers spoke eloquently for an hour. At the end a questioner raised her hand. 'I did notice one thing,' she said, 'that worried me rather. You quoted from the following people: Mao Tse-tung, Betty Friedan, the Naked Ape column from the *Guardian*, the *Observer*, an unnamed young woman, a child psychologist, another unnamed psychiatrist. You didn't actually quote once from the Bible ... What worries me is that you were very clear on what you said women wanted. You didn't make it at all clear whether this is what God wanted.'[12] This kind of thinking is bound to lead us into error, with feminism as well as with anything else.

Let us take an example. There is an assumption nowadays that we ought to be 'fulfilled'. What we mean by fulfilment is a sophisticated form of happiness. Not the instant happiness of having a good meal, but the rather more long-term happiness of being in appropriate employment or living with the person one is in love with. Now a non-Christian is 'wise', from the world's point of view, to seek this kind of happiness. If you do not believe in an afterlife you must of necessity want your present one to be good; and it is sensible not only to seek immediate happiness but also a more lasting form of satisfaction.

A Christian is not always wise to do this. We expect another life after this one, and longer-term happiness still. Just as a non-Christian will sometimes put aside instant happiness (going out for the evening) in favour of more long-term happiness (studying to become a doctor), so we will sometimes put aside earthly fulfilment for the sake of eternal blessings. It is not always right, for example, to live with the person you love. She may be married to someone else. So a Christian is sometimes called to forgo great fulfilment on earth for the greater fulfilment still of obedience to God's commands.

The society we live in is most unsympathetic to this. It will try and persuade us we have a right to immediate 'fulfilment'. It will tempt us to believe we deserve temporal satisfaction. We 'Christianise' the philosophy by pretending there is some kind of obligation on us to be challenged and stimulated; the parable of the talents, for example (Luke 19), is supposed to be telling us to use our abilities. If you are a good pianist you must play the piano for the Lord. This is not what the parable says at all; a talent is a coin; the coin we are to use and invest with profit is the gospel. Of course if you can give yourself or others pleasure by playing the piano you should do so. But you have no more *duty* to than you have duty to enjoy good wine. You will never find a parable commanding you to do this. It is common sense. It is good to be happy and fulfilled. It is how we are created to be. But it is not a priority. It is not our Christian obligation. And worldly fulfilment is not our overriding ambition. Why, it would leave us nothing to look forward to: Christianity *is* 'pie in the sky when you die'.

These assumptions about self-fulfilment are not the responsibility of feminism. Everything in our society is telling us to look after 'number one'. When a man gets bored with his wife he leaves her. When a child finds his parents' authority irksome, he rejects it. Self-gratification is the tyrant of our age. It is not simply feminism which propagates the idea. The supposedly 'Christian' anti-feminist position argues along the same lines; a book actually entitled *The Fulfilled Woman* promises you the ultimate in satisfying experiences if you become a door-mat for your husband to wipe his boots on. This argu-ment is neither convincing nor particularly Christian. We do things because they are right, not because they will necessarily be satisfying.

This desire for self-fulfilment is a disease of our time. But the point is this: modern secular feminism, being a child of our time, has the idea coursing through its veins – not so much because it is feminism, but because it is modern and secular. This is why we must be wary.

I have a Christian friend whose husband wanted to go abroad. This would have involved considerable sacrifice for her; she had work she loved and was good at. It was quite unjust of him to see his job as much more important than hers; it was absurdly selfish to expect her to embrace unemployment so his work could take the turn he wanted. Being no fool she realised this, and the very realisation put her into a dilemma. The voice of feminism, the voice of sexual justice and equality, told her it was quite unreasonable to give in to her husband's wishes.

And the voice was absolutely correct. It *was* unreason-able. There is compelling logic in the argument. But there is also a deeper, more compelling logic which calls out to any Christian making a decision. Her own happiness, her work, her fulfilment and her achievements are not the only consideration. There is also a matter of love, and respect, and self-sacrifice and submission to bear in mind. In the end she put her husband before herself and gave in to his wishes instead of her own.

This is the kind of pressure we can find ourselves under. Feminism is right to fight for equality for women and men. It is wrong if it ever tempts us to see that equality in terms of our own fulfilment, assertiveness or rights. 'For the desire for *self*-fulfilment, *self*-achievement, *self*-growth and *self*-service is what has produced chauvinism in men. For women to travel further down the same road can only make the situation worse.'[13] These ideas are bound to make us unhappy and frustrated, and they are the kind of ideas we absorb without noticing.

A couple I know were going out for a meal together. He wanted to go by car, she on foot. They both found themselves under pressure to insist on their own way. She had heard from friends and colleagues that women are always making way for men. They have only themselves to blame if they are bullied and walked over like doormats. She ought to 'assert herself'. He had heard, on the other hand, that men should wear the trousers. Only fools are henpecked. Men should never give in to women; he should also 'assert himself'. In short, they had both been persuaded that they had a duty to be selfish. These ideas are communicated in the most subtle of ways: they come about through a chance word or barely spoken attitude. If this couple had stopped to think they would both have realised that it is Christlike to give in, and they need not have ruined their evening.

I have pursued the question of fulfilment because it is a good example of the many assumptions in our culture which are profoundly anti-Christian. They are starting to creep into Christian thinking: 'Love your neighbour as yourself' now tends to be expounded as first 'love yourself'. This is where we must resist the influence of the women's movement. We are in danger of being convinced that we cannot be happy if we lay down our lives for one another. Yet this is exactly what Christ's example tells us to do. My friend's meal out was spoilt because she was told she must have her own way in order to enjoy herself. This can happen in more serious ways. To take a well-worn example, many women are made to feel ashamed for staying at home as housewives; yet they have often made the decision to do so through purely unselfish motives, laying aside other work they enjoyed because they believe their small children need them at home. And then they are made to feel inadequate for giving up the stimulation and challenge and money of the work they did before. The world tells them they are foolish to have put others before themselves.

It is important to understand, though, that feminism itself is not answerable for this. Indeed it is not really genuine feminism. It is our own selfishness assuming a feminist voice. One can be tempted by it every day. 'It is unfair to change more than your share of the nappies.' 'It is ridiculous for you to tidy away his gloves.' 'It is not right for your work to be put second yet again . . .' and so on. This is not feminism. It is our own sin and the egotism of our age disguising itself as sexual justice. But because it disguises itself quite well, we must be careful not to fall for it.

There is much in secular feminism that is right: its basic fight for sexual justice puts us to shame. But we will also come across underlying worldly assumptions, in this, as in any secular movement, and it is these we must be particularly wary of.

CHRISTIAN FEMINISM

Christians ought to be prominent in any pursuit of justice. But there are inevitably aspects of secular feminism we cannot endorse. So what will characterise a Christian involvement in the cause?

A biblical outlook

A truly Christian approach will reject all that is false. On one hand this means jettisoning the additions to scripture we have accumulated over the years. Adding to God's word was the first mistake ever made: 'Did God say, "you shall not eat out of the tree?" ' (Genesis 3:1). 'We mustn't even touch it,' Eve replied, going beyond God's prohibition. Additions to scripture are dangerous. Like Eve's, they can be precursors to a fall. Among them we would include all the old wives' tales: women should stay at home with the children; men are natural leaders; husbands should assert their 'headship'; men are more objective; women should not be the initiators – and so on and so forth. Some of these are half truths. Some are similar to something taught in the Bible. But none is scriptural, and all are to be found in popular Christian paperbacks. There are still plenty of books being published telling Christian women to be fluffy little housewives. These notions are fair enough as someone's personal opinion or observation, but when presented as biblical teaching, they should be ruthlessly exposed.

On the other hand, Christian feminism will reject the secular assumptions of our age. We are called to be holy, different from the world around us. We will not swallow many of the things our fellow feminists may take for granted. The following should go on the list of new wives' tales to be abandoned: you must not sacrifice yourself for other people; you should assert your own rights; you must not let your husband or anyone else take advantage of you; you should stand up for yourself; you must be fulfilled – and so on. These lies are just as bad as the others, and may be more likely to deceive us in the years to come.

A concern for others

But what should characterise a Christian alternative above all is a Christian love for others. In the last century, feminism fought for the less articulate. Its battles were for slaves, prostitutes and paupers. Sadly, the feminism of today seems to have lost much of this spirit. The campaign for abortion exemplifies this: the cry for mercy from the unborn falls on deaf feminist ears.

There are plenty of people in the world in need of philanthropic feminism. Millions of girls in Sudan (and even many Africans in this country) are still subjected to the brutal mutilation of female circumcision.[14] Tiny girls of six cannot walk for weeks, or relieve themselves without excruciating pain for months, because of the 'operation'. They will never feel sexual pleasure. They cannot give birth without being surgically opened and then sewn up again. I have even heard that a frustrated groom may take knife to his bride on their wedding night if her vagina has been made too small. Is this not an appropriate cause for Christian feminists? If we do not care about such issues, who will?

It is probably true to say that wherever men suffer injustice in the world women are likely to suffer more. Wherever there is poor education, women's will be poorer. Wherever there is exploitation of labour, women tend to be exploited far more. And wherever there is starvation women are likely to be fed after their menfolk, and then pass half their portion to the children. Again, if Christians do not concern themselves about such injustices, who will?

Not that we are short of needs far nearer home. One London woman in six has been raped. Half those rapes have included violence.[15] These women may turn to a rape crisis centre, but if they do, they are unlikely to find any Christians there. They will find feminists who are often aggressively misandronous[16] and also often anti-Christian. Clearly this is another place where we need Christian feminists.

We also need to help people to become more aware of sexual abuse. Rape and incest are still not taken seriously in our society. I heard a barrister on the radio recently say that a thousand pounds – less than one would receive for losing a couple of front teeth – was perfectly adequate compensation for 'not serious' forms of rape. By this he did not mean a girl who had led a lover on and then changed her mind. He only meant that she had not been beaten up, stabbed to death, or left bleeding in a gutter. This attitude is still common amongst lawyers, judges and even some members of the police. As it is, the chances of any rapist being convicted are less than 2 per cent,[17] and even when rape is proved beyond any doubt and sentence is given, the penalty is often so lenient the victim will still be suffering the effects of her ordeal years after her assailant walks free. There is very little deterrent to protect women from sexual abuse. Presumably this is because those who make our laws do not realise that rape is a serious crime. Christian feminists must put this right, and urge society to treat it with appropriate abhorrence.

An involvement of men

In all these struggles there is another quality which ought to make Christian feminism distinctive. If it is motivated by a concern for others, as it should be, it is a cause which should appeal to Christian men as much as to women. We tend to think of feminists as women. Why? Because women are concerned about women's issues. Plenty of Christian men are happy to claim that their sex have a kind of umbrella 'headship' over women which is expressed in 'loving responsibility'. Why, then, have they not translated this loving responsibility into active feminism? Women tend to be physically weaker than men. This means they are liable to physical abuse. There is serious domestic violence in our society, and it is not confined to the secular world; in Christian and non-Christian homes alike, hundreds – possibly thousands – of women are subjected to sickening levels of systematic torture.[18] As we saw in chapter 3, if women are to be treated as equals, they will sometimes need protection. It is ironic that those men who shout loudest about headship (and the responsibility it entails) are often those least likely to be doing something about this protection.

Many feminists do not welcome men in their campaigns. I believe Christian feminists should. If a woman suffers violence from her partner she will almost certainly find it hard to relate to the opposite sex. She will eventually need loving men as well as loving women around her. If the only refuge available is staffed entirely by women, and she is cared for only by women, there is a real danger she will grow to distrust most men. Christian men need to care about so-called women's issues as much as Christian whites should care about racial apartheid.

We also need to do much in terms of campaigning on behalf of men. As husbands, and particularly as fathers, men are seriously discriminated against in this country. A man does not have the automatic right to paternity leave, whereas a woman having a baby can claim several months' leave at almost full pay. Many men's working hours are such that they barely see their young families at all. We have a number of friends who leave for work at seven and get home again twelve hours later; presumably, until their children are teenagers, the fathers hardly meet them on a normal day. Because men are seen as 'workers', not husbands and fathers, they are not free to choose a civilised working day and spend the rest of their time bringing up their families. Again, Christians should be the ones to be saying that there is more to a man's life than a large salary.

These tasks may sound daunting. But I knew of a church, which was in no way exceptional, which had two or three women in the congregation, as most churches probably have, who had been badly treated by their husbands. It occurred to someone in the church when they were going through the worst that they may have had no one to turn to. To tell the vicar would have been difficult; partly because he is a man, and partly because it would have felt disloyalty to their husbands. To tell anyone else might have started gossip. To go to a secular rape crisis centre would never have occurred to them, and they might have been told outright to leave home, and received little sympathy for their Christian convictions; a woman who was still committed to her husband despite his aggressive tendencies would probably be seen as hopelessly oppressed by sexist indoctrination. So the suggestion was made to have a church-based domestic crisis centre, providing two or three people – probably a married woman and a married couple – trained together in a small group. Anyone with domestic problems, whether beatings and incest or simply distressing rows, could ring and ask for help. She, or her husband, would be guaranteed confidentiality, anonymity, and a listening Christian ear.

We need Christian feminism. The Church needs it and society needs it. Christian feminists could be exposing what sexual permissiveness does to women. Christian feminists should be asking how abortion exploits a woman. Christian feminism ought to be fighting pornography. Above all, Christian feminism should be distinguished by its concern for others and *their* rights.

A more Christian behaviour

In a sense, however, there are more basic changes to be made. This book has been trying to illustrate some of the unbiblical attitudes we have about the sexes. Those of us who cannot work in the Sudan, for example, to change attitudes about female sexuality can still do a great deal to make our behaviour nearer home more Christian.

At work Christians often need to show far more respect for women. As we have seen, we need women as well as men in all aspects of employment if we are to benefit from God's design in creation. Presumably we still have fewer women MPs and executives and professors partly because we are more reluctant to vote for them, employ them, or educate them. Christian employers should ensure that they are not passing over women suitable for positions of responsibility. Christian husbands should ask themselves if they really are promoting and supporting their wives' work. Christian parents should give their daughters confidence in seeking higher education and more demanding work.

At a more mundane level, we could be setting a better example at work. Christian men are unlikely to subject their female colleagues to sexual harassment, but they are only too likely to show disrespect to female superiors; I have frequently noticed how bad Christian men are at taking orders from a woman. And they are also only too likely to display ugly sexist attitudes. I was working in a theatre company with one other Christian. He was the only one who had never made the coffee, washed up the mugs, or made a cake for anyone else's birthday. It proved to be a very offputting Christian advertisement for those who were working with us.

Our Christian homes could also show far more equality and interdependence. Christian husbands are sometimes not as good as they could be at nourishing and cherishing. Many appear to think it their duty to put themselves before their wives. Some do not seem to recognise their more mundane domestic responsibilities at all. We knew a minister whose wife, after years of running the home, had to take on a full-time job because they could not make ends meet. She was on her feet all day, but he still expected her to cook all his meals, do all his washing up, rear his children and do all his house-work when she came home in the evening. He would sit impatiently in his study waiting for her to come home and make him a pot of tea.

As I hope was made clear, men are seen by God to have the same duty to the home as women. Women's outside work is as important as men's. And because husbands are to lay down their lives for their wives it is their duty to further their wives' work, encourage their careers and make sure the women are not doing more than their share in the home. Men whose wives are housewives should be offering just as much support. A friend of ours is bringing up her tiny children almost single-handed at the moment because her husband's job keeps him away from home several nights a week. The children are proving difficult and she is under pressure. Yet recently the church expected him to be away for an entire weekend on a PCC conference.

And of course our churches themselves could show far more sexual interdependence. As we have seen, the Church tends to divide its responsibilities into men's and women's work. Whether or not we believe in women's ordination we should be encouraging far more women to study the Bible seriously and equip themselves to train others in Christian behaviour, as Paul says they should (Titus 2:4,5). I know an Oxford graduate who has sat through weekly Bible studies for four years and has never been asked to lead one. She is far more competent to lead them than some of the people she has to listen to. She gains nothing from the meetings apart from humility and a deep sense of frustration. If the reason she has not been asked to lead is because of scruples about women teaching men, she ought to be put in charge of a women's group before her mind atrophies altogether.

We should also be more concerned about evangelism to *men* in churches where they are outnumbered. The domestic image of the Church, the plethora of women's activities, and the expectation of the congregation to sit in the pews taking orders while the vicar does all the work, all help to serve as deterrents to men.

Christian feminism, then, should be biblical and altruistic. We should know what God says about the sexes, and be confident in the knowledge. We should show a concern for others who suffer from sexism, rather than for our own rights. We should include among our feminist ranks, and indeed be caring for, fellow men as well as women.

Indeed any Christian behaviour should be all these things anyway. If the Church were truly faithful, we would out-feminist the feminists. If we were really loving our neighbours we would be more genuinely concerned for sexual justice than the most militant of feminine extremists. If we were the body of believers we ought to be, there would be more sexual liberation in our ranks than anywhere else in the world.

Liberation

'Women's Liberation', as the name suggests, is all about freedom. And genuine freedom is not so much freedom to choose, but freedom to be oneself. We are not free if we are living in rebellion against God, no matter how much choice we have in the matter, because we were made for His service, the service which is perfect freedom.

The freedom we need is freedom to be our true selves, to be what we were made to be, to be the image of the God who created us. Men and women are different, and should rejoice in that difference and appreciate it. We are equal, and should promote that equality far more than we do at present. We are interdependent, and Christians should always be working in sexual harmony and partnership.

But above all, we are made to love. We are made in God's image, and He is Love Itself. The way we relate to one another should speak of concern and gentleness and humility. This is more important than all the rest.

ELEVEN

Back to the Image

'Remember Freud's dying words: "Good grief, good
grief, what do women want?" '
'Those were Freud's dying words?'
'Just before his wife shot him.'[1]

Man was digging the garden. He was having a jolly good
try, but something was seriously missing. His ideas all
seemed incomplete. He would plough up the earth, and
then not think to plant it. He would collect up the fruit,
and then not know what to do with it. He grew
vegetables, and then puzzled over how to use them.

'This is hopeless,' God said to Himself. 'This man
can't cope. He's not behaving like us at all. This human
being, who is supposed to resemble us, is only half
there.'

So God decided to complete the picture. He would
make a perfect counterpart to man, someone who could
help him in the work, so that together they would be His
true likeness.

He would have to make somebody equal: the animals
would not do at all. He would have to make somebody
different: another man would simply double the problem.
And he would have to make someone who had some
deep connection with the man, someone who needed
him as much as he clearly needed in return; it would be
absolutely no use making him a partner, a different, equal
creature who complemented him beautifully, if the two
ignored each other and went their own separate ways.

No, they would have to be inseparable; they needed to be part of one another.

God had a brainwave. He decided to use a bit of the man himself. That way they would always want to be together. He would only find himself complete in her, and she in him.

God was looking forward to showing the man his new companion. He knew Adam would be excited. 'At last!' he would say. 'Here's part of me! My other self. My counterpart. I'll call her after me.' God anticipated it with pleasure.

He took her by the hand and led her to the man. 'Wake up Adam,' He said. 'At last I've got a friend for you.'

The man sat up and rubbed his eyes. Then he felt his side. 'Bother!' he said out loud. 'I say,' he asked God, 'you haven't seen a spare rib on your travels, have you?'

'Adam,' God said patiently, 'I have made a friend to help you. Aren't you pleased?'

He looked at her. Then he looked at God. 'What was wrong with the way I was doing it?' he asked crossly.

God was starting to feel discouraged. 'You'll do a lot better together,' He explained.

Through his resentment, the man looked at the not-quite-man. He could see that the new creature was in some ways like himself. So far he approved. But in other ways she was not like him at all. Of this he disapproved very strongly.

'She seems to have bits missing,' he said to God, rather critically.

God thought it better to leave them to get to know each other. This they did, in a manner of speaking.

'Look here, Notquiteman,' the man said to the woman. 'I've started to work on this garden, and you'll only mess it up, so why don't you find something else to do while I get on with this? Do some knitting or ironing or something?'

The woman looked puzzled. 'We don't wear clothes,' she said.

'Yes dear,' the man said absent-mindedly. 'Don't trouble me now, there's a good girl.'

He wandered off, scratching his head for the twentieth time over what to do with the cauliflowers.

Some time later, something wonderful happened to the man. His life was transformed. The woman bore him two sons.

'At last,' he said when he saw them. 'They are the bone of my bone and flesh of my flesh. They shall be called men because they were taken out of me.'

He was thrilled. He took Cain and Abel off to the garden to help him with the work God had given him to do.

God was walking around one day, when He thought He would have a look to see how they were all getting on.

Out in the garden there were three men, digging over the soil, but not thinking to plant it, gathering pyramids of melons which were rotting in the sun, storing sacks of decaying vegetables, building mountains of butter, and digging lakes of milk, and the whole lot was going to waste because they had no idea what to do with it.

It all seemed pretty futile to God. Still, He was glad the earth produced such plenty, as He had designed it to. 'At least you don't go hungry,' He said to the men with satisfaction.

'Don't go hungry?' Adam said. 'We're always hungry! That's why we can never stop working. We never have enough. We're constantly struggling to provide for our families. Now leave us alone. We're busy.'

God grew angry. 'Why isn't the woman helping you? That's what I made her for. Where is she?'

All the three men burst out laughing. 'The women!' they all said in unison. 'They couldn't help. If we can't cope, what can they do? What a suggestion. The women! Ha! Ha! Ha!'

God left them, and went looking for the woman.

Eventually He saw her, sitting inside the kitchen, talking to her daughters.

'You know,' she was saying, 'we could cut open those melons and dry the seeds; then next year we could plant some more.'

'Yes,' said one of the girls, 'and if we could think of some way of turning the soil, of digging it over like the men do, we could plant wild grasses, and grow corn, and eat it through the winter.'

'You know,' said the third, 'there's plenty of food here, if only we could organise it properly. We could cook all those vegetables for supper, if they weren't being stored for something, and have fruit for pudding.'

The men outside paused for a moment and looked towards the house. 'Women!' they said. 'They do nothing but gas all day.'

The women looked out of the window, and sadly shook their heads. 'Men!' they said wistfully. 'They never listen.'

Notes

Page viii.
1. Exley, Richard and Helen, eds *What is a Husband?* (Exley Publications Ltd., 1977), p. 4.

ONE

1. M.D.W. July 1984, *A Fully Human Priesthood*, Oliver S. Tomkins, p. 9. *The Ordination of Women to the Priesthood*, 'General Synod, a background paper', by Christine Howard (UO Publishing, 1984).
2. E.g. *The Total Woman*, Marabel Morgan (Hodder & Stoughton, 1973); *For Women Only*, Evelyn R. Petersen and J. Allan Peterson, eds (Tyndale House Publishers, 1974); *Let Me Be a Woman*, Elisabeth Elliot (Hodder & Stoughton, 1979); simply *Woman*, Dale Evans Rogers (Hodder & Stoughton, 1981) and even *Queen Take Your Throne*, Eileen Wallis (Kingsway Publications, 1985) . . . not to mention *Who's Stopping You Being a Woman?*; *Who'd Want to Be a Woman Anyway?*; *Weeds, Wets, Wimps & Women*, etc. etc.
3. See John Stott, *Issues Facing Christians Today* (Marshalls, 1984), chapter 1, 'Involvement: Is it our Concern?'
4. For example see Mark 1:32–8, when He deliberately turned His back on Capernaum, where crowds were queueing up for healing, so that He could go on to preach, because 'That is why I have come' (verse 38).
5. *Women in the Bible*, Mary J. Evans (Paternoster Press, 1983), p. 17.
6. ibid., p. 16.

TWO

1. Jonathan Cape Ltd., 1979, p. 180.
2. In fact I have been unable to find this quotation in my copy of *1066* – but if it isn't there it certainly ought to be.
3. For example that excellent, and anti-'Women's Lib' book, *The Female Woman*, Arianna Stassinopolis (Davis-Poynter Ltd., 1973).
4. Which is partly what *The Cinderella Complex*, Colette Dowling (Fontana Paperbacks, 1982) is trying to do.
5. Augustine, *De Genesi ad Litteram* ix, 5 cf. vii, 3. 'I do not see in what way it could be said that woman was made a help for man if the work of childbearing be excluded.'
6. *The Female Eunuch*, Germaine Greer (Granada Publishing Ltd., 1981), p. 277.
7. *Voyage to Venus*, C. S. Lewis (Pan Books, 1953), p. 186.
8. Cf. *The Turning Point*, Fritjof Capra (Fontana, 1983), p. 21.
9. Hestia, Hero, Aphrodite, Cybele (or Rhea), Pallas Athena, Artemis, Persephone, Demeter, and so on and so forth.
10. An idea to which feminists – understandably enough – take objection. Cf. *The Second Sex*, Simone de Beauvoir (Jonathan Cape, 1972), pp. 14–16. 'He is the Subject, he is the Absolute – she is the Other.'
11. E.g. *The Times*, Letters, 13 October 1983: 'For many women the language of worship is increasingly hurtful and offensive in its use of "man" to describe us all. The *purpose* has not been to assert the superiority of the male sex, but this has been one of the harmful *results,* as recent studies of language and its effects have established.' Ms Jean Mayland.
12. This, of course, is why Elaine Morgan called her book *The Descent of Woman* (Bantam Books, 1972). See p. 3: ' . . . "man" is an ambiguous term. It means the species; it also means the male of the species. If you begin to write a book about man or conceive a theory about man you cannot avoid using this word . . . before you are halfway through the first chapter a mental image of this evolving creature begins to form in your mind. It will be a male image. . .'
13. E.g. Hosea 1:2; 2:2–13.
14. E.g. Ephesians 5:25–7; Isaiah 54:5–7; Hosea 2:14–16, 19–20.
15. C. S. Lewis sometimes gets dangerously near this idea, for example in saying: 'God is so masculine that all creation is feminine by comparison.' Quoted by Elisabeth Elliot in *The Mark of a Man* (Hodder & Stoughton, 1981), p. 51.
16. A fascinating study of this has been done in *Gynomorphic Imagery in Exilic Isaiah (40–60)* by Leila Leah Bronner. She

quotes a number of striking biblical images 'comparing God's actions to that *[sic]* of a mother bearing, caring *[sic]*, carrying and comforting her children'. For example Numbers 11:12; Deuteronomy 32:18 (the word translated 'begat' – RSV – more often means 'give birth to', while the next line means 'to bring forth with pain or sorrow'. It is used to describe a woman giving birth); Deuteronomy 32:11 ff.; Isaiah 42:14; 46:3; 49:15; 66:13.

17. In *God in the Dock*, C. S. Lewis (Fount Paperbacks, 1979), 'Priestesses in the Church'.

18. John Stuart Mill, *The Subjection of Women* (MIT, 1970), pp. 27–8. 'If women have a greater natural inclination for some things than for others, there is no need of laws or social inculcation to make the majority of them do the former in preference to the latter.'

THREE

1. Misquotation, of course, from *Animal Farm*, George Orwell (Penguin Books, 1945), p. 114.

2. 'Gratian, a jurist from Bologna, said: "The image of God is in man and it is one . . . he has the image of God . . . woman is not made in God's image." ' *Not in God's Image*, Chrysostom, p. 130.

3. The early fathers, for example, often implied that woman was more to blame because she sinned first – Tertullian called women 'the devil's gateway' (*'De Cultu Feminarum'*, I, i, in *Migne, Patrolosia Latina*, I, cols 304–5). The Victorians did the opposite by suggesting that women were, by nature, less sinful and therefore ought to have higher moral standards than men.

4. Although this has always been a mystery to me. I am sure pornography can have a very harmful effect on children, but I am equally sure it has a far worse effect on their parents.

5. *Are Women Human?* Dorothy Sayers (Downers Grove, Ill. InterVarsity Press, 1971).

FOUR

1. Jose b. Johanan of Jerusalem (*circa* 150 BC), quoted in *Women in the World of Jesus*, Evelyn and Frank Stagg (The Westminster Press, 1978), p. 52. The Mishnah, of course, is not

first century – being completed in about AD200 – but it is a compilation of all the earlier Jewish Oral Law, which would have been extant in Jesus's day.

2. According to the School of Hillel, ibid., p. 51.
3. See *God & Women*, Dorothy Pape, Mowbrays (IVP, 1976), p. 22.
4. Again this (appearing in public with unbound hair) was something for which one could be divorced. See *Women in the World of Jesus*, Evelyn and Frank Stagg (The Westminster Press, 1978), p. 51.
5. Often without meaning to or realising it, teachers consistently favour boys in science and maths classes, as was shown, for example, in *The Sunday Times*, 6 November 1983, p. 9. 'Girls Minus Boys Add Up Better.'
6. Quoted by James Dobson in *Straight Talk to Men* (Hodder & Stoughton, 1981). Though this is a well-known quotation of Steinham's I have been unable to trace its origin and therefore read it in context; I hope I do not do her an injustice.
7. *The Gift of Feeling*, Paul Tournier (SCM Press Ltd., 1981). Throughout.
8. *The Turning Point*, op. cit., p. 19, and pp. 18–19.

FIVE

1. E.g. Catherine Marshall in *A Man Called Peter*, quoted in *The Christian Family*, Larry Christenson (Fountain Trust, 1971), pp. 33–4. Also Christenson himself, op. cit., p. 47. And this is James Dobson's assumption in *Straight Talks to Men* (Hodder Christian Paperbacks, 1981). E.g. pp. 101–2.
2. 1 Corinthians 7:32,34–5.
3. See Dobson, op. cit., pp. 109–10. Though he gives some excellent advice in these pages, he does overlook the fact that we cannot simply go back to the shared labour of previous years by being more friendly with our neighbours.
4. Praying mantis, I believe, as well as certain spiders.
5. See *Ascent of Women*, Elisabeth Mann Borgese (London: Macgibbon & Kee, 1963), p. 11. 'Amongst fish, in general, the male is more absorbed by the service to the species than the female . . . The male is the homemaker. It is he who builds the nest, takes care of the eggs, and keeps the young in the nest until they are able to manage for themselves.' She quotes the three-spined sticklebacks as an example of this among fish; she also mentions the quail, the male of whom goes broody and sits on the eggs to hatch them out.

6. *Equal Woman,* Myrtle Langley (Marshall Morgan & Scott, 1983), p. 24.
7. ibid., p. 169. Interestingly, it is the men amongst the Alor who want to have children, although it is their leisure which is likely to be interrupted. 'We men are the ones who want children,' they say. 'Our wives don't. They just want to sleep with us.' Possibly this puts paid to one of those 'differences' we have come to think of as innate – that men want sex and women want children. It is easy to see that the Alor men, like Western women, achieve significance through looking after their children because it is the only job they are expected to do competently.
8. See *Housewife,* Ann Oakley (Pelican Books, 1980), chapter 2, 'Women's Roles in Pre-Industrial Society'. It is not peculiar to modern Western culture to divide labour into men's and women's work, but the *particular* roles we tend to think of as 'traditional' or even 'universal' are neither.
9. See *Inventing Motherhood,* Ann Dally (Burnett Books Ltd., 1982).
10. The fact that Paul singles out women, rather than men, to support vulnerable members of the Church seems to give problems to commentators. It is no doubt because of this that a few versions render the verse 'if any believing man or believing woman...' See *A Commentary of the Pastoral Epistles,* J. N. D. Kelly (Baker Book House Co., 1981), p. 120.
11. See K. H. Registorf, *Theological Dictionary of the New Testament, vol. II,* p. 49. The word 'denotes the "master of the house" who has control over the household in the widest sense'. Here, of course, the word is in the feminine form.
12. 'Working at home, domestic.' *A Greek English Lexicon of the New Testament,* William F. Arndt and F. Wilbur Gingrich (University of Chicago Press, 1957).
13. To 'be at the head (of), rule, direct ... manage, conduct ... be concerned about, care for, give aid.' ibid.
14. *Dictionary of the Bible,* J. Hastings, ed. (T. and T. Clark, Edinburgh, 1906), vol. I, p. 848.
15. ibid., also p. 848.
16. Which is what James Dobson, in one of his teaching films on the subject, analysed as the most common cause of complaint amongst housewives.

SIX

1. Works of Chrysostom. *Not In God's Image*, op. cit., p. 141.
2. *Lysistrata*, Aristophanes.
3. For example C. S. Lewis. Or John Stott, who says, 'If all ordained Christian ministry inevitably has this flavour of authority and discipline about it, then indeed I think we would have to conclude that it is for men only.' *Issues Facing Christians Today* (Marshall Morgan & Scott, 1984), p. 254.
4. In his *First Blast of the Trumpet against the Monstrous Regiment of Women* (London, 1878), p. 17, ff. God, he said, has taken from women 'all power and authority, to speak, to reason, to interpret or to teach, but principally to rule or judge in the assembly of men . . . therefore yet again I repeat that, which I have affirmed: to wit, that a woman promoted to sit in the seat of God, that is to teach, to judge, or to reign above men, is a monster in nature, contumely to God, and a thing most repugnant to his will and ordinance.' Mind you, of course, Knox was a zealous Calvinist, and Mary Tudor was on the throne. (Apparently he regretted his Blast a few years later, when her younger sister took over . . .)
5.   ' . . . there thou may'st behold
   The great image of authority; a dog's obey'd in office.'
   King Lear, IV:iv.
6. C. S. Lewis, *God in the Dock*, op. cit., p. 93.
7. R. E. Clements, in his *Commentary on Isaiah, 1–39* (Marshall Morgan & Scott, 1980) – New Century Bible Commentary series – prefers the NEB and Good News renderings: 'instead of *women* (Heb. *nasim)*, we should read 'usurers', as attested by LXX and Targ.' See also the *Journal of Theological Studies 38* (1937), p. 38, G. R. Driver.
8. J. K. Mozley in *A New Commentary on Holy Scripture* (SPCK, 1929), p. 503, says that verse 10 'is one of the most disputed as to its meaning of any that St Paul has written'. Hardly anyone dares approach this passage without some reference to its obscurity. William J. Martin ('1 Cor. 11:2–16: an interpretation', in *Apostolic History and Gospel*, edited by W. Gasque, Exeter, 1970, pp. 230–41) says 'That this passage is difficult no one would deny.'
9. This is the implication in *Eve's Story*, Eric and Joyce Lane (Evangelical Press, 1984). E.g. pp. 120–1, and in Larry Christenson, op. cit., pp. 37–8.
10. *Man and Woman in Biblical Perspective*, James B. Hurley (InterVarsity Press, 1981), pp. 182–3.
11. Because of tensions between this passage and some verses

later in the letter some throw doubt on this. But this is a very small minority view. Most people point out that Paul's entire argument is rendered absurd if women are not in fact to prophesy. A few suggest that in that case perhaps Paul is talking of private gatherings. The presence of the angels, however, probably implies formal public worship (see M. D. Hooker, 'Authority on her head', pp. 412–3; also Dick and Joyce Boldrey, *Women in Paul's Life*, p. 14; and J. A. Fitzmyer, 'A Feature of Qumran Angelology and the Angels of 1 Cor. XI.10' (*New Testament Studies*, IV, 57–8), p. 55. Fitzmyer also quotes G. Kurze, *Der Engels- und Teufelsglaube des Apostels Paulus* [Frieburg im B.: Herder, 1915], p. 12). However, no one, as far as I know, doubts that men are present; so whichever way one interprets the situation, women have authority to pray and prophesy in front of men.

12. Such as Hurley, op. cit., p. 176. For a full examination of the word *exousia* see: *The Epistle To The Corinthians*, C. K. Barrett (Adam & Charles Black, London, 1973), p. 255. Also 'Authority on her head: an examination of 1 Corinthians XI', 10, M. D. Hooker (*New Testament Studies*, 10, 1964), pp. 190–220.

13. *Women in Paul's Life*, Dick and Joyce Boldrey, p. 15.

14. M. D. Hooker, '*Authority on her head*', pp. 410–16, p. 413.

15. *The Cities of St. Paul. Their influence on his life and thought*, W. M. Ramsey (London: Hodder & Stoughton, 1907.)

16. *1 Corinthians 11:2–16: An Interpretation*, William J. Martin, p. 239.

17. Hurley has had great fun trying to work out exactly what it was Paul had in mind to cover the woman's head. A veil? Some other covering? Or simply a suitable hairstyle? See James B. Hurley, op. cit., pp. 168–71. Also 'Did Paul Require Veils or the Silence of Women? A Consideration of 1 Cor. 11:2–16 and 1 Cor. 14:33b–36' (*Westminster Theological Journal* 35, 1973), pp. 190–220.

18. Though, possibly, the Corinthians' irresponsible use of languages tends to render this interpretation more, not less, convincing.

19. See particularly Eric and Joyce Lane (op. cit., pp. 101–3) who are obviously aping, though not acknowledging, Hurley (op. cit., p. 188 ff.).

20. See *A Greek English Lexicon of the New Testament and Other Christian Literature*, William F. Arndt and F. Wilbur Gingrich (University of Chicago Press, 1957), where the word in Timothy can be rendered 'quietness, rest', whereas in 1 Corinthians 14:34 it is to 'be silent, say nothing, stop speaking', etc.

21. Quoted in C. K. Barratt, op. cit., p. 333.
22. This is Hurley's idea (see above, note 19). He argues that Paul is saying women should not exercise authority by judging the prophets. But if verses 34 and 35 came after verse 40, they are not in the context of prophecy.
23. See Romans 3:27 and 7:21, where Paul himself uses the word law to mean a principle ('On what principle?' RSV. Also Acts 23:29, where it may simply mean Jewish law generally. See also *A Greek English Lexicon*, op. cit., p. 544: '1. gener., of any law . . . 2. *a rule . . . principle, norm . . .*'
24. Cf. *God & Women*, op. cit., p. 132.
25. See *To Corinth with Love*, Michael Green (Hodder & Stoughton, 1982), pp. 159–60.
26. N. J. Hommes, 'Let Women be Silent in Church', *Calv. Th.* J., 4 (1979), p. 19.
27. J. A. Anderson, 'Women's Warfare and Ministry', p. 30. Both quoted in *Women in the Bible*, Mary Evans (Paternoster Press, 1983), p. 103.
28. *Women in the World of Jesus*, op. cit., p. 53.
29. ibid., p. 43.
30. Julian C. McPheeters. Quoted in *God & Women*, op. cit., p. 124.
31. ibid., p. 132.
32. ibid.
33. *New Bible Dictionary* (InterVarsity Press, Leicester, Second Edition, 1982), p. 636.
34. See *A Greek English Lexicon of the New Testament*, op. cit., p. 15: 'adelphos . . . the pl. can also mean brothers and sisters'.
35. 'Priestesses in the Church', C. S. Lewis, op. cit., pp. 88–9.

SEVEN

1. The Zondervan Corporation, 1980, pp. 11–12.
2. Perhaps it would be more biblical if the groom, rather than the bride, were given away, by *both* parents . . . ?
3. See G. Lloyd Carr, *The Song of Solomon*, The Tyndale Old Testament Commentaries (InterVarsity Press, 1984), p. 20: 'Solomon's name is introduced here in what has been called a "literary fiction" . . . the "great lover" in Israel would naturally appear in the poem whether or not he really had anything to do with it. Similarly, Don Juan would conjure up the same picture in later love poetry.'
4. *The Four Loves* (Geoffrey Bles, London, 1960), pp. 119–21.

5. See G. Lloyd Carr, p. 88: 'One of the unusual features of the Song is the major place the words of the girl have in it . . . Our contemporary attitude where the girl is on the defensive and the man is the initiator, is in direct contrast with the attitude in the ancient world.'
6. Wives take note: 80 per cent–90 per cent of men initiate sex almost every time, but 30 per cent–33 per cent wish that women did! *The Hite Report on Male Sexuality*, S. Hite (Macdonald, 1981). Quoted in *The New Internationalist*, April, 1986, p. 10.
7. *The Four Loves,* op. cit., p. 120.
8. Though, to be fair, those who argue this are saying there is therefore no particular behaviour associated with the concept. The most well-researched discussion of the subject is S. Bedale's 'The meaning of *kephale* in the Pauline Epistles', *Journal of Theological Studies* 5, 1954, pp. 211–15. Other treatments of the subject tend to be derived from (and are often misunderstandings of) Bedale.
9. *Mere Christianity,* (Geoffrey Bles, 1952), book III, chapter 10, p. 108.
10. See note 10 to chapter 5. Another use of the same root in the New Testament is in Matthew 10:25 – translated 'head of the house' in the NIV.
11. *The Four Loves,* op. cit.
12. Quoted by C. S. Lewis in *The Four Loves,* op. cit., p. 111.
13. R. A. Torrey's book *The Power of Prayer* (Zondervan Books, 1971), actually includes two chapters entitled 'How To Pray So As To Get What You Ask', and 'Who Can Pray So As To Get What They Ask?'
14. Patricia Gundry, op. cit., p. 34.

EIGHT

1. See, for example, *The Life and Times of Jesus the Messiah,* vol. I, Alfred Edersheim (Longmans Green & Co., 1897), p. 353. Edersheim explains the 'ardent insistence on marriage amongst Jewish society of the time'. See also Evelyn and Frank Stagg, op. cit., p. 50: 'The Mishnah made the bearing of children a duty: "No man may abstain from the law *be fruitful and multiply* unless he already has children" (Yeb 6,6).' See also C. K. Barrett, 'The First Epistle to the Corinthians', *Black's New Testament Commentaries* (Redwood Press Ltd., 1968), p. 161: '. . . marriage appears

to have been obligatory for a Jewish man.'

2. *Greek English Lexicon,* op. cit., gives the following meaning for the two words:

   a) 'be present, have come, impend, be imminent', w. the connotation of threatening.

   b) 'necessity, compulsion, distress, calamity, means of compulsion'.

3. For example *Sex and that: what's it all about?* (Michael Lawson and David Skipp, Lion, 1985), a Christian book for teenagers, confirms the view that 'normal' people must have some kind of kiss-and-cuddle with their boyfriend or girlfriend: 'Even these days some of us need to be told that we are allowed to kiss and hug!' (p. 51).

4. These verses (particularly 36 and 37) are quite difficult to understand, and have different interpretations put on them. See, for example, C. K. Barrett, op. cit., pp. 182–5.

5. See Edersheim, op. cit., pp.149–50.In Corinth – among the Jews at any rate – it would presumably have been standard procedure for the single people to be engaged to somebody by their parents. This amounted to marriage in every legal way, although the couple would not yet live, or usually sleep, together.

6. *Bash – A Study in Spiritual Power,* John Edison, ed. (Marshalls, 1982), p. 58.

NINE

1. Gary Collins, *Christian Counselling,* (Word, 1980), p. 316, quoted in *Homosexuality, What Does the Bible Say?*, David Field (UCCF Booklets, 1976).

2. Laws 839–40, *The Collected Dialogues of Plato,* ed. Edith Hamilton and Huntington Cairns (Princetown University Press, 1961), pp. 1404–5. Plato also includes other forms of immoral sex, for instance, bestiality.

3. 'Thought for the Day', in the *Today* programme on Radio 4, 10 October 1996.

4. Thomas Schmidt, *Straight and Narrow* (IVP, 1995). Other books which are also helpful are Stephen Green's *The Sexual Dead End* (Broadview Books, London, 1992), *Homosexuality and the Politics of Truth* by Jeffrey Satinover (Baker Books, USA, 1996), *Out of the Blue* by Martin Hallett (Hodder & Stoughton, 1996), and *Homosexuality: A New Christian Ethic* by Elizabeth Moberly (James Clarke, 1983).

5. See the *Daily Mail*, 8 August 1997, 'The out-of-wedlock baby boom. Almost half of all British babies are now conceived out of wedlock, figures revealed yesterday.' The damage done to children, and therefore society as a whole, as a result of increased illegitimacy is alarming; see, for instance, *Broken Homes and Battered Children – a study of the relationship between child abuse and family type*, Robert Whelan (Family Education Trust, Oxford, 1994).

6. Richard Holloway, Bishop of Edinburgh, apparently advocates unfaithfulness, serial monogamy and homosexual quasi-marriages, but also, paradoxically, claims that none of this is any of the Church's business (according to the *Daily Telegraph*, 18 August 1997, 'Bishop's marriage views "liberalism gone mad" ').

7. It was a very interesting and informative evening. The same priest made no secret of the kind of lifestyle he, at any rate, is arguing for in wanting a more relaxed attitude to homosexuality. 'I don't have a partner,' he said at one point, 'but I do have sex.'

    I felt all our 'sophisticated' arguments were summed up by a young black man who stood up towards the end of the proceedings and made the most profound statement of the evening, roughly along these lines: 'I have very poor English, so you must forgive my simple question, and please don't give me clever answers because I don't understand them. But please will you well-educated people tell me, in easy words, very simply, yes or no, does God say anywhere in the Bible that a man can marry a man?' There was a stunned silence from the panel. It was eventually broken by the one word 'No'. Our opponents said nothing. There was nothing more to be said.

8. In *The Colour Supplement* with James Whale, with fellow guest Iain Bainbridge, Talk Radio, 14 September 1997.

9. Try, for instance, Michael Vasey's *Strangers and Friends* (Hodder & Stoughton, 1995). Perhaps you will be more convinced than I was.

10. See also Henri Blocher, *In the Beginning* (IVP, 1984), particularly 'Man and woman' p. 103: 'Immediately we can understand why the apostle Paul makes a close association between idolatry and homosexuality (Romans 1:22–27). This sexual perversion as a rejection of the other corresponds to idolatry in its . . . rejection of the Other; it is the divinization of the same.'

11. I was involved in a television programme, *Central TV Live*, early in 1997. I learnt a great deal from the evening, and a

lesbian there, who was much older and more experienced than the rest of us, said it is commonly difficult for lesbian couples to maintain sexual momentum and interest if the relationship has been stable for some years.

12. See, for instance, the letter from Peter Tatchell (of the militant gay pressure group OutRage!) to the *Guardian*, 26 June 1997, in praise of sex with children as young as nine.

Considerable research has been done on the links between homosexuality and underage sex. For instance K. Freund *et al.*, 'Pedophilia and Heterosexuality v. Homosexuality', *Journal of Sex and Marital Therapy*, 10 (Fall, 1984), p. 197. Also P. Cameron, 'Homosexual Molestation of Children: Sexual Interaction of Teacher and Pupil', *Psychological Reports*, 57 (1985), pp. 27–36. Also *Psychological Reports* 1996, 79, 385–404, Family Research Institute, PO Box 62640, Colorado Springs, Co 80962.

It is an emotive subject, and we must be very wary of drawing the wrong conclusions. I would happily entrust my children to any of my gay friends (with the exception of one who is mentally disturbed).

Nevertheless, statistically there seems to be a link. Most studies show that about a third of sexual crimes against children are homosexual. This does not necessarily mean they are committed by homosexuals (it is possible that offenders simply do not care what sex their victims are). However, on the assumption that they are, and that 2 per cent of the population is homosexual, this would mean that a homosexual is over twenty times more likely to abuse children than a heterosexual. See Schmidt, op. cit. pp. 114–15 and references p. 205.

Anecdotal evidence also suggests a link. It is not unusual to find gay campaigners in favour of lowering the age of consent, or even doing away with it altogether.

13. See notes 1 and 4: e.g. David Field, op. cit., pp. 13–16; Thomas Schmidt, op. cit., chapter 5.

14. *Out of the Blue*, op. cit., p. 58.

15. BBC's *Radio 5 Live*, 9.00–10.00 a.m., 14 July 1997.

16. See A. C. Kinsey, W. B. Pomeroy and C. E. Martin, *Sexual Behaviour in the Human Male* (Philadelphia: W. B. Saunders, 1948), p. 483; A. P. Bell, 'Homosexualities: their range and character', *Nebraska Symposium on Motivation 1973* (Cole and R. Dienstbier (eds), U Nebraska Press); W. M. King, *The etiology of homosexuality as related to childhood experiences and adult adjustment*, (Ed. D. thesis, Indiana University, 1980). The study in 1983 was done by the Family Research Institute; see

P. Cameron, K. Cameron and K. Proctor, *Psychological Reports*, 64, 1167–79. All quoted in *What Causes Homosexual Desire and Can It Be Changed?*, available from Facts Matter, PO Box 62, Royston, Hertfordshire, SG8 7UL.

17. 'Human sexual orientation: the biologic theories reappraised', *Arch. Gen. Psychiatry*, 50, 1993, pp. 228–39. Quoted in *Born What Way?* FRI, available in UK from Facts Matter, see above.

18. See Cameron, op. cit. Also *Is Homosexuality Learned?* Paper presented at Eastern Psychological Assn., 15 April 1994, ibid.

19. Quoted in the *National Association of Research and Therapy of Homosexuality Newsletter*, September 1993. Also, *Wall Street Journal*, 9 January 1997:

   Suppose that a young man, seeking help for a psychological condition that was associated with serious health risks and made him desperately unhappy were to be told by a professional he consulted that no treatment was available, that his condition was permanent and genetically based, and that he must learn to live with it ... How would this man and his family feel when they discovered years later that numerous therapeutic approaches have been available for his specific problem for more than 60 years? ... How would [he] feel if he discovered that the reason he was not informed ... was that certain groups were, for political reasons, pressuring professionals to deny that effective treatment existed? (*Don't Forsake Homosexuals Who Want Help*, Socarides *et al.*)

20. A. C. Kinsey *et al.*, op. cit.

21. Interview with Rupert Everett, *Daily Telegraph*, 9 September 1997.

22. See for instance: P. Painton, 'The Shrinking Ten Percent', *Time*, April 1993, pp. 27–9. P. Rogers, 'How Many Gays Are There?' *Newsweek*, 15 February 1993, p. 46. A detailed critique was done by J. H. Court and J. G. Muir, (eds), *Kinsey, Sex and Fraud: The Indoctrination of a People* (Lafayette, LA: Huntington House, 1990).

23. Most modern studies put the figure at less than 2 per cent. Schmidt, op. cit.: '... more than a dozen recent studies ... consistently put the incidence of homosexual studies at around 1 per cent' p. 102. (All referenced by Schmidt, p. 296.) The National Opinion Research Center in the US studied 7,408 subjects in the period 1970–90 (mostly 1988–90) and concluded an incidence of 1.8 per cent male-to-male sex in the previous year. E. O. Laumann *et al.*, *The Social Organisation of Sexuality* (University of Chicago Press, 1994), studied

3,000 subjects and found 2.8 per cent of sexually active men had had at least one male sexual partner in the previous year.

24. Schmidt, op. cit., pp. 105–8.
25. Edmund White, *The Farewell Symphony* (Chatto & Windus, 1997), p. 43.
26. See *Homosexuality, the Medical, Social and Religious Implications*, report by the Maranatha Community, 102 Irlam Road, Fixton, Manchester M41 6JT, 1997.
27. See note 26. See also Schmidt, op. cit. Or, if you can bear it, *The A to Z of Gay Sex*, which gives advice on sex in public lavatories and group sex in a 'daisy chain' (both illegal); use and consumption of urine ('golden showers') and excrement ('rimming', with the tongue inside the anus); 'fisting' (using the fist instead of the tongue) and worse.
28. Paul Cameron, William Playfair and Stephen Wellum, 'The Longevity of Homosexuals: Before and After the AIDS Epidemic', *Omega Journal of Death and Dying*, vol. 29, no. 3, 1994. Quoted in *Medical Consequences of What Homosexuals Do*, Family Research Institute Inc., PO Box 62640, Colorado Springs, Colorado 80962, USA. Available in UK from Facts Matter, as above.
29. Schmidt, op. cit., p. 110 and following.
30. Cameron, op. cit.
31. Schmidt, op. cit., p. 127.
32. Of British men, 70 per cent think homosexual acts are always or almost always wrong. See 'Sexual behaviour in Britain', *The National Survey of Sexual Attitudes and Lifestyles*, K. Welling, J. Field, *et al.*, (Penguin 1994), pp. 183 and 253.
33. For instance True Freedom Trust, PO Box 3, Upton, Wirral, Merseyside L49 6NY, telephone: 0151 653 0773. Also Courage, PO Box 338, Watford, WD1 4BQ, telephone: 0181 420 1066. Also U-Turn Anglia Trust, PO Box 138, Ipswich IP4 4RP. Exodus International North America, PO Box 2121, San Rafael, Ca 94912, USA, telephone: 415-454-1017. Exodus South Pacific, PO Box 308, Fortitude Valley, Queensland 4006, telephone: 07-371-4705.
34. I hesitate to suggest any supplementary action, in case the call to prayer then goes unheard; it is always easier to do anything else than pray. Nevertheless, we must also support those who are standing firm in a difficult political climate. Dr George Carey, the present Archbishop of Canterbury, has made his orthodox position quite clear. We should thank God for him in our prayers, and lift him to God for support. A letter to encourage him would not go amiss.
    In addition, there are a number of pressure groups forming

for those who want the Church of England, or society, to return to a more obedient walk with God. Forward in Faith is an Anglo-Catholic organisation, and Reform is Evangelical; both are Anglican, and they have similar aims and often work in tandem. CARE works for Christian values in society. Some may seek membership of these, or even make the sacrifice of standing for General Synod.

I consider it unlikely that the unthinkable will happen, and that the Church of England will go against all biblical teaching and Christian tradition on the subject to say that it is acceptable for members of the clergy to be practising homosexuals. But it is a danger. It has already happened in the Episcopalian Church in America. 'For evil to flourish it is enough that good men do nothing.'

35. The *Sun*, 15 July 1997.
36. For instance in the children's television programme, *Love Bites*, in the summer of 1997.

TEN

1. Actually this is not anon. at all. It was said at our breakfast table not very long ago.
2. Op. cit., pp. 113–20.
3. ibid., p. 114.
4. *The Mark of a Man*, op. cit., p. 25.
5. See *Faces of Feminism*, Olive Banks (Martin Robinson & Co. Ltd., 1981), chapter 2, 'The Evangelical Contribution to Feminism'.
6. ibid., pp. 17–25, and pp. 74–5: 'the feminists tended to see the propagation of birth control techniques as leading to an inevitable degradation of morals, since it would encourage extra-marital sexuality.'
7. Elaine Storkey, op. cit., p. 116.
8. *The Mark of a Man*, op. cit., p. 84.
9. *Understanding the Male Temperament* (Fleming, H. Revell Company, 1977), p. 22.
10. *Issues Facing Christians Today*, op. cit., p. 236.
11. ibid., p. 235.
12. *Sexual Oppression*, Greenbelt, 1983. (*Pace* Osborne)
13. Elaine Storkey, op. cit., p. 170.
14. See *The New Internationalist*, April 1986, p. 16, which quotes F. P. Hosken, 'Female Sexual Mutilations: the facts and proposals for action', *Women's International Network News*, 1980,

and A. Thaim, 'Women's Fights for the Abolition of Sexual Mutilation', *Int. Social Science Journal*, vol. 78. 'At least 74 million young girls in the world have had their clitorises removed ... Approximately 70% of women living in N. Sudan, Djibouti and Somalia have been infibulated. (Infibulation is the removal of the internal and external vaginal lips and the sewing shut of the vagina, leaving just a tiny opening for urine and menstrual blood ...) Deaths due to infibulation ... are estimated at 6% a year.'

15. S. Brownmiller, *Against Our Will* (Penguin Books, 1976). Quoted in *New Internationalist*, April 1986, p. 17.

16. I am sick of there being no counterpart to 'misogynous'. This is it.

17. As note 15. 1 in 2 rapes are reported; 51 per cent of reported rapists are caught; 76 per cent of these are prosecuted, and 47 per cent of them are acquitted. I make that about 1 in 60 rapists convicted. *The Fulfilled Woman*, Lou Beardsley and Tony Spry (Bantam Books, 1975).

18. See *Family* magazine, June 1984 and April 1985. *Family* (which is designed for a Christian readership) put out a questionnaire in June 1984 asking whether any of its readers suffered from domestic violence. The response they received – from women who regularly experienced extreme violence from professing Christian husbands – was staggering. The report was published in the same magazine in April 1985.

ELEVEN

1. From a T.V. programme entitled *Just Wait Till Your Mother Gets Home*.

Straight Talk to Men

Caring for Your Family in a World of Pressure

James Dobson

In *Straight Talk to Men* James Dobson explores what it means to be a man today. Is he supposed to be stoic and strong, or tender and emotional? Should he provide leadership for his family, or is there nothing to distinguish his role from his wife's?

Dr Dobson looks at men's relationships with their children, and what makes a good father. He explains what men can know about their wives that can help them build a good marriage. He explores men's attitudes to work and how they can deal with financial and time pressures to maintain a good family life. He also defines why men need to re-establish the priorities of their lives at different stages.

This highly successful book is full of clear and practical advice to all men for building family life in today's pressured world.

Dr James Dobson is president of Focus on the Family and internationally renowned for his insights into family issues. He is the author of many bestselling books including *Emotions: Can You Trust Them?* and *How to Build Confidence in Your Child*.

ISBN 0 340 69484 X

Equal and Different

Male and Female in Church and Family

Michael Harper

Equal and Different assesses the wide-ranging and controversial topic of male and female roles in the Church, family and society, to define where we are at the turn of the millennium. It explores the biblical record, the lessons of history, the impact of feminism and the nature of the family. This updated and revised edition also looks at the question of women as bishops which is set to become increasingly important.

'A powerful and widely researched book ... a major contribution to the ongoing debate'. *Renewal Magazine*

Michael Harper is Dean of the new British Antiochian Orthodox Deanery and Chairman of the International Charismatic Consultation on World Evangelisation. He was previously Canon of Chichester Cathedral and Director of the Fountain Trust, and is the author of numerous books including *The True Light, Let My People Grow* and *Walk in The Spirit*.

ISBN 0 340 69439 4

Loving Against The Odds

For Every Man and Every Woman in Every Marriage

Rob Parsons

'The last thing any of us needs is to be offered a handful of easy answers from someone who gives the impression that if we had a marriage like theirs life would be perfect.'
Rob Parsons

Here is a book for all couples – those with strong marriages who want to protect their relationship, those going through difficult times, and those considering marriage.

With humour and honesty it deals with issues that are relevant to every marriage, including: communicating more effectively, overcoming financial pressure, why interest in sex sometimes dies, the affair, and dealing with conflict.

'This is not just an honest book; it's a book filled with hope and compassion – with understanding – and with down-to-earth advice bursting out of every chapter.'
Fiona Castle

Rob Parsons is Executive Director of Care for the Family, and is also the author of *The Sixty Minute Father*, *The Sixty Minute Marriage* and *What They Didn't Teach Me in Sunday School*.

ISBN 0 340 59315 6

The Search for Intimacy

Elaine Storkey

'The need for intimacy is not a new discovery . . . It is intrinsic to being human. But the depth of the search for intimacy is new to our present age.' *Elaine Storkey*

Drawing on sociological and biblical perspectives, Elaine Storkey explores the meaning and importance of intimacy, looking at childhood and adult relationships, friendship, marriage, and differences in outlook between men and women. Barriers to intimacy can be surmounted: personal knowledge is crucial, as is knowledge of God, 'that great source of intimacy which will sustain us and take us into deeper relationships with others'.

Elaine Storkey is Executive Director of The Institute of Contemporary Christianity. A regular broadcaster, international speaker and member of the General Synod of the Church of England, she is the author of *What's Right With Feminism* and *Mary's Story, Mary's Song*.

ISBN 0 340 48899 9